CLOUDS BEFORE THE SUN

When Helen Schofield's sister dies in a tragic accident, leaving behind a baby daughter, Helen knows that only she can be trusted to tie up her sister's affairs. Against her staid fiancé's wishes, she travels to Cornwall alone. When her sister's farm proves impossible to sell, Helen refuses to let Beth's inheritance slip through her fingers. With the help of her new friend, Agnes, she vows to make a success of the farm herself – despite the rumours of a curse hanging over it.

To my father,
for all the fun I had growing up on a
Cornish farm,
and to Norman, as ever.

Clouds Before The Sun

by

Janet Wright Matthews

Magna Large Print Books
Long Preston, North Yorkshire,
BD23 4ND, England.

British Library Cataloguing in Publication Data.

Matthews, Janet Wright
Clouds before the sun.

A catalogue record of this book is available from the British Library

ISBN 0-7505-1703-4

First published in Great Britain in 2000 by Severn House Publishers Ltd.

Published in Large Print 2001 by arrangement with Severn House Publishers Ltd.

Magna Large Print is an imprint of Library Magna Books Ltd.

Printed and bound in Great Britain by
T.J. (International) Ltd., Cornwall, PL28 8RW

One

'I'll kill him! God help me, I'll kill the swine with my bare hands!'

James Trethowan leaned forward in the driving seat of the two-wheeled dogcart, urging the sweating pony on with voice and whip. His anger was an all-consuming fire, throbbing through his brain, driving him on. That man! How dare he? How dare he!

It was too much to bear. Furiously, he cracked the whip again and the pony increased her pace under the quiet stars, hooves pounding along the rutted Cornish road. The dogcart bounced and rattled as its wheels caught against stones and pot-holes. Beside him, James could see his wife, her face a white blur in the dim light, clinging with both hands to the side of the cart, sobbing with fear, but he was beyond caring. All his thoughts were concentrated on the journey's end, on the confrontation to come. 'That swine! That unspeakable...' Words failed him and he lashed again at the terrified pony.

'Slow down! Slow down! You'll kill us!' Mary's voice was high with fright as the cart hurtled down the twisting track, the wheels at times only inches from the granite-faced Cornish hedges. 'For God's sake James, slow down.'

'He knew!' James was too angry to listen to her. 'The swine knew what he was doing all along. It was deliberate, damn his eyes. Deliberate!' That letter – dear God, when he had opened that letter, realised the reasons for what had happened, knew who was to blame and why...

The cart bounced again as the wheels caught in a rut, throwing them both into the air. The pony did not check her pace. Normally, she was used for carrying hens and butter to the market in Penzance, pulling the cart at a sedate dogtrot. Now, the cracking whip, the bouncing, rattling cart had panicked her. Ears flat, eyes starting, she bolted, foam-flecked, through the darkness, her tortured breathing audible even over the thunder of her hooves, the rattle of the cart.

'James, please.' Mary's voice rose in terror. 'Slow down. Remember Beth; remember our child.'

'The farm, my animals, gone, destroyed by that bastard! All my work, ruined!' The cows that he had lavished such love on, the butter he produced which had such a good reputation – and Anna. Anna, the great mare who had cost more than he could afford; Anna, a seventeen-hand giant of a horse but so gentle a child could play with her; Anna, already pregnant with the foal, the start of the herd which would make Tregurtha Farm famous throughout Britain for the quality of its heavy horses; Anna, lying dead and rotten in the great pit he had dug to bury her, weeping almost as if it had been his own child that he was burying.

But Mary's words had got through to him. Behind the blazing fury that blinded him he saw for a second a picture of Beth as he had left her in her cradle, helpless, chubby, the future.

Whatever his feelings he had to think of her, of Mary, of their safety. Common sense reasserted itself. He sat up straighter, his fingers tightening on the reins as the pony rounded the sharp bend leading down into the town of Madron.

The escaped sow was right in the centre of the narrow road, surrounded by her piglets. 'Whoa!' He threw himself backwards, dragging on the reins, trying to stop the wild gallop, to regain control of the frantic horse. But the pony was too worked up. She pulled at the reins, tossing her head, fighting for her freedom.

The sow charged.

Her instinct was to protect her young and she was already upset by a close encounter with a fox. This huge, racing animal was a danger to her young and she responded instinctively. Head down, screeching wildly, she flung herself at the galloping pony.

It was too much. The pony reared, twisting round on her hind legs, her scream of terror splitting the darkness.

'Whoa girl, steady–' But his voice was drowned out. The mare flung herself round, trying to get away from the new terror and the cart tipped, fell...

James saw his wife's body leave the seat and he reached for her instinctively but he was helpless. The cart fell sideways dragging the pony with it and the two passengers were thrown, like boneless puppets, head first into the granite wall.

'Such a tragedy.' The Reverend Ezekiel Hardcourt shook his head sadly. 'It is a message to us, my dear Helen, to remind us that God may call us to his bosom at any time.'

It was an even clearer message not to drive too fast, Helen Schofield thought. The letter from the Vicar of Madron announcing the death of her sister and brother-in-law had been quite specific about the speed of the dogcart. But her fiancé had a rooted dislike of what he described as her 'levity' so she left the thought unsaid. The remainder of her news would upset him enough anyway.

'There is, of course, the problem of my niece, Beth.' She did not want to see his face darken at the thought of the child and fixed her eyes instead on the over-large gilded looking-glass above the mantelpiece. In it, the reflected room looked strange, its familiar outlines softened and dark. And in the midst was her own figure, her face drained of colour by her dark hair and the new black mourning clothes that she wore, as crowlike as her fiancé in his clerical garb.

'She has inherited the farm, surely her father's family are the best people to look after her.' Ezekiel Hardcourt said swiftly. 'Presumably they are country folk who can bring her up to the station in life to which she was born. When she married beneath her, my dear Miss Schofield, your sister denied her offspring the position in life which would have been theirs had she married more wisely.'

She had never agreed with Ezekiel about her sister's marriage. Mary might have been stigmatised by Grandmama and Ezekiel as flighty and silly but Helen knew how happy she had been during her brief marriage. Her letters had been full of her delight in her husband, her joy in the baby. Helen might be the sensible, clever sister but she sometimes wondered whether silly, flighty Mary hadn't made the better choice after all.

But now Mary was dead and, as so often in their youth, it was Helen who was left to sort out the problems she had got herself into. 'James Trethowan had no relatives,' she said baldly, unable to think of a way of dressing up the information more palatably. 'I am the baby's next of kin.' She watched to see what his reaction would be.

He looked frankly appalled. 'You're going to bring the child here?'

Glancing around the dark parlour Helen had to admit that there was good reason for his dismay. The small room was packed with furniture more suited to a larger house, with every vacant space colonised by tables holding treasured memorabilia. Even the walls were almost hidden by gloomy ancestral portraits frowning down in permanent disapproval. Her own modestly spreading skirts were a constant threat in the cluttered space and the thought of a small child in the room was enough to make the bravest heart quail.

She decided to inflict the second shock while he was still reeling from the first; that way she would only be lectured and advised once. 'Yes, indeed.' Her voice expressed nothing but delight in the prospect. 'And I shall be collecting her as soon as possible.' She folded her hands in front of her and waited for the explosion.

'Collect her?' Ezekiel Hardcourt looked for a moment as if he had lost his breath. 'You are going to Cornwall,' his voice rose from its usual controlled, religious tone, 'to collect a child?' It was almost a squeak.

Helen fought against a tendency to smile. 'She can hardly make the journey alone,' she pointed out.

'But there must be servants, friends, someone…'

'There is a relative,' she reminded him gently. 'Me.'

He was still rocked by her announcement. 'All that way. It will take you days.' His face tightened as a worse thought came to him. 'My dearest Miss Schofield, you'll take a companion? You won't go alone?'

Helen swallowed. She had never even walked the length of the street unless accompanied by her sister or a maid. Despite living in straitened circumstances, their distant relationship to the Earls of Grampound meant that Grandmama insisted they had to keep up standards. If the Earl's daughter never walked abroad without at least a maid, then neither could she – even if the Earl's income was in the tens of thousands of pounds a year while she and Grandmama survived on less than two hundred pounds a year.

To travel three hundred miles all alone, to bring back a baby when she had no experience of small children – she felt her stomach lurch nervously at the thought, but underneath she was also aware of a thrill of excitement.

To be out of this small, claustrophobic house, to be away from the unceasing demands of her grandmother, of her constant reminders to hold herself straight, speak softly, remember that she was a gentlewoman – despite the fear, she could feel the attraction of the adventure. But it would never do to let Ezekiel see what she was thinking. He would only think her ill-bred for wanting such things.

She laughed lightly. 'Mr Hardcourt, you know our situation. Our finances will scarcely bear the cost of a journey for myself, and as for Grandmama – in her state of health I could never deprive her of the services of our only maid.'

He took her hand in his, his thin fingers cold and bony against her skin. 'Alas, that my living has not yet come through. If I had already claimed you as my own I could have accompanied you. As it is–'

'As it is it would be most improper,' Helen said swiftly. She smiled at him, anxious to change the subject. 'I don't suppose that you have heard anything from your noble cousin?'

'I had the honour to receive a letter from Lord Carnglase this morning.' His face glowed. 'He is coming to London for a few days and wishes me to call on him to discuss a living he has in his gift.' He took a deep, satisfied breath. 'And he has begged the honour of meeting you too, my dearest.'

No honour, Helen thought cynically. Just a precaution to make sure that she would be a suitable wife for the new vicar. Not that there was any doubt of that. Ezekiel was as poverty-stricken and as well-born as herself. Where else would he find a wife who was a suitable match and yet not so rich that she would refuse to marry an impoverished clergyman? Where else would she find a suitable husband, tied as she was to the apron strings of a proud, sick, poor grandmother and lacking the beauty with which her younger sister had captured the ineligible Mr Trethowan?

Helen gazed into her future with a sinking heart. It was not that she did not want to marry Ezekiel Hardcourt, it was the predictability of it all that was so depressing.

Now she was her grandmother's companion, on marriage she would become a vicar's wife. Her life stretched before her, respectable, dutiful, dull. Their wedding day could not be far removed now. Once Lord Carnglase had approved her and given Reverend Hardcourt his living there would be nothing left to wait for. He would move from his curacy in the East End of London, she would join him as his new bride, Grandmama would leave this poky house for the greater style and freedom of the Vicarage and everything would be wonderful. She sighed.

Ezekiel Hardcourt moved nearer, took her hand again. 'I hope that sigh is for us, dearest. You have waited so patiently, as becomes the future wife of a man of God. But it will not be long, I promise you, before I can claim you for my own.'

She smiled but made no answer. The future vicarage seemed to loom over her, black and forbidding. But before that there was the trip, her adventure. It lay across her future like a ray of sunlight in a dark room. After, marriage, respectability, duty. First, this brief flash of freedom, of making her own decisions, not deferring to grandmother or fiancé for one brief, glorious week.

She glanced at the ornate clock in the centre of the cloth-covered mantelpiece. 'You mustn't miss your parish meeting,' she reminded him.

'You'll be back soon from Cornwall?' There was anxiety in his voice and she softened towards him.

'As soon as possible,' she assured him. 'I shall collect my niece, put the farm in the hands of an agent and come straight back.' Helen smiled up at him. 'Will you miss me?'

'Very much. And, of course, Lord Carnglase will be in London any day now and wishes to see you. You would not wish to disappoint him.'

'Of course not,' she said quietly.

He leaned forward and kissed her forehead. His lips were dry as paper against her skin. 'A good journey, dearest.'

'Thank you, Mr Hardcourt.' She had a sudden memory of the book she had read this morning. Grandmama did not approve of novels, nor of wasting candles in the bedroom, but now that the days were lengthening she would wake early. Wrapped in a shawl, she would huddle under the window to catch the morning light and lose herself for a precious hour in someone else's life.

Even after eight years, she remembered, Anne Elliot's heart would flutter at the sound of Captain Wentworth's voice, or a glimpse of him in the street. Surely she should feel more at the chaste kisses of her future bridegroom than mild embarrassment? But novels were not real life, of course. It was probably for arousing such false expectations that Grandmama had banned them.

She smiled at him more warmly, to hide the guilt she felt. He responded by tightening his grasp. 'Once we are married, my dearest, your little niece is, of course, welcome to make her home with us.'

She had wondered if he would accept Beth and his prompt offer overwhelmed her. He was so good, so kind; she, with her cynical, disbelieving mind, was totally unworthy of a man like him. She smiled warmly, her face lighting up with pleasure. 'That is very generous of you, very kind.' Their courtship had always been properly conducted, as befitted a clergyman and a well-bred lady, but she could not contain her happiness at this sign of his love for her. Impulsively, she leaned forward and kissed him briefly on the cheek. It was the merest touch – but it was too much.

She felt the shock and horror that ran through him at her forward behaviour and pulled back instantly, but it was too late.

'Miss Schofield!' His voice shook with distress.

Relegated from 'my dearest' to 'Miss Schofield' by her shameless behaviour, Helen could only hang her head, feeling her face flame with embarrassment at his displeasure.

'I – I'm sorry. I couldn't help myself.' She forced herself to meet his eyes. 'It was so good of you...' She tailed off under his outraged stare.

'I hope, Miss Schofield, that you know me well enough to realise that I will always do my duty.'

Even in the midst of her distress her unruly mind threw up the thought: *'Duty' is a cold word* to *use about a small baby.*

'So you were the belle of the ball, Theo?' Anthony Ledgerwood smiled fondly at his sister. As if she could ever be anything else with her ethereal fairness, her eyes of angel blue, the slight figure that seemed almost too frail for this workaday world.

She smiled, her enchanting face lighting up with mischief. 'Would I ever admit to such a thing! Even if it were true.' But the serenity of her face showed that the words were mere politeness. She had always had an accurate appreciation of her own worth. 'My only regret was that you weren't there, Anthony,' she added, her face falling. 'You would have enjoyed it so much. *Everyone* was there.'

Even after all these years he could still feel the hurt of his exclusion from polite society, almost like a kick in the stomach. These pleasures should have been his; this should have been his world; instead he was excluded from it for ever – and through no fault of his own.

He was certain that his face had showed no sign of his feelings – after all these years he had schooled himself to show only what he wanted to show – but Theo was not fooled. All those years when, as children, they had clung to each other in an alien world had made them almost preternaturally aware of each other's feelings.

'Oh, Anthony, I'm so sorry.' She flung

herself to his feet in a flurry of expensive skirts. 'I shouldn't have said that.'

He stroked her fine curls with a gentle finger. 'Don't worry, sister mine. I'm just glad that you were able to rejoin the fashionable world. That's one advantage of being a woman.' His laugh was harsh even in his own ears. 'You take your husband's position in society. Even if I married one of the Queen's daughters I would still be only an apothecary, scarcely even a professional man, certainly not a gentleman.'

'It's so unfair!' Her pretty face darkened. 'Robert's father was only a miner yet *he's* accepted everywhere; you're the son of a gentleman and landowner yet you are not. What has he got that you haven't?'

'Money.' It was the obvious answer. But even though Robert was a landowner and the owner of a mine, it was scarcely enough to overcome the misfortune of his birth. Anthony made himself smile at his sister. 'And where is dear Robert? Avoiding me as usual?'

'At the mine.' Theo wrinkled her pretty nose. 'I don't know why he goes; he wouldn't recognise a mine shaft if he fell in one. He says his father always kept an eye on the mine and his employees and so should he. He just won't see how – how *low* it is.'

'Many wives would be delighted to have a

husband who was away all day.' Anthony Ledgerwood rose to his feet. 'I must go. We working men, you know...'

'Don't say that!' She was half joking but he could see the flash of temper in her eyes. She rose to stand beside him, a smaller, feminine version of himself. 'If you had money–'

'I'm doing my best, Theo.' He had sufficient control of his expression to make a humorous face at her. 'Apothecaries at the tail end of Cornwall are not renowned for their vast incomes, you know.'

She was thinking about his problem. 'If you married a rich woman, a woman with land of her own, then it would be yours, wouldn't it? And you could be a gentleman again.'

'Women like that are few and far between, my lovely. And unlike men, they are inclined to have their heads screwed on. Robert might have married you even though your only fortune was a pretty face but a woman wouldn't do a thing like that, I can assure you.' As he had discovered from bitter experience.

There was a small crease between her perfect brows. 'But there must be one...'

Two

'Could you carry my bags in, please?' After two days travelling Helen's main impression of adventures was that they were tiring and astonishingly uncomfortable.

'Sorry, ma'am. In a hurry, ma'am.' The soft Cornish accent couldn't hide the carrier's anxiety. 'Got to get back before dark, see.' He dropped her portmanteau in the porch of the house and hurried to the cart with the patient horse standing heavily in the shafts. Another second and he was gone, leaving Helen alone in front of the strange building.

There was no doubt that this was a farm. She had always thought that cows mooed but these were bellowing raucously. Perhaps that was why no one answered her knock, she decided, because she could see the dim reflection of a light in one of the downstairs windows. Uncertainly, she pushed the door open. She was in a large, untidy hallway, lit only by a sliver of lamplight that edged round the corner of a half-closed door. Taking a deep breath she pushed it open then stopped, appalled, on the threshold.

'What on earth do you think you're

doing?' Helen's voice echoed through the large, stone-flagged kitchen. The single oil lamp seemed to merely heighten the gloom, emphasising the unswept floor, the papers piled untidily on the dark dresser, the shotgun propped in a corner. By a table littered with unwashed dishes a slatternly woman jumped nervously and the crying baby she was feeding from a black bottle almost slipped from her grasp.

'Are you giving that child spirits?' Horror overcame tiredness and her reluctance to accost a strange woman in such a manner. The child must surely be Beth. Helen stepped swiftly forward, cast her shawl over a grimy chair-back and took the bottle from the woman's lax grip. The pungent smell made her grimace with disgust. 'How could you!' She slapped the bottle down on the greasy table and stared at the woman through blazing green eyes.

The woman climbed unsteadily to her feet, the child held loosely in her arms, and dropped an approximation at a curtsy. ''Tes only a drop of medicine,' she protested in a slurred whine. 'For her teething, see. To quiet her.'

'And I suppose you're teething as well,' Helen snapped. The smell of spirits on the woman's breath was enough to rock her back on her heels. Disturbed by the strange, angry voice, the child screamed louder and a frantically waving arm hit the woman in the face, loosening her already slack grip.

Helen dived forward, clutching at the small body as it slipped dangerously down the woman's hip. Her niece; Mary's only child! She hefted the baby quickly in her arms but the child showed no gratitude for her rescue. If anything the screaming increased in volume, the firm little body thrashing and writhing as if determined to be put down.

Helen had imagined her first meeting with Beth. She had seen herself cooing over the cot of a sweetly smiling cherub. She had never imagined for one moment that the child would be this screaming, wriggling banshee!

She hitched the child more securely in her arms and raised her voice above all the noise. 'I am Mrs Trethowan's sister. I shall expect you to leave in the morning. In the meantime, I need a bed made up and some food. Please call one of the servants; then you can go and pack.' She had never given orders before except to Grandmama's little maid, Millie, who was more of a fellow sufferer than a servant, and the sudden echo of her grandmother's voice caught her by surprise.

The woman smiled slyly. 'There aren't no servants left,' she said and Helen caught a glimpse of malicious pleasure in her red-veined eyes. 'They've all run off, said the place was cursed, like. I'm the only one here. If you do sack me you'll have to do it all yourself.' Unsteadily, she drew herself up to her full height. 'You didn't ought to be so cross. You should be thanking me with all your heart and soul for looking after the baby, not complaining because I tried to soothe the poor little mite with a drop of liquor. Liquor what I paid for myself, mind,' she added, her voice becoming a whine.

Helen felt her heart sink. She was tired; two days travelling by rail and steamer and then being trundled through Cornish lanes on a jolting carrier's cart had left her bone weary and hungry with a nagging headache. She had been looking forward to food, warmth, comfort. Instead...

The abandoned look of the farm; the bellowing of cattle; the reluctance of the carrier to bring her here and the speed with which he had departed; all these signs should have warned her that her vision of a comfortable homecoming were a dream. Resignedly, she hefted the still screaming child over one shoulder. 'What do you mean, run off?' she demanded. 'Why should they go?'

''Tes the curse, see!' The maid moved forward, her eyes wide. 'Brem bad it is. Ill luck comes to all what lives here.' She glanced over her shoulder at the shadows gathering in the corners of the large stone-flagged kitchen as the sun set.

'Don't be ridiculous.' Helen was too sensible to be frightened by the wild tales of a half-drunk servant. 'There are no such things as curses – as you know very well.'

'Not where you do come from, maybe, but down here...' The woman moved closer. 'Then there were the accident. Him and her both. What were that if it weren't a curse, then?'

'It was an accident,' said Helen crossly. 'As you've just said yourself. You're not trying to tell me that perfectly respectable servants ran away because of stories a child would laugh at?'

The woman's face darkened. ''Tes true, as you'll find out. There's just me left. In terror of me life,' she added, eyeing Helen carefully. 'Risking me immortal soul for the sake of the little one there.'

It was too much. 'Your immortal soul is in more danger from your drinking than from this nonsensical curse,' Helen declared roundly. 'Now, what about some food?'

'I bin sacked,' the woman announced. 'Food idn't my problem any more. 'Tes all down to you now.'

She turned on her heel with a flourish and lurched unsteadily to the door.

Helen felt too tired to face a cold, cheerless evening without food and with a screaming child to cope with. Feeling that she was putting her own immortal soul in danger, Helen said quickly, 'Work for tonight and I'll write you a reference.'

The woman paused. 'A good one?' she enquired cautiously.

'As good as I can.' After all, she had stayed with the child when the others had left. At least Helen could say she was loyal. But she didn't want to spend the evening with a drunken, resentful servant. 'Is there a parlour I can sit in? There must be another room in this place.'

''Tes just for best,' the maid said. 'The master never used it for everyday, like.'

Holding the child, Helen began to explore. It was difficult to reconcile the damp, decrepit house with the glowing descriptions Mary had written of her new home. But perhaps, having eloped, she felt that she could not let slip anything that made it sound as if she had regretted her actions – not even to her only sister. 'Oh, Mary,' Helen breathed, her heart going out to the foolish, beautiful girl-child she remembered so well, 'you could have trusted me.'

The parlour, when she found it, was cold and damp and covered with dust. A faint smell of mushrooms suggested that it was seldom used. Helen's dream of handing a successful, working farm and comfortable house to an agent who could speedily let it, to bring in the much-needed money to help with Beth's upbringing, was quickly fading. The house seemed barely inhabitable, and what use was the farm with no workers?

At least being carried around seemed to soothe the child. Her screams had dropped to an occasional whimper and she laid her head on Helen's shoulder, one pudgy fist thrust into her dribbling mouth. The soft summer night was drawing in quickly now. Helen decided that more walking around might send the baby off to sleep, and the bellowing of the cows outside reminded her that she had more responsibilities than just the house.

Though what she could do about cows, she did not know. Beth presumably needed milk but, in Helen's experience, milk was something which turned up outside the back door each day in large churns pulled on the back of a cart. She knew that originally it had come from cows but the process by which it had transferred from one to the other was a complete mystery to her.

She sighed when she saw the farmyard. A brief hope that her unknown brother-in-law might have spent all his money on the farm rather than the house quickly faded. Not even the twilight could soften the view of tumbledown buildings – their shaggy thatched roofs growing everything from grass to a small tree surrounding a muddy, rutted yard with a manure heap in the middle. An evil-looking rooster, balanced on its peak, eyed her speculatively. He looked as if any attempt to feed him might leave you with less fingers than the ideal. Helen gave the noisome heap a wide berth and headed, rather nervously, for the dark shed from which the bellowing was coming.

Inside, it was even darker. White, ghostly shapes in the dimness made her start before she recognised them as the white markings on cows. You're just tired, she told herself, waiting for her heart to stop thumping. You're letting those stupid stories get to you. Taking a deep breath, she moved further into the shed, praying that the cows, with their wide, curving horns, were less dangerous than they looked.

The small figure that leapt up from beside the cow made her gasp with fright and set Beth off wailing again. But the stranger seemed as frightened as she was herself.

'I weren't stealing,' the figure explained, shrilly. 'I weren't, honest I weren't.'

'No, I'm sure you weren't.' Helen patted Beth's back absently as her eyes took in the small urchin staring up at her, eyes huge in a pale face under riotous curls which glowed red even in this poor light. The cow beside her moved suddenly, lunging forward with a hind hoof, and the strange child slapped her swiftly on her bony rump. 'Quiet, Daisy.'

'You know the cows?' Helen was unsure where to start.

'I takes 'em round the lanes, feeding,' the child explained. She scratched at the dung-covered floor with a dirty foot. 'I do know I shouldn't be here but...' She paused then her voice grew stronger. 'It were their bellowing, see. I couldn't bear to hear poor creatures in agony like that so when I could get away from Ma I came up here to milk them. Just to ease them,' she hurried to reassure Helen. 'The milk I took is in the dairy, right and tight. Daisy here is the last one.' The cow mooed, moving uneasily, and the child glanced at her. 'She's still full to bursting. She'll kick the bucket over if I don't get on with it.'

'Carry on then,' Helen said weakly. She was out of her depth here. The child seated herself on a three-legged stool, her head buried in the side of the cow and immediately liquid began squirting into the wooden bucket through her capable, small hands, singing as it frothed up in the milk already there.

'I – I'm very grateful to you for taking the trouble,' Helen said, knowing that she could not do what the child was doing. Although it all seemed to be happening so easily she was sure that there was a knack to it that she did not possess and besides, there was something so – intimate – about the whole business. Looking away from the bursting udder, the pink, swaying teats, she realised that the cows were much quieter than when she had arrived at the farm. Only one still mooed, head stuck out as she bellowed her unhappiness to the world. 'I thought you said that this was the last to be milked,' she said, glad to make a contribution to the conversation.

The child raised her head briefly from the cow's side. 'That's Blossom,' she said calmly. 'She's troublesome. T'aint milking she do need, 'tes a bull.'

Helen swallowed. 'Oh! Really?' Her heart quailed at the thought of taking a cow (how? On a lead like a dog?) to a bull. Did the farm own one? And if not, how did one raise the subject with another farmer? Nothing about this strange new world in which she found herself seemed compatible with the ideas of ladylike behaviour as maintained by her grandmother.

She looked again at the strange child whose fingers moved so competently amongst the rubbery teats of the cow and took a deep breath. 'You couldn't – I mean, if I were to employ you–'

'Me?' The young voice squeaked with surprise. 'To look after your cows?'

'Yes. And any other animals,' Helen added swiftly. 'Er, do we *have* any other animals?'

'Oxen, pigs, chickens, ducks,' the child chanted swiftly. 'There used to be a couple of horses but they – died.'

The pony involved in the carriage accident that had killed her sister and brother-in-law had broken a leg and been shot, Helen remembered. At least that was one less problem. 'Can you do it?' She hoped that her voice did not betray the eagerness she felt.

'If Ma says I can.' The girl finished her milking and stood up, pulling stool and bucket easily out from under the cow's belly. Patting the hiccuping Beth, Helen followed the girl out into the yard. Her rumbling stomach reminded her of another problem. 'What about feeding everything?'

'Done it already.' In the lighter yard Helen could see that her new employee was only about eight, skinny and barefoot. She heaved the heavy wooden bucket across to the dairy and poured the milk into a single, big churn. 'Going to make butter and all like before, are you?'

Helen had had enough of being made to feel incompetent by an urchin not one quarter her age. 'I'll decide later on,' she said loftily, trying to hide the plummeting of her heart at this new problem. Running a farm was more difficult than she had ever imagined.

She hadn't impressed her new employee. 'Milk'll be turned by then,' the child said calmly. She stood on tiptoe, reached down a metal tin and scooped up some of the fresh milk. 'Here. You'll need 'un for the baby.'

Helen trailed behind the child out into the yard again. Beth was still grizzling softly, her hand in her mouth, and had dribbled a wet patch all over Helen's shoulder. Suddenly, tiredness and ignorance got her down. 'Oh, Beth' – it was almost a wail – 'why won't you stop crying?'

In this as in everything else the child was an expert. She stopped where the lamplight from the kitchen flooded out. 'She's teething, see.' To Helen's horror she pushed a grimy finger in between the baby's lips, turning her head and opening her jaws so that Helen could see the bright red, inflamed gums broken by small, white patches.

'There's her teeth coming through. She'll be all right once that happens but you won't get much sleep until they do.'

Helen had a fleeting moment of sympathy for her drunken, sacked servant but forced it down. 'Isn't there something I can do to help her?'

'You could cut a cross over where the teeth is.' Seeing Helen's instinctive revulsion, she added, 'Or you could give her something to chew; an old bone, something hard and smooth. Calves chew the tops of doors and it do seem to help them.' She turned to go.

'Wait.' Helen hoped she didn't sound panicky. 'When I come to see your mother tomorrow, where do I come?'

The girl pointed. 'Further on down the lane and past the works. It's the only cottage.' Then she was gone, merged into the darkness.

Helen stared after her. Life on a farm was nothing like she had imagined – but it looked as if she had found one ally.

Three

'Shoes mended.' 'Buy your butter here. Straight from the cow.' 'Fresh fish, Miss? Lovely fried for yer supper.'

Helen ducked swiftly away as a fat lady with no teeth wearing what looked like an old straw basket on her head waved a large wet fish right in her face. She had been thankful to be able to leave Beth with Jenny's mother; she didn't want to burden herself with a dead fish before her meeting with her brother-in-law's attorney.

Above her towered a handsome domed building behind a classic portico, a combination of Council chamber and court. All round it, ignoring the classic elegance behind them, the street vendors clustered, shouting their wares in the uninhibited voices of those who spend most of their lives out of doors.

After the quiet of the countryside, the bustle of Penzance was overwhelming. Helen had planned to spend the hours before her appointment with Mr Brownfield exploring the town but she found the teeming life of the market intimidating.

She turned off down one of the meandering roads. In the distance the sea sparkled, blue, inviting; the ideal place to pass a few hours before the meeting this afternoon. As a woman alone she needed somewhere quiet to pass the time. The calls of the street vendors faded as she left the market area but the bustle of people didn't lessen.

The harbour was a seething mass of boats and people. Boys moved small rowing boats along by the seemingly magical means of waggling an oar over the back – stern, she reminded herself, and smiled as she thought again of Anne Elliot. Three days ago, Anne's fictional life had seemed so vibrant to her, but since then, her own had changed beyond recognition.

She knew that, as a well-bred lady, she ought to have been prostrate with nervous exhaustion but instead she found herself glowing with an inward excitement. It was actually fun to meet all these difficulties and surmount them. Not that the problems in the future didn't loom alarmingly, but then, she told herself, a week ago she had doubted her ability to travel to Cornwall without a companion. Now, with Jenny employed to look after the animals and Jenny's mother minding Beth for the day, she felt she was surmounting her problems.

Once she had instructed the attorney to rent or sell the land she could take the child and leave, satisfied that she had done all that she could. A few more days and she could be back in London again.

But for now, she was determined to wring every last particle of enjoyment out of her adventure. She stood outside the white-painted Custom House with its own steep flight of steps leading down to the harbour and prepared to enjoy the sunlit scene in front of her.

One boat was unloading fish at the small pier, another was taking on board silvery ingots that were probably tin and it was all done with many shouts and comments which her unaccustomed ear could not translate but which were almost certainly unsuitable for a lady to hear. Close by, the doors of the Dolphin Inn opened and two men staggered out, shouting. This was no place for a lady, she realised.

Driven from the harbour area she wandered along the seafront, past the outcrop of rocks that were still crowned with a battery of guns and on past small, tidy cottages, built only yards from the sea.

It was quieter here but there was nowhere for a lady to sit. She wandered further on. The sun beat down and she knew that Grandmama would scold her for letting herself become tanned but it had seemed ridiculous to walk through the countryside clutching a baby and a parasol. Besides, with her dark colouring she would never achieve the fashionable whiteness.

On the far side of the town the houses gave way to a wide swathe of sand dunes between the sea and a road. With a satisfied sigh, Helen sank into the shade of a dune, gazing out across the blue curve of Mounts Bay.

Three days ago she had never walked to the end of the street alone; now she had travelled three hundred miles, sacked her first servant, employed her first farm-hand – the very thought of applying that term to the urchin, Jenny, made her choke with suppressed laughter – and walked three miles, totally alone, to a strange town. And, this afternoon, she had an appointment to see her brother-in-law's lawyer. And then...

What was that woman doing? Suddenly, Helen was on her feet, her attention on the thin figure wading, fully clothed, into the calm waters. Surely she couldn't be...

Helen paused in a welter of indecision, biting her lip, the well-bred woman's inborn dislike of interference with a stranger's actions holding her back. After all, she knew nothing of life by the sea. Perhaps the woman was – was – catching crabs or something.

She glanced both ways, hoping to see another person, but the stretch of coast between Penzance and Newlyn was empty. She looked back. The woman was deeper now, the small, incoming waves lapping well above her knees as she took another step forward into the sea.

Better to look a fool than risk standing by while another took her own life. Hesitantly, Helen stepped forward onto the damp sand. 'Excuse me...'

If she needed an answer she had got it. The woman cast a frantic look over her shoulder and began to hurry forward. In an agony of indecision, Helen glanced around again. Still no one. It was down to her.

'Please, you mustn't–' She pulled off her boots, snapping the laces without a second thought, then moved into the sea after the woman, trying to lift the skirt itself free of the waves even though her petticoats hung into the water. 'Come back. Tell me about it. Perhaps I can help you.'

The woman was almost up to her waist now, moving more slowly, but Helen found it impossible to catch her up. The layers of wet petticoat clung round her legs, tying them together while at the same time they caught the flow of the sea. The little waves, which had looked so gentle and kindly from the shore, pulled at the yards of material, dragging them forward and back and making her stagger drunkenly. She caught her foot on a hidden rock and tripped, falling forward. The cold water rushed over her, soaking her to the skin and taking her breath away. With an effort she regained her feet and carried doggedly on. 'I'm sure I can help you. If you've been deserted by a man–' It was the most likely explanation.

The woman gave a harsh laugh. 'Deserted! Oh, God! Would that I were.' She stepped forward again, almost breast-deep in the surging sea.

'Why won't you let me help you?' Helen cried, forcing her way through the waves. It was like a nightmare. No matter how hard she tried she could not move quickly enough. The woman was always a few feet in front of her, always just out of reach. And the sea was getting dangerously deep. If she went any further she would be in danger herself.

The woman must have realised this too because she turned and for the first time Helen saw her face. It would have been pretty if it were not so thin and careworn. 'Go back,' the woman cried. 'You can't do nothing for me. Go back. Don't risk yourself.'

'Come with me.' Helen forced her legs another couple of paces through the cold sea. 'At least let me help.'

Her foot tripped against another stone just as a larger wave than usual surged against her. For a second she struggled frantically to keep her balance but it was too late. She fell forward into deep water and the surging sea, pulling and dragging at her wet clothes, swayed them up, over her arms, her head.

Choking, struggling, Helen tried to gain a foothold but the hindering petticoats were everywhere, blinding her, tying her arms. The waves rolled her over so that she no longer even knew which way was up, which way was shorewards. Panic rose as the water entered her mouth, her nose. Gasping, she breathed salt water which burned and choked her, filling her lungs with fire. She struggled frantically, uselessly, against the hampering cloth. She was drowning. She was lost.

The pain brought her to her senses. Something, someone, had grabbed a handful of hair and was pulling. She was aware of the sensation of movement, then that her head was above the water, but her thick skirts clung to her face, smothering, suffocating. Then the material was flung back and light, blessed light and air reached her.

She choked and coughed, clinging to her rescuer as the waves surged and eddied against their joined bodies. Tears and salt water blinded her. Through her laboured breathing she could vaguely hear a soothing voice. 'There, there, my handsome, you'll be all right dreckly.'

Hands forced her to move and she was half carried, half staggered blindly onwards, stumbling as the waves took her. Then the sea was shallower, the waves pulling only at her calves, her ankles.

She fell thankfully to her knees on the wet shingle, retching as her body tried to expel the water she had taken in. As her senses returned she could feel a warm body next to hers, an arm supporting her, a voice reassuring her. More than one voice.

Blearily, she raised her head. Where before the beach had been empty, suddenly, when she needed privacy, there were people all round, staring at her, talking about her. She was suddenly aware that her bonnet was gone, her chestnut hair hanging loose and wet about her shoulders, her newly bought mourning clothes ruined.

She coughed and retched again, longing for privacy, longing for warmth and dryness, aware that the arms holding her belonged to the woman she had followed into the sea.

'There's Doctor.' A louder voice than the rest cut through her coughing.

A new face appeared, male, handsome,

bored. 'Nothing for me to do here. Keep her warm and dry. No exertion.' She knew already that without pay he would do nothing and she *was* improving.

'What did she go into the sea for?' a voice demanded. 'Off her head, is she?'

Helen felt the thin figure beside her tense and knew that she had to protect her. Suicide was against the laws of man and God. With an effort she raised her head. 'My dog.' Her voice was rough and croaky and the excuse weak but it was all she could think of on the spur of the moment. 'He went into the sea. I thought he would drown.'

She collapsed, coughing again, but she had said enough. The buzz of conversation grew louder. 'Risked herself for a dog, did she?' 'Brem mad these up-country folk.' 'As if a dog can't look after 'isself.' The crowd turned, staring out to sea, some exclaiming over the loss of a dog, a few even seeing its head here and there in the sparkling waves.

Helen pushed herself up and forced a tremulous smile. 'Thank you.'

The woman stared at her bitterly. 'You've nothing to thank me for. It were all my fault. It always is. All I do is bring trouble to them about me. T'were better I were dead.'

'No.' Helen had to keep the woman with her; she was too weak to stage another rescue attempt. 'You can't leave me like this.

I've got – I've got to get back to town.' She struggled to her feet and stared down at the ruin of her clothes. 'How can I see a lawyer like this?' Her voice was almost a wail.

The woman sighed. 'You can have my spare clothes.' Her voice grew bitter. 'God knows, I'll never need them again. And *he* has no use for them.'

Helen limped over to her boots and forced her cold, wet feet into them, knotting the broken laces together to keep them on. 'He?' she queried.

'My husband.' The woman's voice dripped hatred. 'My man. My *owner.*'

So it wasn't the prospect of an illegitimate child that had driven her into the sea. Helen held out her hand, still wet and shaking slightly as a result of her experiences. 'Won't you tell me your problem? And your name.' She laughed, her voice still hoarse from the water she had swallowed. 'It feels wrong to be owing my life to a person whose name I don't know.'

For a moment she thought the woman would refuse, then she shrugged. 'What do it matter? And I owe you something, after all. You could have told them back there' – she nodded over her shoulder at the dispersing crowd – 'what I were about and that would have meant prison for me. My name's Agnes Penhaligon.' She stopped, obviously waiting for a response.

Helen could not give one. 'Should I know the name?' she asked.

'The rest of the world do,' the woman said, angrily. 'George Penhaligon, the great seer. George Penhaligon the mystic.' Her voice hardened. 'George Penhaligon the brute,' she snapped.

Helen was beginning to get an inkling. 'He beats you?'

'When he can find me. I left him after he hit me when I were expecting and I lost the little one.'

Helen winced. 'I don't blame you,' she said, though she knew that many would. Women were expected to stay with their husbands through thick and thin. It was in the marriage service. 'For better or worse.' It was hard to think of anything worse than losing a child like that because of the violence of your husband but that didn't matter. The promise had been made and women were expected to keep it.

'That isn't all.' Agnes walked beside her towards the town and Helen was aware of the sight they made, both wet through, clothes and bonnets ruined. 'I left, went to another town, got myself a job as a maid. Earned a bit I was keeping, like. Then *he* came.' Again her voice was harsh with hate. 'He hunted me down, beat me up, took all the money I'd earned and left again.'

'But surely,' Helen protested, 'you could

have gone to the magistrates. That was your money, money you'd earned without him.'

The woman laughed. 'It were *his* money,' she said. 'We're one person, him and me, for ever. A lawyer told me that, and a vicar. Any money I earn, he can take.' She sighed, her shoulders drooping. 'I ran away again; it happened again. And again. Then I came here.' She nodded at the outskirts of Penzance, looming in front of them. 'I changed my name, lied about where I come from. I thought I'd got away.' Her voice rose. 'I'd money put aside. I were going to get out of service, start up as a dressmaker, work up to a shop.'

Her voice broke. 'He found me again. Took it all. Every penny I'd saved. That's when I decided it weren't no use. No matter what I do, he'll find me, he'll get it. And I *won't* work for a man what killed my babby, I *won't*, I *won't!*' Her voice rose hysterically.

'Of course you mustn't.' They were weaving their way through the back streets now, amongst men and women whose clothes were little better than their own. 'But you mustn't kill yourself either. That way he's won.'

Helen stopped and held out her hand. 'Come and stay with me. I can't pay you but I can offer shelter for a few days. On a farm, off the beaten track. No one need even know you're there. I shall have to go back to

London in a day or so but that will give you time to think about what you're going to do, where you can go.'

She smiled at the thin, set face beside her. 'I need help.' Her voice and face were luminous with the truth. 'I've got a seven-month orphan baby to look after, a farm of animals and a filthy house. The servants and farm hands have all run away and my only helper is an eight year old child.'

She put her hands on Agnes' damp sleeve. 'You saved my life just now,' she said quietly. 'You have some responsibility for me, as I have for you. If you agree, we can help each other now, as we did in the sea. Please.'

There was a long silence and she had almost given up hope when Agnes said gruffly, 'Suppose I could help you out for a day or two.' She sniffed. 'The sea won't go away, that's for sure.'

Helen turned away to hide her relief.

Four

'So you see,' Mr Brownfield said awkwardly, 'there really is no possibility of letting the farm as you suggested.' He let his gaze drop from the cobwebbed corner of the ceiling to his client for a second, almost visibly shuddered, then looked away again.

It was a good thing, Helen decided, that when she had arranged this meeting with the clerk earlier on she had looked respectable. She had seen the shock in his face when she had arrived this afternoon and realised that, looking as she did, she would never otherwise have been admitted.

Not that she blamed Mr Brownfield, or his clerk. Agnes might be a good needlewoman but her clothes were made for a smaller frame and Helen was aware of a constriction around the chest warning her that one deep breath would pepper the room with buttons. Green was not the colour for a mourning sister to wear either. She dismissed the thought. Her mission was more important than her dress.

'Mr Brownfield,' she said steadily, 'I think you misunderstand me. The farm *must* be let. And soon. I have engagements in London in the near future that I must carry out.' What Ezekiel Hardcourt would say if she missed her interview with Lord Carnglase did not bear thinking about.

'Miss Schofield, it is *you* who do not understand.' He still stared at the corner of the ceiling but she could see lines of irritation deepen around his mouth. 'The Cornish are a very superstitious race. Regrettable, I am sure, but it is a fact of life. And with the reputation of that farm you will not get anyone to work there. It is, in effect, unlettable.'

He must have meant what he said because he actually lowered his gaze and Helen was aware of a pair of uncomfortably intelligent eyes watching her.

'It is the history of the farm that is the problem, you see. Your brother-in-law's grandfather won it from the previous owners in a card game – unlucky for the original owners – then died almost immediately. His son inherited it and came to live there but again, tragedy struck. Within months his wife died in childbirth, together with the baby boy she was carrying. He took to the bottle, I am afraid, let the land go to rack and ruin and died drunk.'

'Things like this happen all the time,' Helen said impatiently.

'I haven't finished yet.' He stared at her reprovingly. 'Then your brother-in-law inherited the land, married your sister and had a child. He decided to concentrate first on building up the stock by selective breeding but he, too, had bad luck. Calves he had pinned his hopes on died; workmen became ill just when they were needed for important work; a magnificent working mare, that he spent more on than he should and from which he was planning to breed, died; cows have been ill and given less milk that he anticipated, and finally he and his wife were killed in an accident.' He cleared his throat. 'Would you deny that there is good cause for the superstition?'

Helen's heart sank at the catalogue of disasters. Listed like that she could understand why uneducated people might think as they did. 'What do you advise me to do?'

'Stop hitting your head against a brick wall.' He smiled briefly. 'Sell the animals for what you can get, take the child back to London with you and cut your losses.'

'And the land, the farmhouse?' she asked.

He shrugged. 'I doubt that you will get a tenant for the house, isolated as it is and close to the calciner. As for the land–' He sighed. 'That will revert to the moorland from which it was originally claimed. If you look around at the moors you will see numerous traces of fields which have been abandoned. This farm is not the first to which it has happened and I fear it will not be the last.'

'And my niece?' she asked, swallowing the bitterness inside her. 'This farm is her inheritance. What will happen to her?'

He shrugged again but his face showed compassion. 'Apart from what she will get from selling off the cattle I am afraid that she will lose it all.' He cleared his throat. 'It might even be considered another sign of the curse at work. If she were older, of the opposite sex, she could work it herself, struggle through alone for a few years until she could persuade people that the curse had lifted. As it is...' He spread his hands helplessly.

Helen felt a bubble of anger rise within her. 'As it is she will be virtually a pauper,' she snapped. She thought of her small niece, so helpless, with all her life in front of her, and the inheritance, which should have made everything smooth for her, taken away, lost, because of the superstitions of the ignorant.

Instead of growing up with money for her education and an income to attract a wealthy husband, she would be like Helen herself, little more that an unpaid servant in a relative's house until she herself could scramble into some sort of union with the first man who proposed to her.

Poor little Beth. And just because she was the wrong age, the wrong sex... Helen sat up straighter. 'Tell me, Mr Brownfield, is there any money?'

Her shrewd eyes narrowed. 'A little,' he said reluctantly. 'As I said, too much has been spent recently on the purchase of high-quality animals but there is some capital. The sale of eggs and butter and cheese, together with sides of pork, have been providing the farm with the day-to-day income but of course, since the accident...' His voice faded meaningfully.

She knew nothing of cheese and butter-making. Helen ignored the thought. 'Has the sale of these items been affected by the so-called curse on the farm?'

He was looking at her with more attention now. 'It appears not, Miss Schofield.' He raised a bushy eyebrow. 'Are you thinking of continuing with the farm?'

She climbed to her feet, her face set. 'If that is what it takes to save my niece's inheritance, Mr Brownfield, then that is what I shall do.'

'And your engagement in London?'

She had forgotten she had mentioned it. Ezekiel would be very upset if she missed seeing his patron.

She dismissed the thought. There would be other opportunities. Surely if she could keep the farm running without a disaster for just a few weeks then people would believe that the curse was lifted. At the very least, there was a better chance of letting or selling a working farm than one that was abandoned.

'It will have to be postponed.' She saw the doubt in his face and continued, 'I already have one person to help with the cattle so I shall not be totally alone.'

'Then I can only wish you luck.' He too rose heavily to his feet. 'Presumably you are not planning to run the farm permanently?'

'An emergency measure only,' she confirmed. 'So if you can advertise it for sale or rent I would be grateful.'

He bowed. 'Knowing what you have taken on, I can only admire your courage, ma'am.'

I wish I knew what I had taken on, she thought as she held out her hand to him. But it had to be done, and she was the only one who could do it.

He ushered her out of his office with a ceremony that contrasted so starkly with his reception of her that Helen realised that she had managed to offset the bad first impression created by her rag-bag of ill-fitting clothes and was secretly heartened. Whether what she was doing was wise or not, at least she had managed to impress a shrewd old lawyer.

As they moved into the waiting room a gentleman rose politely to his feet, and her belief in Mr Brownfield's respect was reinforced when, instead of hustling her swiftly out, he stopped. 'Miss Schofield, may I make known to you your nearest neighbour, Mr Ledgerwood.'

Looking up, she found herself looking into the blue eyes and handsome face of the young doctor from the beach.

'Oh.' For a second her social training deserted her. Helen was only aware of her over-tight, brightly coloured clothes, of her still wet hair bound up under a cheap bonnet. Then sense returned and she realised she was staring at him like a child at a lollipop.

Blushing, she dropped a swift curtsy. 'How do you do, Sir. I – I am afraid that I have not yet had a chance to visit any neighbouring houses.'

'Oh, he doesn't live by you,' Mr Brownfield intervened swiftly. 'My fault. I meant that he is part-owner of the calciner that is built just by your bottom fields.' He shook the young doctor's hand. 'How is it doing, Mr Ledgerwood? Is it a success?'

'My brother-in-law and I are going over the first six months' figures tonight, but' – he smiled, showing strong white teeth, – 'my impression is that it is doing very well, very well indeed.'

He turned back to Helen. 'And you are the new owner of Tregurtha Farm?'

'No,' she corrected him swiftly. 'That is my niece. I am merely her guardian.'

He was looking at her closely now, not with the merely passing glance of a chance-met stranger, and she saw his glance touch her wet hair, drop to her face, saw recognition dawn.

'But you – aren't you the lady I attended at Wherry Town beach?'

Her blush deepened and she felt the heat spreading through her body. 'I...' What could she say, how could she explain herself? She tried again. 'I–'

'And your little dog? I hope he was rescued.'

Guilt and embarrassment almost robbed her of her voice. 'No.' It came out in a strangled gulp but luckily he took it as a sign of grief and his warm fingers clasped hers in sympathy.

'You mustn't let it prey on your mind, Miss Schofield, indeed you mustn't. Though I know how ladies dote on their little companions.' He smiled at her. 'I think that it is a sign of their maternal feelings coming to the fore, even before nature gives them a better subject for such devotion.'

The touch of his hand, his smile, his words, all deprived her of her power of speech. It was a relief when he turned to Mr Brownfield to explain how they had met before and when he turned back, expressing concern that she was not following his instructions regarding warmth and rest, she was capable of once more responding as she ought.

'You have your maid with you at least,' Mr Ledgerwood continued, turning to where Agnes sat silently, a carpet-bag containing their wet clothes at her feet. 'I'm sure she will see that you get home quickly and act sensibly.'

Agnes dropped a small curtsy. 'As you say, sir,' she responded, her face and voice expressionless.

Helen made an effort to act like a proper

lady – and a guardian. 'You mentioned a calciner by my land, Mr Ledgerwood. Forgive my ignorance, but is that the long, low building with a high chimney that I passed this morning?' Ladies did not mention such things or she would have spoken of the stench of garlic that surrounded the building, even as far as the Trahairs' tiny cottage.

He showed a disconcerting aptitude to read her mind. 'You noticed the smell? But garlic is very health-giving, you know. It is unpleasant but there is nothing to worry about.'

She was relieved to hear it. When Mrs Trahair had offered to look after Beth for the day Helen's only concern had been the unhealthiness of the overpowering smell. Apart from that the cottage was poor but clean and the thought of going through an interview with a lawyer with a screaming child on her lap was enough to make her accept swiftly.

But there was still something she did not understand. 'You're cooking garlic in that building?'

As soon as the words were spoken she knew that she had said something stupid. Both men roared with laughter and she found herself blushing again in annoyance at her ignorance. She could even hear the clerk sniggering softly in the background.

But again, it was the young doctor who acted swiftly to save her feelings.

'It was very foolish of me not to explain properly, Miss Schofield. In this area, mining and its associated industries are of such common interest that we forget that other people do not share our concerns. A calciner is simply a huge oven. When it is mined, tin is often combined with other elements which can make it brittle so we heat the ore in order to drive off these elements before the tin is smelted.'

As simple as that! Helen smiled at him, grateful both for the information and for the kind and unpatronising way it was given.

As she walked to the door Anthony Ledgerwood moved swiftly to open it for her, delaying her for a second as she was about to pass through by a touch on her sleeve. 'My work takes me all around the neighbourhood as you can imagine, Miss Schofield. If I am passing the farm, will you allow me to make a brief visit – to make sure that you have suffered no harm from your unfortunate immersion this morning?'

What was the matter with her? She could feel herself blushing yet again. Stammering slightly, Helen gave her permission and made her way swiftly out of the house, Agnes following silently behind her.

'What a handsome man!' Helen managed to keep her thoughts to herself for some time but as they were entering the village of Madron she could contain herself no longer. 'So kind, so polite.' Another thought struck her. 'He is very much the gentleman, isn't he, for an apothecary?'

Agnes's face did not lose its habitual cold expression. 'Seems to me he were a brem lot more attentive to a land-owning lady than he was to some drowning female,' she observed sourly.

Helen just laughed.

Five

'Money!' Anthony Ledgerwood leaned back in his chair, a broad smile on his handsome face. He stretched both hands into the air, making a grasping movement with his hands. 'Money!'

'You can't be that poor. I pay you well over the odds for the work you do at the mine.' His brother-in-law, Robert Polglase, eyed him cynically. Like his sister, Anthony had a well-developed love of money, but where Theo was an expert at spending it, Anthony just seemed to like the stuff for its own sake. 'Anyone would think that you were hovering at the door of the poorhouse, not one of the best paid doctors in the district,' he added dryly.

'All doctors are hovering at the poorhouse door,' Anthony responded. 'This,' he leaned forward and tapped the pages of accounts spread out on the table between them, 'only moves me a few steps further away.'

A few steps! When Robert needed every penny of his half of the profits to keep the mine working. Were the rumours about Anthony's gambling true? he wondered, not for the first time. He was a single man with a good medical practice in addition to his retainer as mine surgeon – and half the time he ate his dinners at Robert's expense anyway. Why should he always plead poverty?

'You were able to afford to pay a fifth of the calciner's building costs,' Robert reminded him tartly.

That still rankled. He had come up with four-fifths of the cost while Anthony had only paid one-fifth – and he still only got half the profits. Anthony had argued that it had been his idea, that only he had the knowledge to design the works. In addition, he had pointed out that Robert would get the benefit from tin ore free from the contamination of the arsenic that made the processed tin brittle; surely, therefore, it was only fair that they should split the profit made by selling the purified arsenic between them? All true, but Robert knew that he would never have agreed to such a division of profits if Theo hadn't been so determined. Now that he saw the actual figures, the inequality of it was even more obvious.

Despite his wife's persuasions he had managed to get Anthony to put some money towards the works, had argued that unless Anthony paid his fifth then they would not split the profits from the sale of the arsenic equally, never thinking for a second that a country doctor would be able to put up the money. And here he was, hoist with his own petard. As if he didn't need that money desperately himself...

'Never underestimate a Ledgerwood.' Anthony smiled brilliantly at him, his blue eyes and handsome face a masculine version of his twin sister's. 'I would have thought Theo would have taught you that by now.'

'And what would Theo have taught you?' On cue she had opened the door to the study, smiling round the corner at them. 'You know I never do what I am supposed to. Including not interrupting.'

She came further into the room, her blonde curls and blue silk dress that exactly matched her eyes lighting up the dark study. 'Do you know, Anthony, that strict husband of mine *forbade* me to come in here, even though he was only having a talk with you.' She came lightly round the table, the wide sweep of her skirts only emphasising the narrowness of her waist and her pale fragility. 'But I forgive you, you old bear.' She leaned over his chair from behind, twining her arms around Robert's neck, dropping a kiss on his dark curls.

Too late he realised her motives. His hands moved swiftly to cover up the sheet of figures on the table but he was too slow. She had eyes like a hawk's where money was concerned.

'Good heavens! Has the calciner done that well?' He felt the softness of her breasts as she leaned over his shoulder to pick up the accounts, smelled her perfume. 'How wonderful. We'll be able to have new drawing room curtains and re-cover the chairs. That blue has faded so badly it's almost grey; it makes me look really haggard.'

As if anything could dim her vibrant beauty, and well she knew it. He hated denying her anything but he had to put a stop to this as quickly as possible. 'Theo, you know that the mine is doing badly. The whole point of the calciner was to give us another source of income for when the price of tin was down–'

'The whole point of income is to spend it,' she broke in swiftly. 'And you can't say now that we don't have it, can he, Anthony?' Theo turned to her twin brother with a small pout.

He agreed with her as usual. 'These *nouveaux riches* are all the same, always tight with their money.'

Robert felt himself redden under the slur as he always did. Ever since they were boys together at Harrow, Anthony Ledgerwood had never lost a chance to throw in his face the fact that his father was just a miner who had made good. Yet if *he* responded in kind, if *he* ever mentioned their father, he was met with floods of tears from Theo and allegations of lack of breeding from her brother.

Not that they could be proud of a gentleman who had run through his money before shooting himself and leaving his children to be brought up by a distant relative, surely. But in their eyes the important word was 'gentleman'. The fact that they had been raised by an uncle who was only an apothecary and who had to scrimp and save to keep Anthony at public school before entering him in his own profession in order to earn a living was something which neither of them ever mentioned.

Robert sighed, wishing, not for the first time, that Theo was less close to her brother. And that she had not inherited her father's attitude to money. He sighed again. He had been unable to believe his luck when she had accepted him, she was so beautiful, so light-hearted, so elegant.

She put the paper back on the table and ruffled his hair playfully. 'There, Robert, so sad that you are. It's a good thing that

Anthony is staying to dinner or I'd have to put up with your moods all by myself and you know that always gives me a headache.'

'But I thought–' Robert bit off the rest of the sentence. He was certain he had told Theo that he was not having Anthony to dinner tonight, but Theo had manoeuvred him into a corner, got her own way, as she always did. He sighed again. If he brought up the subject of the money from the calciner Anthony would support Theo as always; if he left it, then before dinner was over they would, between them, already have planned how the money was going to be spent and when he put his foot down he would be met with tears and recriminations from Theo.

But this time he would have to put his foot down. Things were too bad at the mine for there to be any other course of action open to him. Much as he hated depriving his beautiful Theo of anything she had set her heart on, she must be made to see reason this time. He could not put men out of work just so that she could redecorate the drawing room.

He was aware that she was smiling down at him. 'I was so sure the figures would be good that I had Carstairs bring out some champagne so that we can drink a toast before dinner.' She took his hand in hers, her slim, white fingers dwarfed by the broad palm that he had inherited from his working-class ancestors. 'Come on, Robert, come and enjoy yourself. Stop worrying about silly mines and calciners and things as if you were some sort of clerk.'

It was only because he worried about the mines and the calciner that they could afford to buy champagne. Robert knew it was pointless trying to make Theo understand this. She was all woman, soft, sweet, incapable of understanding the concerns that men had – but that just made her even more feminine and lovable.

In the small salon that she had made her own, Theo raised her glass. 'To the calciner,' she said, 'and all its lovely profits.' Her blue eyes twinkled at Robert over the sparkling, golden liquid. 'And to my new curtains.'

Robert put his glass down untouched. He could not drink to that. Theo would use it as a sign that she had got her own way and he couldn't let her. Not this time.

'Robert?' Her voice was suddenly sharp. 'You're not drinking.' She moved closer so that her full skirts brushed up against him. 'You're not going to be a stingy old husband, are you?' Her voice was low and caressing despite the words, her blue eyes were opened to their widest extent. It was a look Robert knew well from the early days of their marriage, a look that promised all sorts of things – if he did as she wanted.

For once he was glad for Anthony's intervention. Holding the champagne up to the lamp so that he could enjoy the flicker of the flame in the faceted sides of the cut glass, Anthony had taken no interest in his sister's actions and now he said, casually, 'By the way, I met our new neighbour today.'

Theo stood motionless for a second, then, as if realising that the moment for cajoling Robert had gone, she moved away to settle in her own chair with a graceful swirl of silk skirts, leaving Robert to follow up his brother-in-law's lead.

For a second Robert did not know who Anthony meant. 'But surely,' he began, 'the Nancarrows–' Then realisation came. 'You mean Tregurtha Farm. Has it been let, then?'

'Not yet. I met the child's guardian, who had come to see Mr Brownfield about the farm. She is very much the lady,' he added, softly.

Robert knew that this was another dig at him but ignored it, as he had ignored so many throughout the years. 'I am glad the child has a protector,' he said heavily. 'That was such a tragedy. Two young parents killed so suddenly in that way. Dreadful.'

Theo giggled. 'Racing in a dogcart,' she said. 'I'm surprised you can make them go fast enough to overturn.'

Robert disliked her levity but it would be

disloyal to reprimand her in front of her brother. 'Is she young?' he asked. 'I feel sorry for young children sometimes when they are brought up by elderly relations. They seem to miss out on their childhood somehow.'

'Very young,' Anthony confirmed. 'Only a couple of years older than the child's mother, from the look of her, but completely different. There's nothing of the flibbertigibbet about her.'

'And pretty?' Theo broke in swiftly. 'Is she as pretty as me?'

Anthony paused and Robert found himself holding his breath. Since she had clawed her way back into society by marrying him, Theo had gloried in being the youngest, most attractive lady in the area. Now, after seven years of marriage, he knew that she was aware that time was passing, that soon she would no longer be the reigning belle. Not that it mattered to him but he didn't want to see her hurt.

Anthony considered for so long that Robert knew that he was deliberately teasing his sister, before he said slowly, 'Well, she's dark.'

Robert felt the tension in his wife ease. A dark beauty would not be such a rival.

'Actually,' Anthony confessed, 'it was difficult to see what she was like. When I saw her she had just had a soaking. Her dog had gone into the sea off Wherry Town and had drowned. She and her maid had gone in after it and when I saw her she was wearing some old clothes that someone had lent her. But, despite that, you could see that she had class. When she is correctly dressed–'

'Fancy getting your clothes all wet just for a dog,' Theo said, with a derisory hoot of laughter. 'She must be a fool.'

'She must have loved her dog,' Robert corrected. He had owned dogs until his marriage but Theo had soon made him get rid of them, complaining bitterly about their smell and the hairs they shed on her new carpets and chairs. He felt a momentary pang but pushed it aside. A wife's happiness was more important than any dog, of course, but even so... Still, it was sad that this unknown lady should lose her dog so soon after the death of her sister.

'I suppose that she will take the child away with her,' he said, tearing his mind away from the sad vision. 'She will hardly want to farm the land herself.'

'Brownfield said that she had come to him about letting it,' Anthony admitted. 'But then, of course, she has a vested interest in getting a good price for it.'

Robert nodded. 'The child will need educating and girls cost money.' He was about to say that they needed money for a dowry but bit the words back quickly. He had married Theo because he loved her and had never mentioned the fact that she had been penniless when he took her as his own. Theo was hypersensitive about her former poverty and could read references to it where he had intended none.

Anthony shrugged. 'I would think she has a closer interest than that. The baby can't be more than six or seven months old. Small children can die of so many things: dysentery, cholera, even a bad cold can go to their lungs and carry them off. If that happened then the aunt would inherit the farm. You can't blame her for taking an interest in it.'

Robert was horrified. 'I'm sure that possibility hasn't even crossed her mind.'

'Then she's an even bigger fool than I thought her already,' Theo said coldly.

Robert gazed down at his almost untouched glass of champagne. Poor lady, he thought. He would go and offer her his condolences – and any help she needed. It was the least he could do in the circumstances.

The peal of the doorbell startled them all. No one paid calls at this time of night, just as people were sitting down to dinner. In sudden silence they listened to the footsteps of Carstairs, the butler, as he made his stately way to the front door.

The unexpected visitor was less patient. The bell pealed again, then there was a thumping sound as if someone was hammering on the door with their fists.

'What on earth–' Robert put down his glass and hurried to the hall.

It was dark outside now and for several seconds he could not see the visitor behind Carstairs' broad figure, just hear a high-pitched voice demanding instant entry.

Then there was a scuffle. A small figure ducked under Carstairs' arm and, erupting swiftly into the hall, ran straight into Robert, rocking him back on his feet.

'Careful.' Automatically, he clutched the figure which he now saw to be a small girl with a blazing head of red hair and a face that was one huge freckle. 'Don't be upset. Just tell me what you want.'

'Oh, sir.' She gazed up at him, her dirty hands twisting her thin cotton skirt nervously. 'Oh, sir, is Doctor here? 'Cos my granda's been taken awful bad and we need him quick.'

Six

Helen hurried through the growing darkness. Beside her, the long, low, windowless building of the calciner stretched out, ending in the tall chimney.

In this light she could not see the thick,

white smoke that dropped heavily from its top but she could smell it, a garlic-scented stink that seemed to fill the small valley. It had been her only fear when Jenny's mother had offered to look after Beth for the day.

Anyone with the slightest experience of children would be a better guardian than herself, Helen knew. Her only concern had been the dreadful smell. Surely it couldn't be healthy?

'Don't you worry about that, m'dear,' Mrs Trahair had said comfortably, reading the doubt in her eyes. 'My husband has bin working there ever since it started up and you won't see a healthier man than he anywhere in Cornwall.' It was true. Behind his shy smile, Mr Trahair's face was pink and healthy, the skin clear, hair shining with health.

The thought of carrying the surprisingly heavy child a couple of miles into Penzance and visiting an attorney with Beth screaming and wriggling in her arms was daunting. Helen had accepted with relief, promising to come back from town soon after midday. And now it was almost dark. She increased her speed, the noise of her feet muffled by the small stream that ran along the bottom of the valley.

Helen could hear Beth's anguished screaming as she turned into the cottage gate but no one seemed to be bothering with her. Instead, there were raised voices, feet scurrying on the earthen floor. If they were neglecting the baby...

Not stopping to knock she pushed the door open, stepping through into the golden lamplight.

On the rough wooden table, safely ensconced in a wicker basket, Beth screamed ceaselessly, her face red with fury. With a swift movement, Helen snatched her up, cradling her gently as she opened her mouth to complain about the child's treatment – but the words died unsaid. It was obvious something was wrong. Very wrong.

A small fire burned smokily in the hearth and its fitful flames lit up the figure of an old man, lying back weakly in the corner of the black oak settle drawn up in front of it. Even in that uncertain light Helen could see that his face was strangely yellow and running with sweat. Mrs Trahair stood beside him, one arm supporting him, an earthenware bowl held in front of him and Helen felt her stomach lurch as she caught the scent of vomit even through the smell of the calciner and the pilchard oil burning in the lamp.

The woman turned. 'Thank God–' Her face fell. 'I'm brem sorry, Miss. I thought it might be our Nat back from the mine.' She started to climb to her feet but Helen waved her back with a gesture. 'Don't worry about me. Is the old man ill?'

She nodded, her face drawn. "'Tes old Da. Sick as a shag he bin for days and that yaller! Colour of that there train oil,' she added, pointing to the thick, yellow pilchard oil burning in the lamp.

'You should have said.' Helen felt uncomfortable. If she had known she would never have left Beth here. Apart from the extra work for Mrs Trahair there was the danger that the baby might catch whatever it was that the old man was suffering from.

The other woman dismissed this with a wave of her hand. 'He weren't too bad this morning, see, better if anything, so I made him a nice broth of nettles for dinner.' She eyed Helen warily, twisting her thin, red hands in her threadbare apron. 'Out of your lower fields, they were, but I didn't think you'd mind, him being so ill and all.'

'Of course not.' Helen wondered if she really meant stinging nettles. Surely they weren't edible?

'Brem good they are in the spring. Perk your blood up something lovely. But he's bin so bad this afternoon, I don't know where to turn for the best.'

As if to support his daughter's words the old man began to retch weakly. Helen hastily turned her eyes away. 'Have you called an apothecary?'

'And how could we afford one of they?' Mrs Trahair asked bitterly, tending her father with rough care. ''Tes all we can do to keep body and soul together as it is.'

Eyeing the old man, who, exhausted by his bout of sickness, was leaning back in the settle, Helen's disrespectful mind threw up the thought that his soul and body wouldn't be together very much longer if he didn't receive some sort of professional help.

The yellowness of his skin couldn't disguise his pallor, and sweat plastered the thin strands of white hair across his scalp.

'If I were to pay...' she offered. It was, strictly speaking, her niece's money that she would use, but surely no right-thinking person would object to it being spent in such a case? 'But–' she glanced down at the baby in her arms. It would be stupid of her to try to find an apothecary herself as she was a stranger here. She had no experience of nursing, either, but it would make sense for Mrs Trahair to go for the doctor and leave her to look after the old man. She took a deep breath, closing her mind to the mingled smells of the small cottage. Needs must...

Before she could speak the door burst open, banging back against the rough wall of the cottage. 'You didn't come to look after the animals!' Jenny stood in the doorway, her face showing the disgust she felt. 'I went to the house and some woman told me you were here – but you never came to the cowshed. *Every* farmer visits his animals first thing. I were waiting and waiting for you to–'

She broke off as she took in the scene before her. 'Granda!' It was a childish wail, the first sign that Helen had seen of the child acting her true age. 'Granda, what's the matter?' She dived across the room, threw herself at the old man's feet, taking his limp, yellowish hand in her own and holding it against her cheek. 'Oh, Granda!' Her voice broke.

'Child.' His voice was weak and thin but the ancient fingers moved to stroke her cheek gently. 'I'm brem glad you've come in time to say goodbye to your old Granda.'

Jenny clutched the gnarled hand more tightly, tears pouring down her freckled face. 'Not goodbye, Granda,' she pleaded. 'Not goodbye.'

Helen felt her own eyes moistening in sympathy but she fought for control. Action was needed if there was going to be any chance for the old man. 'Jenny.' Her voice didn't quaver. 'I want you to get a doctor for your grandfather.'

'Doctor?' The child looked up, eyes wide. 'A doctor?'

'Yes. It has to be you. You know where to find–' Helen broke off. A memory of the handsome young man she had met twice already today nudged at her. 'Do you know a Doctor Ledgerwood?'

The child was on her feet, her face alight now that she had something useful to do. 'He's the surgeon up at the mine. He's *expensive!*' Her voice was awed.

'Never mind that. Do you know where he lives?'

She nodded but her mother broke in, 'He do go to dinner at the Polglases', often as not. Try there first.'

'I'm gone.' The child raced through the door, leaving it open and disappeared into the darkness, her bare feet silent on the beaten earth of the track.

Helen laid the screaming baby back in the basket and approached the old man nervously, forcing down the distaste she felt at being so close to sickness. She knelt by his feet and looked up at the older woman. 'Tell me what I can do to help,' she begged.

'Good heavens!'

Helen stopped abruptly in the doorway of the kitchen, surprise breaking through even her bone-deep weariness. 'I hardly recognised the place.'

'I've just tidied a bit and rinsed through the clomes.' Agnes put away the last of the dried dishes then came forward and lifted the sleeping Beth from her arms. 'You bin a brem long time. I were worried.'

'Oh, everything's gone wrong today.

Except for this.' Helen dropped wearily into a chair and surveyed the kitchen with pleasure.

Agnes could not have stopped for a moment since she had left to collect Beth. The room which had depressed her so much last night was transformed. With the dirty dishes gone and the tabletop scrubbed to a new whiteness, the room no longer looked as if would contaminate anybody who entered it. The great black range warmed the room against the chill of the early summer evening and in the soft lamplight the plates on the Cornish dresser gleamed softly. Even the stone flags, swept clean of crumbs and debris, seemed to glow warmly.

Agnes glanced at the sleeping child. 'I'll put her down, shall I?' She paused at the door. 'A young girl, Jenny she said her name was, was here looking for you.'

Helen groaned. 'I know. I've managed to get myself in her black books. Apparently, I should have gone round all the cowsheds and pigsties and Lord knows what, as soon as I got home. Instead, I changed my dress and rushed off to get Beth. I gather I'm beyond reproach.'

'A good farmer looks after his beasts.' Agnes left and Helen groaned again. A good farmer! But she wasn't a farmer. Or a mother. Or a nurse. And today, she had been expected to be all three. She was aware that she had not shone in any of the roles.

She wasn't even any sort of a housewife, she decided, looking round the sparkling kitchen again. Admittedly the sacked maid had merely flounced off this morning, after taking her money, but Helen realised she should have made more attempt to clear the room up, as well as looking after her niece.

To think that she had always thought that she was well-educated! All that reading, all that learning hadn't fitted her for real life at all. And she was locked into this life for the foreseeable future. She had to keep the farm going somehow, until she could find a tenant for it. And what would Ezekiel Hardcourt say when he learned of her change of plans? He was expecting her back any day to be approved of by Lord Carnglase. She dropped her head wearily into her hands.

'You do want something in your stomach,' Agnes announced, coming softly into the room. 'You must be brem empty after all you bin through today. Have a dish of tay and I'll fetch you up some dinner dreckly.'

'You don't know all of it,' Helen muttered. 'When I got to the Trahairs I found Jenny's grandfather was ill. We had to call in a doctor. That's why I was so long.'

Agnes halted, the brown teapot in her hands, her hard face inscrutable. 'I wonder if I can guess what doctor you called on, then?' she said, tartly. 'T'wouldn't be any young, handsome surgeon by any chance, would it?'

Helen felt herself redden. 'What if I did call for Mr Ledgerwood?' she demanded. 'He's the only doctor I know round here.'

'And the Trahairs had never heard of any other doctor either, I do suppose?' Agnes snorted. 'Good thing for he, he isn't sixty and bald, that's what I do say. I wouldn't mind betting he do get all his work amongst the young women in this here town.' She slapped a plate of ham and new potatoes in front of Helen. 'Here, get yer stomach round that. T'will put new heart into 'ee.'

Helen hesitated, caught between her hunger and an obscure desire to defend Anthony Ledgerwood from Agnes' attacks. In the silence, the knocking on the door echoed through the house, making both women jump.

Agnes reached out a hand. 'You bide there,' she said. 'I'll get 'un.'

The frozen look on her face brought Helen to her feet, remembering why she had brought the other woman here in the first place. 'What if it's your husband?' she hissed.

Agnes shrugged fatalistically. 'If it's he, there's naught I can do about it. If he's found me, that's it.'

The knocking boomed through the house

again, louder than before. Straightening her shoulders, Agnes moved to the door, leaving Helen standing by the table, listening anxiously. There was a confused murmur of conversation but it did not sound angry and she sank to her seat just as Agnes pushed open the door. 'Mr Ledgerwood,' she announced, her face expressionless.

'Oh!' Helen leapt to her feet again in confusion. She glanced down at the scarcely started meal. 'Mr Ledgerwood, please forgive me for receiving you in the kitchen.' It would never have happened in her grandmother's house, she thought, but then, she had scarcely ever been in the kitchen in her grandmother's house.

The young doctor moved forward and clasped her hand. 'It is easy to see that you are not a country girl, Miss Schofield,' he laughed. 'On a farm, the kitchen is the centre of the house. You have nothing to apologise for. If anything, it is I who should be apologising. You have had a strenuous day and should be able to enjoy your meal in peace.'

'No, really,' Helen protested weakly, aware of the warm clasp of his fingers, of the smile in his blue eyes.

He released his hold on her, pressing his hand instead lightly onto her shoulder to encourage her to sit again. 'Indeed. I have only come to set your mind at rest about the old man. He is still very ill but I think I have pulled him through, on this occasion at least.'

'I am so glad.' Helen remembered his pale face and her fears for Beth. If what he had was contagious...

'Could you tell me what was wrong with him?' she asked.

He seemed to hesitate a second, before replying cheerfully, 'It's what they call down here the 'Yeller Janders', Miss Schofield. Actually, of course, it is the local name for jaundice. In his case, I am afraid, it is simply his age catching up on him, but I have pulled him through this time.'

'I see.' Well, old age was something Beth wouldn't be suffering from for a long time yet. Helen breathed a sigh of relief; then her mind threw up a second, more likely reason for his presence. 'I – er, I told the Trahairs that I would be responsible for your account,' she said awkwardly.

'Miss Schofield!' He seemed to recoil in horror. 'As if I could let you do that! No, in this case I am delighted to be able to assist you in your charitable deed. I am only relieved that I can bring you such good tidings of the patient.'

Helen felt herself blush again. It almost seemed – one would almost think...

He smiled down at her. 'But I am interrupting your dinner and keeping you from your bed, despite the advice I myself gave you earlier.' She protested but he insisted, and within seconds, it seemed to Helen, Agnes had shut the door behind him and returned to the kitchen.

'Well!' Agnes' face showed only dislike. 'Brem strange that was.'

Helen felt an obscure desire to support him. 'I thought it was very kind of him,' she said, hoping that her face did not show the confusion she felt within.

It was understandable that, after her experience with her husband, Agnes would only see the worst in men. Helen decided to help her overcome this. 'It just shows,' she said cheerfully, though unable to bring herself to meet Agnes' eye, 'that Mr Ledgerwood is not simply motivated by money as you suggested earlier.'

Agnes sniffed. 'Then he's a brem strange doctor, that's all I can say,' she snapped. 'Now you eat up that food and get to bed. That man has said only one sensible thing all day and, it seems to me, you're dead set on ignoring it for all the rest of the rubbish he's talked.'

Seven

'These fuel costs are as high as we have in the winter!' Robert Polglase flung the account sheets onto the Count House table with a despairing gesture.

Ben Lanivit, his purser, looked at him sympathetically. 'It's been a wet spring, Sir. I know the sun is out now but it takes time for all the rain we had earlier to percolate the ground. We'll be running the pumping engines on full for a while yet.'

'More costs.' Robert got to his feet and strode to the window. Outside, the surface workings of the mine buzzed with activity. Young boys wheeled barrows of ore from the whim, where it was drawn up to the surface, along to the spalling sheds, where the bal maidens would hammer it into small lumps.

Other boys wheeled the small lumps of ore to the stamps, which pulverised them, or stood with long rakes, watching over the buddles where the heavy tin-rich ore was separated from the lighter stone dust by the action of water.

All these people depended on the mine, on him. And that was without counting all those men underground, risking their lives in heat and dark to work the narrow veins of black tin and bring it to the surface. Sixty people were employed by this mine, and they in turn supported with their earnings perhaps three times as many. If this mine closed all those people would be thrown onto the dubious charity of the Poor Law. If they were lucky.

He sighed, wishing he could lay his aching head against the cool glass. Theo's tears and tantrums had gone on for most of the night. If only she could understand, if only she would realise that, in the long run, putting money into the mine would mean more for her to spend.

He had loved her from the first moment he had set eyes on her, when he was a hobbledehoy schoolboy and she the lovely sister of the sophisticated Anthony Ledgerwood for whom he used to fag.

Marrying her was more that he had ever hoped, more than he had dared to dream. Theo, with her beauty and grace and wit, tying herself down to a man like him, whose father had been a miner, whose mother spoke broad Cornish.

How could he expect a lady like her to understand? When she had married him he had been a rich man. She couldn't be expected to predict that when the price of tin went down his income would halve, but that was exactly what had happened.

If only the price would rise again. It would, of course it would. Everyone said so, the bankers, the smelters, the agents. It would rise. All he had to do was hold on until then.

Behind him, Lanivit cleared his throat, dragging his thoughts back from the endless treadmill of worry about the mine, about his employees, about Theo. 'Yesterday's calciner figures were better than expected, Sir.'

Much better. Good enough to keep the mine going for a few more months, waiting for the price rise, the rise that *must* come. As long as he could keep Theo from spending it all. But he hated to deny her anything. Poor love, she had had a bitter childhood. Her father's bankruptcy, living with an elderly uncle who toiled as an apothecary and saved every penny to educate her brother but spent nothing on her – of course she longed for the fun, the freedom of money. And she should have it while she was young. What was the point of pretty clothes when she was old and haggard? She deserved them *now*.

He could not let her have them. He looked at his employees, toiling in the sun for a pittance that wouldn't cover Theo's glove bill. These were men, or the children of men, who had worked first for his father. He had a responsibility to his wife but he had a responsibility to them too. Theo would understand. He just hadn't explained it very well last night.

Lanivit cleared his throat again. 'Perhaps if we could examine these figures in more detail, sir, I can show you in particular where the money is going.'

Robert could see through this. Lanivit was planning to back him into a corner, to extract a promise that the money from the calciner was going to be spent on the mine and he could not do it. Not until he had explained everything to Theo and made her understand. To act behind her back was disloyal to the woman he loved.

A familiar red-haired figure passed in front of the window and he seized his chance. 'There's Nat Trahair. I must see how his grandfather is.' He hurried bare-headed from the Count House, ignoring the flurry of papers blown to the floor by the speed of his passage, the purser's smothered exclamation. 'Nat, how's the old man?'

The young miner, on his way to working on the 'afternoon core', as the Cornish miners referred to their shifts, stopped unwillingly. 'Just between the driftwood and the hard,' the young miner said, touching his forelock with a scarred hand. 'Don't reckon he's long for this world but Doctor pulled 'un round all right last night.'

'Good. Splendid.' Robert paused. He could remember his father talking to men like this and they were always laughing and chatting together, even though his father was a rich mine owner and the men his employees, but Robert could never do it. He was cut off from them for ever by his educated accent, by the fact that he had never worked down the mine beside them, just as he was cut off from born gentlemen, like Anthony Ledgerwood, because he was not the son of a gentlemen, despite his education. His money and his large house were the only things that made him even half acceptable to the local gentry. No wonder Theo thought them so important. He dragged his mind away from the thought of her.

'If there is anything I can do–' He saw the frown on Nat's face and cursed himself for being so clumsy. These people were proud. They would resent anything that smacked of charity.

'I mean,' he corrected himself quickly, 'your grandfather worked with my father, your father is doing sterling work in the calciner, I feel a responsibility. Perhaps if tonight I call round to see your grandfather?'

'He's too ill,' Nat said swiftly. 'Sick as a shag, he is. He don't want to see nobody.'

'But your mother,' Robert protested. 'Perhaps she would welcome a–'

'She's got her hands full as it is,' Nat broke

in. 'Best thing you can do for she is keep away.'

'I see.' Robert had been subject to too many slights all his life to push in where he wasn't wanted. He was a stranger everywhere. Only in his own house could he relax, be accepted as himself and now that Theo...

There was no escape from his problems. He wished Nat a polite farewell and, shoulders bowed by the weight of his troubles, he went slowly back into the Count House.

'But you can't *go!*'

Helen stared, horrified, at Agnes. 'Besides, why should you? We're miles from anywhere here. How could your husband know where you are?'

Agnes hunched a shoulder. Her face, always cold, now seemed fallen in on itself, as if a greater sorrow than usual was afflicting her. 'He'll know,' she said bitterly. 'I've tried everything, changed my name, moved from one town to another but nothing works. He do always find me. And he'll find me here again if I stay any longer.'

Helen felt her heart sink. Despite her appearance Agnes had been a tower of strength since she had pulled Helen out of the sea. Without her, the farmhouse would seem too big, too empty. Besides, how would she get another job? She had left the last position without giving notice so they would not give a reference. Or was she planning to walk into the sea again?

Helen would not let her do it! Agnes was a good woman, too good to be treated like this. She deserved better. Helen had already found that beneath her gruff exterior she was kind, gentle even with little Beth, and hard-working and intelligent. She would not let this woman be hounded to death by a no-good husband.

'He'll never find you,' she said decisively. 'How could he? No one even knows you're here.'

'That doctor do know,' said Agnes, mulishly, 'and Jenny.'

'Oh, for heaven's sake!' Helen almost laughed. 'You've seen the doctor; you said yourself he was a real gentleman. Does he look the sort who would even talk to your husband? There's no way that your husband would learn where you are from him.'

Agnes wavered slightly. 'There's still Jenny.'

This time Helen did laugh. 'If you were a cow or a particularly well-bred pig then yes, Jenny might talk about you. But as a human – I doubt if she knows that you exist. I think she classes you and me as alternative cow feeders, and very second-rate ones at that.'

She moved forward and put her arm

around Agnes' thin shoulders. 'Your husband will never find you here. And what if he does? Do you think I'd let him hurt you?'

'How could you stop him?' Agnes asked bitterly. 'He's my husband, isn't he? He's got rights.'

There were tears in her usually hard eyes. 'Never mind that he has any light skirt he fancies, never mind that he doesn't support me, he's my husband and when he says 'come' I got to come. That's the law, that is. And if he wants more from me–' she lowered her face but Helen could see the slight blush that rose to the thin, pale cheeks '–well, that's his right as well. And there's nothing I can do about it. Nothing. I'm his until I die. And if that's what I've got to do to get shot of him, then I shall do it.'

She lifted her head, careless now of the tears that were running down her cheeks. 'I won't earn another penny that he can take off me. I won't let him get another second's ease because of my work. Let him starve, let him live off his fancy women. I don't care. He's made my life unbearable and now it's him that going to suffer for it. Not me. Not any more.'

'Oh, my dear.' Helen pulled her closer, her heart torn by the other woman's anguish. To think that a man could bring a respectable woman to this state. For a second she thought of the Reverend Ezekiel Hardcourt.

He would never treat her so. He would never drive her to such despair.

Her unruly mind threw up a thought. Not deliberately. But after a few years of marriage to him perhaps the freedom of death might seem preferable to living in a strait-jacket of convention and propriety. She forced the thought aside.

'I've heard,' she said, slowly, trying to concentrate on ways of keeping the woman from her set course, 'I've heard that the Chinese believe that if you save a man's life then he's your responsibility. And you saved mine. Oh, you did,' she insisted as the older woman shook her head. 'I'd have drowned in the sea if you hadn't pulled me out. Or caught my death of cold if you hadn't lent me some dry clothes. So, you see, you have a responsibility to me.'

Agnes laughed bitterly. 'And if I had, what good would that do you? What have I got that you would ever want? You or anyone else for that matter?'

Helen squeezed her shoulders. 'Your presence,' she said. She waved her free arm around the kitchen, spotless since Agnes' arrival. 'I couldn't do all this. Oh, I helped,' she admitted as Agnes tried to break in, 'but I've never done any sort of housework in my life. If you hadn't shown me, I wouldn't have known how to clean the brass or light the range. And then there's Beth. You can get her to sleep better that I can.'

'She's just teething,' said the other woman roughly. 'She might be teasy as a snake for now but in a day or two she'll be right as rain.'

'You know that,' Helen said, 'but I don't. I wasn't even sure what to feed her before you arrived.'

Again, Agnes tried to play down her role. ''Tes because her ma's died. She's not used to taking food from a spoon yet but she's learning.'

'Agnes.' Time for honesty. 'I need you. I – I need a friend,' she admitted. 'Someone I can turn to, someone I can trust.' She looked the other woman straight in the eyes. 'It isn't because you know things that I don't that I want you to stay. It's just that – that you're *here*, and I need that at present.' She took Agnes's thin, work-reddened hand in her own. 'Agnes, please. For me. As a friend.'

There was a long silence. Helen felt her heart thudding uncomfortably. If Agnes decided to go she had no way of stopping her. Telling the local magistrates about the woman's attempt to take her own life would only get Agnes arrested and imprisoned. Tell no one, and she knew that Agnes would be dead within a few hours.

She wanted to speak, to say something, anything, that would sway the woman's mind, but she knew that she mustn't. She had done all she could. She had offered Agnes a reason for living. It was up to Agnes whether she thought it a good enough reason to continue with her life.

Eight

In the quiet bedroom the guttering candle gave an uncertain light, but no more uncertain than Helen's mind.

How to even begin the letter to Ezekiel? 'Dear Sir' was surely too formal for an engaged couple, 'Dear Mr Hardcourt' too cold. She toyed with the idea of writing to her grandmother, allowing her to pass on the message but dismissed that too. This was her problem. Not that she shouldn't write to her grandmother also. Another difficult letter. She sighed.

A creak brought her head up but it was only the old house settling. But what if she woke tomorrow and found Agnes gone? Helen was by no means certain that she had won the other woman over. Perhaps, she admitted to herself, this late-night letter-writing was only an excuse, to make sure she heard Agnes if she tried to creep out.

She turned again to the letter, her pen

doodling idly as she tried to plan it. There was no doubt about the message, but what tone to adopt? Regretful? Apologetic? Determined? Businesslike?

The trouble was, she admitted to herself, she didn't feel apologetic or regretful. Despite the fact that she had worked harder in the last couple of days than ever in her life before, Helen had enjoyed herself. Because of what she had done, what she had decided, things were different, were better. At home she had never made a decision of greater importance than what gown to wear and even that had been vetoed occasionally by Grandmama.

She dipped her pen and doodled again. Cows, a misshapen pig. Her grandmother had said that you could always tell a lady by her hands, but even in the candlelight she could see that hers were no longer white and shapely. She picked idly at a torn cuticle, smiling. Only two days, two days of cleaning and feeding animals, of looking after a baby and making beds.

She had never been so happy.

That was a fact she would have to keep from her fiancé, because the bitter truth was that these few days were an adventure out of time. Soon, too soon, real life would enforce its demands – and real life meant marriage to Ezekiel Hardcourt. Marriage was her only escape from penury; her grandmother's tiny annuity would die with her and what would Helen's life be then? Being paid a pittance to act as a companion to a succession of old ladies who would discard her, homeless and penniless, when she was too old to carry out their demands with sufficient energy. She shuddered. Ezekiel was offering her marriage, a position in society as the wife of a clergyman, a home for her grandmother – and Beth.

Helen sighed. There was no alternative. Marriage with Ezekiel was her only real option. But first, she had her time here, time to live life as she had only dreamed it could be lived. And it was not only a pleasure, it was her duty.

But neither Ezekiel or her grandmother must ever learn how much she was enjoying herself, behaving – and being treated – not as a lady, the distant cousin of a peer of the realm, but as an ordinary woman. She would have to make regret the theme of her letter, regret that her sense of duty did not allow her to leave the farm in the immediate future. Ezekiel was very strong on duty. She only hoped that he would consider her to be right in putting her duty to her orphaned niece before her duty to himself.

She took a new sheet of letter paper and began to write. 'Dear Sir...'

'You don't love me any more!'

'Oh, Theo, of course I do.' Robert ran harassed fingers through his hair. 'I love you as much now as on the day I married you. More,' he amended quickly, seeing the look in her eyes.

'You can't! Not now I'm old and ugly. You don't care for me any more. You used to give me things, presents, but not any more.' Teardrops glistened on her lashes. 'Not even little things from Penzance.' Her voice rose in a wail.

It was true. With all these money worries he had not thought to buy her the small gifts of gloves or pretty knick-knacks. Guilt suffused him. Admittedly when he went to Penzance now, it was for uncomfortable business meetings with his lawyer or the bank, but he should have remembered.

'I'm sorry, my love. I'll buy them for you in future.'

It was the wrong thing to say. 'I don't want them because I've told you, I wanted you to think of it yourself. And you don't any more and it's all because you don't love me.' Her voice was a fretful howl that assaulted his ears.

'Theo, darling, I do. I do!' He clutched her to him, rocking her in his arms. 'I love you more than anything.'

'Then why won't you let me refurbish the drawing room?'

He knew it would come, of course; they

had been through other nights like this. In the end, whichever route she chose, Theo would end up at her chief concern – spending money.

'I've told you, love. I don't have the money.' He tightened his arms, pulling her closer. 'Look, next time. In six months, that's all. Six months and I'll let you refurbish the room.' He held her away from him so that he could see her stormy face and smiled down at her. 'Six months. I promise. The next lot of profits from the calciner.'

'But you have *this* half-year's profits now!'

He gritted his teeth. 'Theo, we discussed this before. I can't afford it. I have to use that money for the mine.'

'Some love!' she flung at him. '"I love you more than anything, Theo, I'll do anything for you, Theo"!' she quoted at him, her voice cruelly emphasising the faint trace of Cornish in his voice. 'Anything except do what I want! Love me more than anything – except your mine!'

She pulled herself from him, flung herself onto the couch in a flurry of gauzy skirts, abandoning herself to weeping. 'You don't love me anymore. You don't! You don't! Because I'm no longer young enough and pretty enough for you.'

'Theo.' He could feel himself weakening. She knew just how to manipulate him, how to drive him into a corner where he would do anything rather than see her suffer as she did, deny her what she had set her heart on.

He could not do it. But equally, he could not let the mine go down. Even letting some of the men go would cause despair in the families that depended on them.

'Please, Theo, see it my way.' He dropped to his knees beside her, stroking her hair, her shaking shoulders. 'These men – their job is all they have–'

She reared up. 'Men! Anyone can see that you're no gentleman! You put these men before your own wife, before me!'

He stared at her, white-faced. He had always known that he was not her equal by birth but this was the first time she had flung his lowly origins in his face. Here, in his home, his sanctuary from the worries of the outside world, here, at least, he had felt safe from the slights and insults he experienced outside. And here was his wife – his beloved Theo – showing that she despised him, that she, too, condemned him for his birth, for the fact that his father had been a common miner.

He climbed to his feet, waves of sickness running through him. That she should feel like that! That she should despise him!

Shaking, silent, he moved slowly to the door of the room. He had to get out. He had to get away...

Vaguely, behind him, he heard a rustle of clothes but he did not look round. After all these years, thinking that she had loved him, that his money and education made him an acceptable husband to her and–

'Robert!' Her voice was quieter now, almost sounding frightened. 'Robert? Where are you going?'

He did not answer, *could* not answer. His thoughts churned and surged in his head, round and round until he felt dizzy, until he felt sick.

Silence. That was what he wanted. Silence and darkness. It was strangely difficult to walk. His legs didn't seem to belong to him properly. Perhaps they really belonged to that other man, that rich, acceptable man; perhaps he had no right to legs like these, not with his birth.

'Robert!' The voice was a shrill scream now but it was nothing to do with him, it belonged to another world, another man. Lurching slightly, he moved across the empty hall, flung open the door, staggered down the fine flight of granite steps, out of her reach, out of the house, out into the peaceful, gracious coolness of the Cornish night.

George Penhaligon came to with a groan, rolling over on the lumpy flock mattress that was all that the cheap boarding-house in

Penzance provided. The brandy he had drunk that evening throbbed in his head, furring his mouth and coating his dry tongue with a foul-tasting bloom.

He rubbed a hand over his face, hearing the scratch of his bristly chin in the darkness. Too much to drink. But then, he hadn't expected Agnes to have so much money on her. Cow that she was, hiding away in the back end of beyond, changing her name, stashing away all that money – money that was his by rights. Bloody women, they were all the same.

Even his mother! Leaving him like that. Going off with no thought for him, even though he was only a small boy, but what did she care? Nothing. Not for him or his father. He should have learned then that women couldn't be trusted; instead, he'd had to go and marry that damned Agnes.

The brandy fumes, swirling through his brain, brought tears of self-pity to his eyes. Bitches, all of them. Even the one last night...

He remembered now. Small, dark, a whore of course, but worth it. Vague memories of their earlier coupling trickled into his memory. Definitely worth it! Ignoring his throbbing head, he reached across the lumpy bed–

He found nothing.

Swearing, he sat up, struggling to light the

candle by the bed, though he knew already what he would find. The bitch had gone – and taken his money, he wouldn't mind betting! As if he hadn't paid her well enough beforehand. And given her a bed for the night. Not that there was much cash left, he consoled himself, memory oozing slowly back. Buying the brandy and paying her had used up most of the money he had taken out with him last night.

Another awful thought struck him. He staggered upright on rubbery legs, too concerned now to worry about his reeling head, and dragged up the lumpy mattress.

The cache was gone! All the rest of the money he had got from Agnes – gone! Stolen by a bitch with a pretty face and a cesspit of a mind.

He dropped heavily onto the side of the bed, ignoring the way the jolt affected his churning stomach, and buried his head in his hands.

He needed that money, needed it desperately. George Penhaligon, the seer, George Penhaligon, the man who could see behind the veil, who could tell the future, find that which was lost – who would believe that if he couldn't even find enough money for himself to pay his shot? There was always the old line, of course, that his gift only worked for other people, not for himself, but it was a fact that he got more work – and could charge more – when he looked affluent.

Then there was the woman. What if she spread the word that she had taken him for a sucker? He'd have no credibility left at all. And stories like that got around. Even if he moved to the other end of Cornwall, there was a danger of someone passing on the story. George Penhaligon was a name, had a reputation. For the moment.

He groaned again, digging his fingers into his throbbing head. One thing was certain; it had to be Agnes' fault. If she had been a proper wife to him he wouldn't have had to take other women home, pay for what should be his free, by rights. He would have had her.

And, by God, he would. She was his wife. She should be by his side, giving him her money freely. He shouldn't have to hunt her down or slake himself on other women.

Wincing against the pain in his head, his roiling stomach, George Penhaligon lurched to his feet.

The candle was almost burned out. Helen yawned and re-read the last few lines she had written. 'So, while I very much regret that I shall miss meeting your esteemed cousin, my present circumstances preclude my leaving the farm...'

Her hand reached out, without her

volition, and the pen nib scored through the carefully composed prose, digging deep into the paper.

I *don't,* she thought, suddenly angry, I don't regret it *at all.* Lord Carnglase was an interfering snob. She was glad she would not have to meet him, be promenaded before him for approval like a cow in the market. Either Ezekiel Hardcourt would be a good vicar or he wouldn't; who he married had nothing to do with it.

She flung down the pen and it rolled across the page leaving a fine spray of ink blots behind it before falling to the floor. She sighed, running her hands impatiently through her dark hair. Her letter was ruined, anyway, an hour's pen-sucking labour demolished by one second's honest feeling. And that was her last sheet of paper.

Her brother-in-law must have had some. She padded gently into the kitchen which had been the heart of the house. Agnes had tidied things away into drawers of the great wooden dresser that took up almost the whole of one wall but Helen had had no time to sort the drawers out. Striving for quietness, she jerked one open.

As she had guessed from the chaos of the rest of the house, James Trethowan had never bothered with an office, thrusting all papers away willy-nilly. Printed headings caught her eye. Brownfield, Solicitor;

Blacklock's Bank; Sparrow and Tregenza; Smith and Barton, dealers in fine horses. Helen rummaged hastily through and had just found some writing paper when she heard the noise.

She stopped, head poised, listening, aware of the sudden hammering of her heart. All evening, while she had been struggling with her letter, she had been listening – for Beth, for Agnes. But this sound had come from outside.

She swallowed. After all, there were animals out there: cows, pigs, oxen. One of them could have got out, come wandering round the farmyard. But there had been something stealthy about the noise, something deliberate. The sort of sound only a human could make.

Agnes. Dear God, had she left? Had she crept out unheard? Careless of the noise Helen raced for the back door. Locked. The front door – but there was no need to even try that door. It was ajar. Agnes had left.

But she couldn't be far away. Helen dragged the door all the way open and stepped out into the night. Clouds veiled the sky and it was too dark to see any distance.

She had to stop Agnes. The woman would not have crept out like this if she weren't intent on destroying herself. But how to find her in the darkness?

Shout. Even if all it did was panic Agnes into running at least the noise she made would give Helen a lead in tracking her down.

Helen took a deep breath but the sound died unvoiced in her throat.

From out of the darkness came the skin-prickling scream of a woman in terror.

Nine

Agnes' scream ripped through the darkness, sending roosting bird's rocketing into the sky and awakening the answering barks of distant farm dogs.

For a second Helen paused, paralysed with shock; then she turned, racing back into the kitchen.

James Trethowan's rifle was still resting on its pegs, high on the wall. It took only a second to reach it down then she was out of the door again, her hampering skirts caught up in her free hand as she ran blindly up the darkened lane.

She could hear the sounds of a struggle ahead of her; feet kicking against stones, Agnes' voice, panting and desperate, and the deeper tones of an unknown man.

The ground was treacherous underfoot,

full of loose stones and uneven where the animals had trodden in the wet weather. In the darkness it was impossible for Helen to see where it was safe to set her feet. Once she stumbled but corrected herself, forcing herself onwards. She had to get there in time. She had to.

'Stop, or I'll shoot.' The words came out in little more than a breathless gasp. 'I said leave her–'

Under her foot a loose stone turned, throwing her off balance. Instinct made her stretch out a hand to save herself – the hand that was holding the gun.

As if in slow motion she saw the ground come up towards her, saw the gun smash onto the surface of the lane, saw the flash, heard the explosion ... and saw one of the dark figures in front of her crumple to the earth.

'Agnes!' Helen struggled to her feet, feeling sick. If she had killed her... 'Agnes!'

'I'm all right.' Agnes' voice was shaking but strong. 'It were he that you shot.'

'Oh, dear God!' Helen felt cold horror flood through her. 'I didn't mean to shoot him.' Her voice rose in a wail. 'I didn't know the gun was loaded. I only meant to scare him. And now...'

Despite herself, her mind provided the words she didn't want to think about. Murderer. Criminal. Felon. She stopped dead, the gun hanging forgotten from her hand as she contemplated what she had done. To have taken a life – to have killed someone...

Agnes caught her by the arm. 'Don't you worry.' Her voice was a fierce whisper. 'I won't tell no one. No one need ever know. And he deserved it, I tell you. He deserved death a thousand times over. You've got no call to feel bad about it. And you won't suffer, I promise you that. We'll get rid of him, easy as winking. There's old mine shafts aplenty round here. He won't be the first that's been buried deep like that, half-way to the hell he deserves. Why,' – her voice was stronger – 'I'd say I'd done it myself, rather than let you suffer, after all you've done for me.'

'Shot...' Helen struggled to comprehend the disaster that had overtaken her so suddenly. Agnes' voice seemed to come from a thousand miles away, from another universe. Here, in the real world, there was only her – and the man she had killed.

Blindly, she pulled herself free from Agnes' grasp and on legs that seemed stiff and weak at the same time she stumbled forward, the gun still clutched in her hand. The figure lay crumpled on the ground, dark and still. She forced herself to kneel at his side, to touch him.

His face was wet and sticky. Blood. She

swallowed convulsively, burying her teeth in her lower lip as she forced herself not to recoil, not to be sick. She had done this dreadful thing, she must face the facts. She reached lower, touching the man's neck, seeking for the artery ... which throbbed strongly under her fingers.

'He's alive!' Relief made her want to burst into tears.

'Alive, is he?' Agnes' voice was grim. 'Well, he won't be much longer.' She lunged forward, pulling at the gun in Helen's hand. 'Give that to me. I'll put the brute out of his misery. He won't ruin my life no more, I can tell you.'

'No.' Helen had thought she was incapable of movement but this roused her. 'We can't. That really would be murder.'

'Well, he do deserve it.' Agnes dragged at the gun. 'I'll do 'un. You bide in the house. No one will know.'

'No.' They were both on their feet now, wrestling with the gun. What if it were still loaded, Helen thought in a sudden panic. What if it went off again and killed Agnes? 'Drop it.' She released one hand and pushed the other woman hard in the shoulder, simultaneously jerking the gun away with the other hand. To her relief, Agnes staggered back, and almost tripping, was forced to release her hold.

'You won't kill him,' Helen said fiercely.

'Whatever he's done to you he doesn't deserve that.' She looked down at the still figure lying at her feet. They couldn't leave him here all night. He needed help. 'We'll carry him into the house,' she decided.

'Carry 'un yourself,' Agnes retorted. 'I ain't going to put myself out for him, and that's flat.' She folded her arms and stared defiantly into the distance.

'Agnes, for heaven's sake!' Helen could feel her temper rising. 'He needs help.' She thought briefly. 'I helped you when you needed it. Surely you can do the same for him?'

'I wouldn't have needed help if it weren't for that there bugger.' Her face was cold and hard as steel.

'Agnes! I promise you, you'll have nothing to fear from him ever again. I'll – I'll make sure he can't get at you. I'll threaten him with breaking and entering, if you like, or robbery. I'll lie as much as you like, I'll tell him I'll get him put into prison if he doesn't stay away from you. But we can't leave him here to die. And I can't carry him alone.'

There was a long pause. 'Oh, all right.' The words were grudging but they had been spoken. 'But if he shows his face here just one more time–'

'I promise. Now you take his feet.'

The other woman bent forward. 'I reckon he'll be too heavy for the two of us,' she said, her voice sounding more cheerful. 'Reckon this dragging around is probably all that's needed to finish him off for good.'

'Be quiet and lift.' But there was a dreadful truth in the woman's words. It was long minutes later before they manhandled the body breathlessly through the door. The candle she had brought from the bedroom had burned out and the kitchen was in darkness.

'The rug before the range,' Helen gasped shortly. The table would be better but they could never lift him up that high.

She turned away, fumbling for the lamp that had been left on the table and for the matches to light it. As she did so, the man groaned.

'Well, at least he's still alive.' The lamp flared into life and she concentrated on trimming the wick with shaking fingers, turning the flame up slowly so that she did not crack the glass chimney.

Behind her, she heard a gasp.

'What's the matter?' Helen swung round, wondering what horrible sight the light would reveal.

Agnes was standing over the man's body with a face almost as white as his own.

'That's not my husband,' she said, her voice shaking. 'I've never seen that man before in my life.'

She was standing in the yard with chickens pecking around her feet, her dark hair neat and glossy in the May sunshine, her mourning clothes spotless. Even in such homely surroundings she did not look like a farmer's wife. Something about the lift of her head, the set of her shoulders indicated that here was a lady through and through.

Instantly Robert felt his heart drop. Farm women he could deal with, but a lady like this... How they did it he never knew, but he was always aware that they had only to take one look and his humble origins were laid bare. Good clothes, an expensive education –neither helped. He did not even have to open his mouth before he could see the shutters come down across their faces, the look that said 'not out of the top drawer', 'not one of us'.

He hesitated but she must have heard his footfall for she turned to smile at him, moving forward with her hand outstretched.

'My dear sir!' There was no condescension that even his hypercritical ears could hear in her clear, soft voice. 'You should still be in bed. You could do yourself harm getting up with a wounded head.' She paused and to his amazement she looked confused, a faint blush colouring her pale cheeks. 'I – I am not sure – that is, you may not remember last night...'

The combination of well-bred assurance

and embarrassment amused and delighted him. 'I remember coming to and seeing you bending over me but there is a blank before that.'

'We had just brought you in.' She paused, searching for words. 'We were concerned about you but you assured us that it was merely a flesh wound, that you were not badly hurt and did not need an apothecary.' The blush deepened but she raised her head higher on its slender stalk of a neck, staring straight into his eyes. 'I – I realise that I should have insisted but we are only two women alone – there was no manservant to send and I...' Her voice tailed off uncertainly.

He bowed, and was aware as he did it that he was acting less of an hobbledehoy than was his custom with a strange lady. 'Please, think nothing of it. I am merely grateful that you should have been so kind as to have taken me in.' He smiled into her green eyes, trying to dispel the worry that she obviously felt about him. 'I assure you that, except for a sore head, I am quite fit.'

'But I am persuaded that you should see a doctor as soon as possible.' She moved nearer, stretching out a hand to lightly touch his sleeve. 'I had intended that you should remain in bed this morning until we had found out the name of your own doctor and could arrange for him to see you.'

The thought of Anthony, with his handsome face and easy manners, showing him up in front of this woman was insupportable. Anthony would be certain to tell Theo – and how would she take the information that he had spent the night alone in a house with two women? Besides, once Anthony knew he would be sure to spread the story. This lady was too well-bred and too innocent to realise how such a story could compromise her reputation. No, for the sake of both of them he would have to keep his stay here a secret.

'No.' It came out with more force than he had intended. 'I am perfectly well, I assure you, except for a sore head. But...' He paused, trying to search his memory. 'I am not sure how I came by my injury. I remember someone running into me in the dark and I held them, thinking it might be a robber, but after that – there is a blank.'

She took her hand away. Her face first suffused with a violent blush then paled alarmingly but she still met his eyes with steady resolution, standing tall in the bright sunlight against the unlikely backdrop of the farmyard. 'That, Sir, is because – because I shot you.'

For a second he wondered if his head injury was more serious than he had thought. 'You – shot me?'

'I – it was unintentional, I assure you.'

Even her ladylike demeanour could not hide her embarrassment. 'I did not even know that the gun was loaded but I took it with me and fell and it went off and – shot you.' She raised eyes as green as the Atlantic to the side of his head, where the bullet had just scraped the skin in its passage. 'I believe the word is – creased?'

Still reeling from the shock, Robert said, unthinking, 'Good God! I must have bled like a pig.'

Immediately the words were out of his mouth he would have done anything to recall them. They had come straight from his early years, words his uneducated mother would have spoken without pause, though he had learnt better than to do so since then. No gentleman would refer to such a subject in front of a lady. Mortified, knowing that he had condemned himself for ever in her eyes, he dropped his head in shame.

The gurgle of laughter startled him. She had her head back, her eyes narrowed with amusement. 'Oh, you did!' Far from being horrified, she was finding it hard to contain herself. 'The kitchen was bad enough, but this morning, when I came out and saw the marks in the lane–' She sobered suddenly. 'If I had known last night how badly you were injured, believe me, I would never have hesitated about getting a doctor to you, but you insisted that it was not serious.'

'Nor was it.' He smiled at her in genuine friendliness. 'I am glad that you took my word. And more than grateful that you gave me a bed for the night.' But that must definitely be kept from Theo. He shuddered to think what her jealousy could make of that.

Anxious to change the subject, he gestured at the basket over her arm. 'May I carry that for you?'

'Oh, no. It's just eggs.' She smiled up at him again. 'Would you believe how stupid these chickens are? They have a comfortable barn here, with nesting boxes all round, yet the silly creatures go out and lay their eggs in any old hole in the hedge that they can find.'

She picked an egg up, its shell brown against the whiteness of her hand. 'I am a stranger here and know nothing about their habits. And I am only just beginning to find their hiding places. Yesterday, I found a lovely egg, bigger than this, and just such a beautiful brown, and I brought it in for breakfast. And do you know what happened?'

He could guess. His parents had owned a few chickens that had pecked around the cottage when he had been a small boy. 'It had been laid some time ago?'

She wrinkled her small nose in a way that

Theo would never do. 'I think it had been laid just after the Flood! The smell was horrendous. We had to leave the house! And now I am under strict orders from Agnes to shake all the eggs to see if they rattle. But surely that can't be right?' She raised her brows questioningly. 'I was just hesitating when you came out. I don't want to harm a perfectly good egg.'

'It is right,' he assured her. He took the egg from her hand and shook it gently beside his ear. 'You have just saved yourself another disrupted breakfast.'

He held it to her ear and shook it and her eyes widened at the soft knocking. 'It's true.' She sounded amazed.

'It's addled.' He shied the egg into the dung heap in the centre of the yard and took another egg. 'This one is good. Listen to the difference.'

She listened, took an egg herself, shook it. 'Another good one.' Her face was alight with pleasure. 'All my life I have eaten eggs and I never knew that there was so much to producing them – feeding the chickens and locking them up at night so that the fox won't get them. And then finding the eggs and testing to see if they have gone bad...' She gestured helplessly.

Robert could not help laughing. 'You will soon learn all their favourite spots for laying and then you will be able to pick up fresh eggs all the time.' He tested another egg and found it good. 'Are you going to sell eggs in Penzance, Miss, er–'

'Schofield. Helen Schofield.' She held out her free hand in frank friendship. 'Once we can make sure that the eggs are all fresh I suppose that we should do that. My brother-in-law used to, I know, but as we no longer have a pony and trap I haven't really decided yet, Mr–'

Blushing at his ineptitude, he gave his name. He felt so at ease in her company that it was hard to remember that they had only just met. She must think him a real country bumpkin with no more manners than a ploughman. Anxious to amend the poor impression he must have given, he said, 'I was very sorry to hear of your brother-in-law and sister's deaths. It was a dreadful accident.'

'Terrible.' She took another egg, tested it, then dropped it back into the basket and turned to him. 'We were given the news by the Vicar of Madron. He said–' she hesitated, '–he said that the cart was being driven at high speed. Was – was that usual?'

Robert shook his head. 'I never heard of it before. Trethowan was a quiet man who had a reputation for caring for his animals. I often saw him driving to market in the dog-cart and he never went at any speed. I can't imagine him risking his animals like that.

And with a young child at home his behaviour is totally incomprehensible.'

Helen took another egg and shook it. 'Addled?' She held it to his ear and, receiving his confirming nod, hurled it hard into the depths of the dung heap. 'It is more than incomprehensible. I had understood that he loved my sister – and she was always terrified of speed. But there must have been a reason for it.'

'Perhaps the child was ill?' he suggested.

'Then surely one of them would have stayed with her. Or they might have taken her in the cart too in an emergency. But there must have been some reason for their actions.'

'I have heard no rumours.' Robert shook his head. 'I knew of the speed, of course. They were seen on their way from here to Madron and everyone agreed that the pony was galloping wildly and the speed was deliberate. Trethowan was urging her on with his whip – and he was a man who many thought treated his animals with ridiculous kindness.'

'Then the reason must have been good.' Helen paused, staring blankly ahead, then said awkwardly, 'I am a stranger here. I don't know anyone to ask. But you – if you were to hear anything...'

'I will certainly tell you.' Though who would talk to him? Neither the gentry nor the workers would ever confide willingly in him. His only companion had been Theo – and after last night he knew how she thought of him.

The desolation which the shock of his injury, his talk with Helen, had driven from his mind came back and settled on him like a dark cloud. Betrayed. Betrayed by his wife. The woman he loved, the woman he would have died for, despised him.

The pain in his heart was almost physical, far worse than the ache in his head. He could have groaned aloud at the agony of it. Betrayed. Despised.

'Mr Polglase?' The soft voice, the touch on his sleeve seemed to come from a thousand miles away. 'Mr Polglase, are you ill? Is your head hurting you?'

Her green eyes held none of the contempt, the hatred, that had filled Theo's blue ones last night. He swallowed, trying to bring himself back to the present, to act like a man. His eyes fixed on the small, white hand she had laid on his arm, undeniably a lady's hand even though one nail had broken off and two of the cuticles were torn.

He stared at it, taking in every detail as he struggled for control. 'It's nothing.' Dear God, his voice sounded as creaky as an old man's. 'I'm fine. But I ought to be going.'

Going. Going home. To Theo. To coldness and arguments and contempt. Away from this sunny farmyard where chickens pecked around their feet in casual trust and there was laughter and the talk of common, happy things.

He could not bring himself to meet her eye. 'People will wonder where I am.' It was an effort to move, to speak. He could feel Helen staring at him but he could not explain. As if he were only distantly connected to his body he managed to step back, away from her, start to turn round.

'Look, Helen. Look.'

A strange voice. He managed to raise his head, saw another woman with a face he vaguely recognised from the previous night coming through the door, carrying a baby in her arms. She was smiling down at it, immersed in the tiny bundle and it was only when she was a few steps away that she saw him and stopped with a gasp, her face blanching.

'It's all right, Agnes.' Helen's voice was clear and untroubled. 'I am sure you have nothing to fear from Mr Polglase.'

'Nothing,' he assured her automatically, not even understanding the remark.

The woman gave him a doubtful stare, then moved on. 'I wondered why she was sleeping so late this morning, so I went to lift her up and there they were.'

The child waved chubby arms in the warm air, her face pink and beaming under the lace-trimmed bonnet. Then she gave a happy, open-mouthed gurgle, blowing bubbles, and Robert caught a brief glimpse of minute white teeth in the lower gums.

'She's teethed! She's done it!' Helen swooped past him, clutching the child from the other woman's arms. 'Isn't she a clever girl! Isn't she a darling!'

There was no place for him here, Robert realised drearily. Helen had her own life, her own concerns. Just because she had taken him in when he was injured, given him a bed for the night, *treated him like an equal,* it didn't mean that he had any rights to her.

All he could do for her was hide what had happened, pretend that he had cut his head in a fall, never let anyone know that he had spent the night at her house without a suitable chaperon.

Slowly he stumbled to the farmyard gate. There he paused, looking back at the sunlit, Arcadian scene. Helen, glowing and happy despite her mourning dress, gazing with delight at the small white-clad baby in her arms. The sunshine. The peace. He sighed.

'Hello, old boy.' Anthony Ledgerwood's hand dropped heavily onto his shoulder. 'What on earth are you doing here at this hour of the day?'

Ten

'Madame Elise's' shop was smarter than most in Penzance; the bowed window overlooking the Terrace contained a walking-out dress that looked expensive even to George Penhaligon's bleary eyes. How had Agnes got a job in a place like this? Suppressing the surge of anger that she could do so much better than he, George pushed open the door.

'How may I help you, sir?' Even before the bell had stopped jingling the woman was before him, tall and stately, her black skirts sweeping the floor in an arc as elegant as the dress in the window, leaving no doubt as to where the inspiration for the clothes in the window had come from.

George shuffled his cracked leather boots behind the doubtful protection of a bentwood chair, set ready by the high brass and wood counter. 'I'm – er – I'm looking for my wife.' He paused, trying to remember the false name Agnes had been living under. 'Mrs Victor. It's an emergency,' he added swiftly, seeing irritation crease her mouth and tighten the muscles round the neck.

'Your – wife, Mr Victor,' – her eyes swept

coldly over him and he knew that she could see through the superficial smartness of his clothes to the cheap shoddiness of the cloth – 'your wife had the impertinence to walk out on me without so much as a word of warning. After all I had done for her – taught her the correct method of inserting boning, not to mention the importance of the *exact* positioning of seams' – her voice shrilled, the veneer of politeness no deeper than the elegance of his coat – 'and she left me without a *day's* notice. Didn't care about me, oh no, nor my business that I've worked my fingers to the bone to set up. And doing very well it was too, until your *wife* decided to walk out of here and leave me–'

The bell jingled again and she came to a halt, her bony, outstretched finger just a fraction away from his chest. For a second he watched anger war with commerce – then commerce won. The finger dropped, the head came up, poised, the smile returned. All graciousness, she moved forward. 'Mrs Polglase. A pleasure to see you again on this beautiful morning, ma'am. And how may I serve you today?'

The newcomer was a little beauty. For a second George was distracted from his errand. It was unfair that someone with looks like that should have been born into the gentry. If he had an assistant like that, all golden hair and huge blue eyes in a face that an angel would commit a sin for... He dragged his thoughts back to his present problems and stepped forward. 'Excuse me, ma'am.'

'I thought you were leaving, Mr Victor.' The haughtiness was back with a vengeance although the accent stayed true in the presence of a customer.

'Just going, ma'am, just going now. But it occurred to me. My wife. Leaving as quick as she did, she must have wages owed her.'

The figure grew inches taller, swelled. 'Mr Victor. That – person – left without finishing her work. In mid-seam. I have lost business because of her, lost customers. My reputation has been damaged. If anyone is owed money...'

He backed swiftly to the door, bobbing placatory bows. 'Quite understand, ma'am, understand completely. Sorry you've been bothered.'

The jingle of the bell didn't quite cover the final screech, the accent well slipped by now. 'And if she thinks I'm going to give her a reference–'

The door closed behind him with a well-fitting thud, cutting out her voice. George spared a second to wipe his forehead. Old battleaxe. But he had a real problem now. If Agnes had left without getting her pay, she had probably left her lodgings without paying her shot – and as her husband he was responsible for her bills. He daren't ask after her there. And that meant he was at a stand.

He was George Penhaligon, the Great Seer, George Penhaligon who had contacts in the other world, who could see the future, find that which was lost – usually when he had arranged for the disappearance of the object himself – but the one thing he could not be was George Penhaligon, who had to go around asking other people where his wife had got to.

He swore. It wasn't the first time he had had this problem. Why couldn't Agnes act like a proper wife? Do what she was told? Never criticise him? *Treat him nicely?* Instead, she criticised him, argued, objected to his female friends, ran away and tried to keep from him the money she had earned.

He could feel his anger growing by the moment. Silly cow. He'd teach her. He'd been patient up until now, moving in with other women when she left – sometimes before – and enjoying his brief spells of freedom from her carping. But he was getting older, money was harder to come by and so were women. He needed her. And when he found her *this* time he'd teach her a lesson she wouldn't forget. She would never run away from him again, he vowed, thrusting his hands deep into his empty pockets. Even if he had to hamstring her, he'd make sure she never ran away from him again.

But before he could have the pleasure of teaching her a lesson he had to find her. His scruffy hat set at a rakish angle, George Penhaligon set off down Market Jew Street towards the pillared front of the Star Inn. What he needed now was a little inspiration. Surely he could persuade someone in the inn to buy him some.

Robert stood, appalled, his mind racing. If Anthony found out that he had spent the night at the farmhouse he was certain to tell Theo and then there would be hell to pay. Not only for him but for those innocent women as well. He glanced back at the charming scene. He could not let them suffer for taking him in.

Making an attempt at ease he turned to his brother-in-law. 'I didn't know you were such an early bird yourself.'

'Work,' Anthony said briefly, then, his eyes widening, 'What in heaven's name has happened to you?'

Too late Robert remembered his dishevelled state, his coat spattered with blood, his hair still matted against his head where the bullet had given him a new parting. 'I fell.' He gave an unconvincing laugh. 'Went for a walk last night and tripped and knocked myself out. I felt too shaky to try to get home until a short time ago. Stupid really. Theo must be anxious.'

But if Anthony talked to Helen now, she would be sure to blurt out the true story. She had wanted him to see a doctor anyway. He nodded towards the farm. 'You're not going there, are you?'

'Got to keep in with the heiress.' Anthony seemed in good humour. 'I hope you haven't been cutting me out.' He dug Robert in the ribs. 'Theo wouldn't be very pleased, you know.'

His headache and worries were making him slow. 'But the child is the heiress, surely?' Robert said, blinking.

'Pshaw! An orphan child, a few months old. How many like that live to see their majority?' Anthony shrugged. 'Anyway, I've come to give Miss Schofield news of another death. She sent for me to see old Mr Trahair down in the valley. I've just come to tell her that he's found his way to a better world. Though whether Heaven will be strict enough for a miserable old bugger like him,' Anthony added viciously, 'I rather doubt. And if it is, I'm just glad I'm bound for another place. No drinking, no laughter, no pleasures. It's amazing he lived as long as he did. That sort of life would kill me of boredom in a week.'

'He didn't have the money for many pleasures that I remember.' Robert glanced back at the farmyard, now empty except for the chickens. 'Look,' he said desperately, 'don't tell her the bad news now. Come back with me. I – I don't feel well,' he lied frantically. 'While you're there I can pay you for your attendance on old Mr Trahair. And Theo will be pleased to see you, I dare say.'

'Theo has already had that pleasure.' But to Robert's relief the doctor turned and walked beside him back down the lane. 'I saw her in Penzance, just about to go into Madame Elise's.' He laughed. 'She seemed rather cross with you, though now,' he glanced at Robert's bloody head and unkempt clothes, 'I can understand why.'

Theo's anger was always expressed in one way – by spending money. Robert bit back a groan. Still, it gave him a little breathing space. Somehow, he had to keep Anthony away from Helen until he had warned her not to say anything about his being there last night. What Theo would do if she ever learned about that he dreaded to think.

'Now that I have found out how to tell the fresh eggs from the rotten ones,' Helen said seriously, 'we ought to think about selling them.'

'There's all that there milk, too.' Agnes spat at the bottom of the iron and watched the ball of spit career madly across the metal before disappearing in a hissing sizzle. 'Butter was what your brother-in-law used to make from it and brem good it was, too.

Bought 'un, I did, when I had the money. Never needed to put no carrot water in his butter, he didn't.' She thumped the hot iron down on the sheets, smoothing away the creases with long sweeps of her thin arms.

'Carrot water?' Helen looked up from where she was patiently feeding Beth with a mixture of boiled biscuits, milk, eggs and sugar which Doctor Ledgerwood had recommended as a suitable diet for the child.

'To make the butter yellow,' Agnes explained shortly. 'Some people do use marigold flowers, they say, but carrot water's more usual.'

'Good Lord!' Helen had just assumed that butter was yellow, in the same way that she had assumed that all eggs were fresh and that milk appeared in churns. 'You know how to make butter, then?'

Agnes put the cooling iron back in its rest on top of the range and picked up another, hotter one. 'Reckon Jenny and me've got knowledge, between us.' She picked up another sheet. 'But what's the good of us making it? It's got to be sold and that means Penzance and there's no cart like there used to be.'

Helen shrugged. 'Three miles. It's not that far. I'm not going to be able to sell a lot.'

The iron came down with a thump. 'You? You're never going to carry stuff into

Penzance and sell it? A lady like you?'

'Well, you can't go,' Helen pointed out calmly. 'Not with your husband in the area. And if I am going to keep this farm, even for a few months, I need an income. Besides, if we can prove that the farm is a going concern, even after what has happened, then there is more chance of being able to sell it.' She jiggled the baby on her knee. 'Then you'll be a rich little lady, won't you my love?' Beth gurgled happily, almost unrecognisable from the screaming monster that Helen had first seen only days before.

'You can't do it!' Agnes said definitely. 'Whatever would your grandma say? And that young clergyman you're going to marry? Do you think they'll be happy with you acting like you was brung up in some back court somewhere? You've got a position in life and that means you've got responsibilities as well. You can't just go round doing what you want, like you was some bal maiden up the mine.'

'You sound like just like my grandmother.' Helen grinned. 'But there's more than one sort of responsibility. I owe it to Beth to make sure she doesn't lose her inheritance. I can't do that by acting like Lady Muck.' Then she paused, staring at Agnes, her eyes narrowed. 'If I go to Penzance–'

The woman sighed and continued with her ironing. 'Will I run away? Well, I couldn't, could I? Not with the babe here to be looked after. And besides–' she hesitated. 'Last night – when that man caught me and I thought it was my George – I was so frightened. I realised then, you were right. I'm better off here.'

She glanced around the kitchen, the stone flags cool in the afternoon sunlight, the plates shining on the Cornish dresser, a ham hanging from the beam. 'He might find me, but I got a bit of a breathing space.' She shuddered. 'He's out there somewhere. And if he do find me then I reckon I won't need to think that being dead is better than being married to him because I don't reckon there's going to be any difference.'

It never did any good to let Agnes brood about her husband, Helen had discovered, so she changed the subject swiftly. 'It is strange that Mr Polglase should have been outside at that time of night. And strange, too, that he should have caught hold of you.'

'Nothing so strange about that,' Agnes retorted. 'He thought I were a thief, I dare say, and just did what any landowner would do, grabbed me for the magistrates to deal with next court day. And as for what he were doing – well, it were in the lane where I bumped into him, and that lane is the shortest distance between his house and his works.'

'His? I thought – that is–' Helen could feel

herself blushing.

'Thinking of your gentleman admirer, are you?' Agnes asked sourly. 'Dr Ledgerwood's involved in the works, that I know, but I reckon 'tes Mr Polglase owns it.'

'But he wouldn't go there in the middle of the night, surely?'

Agnes exchanged the irons again, filling the room with the scent of freshly pressed linen. 'He might have a reason,' she said, cryptically. 'His wife used to come in the shop where I worked. Looked like an angel she did – and the tongue on her like a fish-seller when something wasn't just as she wanted it. A woman like that can easily drive a man to walk the lanes at night.'

'That's sad.' Helen mopped Beth's face and hands and put her back in her cradle. 'He seemed a nice man, but a bit–' she paused, trying to sort out her impressions of their overnight guest, '–a bit unsure of himself.'

'That's his wife.' Agnes nodded sagely. 'Always putting him down, I expect. A woman like that can sap all the goodness out of a man, bit by bit, like ivy strangling a tree. However strong he is to start with, she'll drag him down in the end.'

'Well, I hope you're wrong.'

Agnes snorted. 'There's one thing I am right about though; he's another one who's seen me here. Oh, I'm not saying he's going to go blabbing to my husband,' she added swiftly, 'but I still reckon that every person who knows – well, that's another step nearer George coming here to get me.'

The sudden knocking on the front door seemed to echo through the house.

Eleven

Helen's heart was hammering. Agnes' fears must be getting to her, she decided, or perhaps it was reaction to the alarms of the night before. It was almost a relief to see the gun that had caused all the trouble last night propped in the corner of the hallway. Swiftly, she caught it up, hiding it amongst the folds of her skirts as she struggled one-handed with the doorcatch.

'Oh!' The last person she had expected it to be. The gun in her hand suddenly seemed to quadruple in size as she gazed, thunder-struck, at Robert Polglase.

As if he had read her mind his eyes went unerringly to the weapon and she saw his face redden.

'Miss Schofield.' He dragged his hat off with a clumsy movement. Helen winced as she saw the band scrape across the wound in his head but he seemed not to notice it, the words bursting from him in a torrent. 'I'm so sorry. I – it was foolish of me. Thoughtless. I should have realised.'

'Realised, Sir?' She was lost.

He gestured at the gun. 'Two women, living alone out here. And after last night. It was wrong of me not to realise that an unexpected visitor must seem – might be considered to be–'

'Please.' She could not allow him to blame himself like this. 'It is not your fault, Mr Polglase. You have nothing to reproach yourself for.' Helen glanced down at the gun. 'It is not gentlemen in general of whom we are afraid but one in particular.' It was not her secret but she was somehow sure she could trust Robert. There was something solid about him; besides, she owed him an explanation for injuring him last night.

She carefully stood the gun back in the corner and gazed up at him, her green eyes anxious. 'It concerns the lady whom you met last night.' Not that Agnes was a real lady but the thought of referring to someone who had helped her so much and been so supportive as a 'female person', as society dictated, made Helen feel nauseous. A lady should be judged by her actions, not her accent.

She took a deep breath. 'She has left her husband and is under my protection. Last night, when you caught her–'

'She thought I was him.' Robert shook his head sadly. 'I can only apologise. She must have been terrified. And you also.'

'You don't – that is, I thought most gentlemen–' She broke off, but he had followed her unspoken thought.

'I don't come from a privileged family, as you can tell, Miss Schofield.' She could hear the bitterness in his voice. 'As a boy I saw many marriages where women were trapped with violent and vicious men, with no remedy, either in law or through the church. I know many men feel differently but I would never blame a woman, in those circumstances, for trying to lead a better life.'

His honesty and compassion moved her and she instinctively held out her hand to him in thanks. 'Then please, believe me when I say that *you* are always welcome here, Mr Polglase.'

Her touch seemed to ease his awkwardness. His big hand enfolded hers warmly, his grey eyes smiled at her without the reservation that had been so obvious when he arrived. 'I remember the lady from last night. She did a sterling job of binding my head and of helping me upstairs. You need have no fear that I would ever do anything to set her husband on her track.'

It was a good thing that the impact of the bullet had temporarily knocked him out, Helen's unruly thoughts reminded her. He would hardly have felt so well-disposed towards Agnes if he had heard her wanting to shoot him dead on the spot.

She controlled the amused twitching of her mouth with an effort. 'Thank you.' She gestured. 'I am being very unwelcoming. Please come in. I am convinced you should not be walking around with a head wound. We are not very smart but' – with a broader smile – 'you know all about that.'

His awkwardness was back instantly and he glanced swiftly behind him before moving past her into the airy quietness of the kitchen. 'I – that is, Miss Schofield...' His voice died away into an embarrassed silence. His big hands turned his hat over and over and she could see, behind the gentleman's clothing, the young village boy he once had been.

In an effort to put him at his ease she settled herself at the scrubbed pine table, folding her hands composedly over the letter to Ezekiel that was lying there. 'Mr Polglase.' She smiled at him. 'I am deeply in your debt for the forbearance you showed after our ill-treatment of you. If there is anything I can do for you, please, just ask.'

He stared at her long and hard then dropped heavily into the wooden chair opposite. 'It's about last night.' He stopped again and wiped his face with a handkerchief.

'Yes?' Helen could feel her heart thumping. Surely he wasn't going to report her for shooting at him?

He put his handkerchief away, then pulled it out and mopped his face again. 'I–' his voice came out in a sudden rush. 'I want to ask you not to say anything about last night to anyone.' Then, catching her startled glance, he explained, 'I have told everyone that I fell down and cut my head. No one knows that I spent the night here and it would be better...' His voice died away in confusion.

A jealous wife, Helen decided, remembering Agnes' description of her. She smiled warmly, regretting that such a pleasant man should have saddled himself with a shrew for a wife. No wonder he had sympathy with Agnes in her situation!

'Of course. Don't worry.' Her unfortunate sense of humour got the better of her. 'I will deny that I ever shot you.'

To her relief he laughed, more at ease again. 'Would you like me to reload the gun for you? It seems the least I can do, under the circumstances.'

'Certainly not.' Her voice rose with horror. 'I would never have touched the dreadful thing if I had realised it was loaded. I only intended to use it as a threat.'

'And if the threat does not work?' He was suddenly serious. 'You are two women alone out here. If that man does discover that you are hiding his wife he is likely to be extremely angry. I–' His voice faltered then strengthened again. 'I would feel happier if I knew that you had some protection you could rely on.'

'And I would feel happier if you could make sure that there are no more bullets lurking in the horrible thing,' Helen said, forthright. 'I managed not to kill you last night. I can't rely on luck like that twice.'

He smiled. 'If that is the only way I can serve you...'

Helen followed him into the small entrance hall and watched as he took up the gun and broke it open. 'It's empty. Are you sure–'

'Certain. I could never shoot anyone, anyway. That is–' She stopped in confusion.

'I know what you mean.' He snapped the gun shut. 'Do you intend to keep it here?'

She opened her mouth to reply but then shut it abruptly as there came a loud knocking on the door only inches away from where they stood.

Their eyes met and held, then Helen dropped hers, feeling breathless. 'Oh, really!' She tried to hide her confusion by bustling past him. 'Anyone would think I lived in the middle of Mayfair.'

'Wait.' He reached out and held her back, his hand a warm band around her wrist.

'Let me answer it. It might be your friend's husband.'

She turned to stare. 'But–' She hesitated. Politeness dictated that she could not say she had guessed about his jealous wife.

He pulled the door open, his broad figure cutting out her view of the person who stood on the step.

George Penhaligon reeled happily out of the Star Inn. Putting an arm around one of the pillars that supported the overhanging portico, he swung himself around till he was facing approximately down Market Jew Street then tacked slowly off, mumbling apologies to all and sundry.

Good ol' George. Never at a loss. He bounced gently off the well-endowed bust of a large lady and continued his walk. No money; win it at cards. No food; get bought it by admir – admir – good new friends. No home; plenty of money for new lodgings. He hiccuped. Good ol' George.

He stopped, leaning against the wall of the Dispensary as a feeling of unease crept into his consciousness. Bladder, he thought. That was the problem. Need a pee.

But not here. His head was clear enough for that. Find a quiet corner, out of the way. Head down some side street, slip into a back yard somewhere. He veered off down a small lane running at right angles to the main street, then again into a narrower passage.

The houses were poor here, no more than tenements, windows boarded up, doors hanging crookedly on loose hinges. In one corner there was a noisome puddle where water seeped up from some underground source. No one would notice a bit of extra liquid, he decided, not in a place like this.

It was as he was adjusting his clothing that he saw the familiar figure slipping past the end of the alley. In his present state it took him a couple of seconds before he could identify it and when he did, his face creased into a surprisingly sober smile.

Not Aggie, as he had first thought, but nearly as good. That little bitch who had robbed him last night. He'd teach her, he decided, setting off after her; he'd show her that she couldn't rob the great George Penhaligon. No one could get away with that.

One hand against the rough granite wall for support, he hurried after the slight figure. He mustn't lose her. And he had to catch up with her somewhere isolated; he knew that.

He didn't want anyone trying to stop him having his fun with the little bitch.

'What the hell are you doing here?'

The self-confident voice was instantly

recognisable: Anthony Ledgerwood. Helen felt embarrassment burn its mark into her cheeks. What would he think of her, closeted here alone with another man? And a married man at that!

Then there was Robert. After he had asked her to keep their meeting a secret!

The least she could do was show some solidarity with him, try to distract Anthony's attention. She moved forward from behind Robert's broad back. 'Doctor Ledgerwood.' Her voice was calm even though she knew that her colour was unbecomingly high. 'How nice to see you. To what do I owe the pleasure of this visit?'

'I'm interested in asking my brother the same question.' The doctor's handsome face was unusually grim; his eyes did not leave the other man.

'B-brother?' Helen glanced from one to another, the full horror of the confrontation becoming apparent. She tried to hide her discomfiture under a light, social manner. 'I did not realise you were brothers.'

'Brothers-in-law.' The doctor's voice was grim. 'Of course there is no blood relationship.' He made it sound as if Robert were a farm animal, Helen thought, recognising the unconscious snub in the words.

Instinctively, she ranged herself on the side of the underdog. 'Mr Polglase very kindly came here to–' She paused, racking her brains desperately for a reason.

'To tell her of old Mr Trahair's death.' Robert's words came out with such a rush that Helen was certain that he, too, had been racking his brains. 'I knew that she had taken an interest in the old man.'

Poor old man. Helen remembered him, so upright and vigorous when she had first seen him and then so swiftly ill. But there was no time to take in the news now. To ask questions or exclaim would be to give the lie to Robert's words.

But for the first time since she had met him she was not first in Anthony Ledgerwood's interest. He said, 'Then, Polglase, as you have performed your self-appointed task, I would advise you to go home. Theo is there and she is – agitated.'

'Just going.' Robert crammed his hat on his head with no concern for the wound. Helen winced. But she had no right to delay him; he was in enough trouble already, from the sound of it.

She held out her hand. 'Goodbye, Mr Polglase. I really am very grateful for your thoughtfulness in this matter.'

Robert took her hand, holding it for a second as if he were going to say something; then, as Anthony Ledgerwood made a small, impatient sound in his throat, he dropped it and fled.

'The great oaf.' Anthony shut the door

behind him and followed Helen through into the kitchen.

'I thought he was very kind,' Helen objected. 'He came right out of his way just to see me.'

He smiled, the ill humour vanishing from his face as if it had never been. 'Who wouldn't come out of their way for the chance of talking to such a charming lady?' When his words received no answering smile from her he went on, with a deprecating bow, 'The truth is, I am angry because I came on just such an errand myself, only to find that I have been beaten to it – and by my own sister's husband.'

His choice of words made Helen's hackles rise. Surely he didn't suspect... Head up, she stared him straight in the face. 'I understand,' she said, calmly, 'that your sister is one of the most beautiful women in the district.'

It made him laugh. 'Don't let her hear you say that,' he advised. 'She is only happy if you tell her she is far and away *the* most beautiful.'

He obviously loved his sister, but the comment made her think no better of Theo. Poor Robert, to be married to someone like that. Changing the subject, she asked what old Mr Trahair had died of.

He shrugged. 'Old age, mostly. He was a good age. Especially for someone who had worked down the mine all his life. Miners usually die young. He must have been tough as old boots.'

For some reason, she was finding him less pleasant than she usually did. His words and expressions seemed marginally wrong and when she asked, 'What about his jaundice?' the words seemed to have a bite to them.

'Jaundice?' He stared at her, his face immobile.

'You told me before that he had jaundice,' she reminded him. 'Is that what killed him?'

Again, a pause. 'Jaundice. Yes.' Then he made a move. 'I should be going. There are other patients who need my skills and my life isn't my own.' He smiled at her, flashing his white teeth, his eyes bluer than ever in the sunlight. 'I hope you don't think that I am a disgrace to my profession, letting myself be tempted out of my way just for the excuse to talk to you?'

Why could he always make her feel so breathless? It hadn't happened when she spoke to Robert. Feeling like an ill-bred schoolgirl she made a negating movement with her hands and swept the letter to Ezekiel off the table and onto the floor.

Politely, he bent to pick it up for her and she saw him glance at the address. Her face flamed again. Young women just did not write to men. 'It's – he's my fiancé,' she stuttered, then realised with an angry start that she need not have spoken. The letter was clearly addressed to the Reverend Ezekiel Hardcourt at the Mission; even young ladies could write to clergymen, and there was no reason for Anthony to suppose that this clergyman wasn't old enough to be her father.

He held the letter in his hands, staring down at it for a second, then smiled up at her. 'You are a long way from the post office here. I have to go into Penzance. May I post this for you?'

What could she say? He always seemed to be able to put her off balance. She nodded, but he brushed away her thanks with a careless gesture. 'You must know that it gives me the greatest pleasure to be able to serve you in any way.'

After he had gone, she wondered at the remark. Wasn't it a strange thing to say to a woman that you had just learned was engaged? But perhaps he was just being gallant, she decided. He always had been polite and attentive to her, ever since they met in the solicitor's office.

Anthony Ledgerwood carried the letter with him all afternoon until he got back to his lodgings. There, sitting in the only comfortable armchair, he read it at his leisure.

And then he burned it.

Twelve

Theo was waiting for him when he reached home with the excited glitter in her eyes that spending money always gave her. 'So you've bothered to come in at last, then.'

Robert's head was hammering in time with his pulse and he felt sick. He should have taken it easy today, not gone off to the farm again to warn Helen. He should have left well alone, trusting to her obvious innocence to silence wagging tongues. Instead, Anthony had seen him there twice – and Anthony, he knew, would make the most of that.

Knowledge that he had failed Helen made him disgusted with himself. Heavily, he dropped into the settee – blue, to match Theo's eyes. God, he was beginning to hate the everlasting blue. Did she see everything in life merely as background for her beauty? Was that why she had married him – because she knew that his brown hair and muscular body were the perfect foil for her blond slenderness? His unusual cynicism sickened him. She was his wife; he had chosen her for better or worse. Such thoughts had no place in a marriage.

Wanting to keep the peace he ignored her question. 'Did you buy anything nice in Penzance, dear?' He saw her eyes narrow and realised immediately that he had given himself away.

'How did you know I was in Penzance?' she demanded. 'You've seen Anthony, haven't you? Where were you?' Her voice rose until he was certain that every servant in the house could hear its screech. 'What have you been doing?'

'Walking, my love.' He would keep Helen's name out of this if he could. He cleared his throat. 'Look, I'm sorry about last night. I expect Anthony told you. I fell and hit my head, knocked myself out completely. Otherwise I would have come back in a short while.'

'That's what you say now.' She wasn't convinced. 'How do you think I felt, knowing that the servants all knew about us? Knowing that even my maid was sorry for me?'

The ultimate disaster for Theo, who needed admiration and envy the way a flower needed water. His head thudded viciously; he couldn't think straight. 'I'm sorry,' he said again, swallowing convulsively against the rebellion of his stomach.

'It's no good saying you're sorry. I'm your wife. If you were a gentleman you would realise...'

The words flowed over him, lost in the bitterness of his thoughts and the pain in his head. He'd been a fool to go out in the sun. Anthony had warned him. Take it easy, lie down. You may find that you're not thinking as well as usual for a few days.

He choked. Not thinking at all, more like. Fool that he was, to risk that lady's reputation a second time. And she *was* a lady.

He stared blankly ahead, not seeing the comfortable saloon with blinds drawn to keep out the afternoon sun but a farmyard, where chickens pecked and squawked and a lady in mourning dress laughed comfortably with him about nesting habits as if they had been friends all their lives.

'–and if you don't even care about your wife's happiness–'

The sun, the exercise, the wound in his head were suddenly all too much. Robert muttered an excuse and leapt for the door, hearing the voice behind him still raised in peevish complaint.

She was moving ahead of him, not bothering to look behind her, not even bothering to keep an eye open for customers.

George Penhaligon followed at a distance. Already the alcohol was clearing in his brain. He had to get her alone if he were to get his money back. She might be a tart but she was local; whatever they thought about her morals, if push came to shove, the townspeople would side with her against him. And there was always the possibility of a pimp in the background.

She turned into a small court, climbed an outside staircase to a dingy hovel. George grinned. Perhaps his luck was changing after all. As long as she was alone in there...

No one was taking any notice of him. Probably they were used to strange men coming and going at all hours of the day. He ran lightly up the steps and knocked. 'You available, love?' He made his voice a shade deeper, trying to suppress the Truro sing-song which she might remember.

'Come on in, me dear.' Although the words were welcoming, the tone was weary, promising only the minimum compliance to earn her fee. Not like last night, he remembered. But last night she had her eyes on his money, the little thief.

He was inside in one quick step, pushing the door to behind him.

'Over here.' She nodded towards the frowsty bed, the dirty covers still rucked up from the last customer, hands already reaching for the fastening of her bodice – and then...

She glanced towards him and he saw recognition dawn in her eyes; saw her open her mouth to shout and he was on her, hands around her throat, strangling the noise before she could call for help, strangling her, strangling Aggie and every other woman who had mistreated him, had lied and stolen from him, who had not shown him the respect his talents deserved.

'Where is it?' His voice was hoarse with fury. 'Where's my money, you bitch?'

She mewed softly, the only sound that she could force past his gripping fingers, nails tearing at his hands, face darkening with congestion.

'Where?' He shook her so that her head and body seemed to be disconnected, the head stiff under his grasping hands, the body lolling madly as he flung her to and fro. 'Where, you little tart?'

She wanted to speak, he could tell, trying to communicate with eyes, with frantically pointing fingers. There. There. He moved his head to see where she was indicating. A string stretched across the corner of the room holding up a blanket.

A final squeeze and he flung her from him, careless about where she fell. Two steps, rip down the blanket. Clothes, a box. He rummaged swiftly. Nothing. He lashed out angrily with his foot.

There. Behind the box. A loose stone in the once-whitewashed wall. George cast a swift look behind him in case the woman was recovering enough to call for help, but she was still huddled on the floor, motionless. No danger from her, at least. He hooked shaking fingers around the irregular stone and pulled it free.

Who would have thought the woman had so much money? Here was even more than she had taken from him. He grinned, pushing the coins deep into his pocket. Serve the bitch right. He would have been on the level with her if she had not cheated him first.

He moved towards her. 'I've got what I came for. Just don't complain to anyone, right? Or I'll have you locked up.' She was silent, unmoving. 'Do you understand?'

Still no movement. He moved towards her, peering through the dim light that was all that percolated through the thick, distorted glass in the small window. 'Do you understand?'

She was thin and dark, lying there with total abandonment. She reminded him of Aggie, Aggie after they had made love, Aggie after he had taught her a lesson. Surely he hadn't chosen this prostitute, out of them all, just because she reminded him...

The thought made him angry and he lashed out. 'Answer me when I talk to you, girl.'

The body lifted slightly with the force of his kick then fell again, motionless and silent. Too silent. Worried, he leaned over her, shook her shoulder, pulled her over onto her back.

'Look, I didn't mean–' But there was no point in saying anything more. She would never answer him, never speak again to anyone. Her head rolled loosely on the floor, at a strange angle to the body.

'I – I didn't mean – I didn't intend–' He backed away, his heart hammering his guilt through his body. 'It wasn't...'

She lay there, a silent witness to his crime. Dear God. Murder. The Assizes. Hanging. The words pounded through his brain. The death penalty. He bit his lips, his hands shaking as he stared at her, so thin, so dark, so like Aggie.

It wasn't fair. He could feel his chin wobble. It wasn't fair. He hadn't meant it. It was her fault. If she hadn't stolen from him, if she hadn't been a whore, if she hadn't looked like Aggie...

To die for a tart – a man like him, with his gifts, his brains, his quick wits.

Only if they caught him. He took a deep breath, trying to think calmly. He was a stranger here. Who knew him? Who would ever guess? She must have had men up here all the time.

All he had to do was walk out quietly. As if he had got what he wanted. Perhaps call a goodbye? Wave? That was it. There was nothing to link him with this, nothing at all.

He pulled open the door. 'Thanks, love.' An easy wave, then down the steps, not too fast, not trying to hide, just turning his head from the only old woman in the court as if he were a respectable man not wanting to be recognised. Then off, still walking at a reasonable pace. Where? The Star. With a bit of luck they would think he had only gone for a piss, would say he had been there all the time. He took a deep breath in through his nostrils, blowing out the stink of the room, of her.

When the door had closed behind him a small child toddled out from the noisome back room. She pulled and shook the body for a while, calling for attention in a low, whining voice before finally giving up and huddling down beside her dead mother.

'I turned out they cupboards in the room Mr Polglase had last night,' Agnes said, coming down with her arms full of material. 'There was a brem lot of old clothes there – and good quality too. Belonged to your brother-in-law's ma, I wouldn't wonder. Look at this.'

She held out for Helen's inspection a black silk dress of old-fashioned cut, obviously made for a large lady. 'I could cut this down for you,' Agnes offered. 'I could make you something far smarter than what you're wearing at the moment.' She eyed the plain mourning dress run up by Grand-mama's cheap dressmaker with disdain.

For a second Helen had a vision of herself feeding the chickens in a black silk gown of Parisian smartness. Foolish, of course. Where would she ever have a chance to wear such a dress? But she knew Agnes by now. If Agnes made such an offer it was because she wasn't planning to leave – at least until the gown was finished.

'That would be wonderful.' Helen smiled up from where she was rocking Beth's cradle with one foot on the rockers. 'If the farm is left to decay all these things will be thrown away. But I feel guilty. You are working so hard and I cannot pay you.'

'I told you,' Agnes said gruffly, 'I don't want no pay. Any money I earn the old devil can get his hands on and I aren't letting him get another penny off me.'

'I'm glad to have you.' Beth was asleep now, her face pink and crumpled under her lacy bonnet. Helen stood and stretched. 'I'm glad of your company. Beth isn't a good conversationalist and Jenny always makes me feel so ignorant. I can feel her despising me every second we're together.'

'She'll be busy at home with her granda dead and all. Her ma'll want her to help I dare say.' Agnes sat in the sunlight that filled the farmhouse kitchen with a golden sheen and spread the flowing skirts of the dress across the scrubbed pine table. 'If I do get a move on, you can wear this here for the funeral.'

Helen's head jerked up. 'What funeral?' Then, realising, 'But I won't go to that.'

'Then you don't know no more about life in the country than you do about cows – or children,' Agnes snorted. 'He were your neighbour and you employ his granddaughter – of course you got to go.' Her usually hard expression softened and she set down the material in a softly shining mass. 'Chapel, I dare say he was, being an old miner. I do love a good funeral.'

'Then you can go instead of me.' Helen was horrified. 'I don't want to go at all.'

Agnes pointed the sharp-nosed scissors with which she was cutting open the seams at her. 'Don't you be so daft. You're somebody now. You've got responsibilities. You got to go or they'll take it as a slight.'

Somebody now! Helen could have laughed. In London, Grandmama was always talking about their position in society but no one knew whether they lived or died. And here she was, temporary caretaker of an almost bankrupt farm on behalf of a baby – and she was a person of importance.

Agnes smiled grimly. 'You Londoners – you don't know what life is like down here. Money is good, of course, but *land* is what's important. You can't never get too much land. God stopped making land a long time ago but he keeps right on making people.'

'But it isn't my land,' Helen protested.

Agnes shrugged, turning back to the black silk. 'No one owns land, not really. You just borrow it for a time. And it's in your hands now, so you've got the responsibility – and the position.'

It was strange to think that until a week ago she had never had any responsibilities, Helen thought. Now they were an integral part of her life. 'Thank God for Jenny,' she said passionately, as a vision of life on the farm without the child's assistance made her shudder. 'I couldn't do anything without her.' Then she cocked her head at the sound of bare feet drumming on hard-packed earth. 'Here she comes now.' She smiled at Agnes. 'Do you think this is my invitation to the funeral?'

But before Agnes could reply the door from the farmyard burst open and Jenny stood panting in the doorway.

One look and Helen was on her feet. 'What is it, Jenny? What's the matter?'

Her red hair clung to a face that was scarlet with exertion. The thin chest rose and fell under the thin blouse. The child was panting so that she could hardly gasp the words out and even when she did, it took Helen a second to grasp the importance of what she was saying.

'The cows – the cows in the bottom field. One's down and another one looks brem ill.'

She threw herself forward into Helen's arms, tears streaking her red cheeks. 'I'm afeared they're dying, Miss Helen. I'm afeared they're dying, just like Mr Trethowan's horse.'

Thirteen

Luckily, it was downhill all the way.

Helen clung to the field gate, panting against the restricting embrace of her corsets. At first sight, she thought Jenny must have imagined the disaster. Six of the cows cropped peacefully at the grass close to the gate, raising great black eyes to survey her with bovine lack of curiosity before lowering their heads to the grass again. The seventh stood alone, head down, legs apart, her tail moving uneasily. And the eighth...

Just a brown heap right at the bottom of the field.

'Oh, no.' Helen opened the gate but it was Jenny who pushed through first, her bare legs red with exertion as she ran down and dropped to her knees, cradling the head in her arms.

She looked up at Helen with tear-drowned

eyes. 'I didn't do anything, honest. I looked after them just as good as always.'

'Of course you did.' Helen crouched by the side of the stricken animal, grimacing. The wind had changed and the foul-smelling smoke from the tall chimney over the calciner blew straight across the small stream and into her face. Perhaps this cow had a sensitive nose. She forced the thought aside. The animal was seriously ill. The fact that she made no effort to rise to her feet even with people around told Helen that.

Jenny's thin body shook with sobs. 'I milked them and everything. I really did.'

'I know, sweetheart.' Helen put her arms around the small body, trying to comfort her. 'I was the one who suggested you put the cows here, remember? So that you had fresh milk to hand if your grandfather needed it. I wouldn't have done that if I didn't trust you.'

It had been a relief. With the old man so ill, the Trahairs would probably have many visitors and could do with the extra milk. And until Helen had scoured the milk containers and butter churns and arranged for the butter to be made and taken to Penzance for sale, the gallons of milk flowing into the farm every day were an embarrassment. Even feeding the pigs on fresh milk, instead of the thin buttermilk which they were used to, had made very little difference. The constantly arriving milk had to be thrown away or the farm stank with the smell as it soured in the churns.

Helen squeezed the child's thin body. 'This is nothing to do with you. Perhaps the cow is just old or something. It's only this one.'

'But it isn't!' Jenny raised her blotchy face. 'That Blossom over there, she's not right. And the ones by the gate – there's something wrong with they, too.'

Helen glanced back at them but could see nothing wrong. The lone cow – Blossom? – wasn't eating or chewing her cud but otherwise she seemed all right and as for the cows by the gate – the child was probably hysterical.

'Perhaps there was a plant or something that she shouldn't have eaten.' Helen wished she knew more about animals so that her attempts to console Jenny were more useful.

'But I looked!' The girl was in tears again, desperate to defend herself. 'I looked all over before I would let they cows in the gate. I was afeared of that after Mr Trethowan's horse died here and all. Then we both of us went round, looking and looking but we couldn't find nothing at all.' She gave a wail of pure misery. 'First Anna – the horse – and now Charity. It's cursed. This farm is cursed.'

'Don't be ridiculous.' Helen knew that she had to put a stop to such wild talk immediately. She would never find a tenant or buyer for the farm if any more of these rumours got around. She climbed to her feet. 'One thing is obvious. The farm may not be cursed but there is something the matter with this field. The best thing to do is to move all the animals out immediately, then we'll do another search. There must be a plant or herb here which is poisonous. It's the only explanation. Come on.' She tugged Jenny to her feet. 'Let's drive the other cows up to the farm. Then...' Her voice tailed off. She hadn't the faintest idea of what to do about Charity. 'I'll decide about this cow later.' She made it sound like a carefully thought out plan, not a course of desperation.

Together they moved back up the hill, away, to Helen's relief, from the stench of the calciner. 'Would you recognise any poisonous plants?'

Jenny sniffed and wiped her eyes on her sleeve. 'The local ones, I would. And so would have Mr Trethowan. And we looked over every inch. There weren't nothing there that could hurt neither cow nor horse, I swear it.'

'But something has harmed the animals.' Helen pulled the gate open then stood back and let Jenny drive the other cows out of the field. She wasn't an expert on animals but now that she looked closer at them even she could see that these cows didn't seem as normal. They were slower, dragging their feet, heads low. Her heart sank. So much for her plans to make butter to sell, to earn some income from the farm. If they were ill, the cows wouldn't give much milk; if they were seriously ill, she wouldn't even be able to sell them to other farmers if the farm did have to be abandoned.

The cows plodded slowly past her and she watched, heart heavy, as Jenny tried to get Blossom to move. The animal seemed sunk in misery and Jenny had to shout and pull at her horns, slap her rump with her hand, before she eventually struggled slowly up the hill to the gate.

'Poor old biddy. Poor old Blossom.' Jenny walked beside the animal, her skinny arm round the animal's neck, crooning sweet nothings into the cow's ear. Helen was amazed to see that the cow responded, moving more freely, as if she took comfort from the child's touch, slowing to a halt when Jenny left her for a second to pull the gate to behind her.

'I aren't never going to put any more animals in there.' The child's voice was fierce, her eyes burned with anger. 'That there's a bad field. I won't *let* you put any more cows in there.'

'I wouldn't dream of it,' Helen said fervently. She watched as the cow waited until Jenny's arm was back around her neck before she began to struggle onwards. 'That cow seems to know what you are saying.'

The girl glanced round with surprise. 'That was why Mr Trethowan employed me, didn't you know? To lead the oxen.' Her thin chest swelled with pride. 'He reckoned I could get more land ploughed in one day than another leader could in a day and a half.'

Helen knew that teams of oxen had to be led around a field, unlike a horse that could be driven, but she had not realised that the leader made such a difference. Then her unruly mind made a thought strike her. 'Wouldn't you have lost your job when Mr Trethowan bought his great horse?'

'He let me look after her all by myself when he were busy.' There was no mistaking the pride in the child's voice. 'He said I were the best stable hand he'd ever heard tell of.'

Of course Jenny wouldn't have done anything to hurt the horse. Helen hated herself for even thinking of such a thing. And there were the cows now, too. She would never have harmed them.

So much death. Cows, horse, old Mr Trahair. Plodding through the next field, Helen said, awkwardly, 'I'm sorry about your grandfather.'

'He were that yeller, poor old man, afore he passed on.' Jenny turned her head. 'I were supposed to be asking you to the funeral come Monday but I saw the cows and I forgot.'

'Of course I'll come.' Thank heaven for Agnes and her timely warning. Helen closed another gate behind them. The smell from the calciner was very faint now – she had never noticed it in the house. Imagine having to live with it all the time as the Trahairs did. Not that it did them any noticeable harm.

Half-way through the next field Jenny pointed to where the granite bones of the country thrust through the soil, great masses of rock in the midst of the grass.

'Mr Trethowan were going to blow they up. He said that with a horse he could plough this field up and use 'un for taties and such except that they gert rocks was in the way. He and my brother Nat got the explosive and all but they never did nothing 'cos of the accident.'

'Well, I won't need to blow anything up,' Helen said firmly. 'I won't be here long enough to plant potatoes anyway.' She glanced around at the high Cornish hedges, thick with flowers and shrubs, any one of which could, as far as she knew, be poisonous. 'Shall we keep the cows in the barn for the time being, in case there are poisonous plants in these fields? I can feed them.' She was already losing her fear of their wide spreading horns and cloven hooves.

'They'll need watering too. I'll come as usual for the milking but just at present–'

'I know. Your mother needs you.' Helen hesitated. 'About Charity–'

'There's a drench for cows Mr Trethowan swore by.' The little girl looked grim. 'I'll try to get it down 'un. If her's not too far gone...'

'And if she is?' What did one do with a dying cow?

'I'll get the farrier to see to 'un.' So much knowledge for a small child. Pray heaven Beth can grow up not knowing about all these things, Helen thought as she watched Jenny's small face droop. 'I'll get old Fred up from Madron. He'll put her out of her misery and take the body for the hounds. Unless you want to salt–'

'No!' The very thought of eating a cow that she knew was repulsive. Besides, it was very sick – and heaven alone knew what with. Anxious to change the subject, Helen asked, 'Did Mr Trethowan have any idea about what had killed his horse?'

'Not that I knew. It weren't no plants that we could find.' The child hesitated. 'He said he were getting bits of the horse to send away but I dunno where. I asked but he wouldn't tell me.'

So he too had tried to shield the small girl from the horrors around her. Helen reached out and held her. 'Jenny, thank you. I don't know what I would have done without you.'

She had meant it well but the result was catastrophic. The tears which had stopped flowed again. The cow stopped, head down and panting as Jenny took her arm from its neck and threw herself instead into Helen's arms.

'It were my fault. I did my best, but–' Her voice rose in a frantic wail, her pink, upset face clashing horribly with her red hair. 'All they animals – I was in charge of they and they're all ill and it were my fault.'

'It wasn't your fault.' But the child would not be comforted. Crouched by the hysterical girl, Helen gazed blankly ahead. For Jenny's sake as well as Beth's she had to find out what had been going wrong with the farm.

This time he should really be drunk but alcohol seemed only to make the truth George Penhaligon was trying to forget more real.

He thrust his hands deep into his pockets and recoiled as he touched coins – coins he had stolen from her. No matter that she had stolen first, no matter that he had intended nothing more than to teach her a lesson, get his own back; because of her he had done the terrible thing, the thing that set any man apart from his fellow men. He had taken a life.

The air in the Star was thick with smoke. The great barrels behind the bar covered the wall. But nothing could stop the vision, the vision of a woman, thin, dark, her head horribly awry.

Looking like Agnes.

That was the stomach-wrenching thing. Agnes. And it should have been Agnes. He knew that now. He had only chosen the whore last night because she looked like his lost wife, he had only been so angry with her because she had done what Agnes had always done – robbed him of what was his by right as her husband. And when he had gripped her neck, when he had thrust her roughly away – it had been Agnes that he really wanted to strangle, Agnes whom he had wanted to punish.

And now he was a marked man. A killer. The mark of Cain. He felt as if the fact of his deed was burned into his forehead, as if his crime was written in blood across his face for all to see. And it was all Agnes' fault.

If he were caught for this, George knew that he would hang. Hang for a worthless trollop. It didn't matter that the very judges who would condemn him to hang would have sent her to prison, vilified her as evil and corrupt, the truth was that he would hang for her death as well as if she had been the purest lady in the land.

And Agnes would be free.

Oh God! It was the nearest to a prayer he could ever remember praying. An incoherent cry from the heart. Let it not have happened! Let me not have done it!

The hand on his shoulder brought him to the present with a nervous cry, though it was not the local constable but one of his earlier drinking companions.

'Reckon I know how you did that trick, now. Reckon I could win this time.' The man swayed slightly, gripping George's shoulder for support.

The perfect mark. Nothing was as satisfying as taking a fool for a second time but for once George did not want to cheat and lie. Revulsion stirred deep in his soul. He wanted time to come to terms with what he had done, he wanted to go somewhere clean, wash away the guilt.

Common sense re-asserted itself. He had to act naturally. His mouth smiled, his cheeks creased. 'Reckon that, do you? How much are you prepared to bet on it?'

Inside, deep inside, unshed tears curdled in the terror of his heart. Outside, his hands felt in his pockets, brushed aside the coins, tainted with her blood, reached for the cards, the cards that served him so well, that could tell past and future when he so desired it.

He would never ask them to show him the future again.

'Stand still, will you?' Agnes pulled at Helen's shoulder. 'How am I ever going to get this looking like anything with you whirling round like a teetotum? You'll end up with a right kerbodgick if you're not careful.'

'But there must be something.' Helen stood obediently still as Agnes pinned the side seams of the bodice to a breathtaking tightness. 'Jenny said that my brother-in-law had sent off samples when his horse died. If he got a reply it might help us.'

'You don't know nothing about a cow when it's in good health.' Amazing that anyone could speak so clearly with a mouth full of pins. 'How do you expect to understand anything some man has written about a dead horse?'

'I could ask him to explain.' She turned her head. 'Agnes, please. I do appreciate what you're doing, but if you would just pull out that drawer and put it on the table I could read while you are doing the pinning.'

'You'll never look like nothing, moving all the time.' But the other woman moved to the dresser, pulled out a drawer full to overflowing with a jumble of papers and set it on the table by Helen's side. 'There. *Now* will you let me get on? It's the funeral Monday and I don't want you looking all poverty-struck. That won't help you sell the farm.'

'You're right.' Helen had never considered this aspect to her dress before. 'Though I don't suppose that anyone who would buy a farm would go to the funeral of someone like old Mr Trahair.'

'Word gets around. And you'd be surprised who goes to funerals round here. It might be different up London way,' said Agnes, dismissing the habits of the capital city with an airy wave of her hand, 'but in Cornwall we take dying seriously.'

Helen buried her teeth in her lip to bite back the laughter. 'I'm so glad.' She realised she was more concerned with the cow than she was with old Mr Trahair. Jenny was the same. But perhaps that was the bitter reality of life for the poor people. However much they loved their old relatives, the truth was that when they could no longer contribute to the family income they still needed food and medicine. She felt her anger rise at the unfairness of it all.

'Stop taking such deep breaths.' Agnes tugged the gaping seam together again with rough hands. 'You won't be doing no running at the funeral.'

'I don't think I had ever run at all before I came here.' Even as a child she had done no more than walk obediently by Grand-mama's side. The thought of going back to that life, to taking Beth back to be reared like that, was depressing. Suddenly, she had had enough of her own problems. She threw the still unread handful of papers back in the drawer. 'What does your husband do, Agnes?'

For a dreadful second she thought she had made Agnes swallow a pin, then the other woman found her voice. 'You know him! I told you the day we met. He's George Pen-haligon.' Despite Agnes' feelings about her husband Helen thought she could detect a trace of pride in her voice.

'But what does he do?'

'He's a seer, idn't he? Most famous seer in all of Cornwall, they do say.' Her voice altered. 'He do say, anyway,' she amended, rather more tartly.

'Seer?'

'Don't tell me they don't have they in a gert city like London?' Agnes sat back on her heels and stared at Helen with wide, brown eyes.

'We might have.' It would not be politic to point out that she had learned more of the lives of the working class in Cornwall in a week than she had ever learned about the London poor. 'What does he do?'

'He sees the future, don't he? In the cards and things.'

Helen swung round, nearly tearing open the straining seam again. 'Really? He can really tell what's going to happen?' No wonder Agnes was so worried about him finding her. If all he had to do was look at the cards... Then her common sense reasserted itself. 'But he doesn't really, does he?'

'Well, sometimes he do.' There was a world of doubt in her words. 'Sometimes he can see all sorts of things. But other times–' She snorted. 'Well, you got to earn a living, haven't you? And you can't always rely on the future.'

If you couldn't rely on that, as a seer, what could you rely on? Helen swallowed a laugh. 'So, what does he do when the cards won't work for him?'

'Plenty. There's card tricks and that sort of thing. He can tell what card you picked just like magic.' For a second Agnes' face was alive and pretty, remembering with pride the accomplishments of the man she married. Then it hardened again. ''Course, they was all tricks, really. And then finding things – there was times he took the things first, just so as to tell people where they was and get a reward.'

The benefits of theft without the risk of disposing of the stolen goods. George Penhaligon was obviously a clever man. But Helen was more interested in his ability to tell the future. 'Can he only see what is going to happen to him?'

Agnes shook her head. 'That's the one thing he can't see, not usually. But for other people he can, as often as not. And all sorts come to him: rich ladies who want to know who they're going to marry, people going to invest in a mine... Course,' she added, 'he do pick up rumours in inns and that. Wonderful what people do say after a few drinks down the kiddleywink. So when a lady comes to ask him who she's going to marry, likely he's heard stories from her groom about her rides round, timed just so as to meet a certain person and things like that. Brem good memory he's got for names and facts and putting two and two together.' Misguided loyalty shone in her eyes. 'I reckon he do be better at that than any of your clever London scientists.'

'I dare say. But Agnes,' Helen turned as she felt the woman finish tacking the seam, 'the very fact that he is what he is makes you particularly safe, doesn't it?'

'I don't see that.' Agnes frowned at the tightly fitting black silk. 'I wonder if I should take in the waist another fraction.'

'No. I'm not a fashion plate, I've got to breathe.' Helen had had enough of a struggle with her grandmother choosing fashions and clothes for her all her life, she wasn't going to be bullied by Agnes now.

'Just think about your husband,' she urged. 'Any other man could ask where you are. He could tell everyone he met that his wife had left him, that he wanted to find her. But your husband can't do that. He can't ask for information about you because people will wonder why his 'seeing' doesn't work. He can keep his ears open, of course, but he can't search for you. So, living here quietly as you do, there's no way he can ever find you.' She smiled triumphantly.

'That's what you do say.' Agnes' face was as dark and withdrawn as usual. 'But that's always been the case. And he's always found me in the past.' She sighed. 'I reckon he'll find me again. And he won't be long about it.'

Fourteen

The soft summer twilight was already fading as Helen made her rounds of the farmyard.

It was becoming routine now, a quiet preliminary before bed. She had chased, as she had every evening, the last solitary chicken from its roosting place in the hedge, where it would be found and eaten by any passing fox, into the noisome recesses of the chicken house and shut it firmly in. She had cast a swift eye over the sows, huddled in a grunting mass in their even more smelly hovel and now it was the turn of the cows.

Her pace slowed. What would she find? But one thought that had crossed her mind this afternoon had been answered. The cows were unlikely to have taken any harm from the stench wafting over from the calciner. Compared to the smell in which most farm animals lived it was unlikely they even noticed.

In the shadowy dimness behind the half-door the cows stood quiet, jaws moving. If only she knew more about the animals, Helen thought hopelessly. At least they were all standing; presumably that was a good sign?

As she turned away there was the sound of hooves on the hard-packed earth of the lane outside and through the twilight a black horse appeared in the gateway to the farm-yard, a tall, top-hatted figure on its back. It was only when the man bowed, removing his hat so that his golden curls gleamed in the darkness, that she recognised him.

'Mr Ledgerwood.' She moved forward, aware that her heart was beating more quickly. 'What a surprise.'

He dismounted with athletic grace. 'I was passing and I couldn't resist giving myself the pleasure of seeing how you were. And your little niece, of course.'

'Oh, there's no problem with us; *we* are both well.' She could not hide the faint bitterness in her voice.

He moved forward. 'But someone isn't?' His voice was concerned. 'Please, won't you tell me your problems.' He smiled. 'That is what we doctors are for, you know. I believe that, like ministers of religion, half our benefit comes from letting our clients talk themselves free of their concerns.'

His honesty amused her. 'Then I am afraid that you could only help if you can talk to animals. My problem is with the cows. Jenny found them this afternoon. One could not rise and she swore that the others were ill, too.'

He hesitated a second before he answered. 'No, I am afraid I cannot help – though, believe me, I would if I could. But cattle are surprisingly vulnerable to all sorts of ills, I understand. We are taken in by the strength of their bodies and find it hard to believe that their constitutions are less robust.'

Helen sighed. 'Of course. I feel so helpless, knowing less than nothing as I do. I have to rely on Jenny for everything–'

'And she is just a child and cannot be expected to know much about animals or their treatment.' He touched her hand. 'I prescribe a night's rest for you. Tomorrow, you will probably find that she was merely imagining things. Perhaps the death of her grandfather upset her and she transferred her worries onto the cows.'

It did not sound like Jenny but he meant well and Helen did not want to argue. 'I am sure you are right. Indeed, I would be quite convinced – if only something similar hadn't happened to my brother-in-law's horse.' She ran her hand distractedly over her hair. 'Jenny said that he had had some tests done on the horse. I shall have to see if I can find the results of those – but all his papers are in such a mess.'

He moved to her quickly. 'My dear Miss Schofield, I forbid it. As a medical practitioner, nay, I hope I may say, as a friend, I forbid it absolutely.'

He waved his hand, indicating the darkening yard, the soft lamplight spilling from the kitchen window. 'It is night, Miss Schofield, it is time for you to rest from your labours. You have taken on so many responsibilities in these last few days. You have had to take on all the cares of an aunt, of a businesswoman, indeed, of a farmer.'

He took her hand in his. His fingers felt warm and firm and Helen's mouth was suddenly dry. 'Please, you are a lady born and bred, anyone can see that. You have been delicately nurtured. Believe me, no one can have a greater admiration for the way you have shouldered these burdens over the past few days, but you have not been reared for it. You must not overtax yourself.'

He smiled down at her, his teeth white in the gathering darkness. 'It seems to me, Miss Schofield, that your pulse is already a little tumultuous. You are doing too much. You should rest.'

Still holding her hand he led her towards the house and she went with him without demur, her knees unaccountably shaky.

At the doorway he stopped. 'Now promise me, no reading; no hunting for papers. Rest, pure rest, is what you need. And indeed, Miss Schofield, I don't hesitate to say that I am certain that even if you disobeyed me you would be no better off. I knew your brother-in-law, as I know most of the gentlemen in this area. A fine man but not, I am afraid, a businessman. I am certain that you will find nothing to aid you in your search. And, most probably, it would be a waste of time in any case. By tomorrow the cows will be swinging their tails merrily again – or whatever it is that cows do to show that they are fit and well. Why, madam' – his voice was lower now, more confidential – 'why risk your health for such a cause?'

His blue eyes burned into hers, his fingers tightened against her skin. 'Believe me, Miss Schofield, I am absolutely in earnest when I say that there is no patient of mine whose interests I hold closer to my heart than your own.'

For once her recalcitrant mind had no opinion of its own to offer.

'Oh,' said Helen, weakly.

'Thank the Lord!' Theo dropped her embroidery with a weary sigh and rose as Anthony entered the silent drawing room. 'I'm dying of boredom here.'

'What, sweet sister? No loving husband to keep you amused with his sparkling repartee?' His blue eyes glinted maliciously down at her.

'Don't be so foolish.' She was in no mood for humour. 'You know he can't put one word after the other at the best of times and recently he's been like a bear with a sore head.'

'Rather literally for the last day, in any case.' Anthony paused. 'Has he told you how he got the wound in his head?'

Theo flung herself onto the sofa. 'Fell over and knocked it, the idiot.' It was hard to keep her anger under control. Bad enough that Robert should have dared to walk out on her like that, but to hurt himself so that he didn't return until the next day, by which time all the servants knew about their argument, was intolerable.

Even her own maid... Theo clamped down on her fury. She needed that wench. Who else would she find who was such a genius with her hair in such a god-forsaken hole as this? But the girl's sympathy had been the final straw. How dare Robert make her a laughing-stock like this?

Her brother seemed uneasy, she noticed. He was dressed in a new frock coat, looking handsomer than she had ever seen him look before but he walked restlessly around the room, moving the lamp a fraction, adjusting the ornaments on the mantelpiece.

She opened her mouth to remonstrate but he spoke first. Back turned as he fiddled with the gilt candlestick he said, awkwardly, 'I don't think Robert's injury was caused by a blow.'

'What then?' She had no interest in how he had hurt his head. Wasn't it enough that he had done it, that he had made her look a fool, that he had gone to bed early yet again with a headache, leaving her to endure the soul-destroying tedium of another lonely evening?

The pause was long enough to register so that she was staring at him inquisitively when he answered.

'A bullet.'

Disbelief made her laugh jeeringly. 'You think someone shot Robert? You must be as stupid as he is. He's a mine owner, for heaven's sake, not some law-breaking fisherman.'

'Not someone else.' His voice was steady. 'I wondered – if he had shot himself.'

Theo felt as if all the breath had been sucked out of her body. 'You thought...' Her mind reeled. 'But how? Why?' Her voice seemed to come from a long way away, creaking like an unused door. Suicide? Robert?

'You're the one who is most likely to know why.' Anthony turned to look at her. 'I haven't said anything before, Theo. God knows, I agree with you most of the time about Robert. But even he must have his limits. And he has always been madly in love with you – ever since he was a gormless schoolboy with scabby knees he has looked on you as some sort of goddess. But eventually...'

'You don't think I have been treating him well?' The laugh was not as light as she had planned. 'I've been as nice to him as he deserves. Mostly,' she added, under Anthony's disbelieving stare.

'So well that you both admit he storms out of the house after a quarrel with you and doesn't come back until the morning?' He looked stern. 'You're a lovely woman, Theo, but there aren't many suitable husbands down here. You're already thirty and no children yet to show for your marriage. Don't think you'll find it easy to get another husband – much less one as good as Robert.'

His words cut her. Raising her chin she snapped, 'A rich widow can always find a husband.'

'Perhaps. But if you've driven him that far how do you know he will leave you a rich widow?'

She fought down panic. 'But there's no one else–' Then common sense reasserted itself. 'Anyway, I don't believe you. You must be wrong. Tried to shoot himself?' The laugh came more easily this time. 'Even Robert couldn't miss from that distance.'

Anthony was still grave, standing over her, somehow menacing in his black coat. 'This time he might have thought better of it at the last moment. But he might try again, Theo. Or he might do – something else.'

Now she did laugh. 'Another woman, you mean? Anthony, don't be foolish.' The gilt looking-glass over the fireplace showed her reflection, softened into ethereal fragility by the gentle lamplight. 'He could no more make advances to another woman than he can fly! Besides, where else–'

She stopped, but he knew her well enough to complete the thought. 'Where else will he find another woman as beautiful as you?' He snorted. 'There are other qualities that a man may look for in a woman, believe it or not.'

The stab of jealousy was almost a physical pain. She could feel herself grow cold as the horror wrapped around her. 'He hasn't – he can't have–' Then, suddenly, it was anger that she felt. She was on her feet, hands stretched into claws, heart hammering. 'Who? Tell me, who?'

Anthony was moving restlessly around the room again. 'I may be mistaken. I just wanted to warn you.' He didn't look her in the eye.

She knew him as well as he knew her. 'But you suspect?' She took a deep breath, fighting to control the emotions that seethed within her. She sat again, smoothing the frown lines from her forehead with shaking fingers. 'Anthony, he is my husband. I need to know.'

Still he didn't answer, moving instead to the window and pulling aside the long festoons of curtains to gaze into the darkness outside. She was forced to plea again before he turned to her.

'I may be wrong, Theo, but twice I have found him near Tregurtha farmhouse. The first time' – he gestured – 'Robert was hurt, pale. He asked me to help him home. I thought no more about it at the time but after...'

'After?' It was hard to breathe. Her whole body was concentrated on his quiet words.

'I went back. I needed to see Helen Schofield. And he was there.' His face hardened. 'I'd told him to take it easy, to stay in bed.' He glanced up. 'It was a bad cut, Theo, and if it was caused by a bullet as I suspected then the impact, even if it just grazed his head, was enough to give him concussion. Yet he still made himself leave his sick-bed to go and see Miss Schofield. I can't help wondering...'

Relief made her say, 'But that woman isn't even very pretty.'

He turned on her, as angry as she had ever seen him.

'For God's sake! There's more to an attractive woman than a pair of pretty eyes. That woman has qualities you can't even begin to appreciate: courage, character, class–'

'Class?' This time the laughter was genuine. 'Are you telling me that Robert has fallen in love with a woman with *class?*' It was laughable. Robert the booby, who could barely keep his head to talk politely to the vicar's wife, who stumbled and stuttered when he met any of the local gentry – him, to fall for a woman with *class?*

Anthony gripped her shoulders, his fingers digging deep into her white flesh. 'Yes, class, you little fool.' He snorted. 'You think class is not talking with a Cornish accent, is being rude to the servants and distant to the workmen. But Helen Schofield is a real lady. You have only to look at her to see that. And a real lady would not try to put Robert down, just because he stuttered a bit; she'd draw him out, make him feel at ease.' He shook her and she could feel her carefully arranged hair loosening under the onslaught.

'I tell you, she has the sort of quality that you never see down here and even your ape of a husband would be able to realise that and fall in love.'

She jerked herself away from him, staggering onto her feet, rubbing her shoulders where his fingers had bruised her. 'And I know someone else who has fallen in love with the bitch.' Unshed tears tightened her throat and made her voice swoop and sink uncontrollably. 'You love her too, don't you? You come here, pretending you're just going to court her just for the farm and all the time–' the tears fell now and she dashed them away, uncaring, '–all the time you're falling in love with her.'

'And if I am?' His voice was cold. 'We, don't all have to be hard-hearted little gold-diggers like you, marrying a man you don't care tuppence for, just because he's got money.' He spread his hands wide, begging her to see things his way. 'Yes, I need to marry her for the land. I'll do everything I can to bring that about, even, God help me, even break off her present engagement. But I want to marry her for what she is, as well, for her mind and her courage and her kindness.'

His turned away, shoulders drooping. 'Today, God help me, she told me about a problem she had and I nearly told her all, I nearly explained–'

But she had no patience with his problems. Her heart felt as if it would burst. The jealousy she had felt when she heard about Robert and this woman was nothing to the emotion that gripped her now.

Robert was merely a husband but Anthony – Anthony had been the mainstay of her life ever since their parents died. With Anthony she could be herself, they could share their innermost thoughts, laugh at acquaintances – even at Robert – together. Together they stood against the world, siblings, partners, friends, allies...

And now he had left her, he had betrayed her, he had changed his alliance to another woman, a woman without beauty or money. *He cared more for this Helen than he did for her.*

The world swayed under Theo's feet. Everything that she had built her existence on reeled and tumbled. Robert, Anthony – both had betrayed her. Once she had been first in both their lives, the woman around whom both had orbited, sharing their money, their time, their *love*.

'Go – go away.' She was almost choking with bitterness.

Now that it was too late, he acted as he had always done, as if he still cared for her.

He took her arm. 'Theo? Are you all right?'

As if she could be all right! As if she would ever be all right again! 'Go!' It took all her effort to force the word past her clenched teeth. Her body shook with the strength of her emotions. 'Just go, Anthony.'

'If you're sure.'

Why didn't he go? Why didn't he get out of her life, take his handsome, betraying face out of her drawing room, leave her before the last, fraying vestiges of her self-control vanished for ever?

He moved with agonising slowness towards the door while her body filled and filled with vile sourness. Her nails dug into her palms, cutting crescent moons of blood and still he hadn't gone, still he was standing there, staring at her.

'Go.' The bitterness filled her completely now. She felt as if the world was wrapped in it, as if, when she spoke, he would see the vileness she was trying so hard to keep from him. She shut her eyes, squeezing them tight, screwing up her face with the effort of control.

The door closed.

For seconds she stood motionless, suspended between the effort of self-control and the emotions within, then she moved. Slowly, her eyes opened, her fingers relaxed. She looked around the room, considering, thoughtful, as if she had never seen it before in her life.

Slowly, legs stiff, she lurched to the window. Her arms moved jerkily out, she clutched the swathes of material in her bleeding palms, and with a scream that echoed throughout the house she pulled the swathes and festoons of material off their hooks, away from the walls, tumbling them in ruins about her slender figure.

'Sitting there, looking like you been piskie-led!' Agnes took the empty plate from under Helen's nose with a jerk and dropped it into the stone sink with a rattle. 'Always the same you are, when you've been talking to that there blamed doctor.'

Helen came to with a jump. 'I was just thinking,' she said defensively. 'You can't possibly know what I'm thinking about.'

'Not about they sick cows. I can tell that by the look on your face.' Agnes clattered loudly in the hot water. 'Nor you didn't go round looking like that after Mr Polglase was here.'

Helen felt a faint drift of guilt. She had almost forgotten that poor man. It was interesting, too, now she thought about it, that Agnes always called him by name, something which she never did with the doctor.

'Poor Mr Polglase.' Helen tried to soothe her angry friend. 'He was very good to us, really. He could have reported me to the magistrates for shooting him like that, if he'd wanted to.'

'He'd have had to explain what he were doing creeping round your farm in the middle of the night.' Agnes paused, up to her elbows in suds. 'Not that what he don't have a reputation for kindness – though some call it softness that I have heard.'

'I wouldn't have thought he was soft.' Helen rested her chin on her knuckles and thought about him. He was a pleasant man – once you had got past his awkward shyness. 'I should think he is a kind husband,' she said thoughtfully.

'Kinder than what that handsome doctor would be, I reckon,' Agnes retorted. She swirled the water around the dishes. 'Not but what that's nothing to do with you, is it?'

'I don't understand what you mean.' Helen felt her face grow red.

'Well, there's that there clergyman up in London. He's the one you're going to marry. Isn't he?' She turned to stare at Helen.

'Yes – yes, of course.' Helen reached out and played with the salt and pepper pots, balancing one on the other, moving them to fit patterns on the cloth. Suddenly her happiness had gone and she felt unreasonably depressed. 'Of course I'm going to marry him,' she repeated more loudly. 'All this is just a – holiday, a brief gap before I go back to where I belong.' She sighed.

'Just as long as you don't forget it.' Agnes stood the last pot on the draining board and reached for a cloth. 'Now, didn't you say you was going to look through those letters after supper?'

For some reason the idea didn't appeal. Helen took the drawer that was lying on the end of the table and slotted it back into its place in the dresser. 'Another time, I think, Agnes. I – I feel too tired just now.'

Fifteen

There was already a crowd of people dressed in black outside the small cottage as Helen made her way self-consciously along the path past the calciner.

At every step her full skirts whispered quality, her petticoats rustled class. The tight bodice, the achingly small waist, even the black jet that adorned her bonnet, all reminded her that she was not here as Helen Schofield, spinster, but as a representative of the land-owning class, an employer of a relative of the deceased, a neighbour.

As she came near the conversation halted,

there were polite bows, heads nodded in acknowledgement. She bowed in return, her feeling of self-consciousness growing by the second.

There was no one she knew. All here seemed to be men, and men of the working class. As she paused, unsure of whether she should enter the cottage or wait outside, a lone woman, there was a stir. Jenny and her brother Nat appeared, one carrying a stool, the other a chair, which they set down outside the door, close to each other. Nat disappeared back indoors and Jenny came to Helen's side.

'I'm brem glad you've come, Miss. 'Tes good to have someone who's a friend, like.' It was an almost unrecognisable Jenny. Her wild red hair had been brushed and severely pulled back, confined under a black bonnet, several sizes too big and soft with age, which almost drowned her white face. Black clothes, also obviously borrowed for the occasion, swept the ground and hung loosely around her skinny waist.

Helen took her cold hand in one of hers. 'You should have known I would come.' She squeezed the hand gently. 'Is this your first funeral?'

''Course not!' The child stared. 'But it's the first from our house.'

The first close relative then. There was another stir and the cottage door opened again. The men removed their hats, heads bowed as the coffin appeared, borne on the shoulders of six men, followed by Mrs Trahair, also in borrowed black. A shuffle, a sideways manoeuvre and the coffin was lowered gently onto the chair and the stool, slightly askew because of their different heights. The bearers moved to take their places in the crowd and a black-clad minister appeared in the doorway behind the coffin. 'Let us pray.'

Head bowed, Helen peeped under her lashes at the people around her. At least now there were faces she could recognise: Mr and Mrs Trahair, Nat and, to her surprise, Robert Polglase, who had been one of the bearers. Jenny's fingers tightened convulsively around hers and she squeezed them in return, trying to put what comfort she could into the small movement.

The extempore prayer came to an end and there was a general rearrangement of mourners. Now, six of the men who had been standing around when she arrived moved forward and shouldered the coffin. The family ranged themselves behind. Helen gave Jenny a little push. 'Go on,' she hissed, nodding with her head at the procession that was taking place. 'Stand with your family.'

Then she realised that she, too, was being summoned. Robert Polglase was indicating with a movement of his head that she should come to stand with him, just behind the immediate family.

Uncertainly she stepped forward. 'But I'm just a stranger,' she whispered. It could not be right that she should be given so prominent a position.

'An employer. Like me.' He stood beside her, head up, replacing his top hat. His smart clothes emphasised the dichotomy she had already recognised in him, accentuating at the same time both his gentlemanly bearing and the thick-set strength that was a relic of his family's background.

The minister moved to the front of the line. 'Now, men, loud and clear. Do your best for our departed brother.' He raised his voice. 'Soldiers of Christ, arise...'

'...and put your armour on.' The bass voices took up the tune. The procession began to move slowly ahead following the minister and the coffin. Under cover of the raised voices, Helen murmured to Robert, 'The bearers look very strong. I suppose they will have to be.'

'Oh, they will carry the coffin in relays, all the way into Madron. That's why there are so many here.' He flickered a tiny smile at her. 'But they are strong. Most of them work down my mine. That's where Mr Trahair used to work when he was younger, in my father's time.' He paused. 'It is said that, at the Battle of Agincourt, the Cornish soldiers had to stand further apart than soldiers from any other county because of the width of their shoulders.'

'I can believe it.' His shoulders, too, showed his breeding. 'But they are fine upstanding men and look very healthy – despite their underground life.'

He nodded. 'Many of them own small boats and go out fishing when they can – or they have gardens around their houses and work in them. That way they provide themselves with good food and healthy exercise in the fresh air. Very few of the miners in my mine look as pale as an outsider would expect.'

They had reached a stile leading across a Cornish hedge. Here the minister stopped and the coffin was laid reverently on the lowest step as another group of six men moved forward and took their places around it. The replaced men moved to the back of the line, the coffin was hoisted again, the singing recommenced and the little procession moved slowly forward.

'Indeed,' Helen felt that she had to say it, 'these are some of the healthiest men I have ever seen in my life. But I suppose,' she added thoughtfully, 'that you will say that I am accustomed to living in a city where men do not habitually have the chance to work in the sunshine or fish on the ocean.'

He sighed. 'I am giving you too pleasant a picture, Miss Schofield. These men are fine and upstanding but these are the bearers. You do not see the cripples, the men whose lungs have been damaged by breathing the smoke from the explosions, or those who have lost their legs or arms in accidents. Some will be at the chapel, for old Mr Trahair was well-respected, but many are dead. Too many.'

'It is wonderful to see so much respect shown to a poor man such as he.' She remembered funerals she had seen in London. Grand funerals, where the coffin was carried on a hearse pulled by six glossy horses with black feathers in their manes, but where the following procession of smart carriages, many with coats of arms on their sides, driven by coachmen in mourning, were almost empty – just the outward show of respect for the dead with none of the honest feeling which pervaded this simple funeral.

Helen glanced again at the minister. He would have to be paid, presumably. She remembered the way the family had tried to avoid the expense of a doctor for the old man. Money was hard to come by for them. Not that she had much herself but even so...

She turned abruptly to Robert Polglase. 'Do you suppose – would they be offended, do you think, if I were to offer to pay for this funeral?' She saw the surprise in his eyes and blushed. 'I – I am afraid I do not quite know the procedure about such things and I would not wish to embarrass the Trahairs or hurt their feelings but this funeral – the minister, that handsome coffin – it must strain their resources.'

'No, no. You mustn't think of it.' His words were hurried and his face suddenly beetroot.

She stared at him, then realisation dawned. 'You have paid for the funeral yourself.'

His face got even redder, if that was possible. 'Their employer...' The words were little more than an embarrassed mumble. 'Old friend of my father's. Long term employees, very respected.'

She smiled brilliantly at him. 'That is so kind of you, so thoughtful.'

'No, really.' He looked so embarrassed at having his little act of charity exposed that she took pity on him, changing the subject rapidly.

'Working for you must be a very healthy occupation, whatever you say of the dangers of mining.' She stared at the small groups ahead of them. 'Look at the people carrying the coffin now, and at Mr Trahair. Their skin is incredibly clear. I can think of ladies in London who would envy them their complexions.'

Robert willingly accepted the change of subject. 'They do look healthy. And, although those men are also my employees, they, at least, are not subjected to the dangers of the mine. They all work at the calciner.'

More evidence that the awful smell need not be unhealthy, that the cow had suffered from something else. Helen tore her mind away from the sick animals. 'Then it must be a very healthy place to work.' She glanced at Mr Trahair, Jenny's father, walking just in front of them. Below his cheap hat his hair gleamed with condition. 'I have only before seen glossy hair like that on a horse, never on a man.'

Robert followed her gaze. 'No,' he said comfortably. 'You would never think that he spent his life dealing with arsenic.'

Theo gazed discontentedly at her reflection in the looking-glass. 'Is Mr Polglase back yet?'

'Not yet, ma'am.' Her maid took up the brush and began to brush out her golden locks. 'I believe I heard downstairs that he said he would be out most of the afternoon, ma'am.'

Most of the afternoon. But what could Robert be doing on a Sunday afternoon? Even the mine was almost shut down on Sundays; the only people there would be those responsible for keeping the pump working, to prevent the mine flooding. There was no sport on a Sunday.

The terrible conversation she had had with Anthony kept running through her brain. Surely not! Surely Robert couldn't really be attracted to another woman? And the possibility that Robert had tried to kill himself?

Theo tried to reason with herself. They couldn't both be right. Either Robert was attracted to another woman or he was so upset by her treatment of him that he had tried to shoot himself. Only one could be possible.

But which one?

The bristles caught on a tangle and she jerked her head away, tears starting in her eyes. 'Silly girl! Why can't you take more care? I don't know why I employ someone as clumsy as you.'

'Sorry, ma'am.' After a pause the brushing began again, more carefully.

Which one? Theo wondered again. If he left her, if he made her look a fool in front of her friends...

'Ma'am!' The maid sounded appalled. Theo glanced at her reflection in the mirror and realised that she was gnawing at her carefully pared fingernails. She snatched her hand away from her mouth. 'Why didn't you tell me before, you stupid bitch? Weren't you paying attention?'

The reflection in the mirror was less satisfying than usual. Theo leaned forward, tugging her hair out of the maid's fingers. Her face looked so drawn! It was all Robert's fault. Staying out all night like that, refusing to let her buy the new curtains and furniture, being out now without a good reason...

There were definitely lines around her eyes. And on her forehead. Theo pressed her temples with her fingers, trying to smooth away the creases between her brows but the moment she took her hands away they came back again. Old. She was getting old. She felt the panic rise inside her. No wonder Robert was seeing another woman! No wonder he was straying.

She could see her future in front of her. She'd be the laughing-stock of the area. The once-beautiful Mrs Polglase who couldn't hold her husband. All those other women whose noses had been put out of joint when she came down here, whose husbands had swarmed around her like bees round a honey pot – they'd laugh. They'd laugh so much they'd split their tight little corsets, the bitches.

'Oh, God!' She set her elbows on the dressing-table and buried her head in her hands to hide the hot tears of shame that burned as they coursed down her cheeks. To have come to this. And so soon. Surely, surely, beauty was more than this? She was only thirty. Her shoulders shook.

Slowly she became aware of a tentative hand on her arm, a hand gently smoothing her hair. 'There, there, ma'am.' The maid's voice was low, consoling. 'Don't let yourself get upset.' A pause. 'I dunno what you're crying about but if it's Mr Polglase – well, men are all the same, aren't they? It isn't worth spoiling your looks crying about them.'

Pity. The pity she had feared. Here, now, from her maid – a pasty-faced female whose only attribute was her ability to dress hair to perfection – and *she* was pitying *Theo!*

Theo lifted her head. 'You little cow!' She snatched up another brush from the dressing-table and hurled it at the maid, hitting her across the head with it. 'Get out!' Her voice rose in fury. 'Get out of here, you little bitch.' She turned and caught up the hair-tidy and threw that too at the girl. 'How dare you! How dare you!'

There was only the bowl of dried lavender left on the surface. She threw that too, covering the cowering maid in a cloud of sweet-smelling seed-heads. 'Get out!' Her voice rose hysterically. 'Get out! Get out! Get out!'

The girl rushed crying from the room and Theo turned back again to the mirror. For a brief second she stared, appalled, at her reflection, taking in her white face, the cheeks a hectic and unbecoming red, the pinched lips, the frown lines that marred her forehead. Then she buried her face in her arms and began to sob. So much beauty. And all gone. So soon.

Sixteen

Theo could not hide her disquiet. 'He was with her again yesterday, for heaven's sake!' Her voice rose with worry. Her argument with Anthony, the way they had parted, was all forgotten. He was her big brother and she needed his support.

Anthony lowered his forkful of food. 'For God's sake, Theo,' – his voice was angry – 'can't you keep him away? You know you can twist Robert round your little finger. Why don't you do it?'

She stared at the uneaten plateful of food in front of her, her eyes prickling. Not even to Anthony could she confess the depth of her despair. The techniques by which she had brought Robert to heel for so many years no longer worked. She had tried tears, smiles, sarcasm – he had met all with a calmness that made her want to scream and did as he pleased.

Now Anthony was cross with her too. Worry and sleeplessness made her snappy. 'Well, you can't be doing too well with her,' she said viciously, 'if she prefers Robert's company to your own.'

He took another forkful of the cold luncheon he ate with her almost every day. 'I have no concerns at all about that.' His voice was calm and she hated his self-satisfied complacency. 'I may very well fail to bring the charming Miss Schofield up to scratch – but it won't be to lose her to your husband.'

He stared at her across the table. 'For heaven's sake, Theo! Helen is a lady through and through. Even if Robert were some kind of Adonis, she would never enter a relationship with a married man. *He* might fall for her but he would never do anything about it. It isn't that that is worrying me.'

'Oh, good,' she said, sarcastically. 'It is so comforting for me to know that even if my husband is in love with another woman she won't have him.' She hammered her fist on the table. 'What about me? What sort of fool am I looking?'

'Oh, stop being so self-centred.' His voice held none of the affection she was accustomed to and she was brought up short, staring at him in shock as he went on, 'It is the calciner that is the problem.'

He stared unseeingly through her, his handsome brow furrowed under the sleek golden curls. 'I'd better go and see her this afternoon. The Munsens' baby will just have to take its chance. It's probably only croup anyway.'

He tapped his fingers irritably on the tabletop. 'Unlike you, Theo, I am not concerned about her relationship with your susceptible husband. Because I know that young lady. She is no fool and she is, heaven help us, honestly concerned to do her best for her niece.'

'A disinterested woman?' Theo could not keep the tartness out of her voice. 'That can't please you.'

He shrugged. 'I could easily be happy with a woman who puts her duty before her own wishes – especially if, as her husband, I am that duty. No, the problem is, if I read the signs aright, that Helen suspects that the calciner is the cause of the illnesses and deaths in the valley – and I don't want her mentioning the possibility to Robert. You know what a soft-hearted fool he is.'

It was laughable. 'How should she? What would she know about it? Besides,' Theo insisted, family loyalty coming to the fore, 'you designed the calciner. You told me once, right at the very beginning, that it was important to get the chimney high enough or you could get arsenic in the smoke which would affect the land around.'

He looked at her strangely. 'At the very beginning, was it?' He crumbled a bread roll in his hand, not taking his eyes off her. 'That would have been before the costs started rising, then.'

'What costs?' she demanded. 'You paid part of the money up front and the works was built for exactly what you said it would be. Even Robert admits you did a good job.' She smiled slyly at him. 'He was hoping that the costs would rise so that you could not pay your twenty per cent. He only agreed to your having half the profits because he was so sure that the building would cost more than you could afford. If you had failed to come up with the money he was going to cut the percentage of the profits you got.'

His mouth twisted. 'It did cost more than I could afford, sister mine. I set it on that rubbishy bit of land because it was the cheapest place – even though, Lord knows, it's about as unsuitable as it could be. And the building cost more than I thought, so much more that I didn't have a hope in hell of paying my bit, even borrowing every penny I could.'

She stared at him. 'But it was built?'

'It was built,' he agreed. 'But to keep the costs down, it was built with a much lower chimney than it should have had.'

His blue eyes, so like hers, refused to meet

her own. 'For the past six months,' he said, his voice strained, 'that calciner has been pumping out arsenic all over the valley. And that includes Helen Schofield's farm.'

'Excuse me, sir.'

George Penhaligon glanced over his shoulder and tensed, the urge to run quivering his knees. A constable. Not that they were a great threat – in themselves. But the police were beginning to see themselves as more than parochial bailiffs. Now they would work together across borough boundaries, even across county boundaries if necessary.

He raised his chin enquiringly. 'You were talking to me, my man?' To be polite was to invite suspicion. Ape his betters, act affronted.

'Sir.' The constable glanced at his pocket notebook then up at his face, as if checking up on information he had got. From that old woman in the court? George felt his head dampen under his hat. 'Could I have your name, sir?'

'You have a reason for asking, I suppose?' Pray God the constable couldn't see his hands shaking. Bodmin jail loomed over him, the gallows, the rope swinging. He had passed by there once, never dreaming...

'We have a description of a wanted man, sir, and you match the description.'

George laughed, all bluff heartiness. 'A

description? Good God, man! If it matches me it must match half the men in the town. Medium height, dark hair, thirties, putting on a little.' He patted his waistcoat and laughed again. In his pocket the money he had stolen from the whore seemed to grow heavier, larger, bulging his coat, crying out its presence to the constable.

'The person concerned said that the man she had seen was a stranger.'

'Me? A stranger?' He tried to look affronted, broadening his accent, trying to hide the mid-Cornwall sing-song in his voice. 'Good Lord! When my wife has been working for months in Madame Elise's dress shop on the Terrace?' Best to stop the enquiries as soon as possible. 'I'll have you know that I'm George Victor, also known, professionally,' he bowed, satirically, 'as George Penhaligon, magician.' He never mentioned 'seeing' to the authorities; fortune-telling was illegal and could end in imprisonment. 'Besides, what has this miscreant you are looking for done? Smuggled a few barrels of brandy, eh? Or poached a couple of rabbits?' Again the laugh. Buff, jovial, *innocent.*

'A woman has been murdered, sir.'

Hearing the word sent a thrill through him but his courage rose. He was always a gambler, always played his best when the stakes were high. 'Good God! In this quiet town. And when would that have been, constable?'

'Yesterday morning, sir. About noon, as far as we can judge.'

'Then I can reassure you at once. I was in the Star Inn at that time, had been for hours, I'm afraid. Playing cards, showing off with some card tricks I know. They'll remember me, I'm sure.'

'And do you have the names of anyone who was there sir? Anyone who can vouch for you for that period?'

A local would know the names, of course. He laughed, playing for time while he thought. Not just a name but the name of someone drunk enough not to have noticed his relatively brief absence. 'Jan Clements. A stable boy at the Polglases'.' The boy had ridden in on the carriage that carried the lovely Mrs Polglase to the shop where he had seen her – and taken advantage of the time she notoriously spent shopping to have a few while he was waiting. Not that her character was as beautiful as her face if what the boy had said was true.

George Penhaligon raised his eyebrows. 'Is that name known to you, Constable?' he enquired loftily. 'They seem a respectable enough family even if their servants do frequent public houses.' The beauty of it was that the boy would not dare to admit he had been drinking heavily during working hours.

'I know the lad, sir.' The constable wrote slowly and carefully in his notebook, tongue protruding as he concentrated. 'That will be all, thank you. For the moment.'

George's heart was thudding erratically with relief. It was part of his ability as a con artist to remember names and facts. And to act. He maintained his composure until the man had saluted then turned away.

He had put the man off the scent – for the moment. But it only took one person in the bar room to remember his brief absence that morning and... It didn't bear thinking about. But to leave Penzance now would be to call attention to himself; best to stay around, acting innocent. Besides, there was Aggie – she was his wife, she should be by his side. This was all her fault. He would not have used a prostitute if she had been here with him as she should have been. All his troubles sprang from one woman or another.

George turned. The constable was standing, watching him. He waved to the man with a cheery insouciance but his heart twisted with fear and anger. It was all Aggie's fault. And, by God, he would make her pay for it when he found her, make her pay for everything.

Theo's eyes widened. 'Anthony, you didn't!' Inside, she felt a stir of pride. He had such courage, such panache. If only Robert was more like him. But poor, pedestrian Robert would never take such risks. He would never lie and cheat, risking all for a fortune.

'But' – common sense reasserted itself – 'how do you think you can get away with it? People will find out and then you will be in terrible trouble.'

He grinned. 'A mistake, that's all. After all, I am a doctor, not an engineer.' His face lit up with mischief. 'If anyone gets into trouble it will be your beloved husband. He owns the calciner, he runs it, he employed me to do the plans. Besides,' he shrugged, 'you are forgetting. I am the local doctor. Old Mr Trahair is ill? Jaundice, I tell them. And so it was, Theo. He was as yellow as a canary.'

'Then it wasn't arsenic that killed him?' She felt a huge sense of relief.

'It might have been arsenic,' he said calmly. 'In chronic cases jaundice can be one of the symptoms.'

'But – but you can't go round poisoning everybody.' The horror of what he was telling her was beginning to sink in.

'It won't be everybody,' he said, unruffled. 'It's been six months now, Theo. The men who work in the calciner are fit and healthy. Old Mr Trahair has died but that may not be anything to do with the calciner. Even the horse and cows on the farm–' he

paused, '–they might have died of anything.'
'But if it's pouring out arsenic–' she protested.
'It's not "pouring" out,' he corrected her. 'Most of the arsenic is captured in the labyrinth at the works. That's where we get all the profit from. It's just that some of it escapes from the chimney. But it's not a huge problem. When there's a wind the arsenic is blown well away. It can fall anywhere – but by that time it's so diluted that it wouldn't harm a fly.'
He waved a shapely hand at the salad dish on the table. 'There is arsenic in the ground all round here, Theo. If you eat anything that has been grown locally you are probably eating a little arsenic – not to mention tin and copper and everything else. You've been doing it all your life and it hasn't harmed you yet.'
She looked at the salad, grateful that her emotions had ruined her appetite. She doubted that she would eat any greens ever again.
'It's only when the weather is still that there could be a problem,' he went on. 'Arsenic is heavy – very heavy. If there is no wind the arsenic comes up the chimney and just drops on the ground nearby. There is a chance – a small chance – that if a man or an animal ate anything that was grown in the vicinity of the chimney that they could

– become ill.'

She was still appalled at what he had just told her. 'But Anthony, you can't let this happen. You have to do something.'

He was watching her carefully now. 'What do you suggest?'

'I don't know.' She waved her hands helplessly in the air. 'You could tell Robert.' The thought comforted her. Robert would know what to do. Robert wouldn't let this sort of thing go on. 'That's right. If you tell Robert–'

'If I tell Robert,' he interrupted, 'he'll close the calciner down.'

'Oh.' Theo hadn't thought of that. 'Well, for a little while, perhaps. Until the chimney is made taller.'

'Which will cost money. Which Robert doesn't have. And while the works are closed,' he went on implacably, 'you'll get no money from the calciner. And it is only the money from the calciner, Theo, that is keeping the mine going at present.'

Theo felt as if all the air had been taken out of the room. Her lungs strained in the tight embrace of her corset. 'Oh, but surely–'

'If you tell Robert a word of this,' Anthony went on implacably, 'you will find yourself rather poorer than I am. Is that what you want, sister mine, not only to be married to a lower-class lout but to a lower-class lout with no money?'

'I – it...' Her voice died away. The thought was impossible. Money was all that made life bearable. Even with her present worries, even though Robert was being horribly mean about the new furniture she wanted, at least she lived in one of the biggest houses in the neighbourhood, had pretty dresses, a smart carriage, servants.

The thought of losing it all made her feel ill. She sat, white-faced, staring at a future that she could no longer take for granted. She felt as if she was standing on the edge of the sea, as if a great wave was coming in to overwhelm her, sweep her away, wash away all the enjoyments of her life.

As if from a great distance she heard Anthony's voice. 'Now do you understand, you little fool? Now do you see why it is so important to keep Helen and your husband apart?'

Seventeen

'Doctor Ledgerwood.' Helen felt her heart leap at the sight of him. He was so handsome, his top hat in his hand, his smart frock coat fitting his slim figure like a glove. Quite as handsome as she had imagined Captain Wentworth, she thought. But you always imagined him to be dark, her unruly thought reminded her.

She stood and gave him her hand. 'I hope you have not come to give me bad news. None of the Trahairs is sick, I pray.'

His gloved hand held hers for a fraction longer than necessary. 'They are all well, as far as I know. But I was concerned about yourself. You never spare yourself; your niece, the farm, even the funeral yesterday – all are tiring and the last time I saw you I was afraid that you were not in your usual blooming health.'

The snort from Agnes, stirring a dish on the stove, almost overset Helen's gravity but she controlled herself. 'Really, Doctor, I appreciate your concern but I am not such a frail creature as you believe me to be.'

His eyes crinkled attractively. 'Perhaps my – respect – for you leads me to be over-anxious where you are concerned. But if you will not discuss your own health then tell me, how is your little niece?'

Helen knew that she was getting as besotted with Beth as those mothers she had always despised in London, endlessly prattling on about their babies as if they were the first person in the world to have a child. She could not hide her feelings as she said, 'She is well, thank you. And a pleasure to have around – now that she has stopped teething.'

His smile was understanding. 'Unfortunately, ma'am, that is a temporary respite only. More teeth will arrive. But if you are ever worried about her you have only to call me. Also, I have a nostrum which is guaranteed to ease a child's discomfort. Allow me to drop some in the next time I am passing. I would not like the little dear to lie awake in pain when a little of my medicine can ease her to sleep.'

Agnes dropped the iron ladle with a clang and bent to pick it up. Her muttered, 'Little dear!' seemed to echo around the kitchen.

Doctor Ledgerwood's kindness was difficult enough to take without Agnes' caustic counterpoint. Helen turned to her. 'Surely Beth's dinner is ready now?'

The other woman snorted again. 'In the way, am I? Well, I won't stay where I'm not wanted.' She picked up a bowl of soft food from the top of the range where it was keeping warm. 'I reckon there's more sense in her burblings than in some others' I could mention.'

'An impertinent servant.' Anthony Ledgerwood's face darkened and Helen realised that he had no sense of humour where he himself was concerned. 'You should turn her off.'

'She is no servant.' Helen waited until Agnes had pulled the door shut behind her with unnecessary force. 'She is a friend, someone whom I discovered in trouble who has been a godsend to me.'

'In trouble?' He moved towards her, his face serious. 'I hope you know what you are doing, Miss Schofield. Some of these rogues are plausible creatures and you are alone out here. If she has henchmen–'

Helen laughed. 'Agnes? No henchmen, I assure you.' The thought of Agnes as the head of a criminal band was too ridiculous to be taken seriously. 'If Agnes has a problem it is quite the opposite. She is in hiding from a violent and abusive husband of whom she is terrified. She says he is a seer – if you have ever heard of such a thing.'

'And you are protecting her?' His face was grave. 'The law, Miss Schofield, is on her husband's side. She married him before God for better or worse and she must stick by her vows.'

'And he vowed to cleave only unto her, and to honour and protect her,' Helen pointed out tartly. 'If he does not honour his vows, why should she honour hers?'

He stared at her, his face suddenly serious and she realised what she had done. A young woman, to disagree with a man! To support another woman against the laws of the land! What would he think of her? He would be disgusted. He could never respect her now, never admire her. She had put herself beyond the pale.

She had a sudden vision of her grandmother's response if she had put such views forward, and Ezekiel's. Their horror would know no bounds. She would be sent to her room for the rest of the day – for the rest of the week! Certainly until she had apologised, and even then the lectures would have continued for weeks, her awful crime being brought up before her until she wanted to scream at the mention of it.

Her heart sank and she felt her hands dampen with shame. She turned away so that he could not see the anguished blush that covered her face. How could she have said such things? Because you believe them, her mind protested, because you have as much right to your opinions as he has to his – or your grandmother to hers.

That thought almost took her breath away. As much right! If she went back to her grandmother's house thinking like this...

If? But she had to go back! She had no alternative.

Her own thoughts occupied her so that it took a few seconds for the strange sounds to come to her attention, then she turned, astounded.

Doctor Ledgerwood was laughing!

Laughing? He, whom she had just thought had no sense of humour? He moved towards her, his hand held out. 'My dear Miss Schofield!' His eyes gleamed as he stared down into hers. 'Such radicalism! Such republicanism! And in so charming and well-bred a lady!' His white teeth flashed. 'I am astounded, Miss Schofield – and impressed. But, I have to tell you, you are wasted on a clergyman.'

'W – wasted?' His words echoed her thought so closely that she felt the blush rise in her face again.

'Indeed. Such a free-thinker should marry a poet or a scientist – or a doctor. Someone who will appreciate the freshness of your mind, who can enjoy the courage with which you reach your own conclusions instead of blindly following ideas that have been taught for hundreds of years.'

'Indeed,' she said, weakly. Her cheeks were still burning and her mind reeled. She felt as if the ground she was standing on was whirling around. Nothing was as she had thought it. He had approved of her! He had laughed! He had said – surely he didn't mean...

His expression changed and he reached out and touched her burning cheek with a gentle finger. 'Miss Schofield, I am sorry. I should not have said what I did.'

She turned away, her head drooping, absurdly disappointed. Of course; what a fool she had been, to read so much into such a light-hearted remark. 'Please don't apologise, Doctor.' Her voice did not shake but it seemed strangled in her throat, as if there was a lump there that she could not force the words past. 'It was good of you not to take offence at my very free speech. It is I who should apologise for such unladylike conduct.'

He caught at her arm, pulled her around to face him. 'Not unladylike,' he insisted. 'That you could never be. And it is I who–' He dropped her arm, turned away. 'Madam.' His voice was as constrained as her own. 'I have forgotten myself. I was carried away by my feelings. You had already told me, you had already intimated that your heart belonged to another...'

'I–' She could think of no response. Her head, her heart, neither seemed to work as they should. She stood in a rainbow whirl of uncertainty, of happiness. The conversation had suddenly moved to new areas. She was in doubt as to his meaning.

She was in doubt as to her own response.

In the midst of her jumbled thoughts the doorknocker sounded like the crack of doom.

She could no more have moved than she could have flown. It was all she could do to control her expression, to maintain the outward calm of a lady, while inside...

Agnes clumped down the corridor, crossed the kitchen to the hallway, opened the front door.

The muffled words meant nothing to her. Helen still struggled to comprehend what had just happened. All she wanted was for the visitor to leave, Agnes to go.

She wanted to hear more from Doctor Ledgerwood.

Agnes returned and stood in the doorway.

'The Reverend Ezekiel Hardcourt,' she announced.

His brush with the constable had made George Penhaligon uneasy. The future seemed to be hanging over him, threatening.

If only he had not seen that tart again, if only he had not – his mind shied away from the word 'killed'. It was so unfair! His stomach churned with the anger that burned inside him. He had not meant to do it. He had been given no warning. Even the dream the night before – that could have been Agnes, not the prostitute. What good was his gift if it didn't help him stay out of situations like this one?

He moved slowly through the bustle of the town. The hot sun seemed to be picking him out, surrounding him with a halo so that he stood clear of all the crowds around him. He felt that his guilt was written clear on his face.

With the instinct of a hunted animal he headed for darkness. The butter market in

Princes Street was cooler and darker, though still crowded. Servant girls offered their wares, their faces pink with health under their bonnets. Eggs of all sizes, brown and white, were piled high in sagging baskets, set out on yellow straw as if they had been freshly laid by an amazingly productive hen with a sense of artistry.

He edged his way through the crowds that argued over the butter, each golden pat marked with a pattern that showed the farm of origin. One careless girl moved to the front of the counter leaving her store of cash unmarked while she set out her wares more attractively. Despite his worries his instincts were as good as ever. He strolled past, his body momentarily between the bowl of money and the crowd and when he moved on the bowl was emptier.

He was too much of an old hand to hurry away. Or to take all the money. With luck it might be several minutes before the girl noticed the loss. Calmly, he moved on, raised his hat briefly to a fat red-faced lady he had bumped into, listened with enjoyment to a lively interchange between two stall holders.

'That's him! I know it. That's him!'

Never run. That marked you out as guilty. His heart thudding, George stopped at a stall that was selling fresh milk, acting as if he had nothing more on his mind than a desire to make a good bargain. 'How much, love?'

'That *is* him!' The voice was right behind him now, a hand caught at his sleeve. His throat was tight with fear but he turned with calm arrogance, brushing at the hand. 'Do you mind, Miss.' He stroked the cheap cloth as if it were pure cashmere.

Not the old woman he had seen in the court, thank God. Not even the careless girl with the money. And no constable. Just a pretty girl, her hair untidy under her cheap bonnet and a heavy-set young man with the skin of a fisherman. Not that he didn't have far more on his conscience than those two little worries. He raised his eyebrows. 'I don't believe we have met, young lady.'

The man took over, snatching off his greasy hat and holding it in front of him like a shield. 'I'm brem sorry to bother you, Sir, but Sue here says – well, she says you're a seer, like.'

George almost sagged with relief. 'Yes.' It came out too readily and he snatched it back. 'Of course, you understand that fortune-telling is against the law.'

The girl's eyes widened. 'Oh, but–'

The young man was more sophisticated. 'I wonder if we could have a word with you outside, sir.' He glanced around. 'Somewhere where we won't be overheard, like.'

An excuse to leave the place. George

followed them to the relative quiet of the outside street. 'You know who I am, then.' The trouble with being a seer was that you couldn't ask questions or people started doubting your credentials. Not that there weren't other ways of finding things out.

'I saw you when I were up in Truro staying with my aunt what married a butcher up there.' The girl was the sort who would tell you her waist measurement if you introduced the subject in the right way. 'When I saw you here I just had to get Billy. I knew you'd be the one we want.'

Billy was obviously her young man, not a brother. Automatically, George noted such clues, stored them up for production later on if necessary.

Still not asking questions, George raised enquiring eyes to Billy's and, as he had expected, the young man burst into an explanation. ''Tes Sue's Freddie, see. He's bin gone these six weeks or more and the voyage weren't supposed to be more than a couple of weeks. Her ma's that worried, having lost her own man that way.'

It was the old, old story. Drowned, of course. A sudden squall, a clipper running down a small boat in the darkness – it happened all the time. But no one paid a seer to see bad news, that was the first thing he had learnt when he started out. What people wanted was hope – and they would pay well for it.

'I'll come, of course. Poor lady. Such a worry for her.' He raised his hand warningly as they burst into grateful thanks. 'I can't promise anything, you understand. This is a gift. It comes from the spirit world, from the great elementals that were here before us. Sometimes,' he shrugged, 'well, they are not like tame dogs to come when they are called. They must be propitiated, and if it pleases them they will assist. But they are chancy and dangerous. If, instead, I anger them...' He let his voice tail off meaningfully.

George always enjoyed giving the warning which he had copied from another con man he'd met long ago. He had no idea what it meant but it always seemed to go down well.

As usual, they nodded solemnly, their eyes wide. He settled his shiny hat more securely on his head. 'That is my problem, not yours,' he advised them, smiling bravely. 'I am willing to run the risk if by doing so I can give comfort to the suffering.'

'Knowing either way would be better than not knowing,' Billy explained as they walked through the back streets towards the area of the town known as the Barbican and George nodded understandingly even though he disagreed. Sufficient unto the day is the evil thereof. Besides, it was safer. The man might yet turn up and George knew he'd look a damn fool if he'd been coming up with some sob story about how the sailor drowned bravely helping a fellow seaman. Whereas, if he'd drowned and they'd heard nothing yet – well, the chances were, they never would. Certainly not enough to disprove the hopeful message he'd give today.

'Up here.' Billy dived into a narrow court and for a second George felt his heart contract with fear. Had he been identified, led into an ambush by friends of the woman he had killed? But the entrance, though similar, led to a wider court, the houses more respectable. He took a deep breath, wiping his palms down the sides of his trousers as he followed the couple into a small whitewashed cottage.

'Here, Ma.' Sue ran ahead, dropping to her knees by an elderly woman whose face showed all the signs of a full-fleshed woman having lost weight recently. Her cheeks were pendulous, the bags under her eyes fallen in. 'Here's that man I told you I saw in Truro, the one who can see the future. He's come to tell us about Freddie.'

'Only if the spirits are willing.' George moved forward, bowing over the woman's rough hand. 'I cannot promise success, ma'am, nor can I know whether the news will be good or bad.'

He smiled at her but his eyes were taking

in every detail of the room; the exotic conch shell balanced on the mantelpiece, the picture of a small boat (a lugger?) carefully worked in wools, a clomen cat, made of pottery and common in mining districts, sitting by the hearth.

'Any news, my 'andsome. Any news. Not to know - that's the dreadful thing.' Tears trickled down her cheeks, winding their way down the sunken valleys of her face. 'And him so young.' Her voice rose. 'What'll I do if he's dead and gone? What'll become of me? 'T'will be the poorhouse and I couldn't bear the shame of that. It'd be the death of me.'

'Now, Mrs Truggan.' Billy stood over her, his kind face red with embarrassment. 'I've told 'ee before, you can come and live with Sue and me when we're wed. There's no need for you to take on so.'

'My last one!' She was rocking to and fro, now, her white apron thrown over her face. 'My last one! All gone! All of 'em – drowned and gone.' Her voice changed. 'I hate the damned sea, I hate 'un. Taking all my men from me. Why ever did I leave home? Just for this unhappiness.'

'There's still me, Ma, you still got me.' Sue knelt by the woman, catching at her hands, tears of sympathy running down her cheeks. 'You still got me. I got a job, I'm earning money.'

But George could see that daughters did not count with the old woman. He heartily agreed with her. Men were the important ones, women were just a darned nuisance. Look at Aggie.

Billy broke in. 'Why don't you hear what this gentleman has got to say, Mrs Truggan? Perhaps you're screeching like a whitnick for nothing. Freddie could be alive and well, for all we know. Let this gentleman tell us.'

'I'll do my best.' He could have done with a few more clues but he had worked before on less. Besides, once he started, the comments and exclamations of his listeners often gave him all the clues he needed. He glanced around. 'I'll need a chair.'

Before they could move he had gone himself, picked up a rickety chair from beside the table. It took him nearer to the picture too but, to his disappointment, there was nothing more to learn from it. He cursed the fact that it was an embroidery; a painting would have shown the name of the vessel.

'You'll have to keep still. I need absolute quiet in order to get in touch with the spirits.' He leaned back in the chair and closed his eyes, his hands hanging loose in his lap.

Not that there was quiet anywhere. With his eyes closed the sounds became magnified, the rumble of cart wheels on cobbles, the squeak and splash of a pump being worked outside, children's voices shouting, the distant sound of voices calling their wares from the street market.

He deliberately closed his ears to the noises, pulling back inside himself. He had the true gift for seeing, but it was a chancy thing, coming at unexpected times, giving dubious information. Better by far to give the messages that people wanted. They paid more for that anyway.

He sank deeper, slowing his breathing. A couple of minutes should satisfy them. People like this didn't have the patience for a long artistic wait. No rattling breathing, either. Once in his early career he had been giving it all he got and some stupid farmer had thought he was having a fit and thrown a pail of cold water over him. It had put him off 'seeing' for weeks.

He dragged his mind back. Think about what you have seen and heard here, use it to frame nice general sentences, sentences which will elicit even more information.

He breathed deeper, slower, his head drooped, fell forward on his chest. 'Wh–?' Sue began but was shushed by Billy with a shake of his head.

Silence. Just George's breathing growing slower, deeper.

His head fell back, his eyelids fluttered, he began to struggle, mouth moving, muttering incomprehensible syllables, eyes turned heavenwards until only the whites could be seen. His breathing became heavier, more erratic, then stopped.

For long seconds he did not move, did not breathe. Then he quivered from head to foot, his body convulsing. He shouted, was on his feet, eyes wide, mouth agape.

'What is it?' The old woman huddled into her chair, terrified, with Sue clinging to her, her head buried in the old woman's lap. 'What have you seen?' She began to cry again, her voice rising in a wail. ''Tes Freddie, isn't it? He's dead. Dead and drownded and we're all ruined.'

'Freddie?' George stared at her, eyes still not focusing properly. 'Freddie?' The name meant nothing to him.

Because it had happened. The unpredictable, impossible thing had happened. He had seen a vision.

But not of Freddie, not of the sea.

He had seen Aggie. Aggie, lying beneath him, her body covered in blood.

And in her side, a knife.

Eighteen

'Mr Hardcourt.' Helen moved forward automatically, her hand outstretched, twenty years of training in polite behaviour coming to her rescue. Internally, she was in a turmoil. Ezekiel here, and at such a moment!

'My dear Miss Schofield.' He bowed over her hand and although his manners were irreproachable she could tell that she was in disgrace with him. 'I am pleased to find you well after all.'

'After all what?' She stared at him, still trying to come to terms with his sudden appearance.

There was a slight cough from behind her and she swung round to see Anthony Ledgerwood reaching for his tall hat. 'I shall leave you, Miss Schofield, as you have a visitor.' There was constraint in his voice too. And not surprising, Helen thought, repressing the desire to run her fingers distractedly through her carefully arranged hair. There could be few things more disconcerting than to have one's proposal interrupted by the fiancé of the lady to whom one was about to propose. If that was what he had been doing.

He took her hand and bowed over it. For a brief but significant second his fingers pressed hers meaningfully. 'I shall come by again to see how – the young lady does.'

He might be referring to Beth or... She inclined her head, fighting down the thrill that ran through her. 'I shall be grateful if you would do so, Doctor Ledgerwood.'

He paused in the doorway, looking at her and for a moment she saw him and Ezekiel side by side. Anthony Ledgerwood was handsome, his fair curls gleaming in the afternoon sunlight, his frock coat admirably showing off his broad shoulders and tall figure, the top hat in his hand shining softly. Ezekiel was shorter, slighter, a scholarly stoop to his narrow shoulders, his clerical suit shabby and his hair already receding from the high forehead.

Then the doctor bowed, turned, was gone.

Helen took a deep breath, trying to quiet her racing heart, and turned to her betrothed with a pleasant smile. 'This is such a surprise–'

'Surprise, Miss Schofield?' He moved into the room, casting a disparaging glance around the kitchen. 'When neither your grandmother nor myself have had the honour of the briefest letter from you appraising us of your whereabouts or situation?'

'But I wrote–' Helen began, then stopped. She *had* written. And she had given the letter to Anthony Ledgerwood. But he was a gentleman; he wouldn't have suppressed the letter. He was going to propose to you, her disobedient thoughts reminded her; he might have had a reason.

'Are you asking me to believe that our Royal Mail is so unreliable that it takes over a week to convey a letter from Cornwall to London in the middle of the nineteenth century?' Ezekiel moved forward, dropping his shabby hat onto the sideboard, stripping off his black gloves and setting them inside the brim. 'I find it hard to believe. Even from such a benighted county as this.'

'You are accusing me of lying, sir?' Helen's chin was raised, her green eyes snapped. After the emotional upsets of this afternoon she was in no mood to act the complaisant little woman.

He stared at her and she realised that it was the first time in their relationship that she had challenged him outwardly. The time she had spent in Cornwall must have changed her more than she had realised. Behaviour and attitudes that she had once adopted naturally now seemed alien and artificial. She swallowed, making an effort to act as he expected, lowering her angry glance submissively. 'My apologies, Mr Hardcourt. I – I have had a somewhat tiring time.'

He moved forward, taking her hands in his. His fingers felt cold and bony. 'I understand. For a lady such as yourself, to have had to live in this backward land – you must have found it a great trial.' He looked round the kitchen, at the plates and copper gleaming on the dresser, the table scrubbed to pristine whiteness, the black Cornish range with towels and nappies hanging over the brass rails, the softly glowing flags under bright rugs. 'But why are we talking in here?' He face altered. 'You do *have* a parlour?'

She had a parlour. And since that first day she had scarcely been into it, except when she helped Agnes with the dusting. It showed how far she had moved from the standards in which she had been brought up that she had not even noticed that she had made the kitchen the centre of the house, as if she were related to farmers instead of earls.

'It is – less comfortable than here.' Best say nothing about the strange mushroom smell and the distinct dampness you felt sitting on a chair – even through layers of petticoats. She freed a hand from his grasp and indicated a wooden chair with arms at the head of the table. 'Please, won't you sit down.'

He lowered himself as if he expected the chair to be somehow contaminated. 'Your grandmother is very concerned that she has not heard from you.'

She translated that in her head to: 'She has no one to run around after her and read her sermons each evening'. 'I am sorry,' she apologised. 'I had expected that you would communicate with her on receiving my letter.' She met his doubting look without flinching. She *had* written the letter. It was not her fault that he had not received it.

'And you could not spare the time to write to her also? After all she has done for you?'

Why did he always have the ability to make her feel guilty? 'I have been extremely busy,' she said defensively. 'I have had the farm to look after, the house to maintain, my little niece to care for. And there have been – problems.' Like old Mr Trahair dying, and the cow, not to mention shooting a man, or almost drowning whilst trying to rescue a woman intent on committing suicide. Not that she could ever tell him about those. He would never understand.

'And your niece being ill, I hazard.' She raised her brows, puzzled and he asked, 'Was that not why the doctor was here?'

Helen felt the blood rise in her face. 'She – has been teething,' she said, opting for the easy way out. 'It can make children unwell.'

'Too unwell to be brought back to London as you had intended,' he remarked drily. He rose to his feet. 'My dear Miss Schofield, I appreciate that you have had problems but they are not yours to deal with. You came only to collect your niece.'

'It wasn't as easy as that.' She resisted the impulse to wring her hands. 'The farm is unlettable, no servants will stay here, the animals are ill–'

'But those are not your problems,' he broke in. 'You are not responsible for the farm.'

'I am responsible for my niece,' Helen snapped, 'and the farm is her inheritance. Without it she will be penniless.'

He waved his hand, dismissing her objection. 'You are making too much of some very minor problems. Any competent agent could let the farm and sell the animals and as for the servants – why, a very respectable-looking woman opened the door to me when I arrived.'

'I took her on myself,' Helen said rashly then cursed herself. It was the wrong thing to say.

'Took her on? You *intend* to stay, then?'

'Until – until I have arranged for a suitable tenant to take over the farm.' She stared at his haughty face, the mouth pinched tight in displeasure. 'You must see that it is my duty,' she pleaded.

'Duty?' For once the word did not work its magic with him. 'And what about your duty to your grandmother? What about your duty to me?'

'Well – I–' Why did he have to make everything so complicated, she thought angrily. It had all been so simple before he arrived.

He interrupted. 'My uncle, Lord Carnglase, is in London. He has been most anxious to see you.'

Of course! She should have known that it was not merely a desire to see her or concern for her that had brought him so far. Despite everything she felt an obscure disappointment that his actions hadn't been brought about by a longing to see her again. If he had really loved her – if he really cared–

'Couldn't you have explained?' she asked wearily. 'As a landowner he must know of the difficulties when a farm is left untenanted.'

'As a landowner he is well aware that there are agents who are more capable of dealing with the problem than a delicately nurtured lady who can have no real understanding of the issues involved.'

He stalked around the kitchen, his dark clothes seeming to dull the gleams from the copper platters, darkening the shadows in the corners of the room. 'Miss Schofield–' he swung round, staring at her through his light, short-sighted eyes, 'I have to tell you that it is the wish of your grandmother, and of myself, if that still has any influence with you, that you should return to London with me immediately.'

The shadows darkened, reaching out for her; the room grew smaller, closing in, stealing away her breath. 'Oh, but...' She hesitated. 'Mr Hardcourt, that is just not possible.'

How could she go? Apart from her responsibility to Beth there were her other commitments. If she left Agnes now, what would happen to her? And Jenny? How could she leave a young girl like her to shoulder the responsibility for the farm animals all alone? Her emotions when she had found the cows ill had shown Helen how much the child needed an adult to make the final decisions.

These are excuses, another part of her mind told her. The truth is, you are enjoying yourself too much. You don't want to go back. She forced the thought away. She would have to go back sometime. A picture of Anthony Ledgerwood rose before her, smiling blue eyes, the touch of his fingers...

It was a few seconds before she was aware that Ezekiel was talking to her, his educated voice seeming out of place in this Cornish kitchen. '–no problem,' he was saying. 'As your fiancé I will act on your behalf, see an agent, set everything in train. You and the child will be able to accompany me back to London within a day or two at the most.'

'*No!*'

It took her by surprise, bursting from her in an explosion of sound. She was astonished to find that she was on her feet, fists clenched, leaning forward, her face white with fury. 'No. You can't do that! You have no right.'

He raised his brows. 'I have every right.' He walked towards her, his hand held out, a forgiving smile on his face.

'I know how it is.' His voice was softer, forgiving. 'I was the same when I first became a curate. Because we have once done something we think that we are the only one who can do it. But that is merely a manifestation of the sin of pride as my superiors were able to point out to me.'

He took her hand in his and she had to repress a shudder at the touch of his cold fingers. 'My dear Miss Schofield, my very dear Miss Schofield.' His voice lowered. 'I know you better than you know yourself. I have studied you carefully, as befits a clergyman who is about to enter a lifelong contract with the woman of his dreams. You are too conformable, I know, to set up your wishes in opposition to my own. You will find that this is merely an irritation of the nerves, caused by the overtaxing of your feminine frame. Once you submit to my wishes, put your affairs in my hands, you will be at peace again, you will be able to relax. And I will shoulder your burden as your betrothed should. In two days you can be back in your grandmother's house, with your little niece. In three you will have met Lord Carnglase, satisfied him as to your suitability for a clergyman's wife.'

He pulled her closer and she could not resist. The flow of words surrounded her, drowned her, beat down any resistance.

He leaned forward and planted a chaste kiss on her forehead. His dry, cold lips seemed to burn. 'My dearest Helen, for so I make bold as to call you. Soon, very soon, we shall be as one. I can understand that you have been seduced by the challenge of managing your own house, after so long living under the government of your grandmother, and I rejoice in it. It shows how right I was to choose you, how well you will soon rise to the challenge of running not only your own house when we are married but also all the multifarious concerns of the parish.'

As he spoke, the plans took shape in her head, solidifying into a cage. Of course, this was what would happen. This was what she had been expecting. This was what he and Grandmama had planned for her. Life as a vicar's wife. Hard-working. Respectable. Respected. There was no other option available to her.

The future settled itself around her like a dark, stifling cloak. It was difficult to breathe, to move.

He put his arm around her waist, leaned over her. She could smell the faint mustiness of his clothes. 'You and your little niece will be safe then. Safe in my protection as now you are safe in your grandmother's.'

Safe. The very word brought her grandmother's parlour before her eyes, the lowered blinds keeping out the sun and the noise from the streets outside, the tables crowding every inch of floor space, the portraits that glared disapprovingly from the walls. It was dark, quiet, safe. And it was a prison. For her, and for Beth.

She seemed to have no power to fight back. Twenty years of ladylike upbringing reinforced his words. This was what she had been bred and reared for. This was what she should expect.

Ezekiel smiled down at her, taking her complaisance for granted. 'And when Lord Carnglase meets you,' he said, his voice fat with satisfaction, 'he will have no hesitation in awarding me the living he has in his gift.'

He only wanted her as a means of getting the living! She tore herself away from him and leaned over the table, head down, panting for breath. The shadows seemed to retreat, hiding in the corners of the room. The sun shone again, the copper plates scattered sunbeams to glisten in patches on the uneven walls.

'You do not need me for that.' She clung to logic as if it were a lifeline. 'You do not need me to enable you to get the living.'

'I assure you' – his face darkened again, the lines deepening in his cheeks – 'Lord Carnglase is anxious–'

'You have your superiors, your parishioners.' She interrupted him ruthlessly, the words flowing more easily now. 'They will vouch for you. No one will deny that you are an excellent priest, a true man of God.'

'Lord Carnglase insists,' he repeated more firmly, 'that he should approve the wives of his clergymen. As your betrothed I cannot take a living without giving him the opportunity to–'

'Look me over.' Helen was beginning to feel light-headed. Relief washed over her, trickling down her spine. 'As if I were a cow.' She knew she should not be saying it but she could no longer control herself. Freedom sang in her veins, bubbling like champagne.

She pushed herself up and stood, smiling at him. 'I have a suggestion, Ezekiel.' His face stiffened as she used his Christian name for the first time – but why not? He had used hers. The smile broadened until she could feel her cheeks aching with it.

'Forget that we are betrothed. I will make an agreement with you.' She took a deep breath. 'Once I have finished here, once I have done all that is necessary to ensure that the farm is able to provide Beth with the security she deserves, then I will arrange to see Lord Carnglase, whenever and wherever he wishes. And if, after that meeting, he does not feel that I would make you a suitable wife I promise that I will not hold you to your engagement. I will release you, completely and utterly.'

The bubbles in her blood seemed to be bursting in her brain. She had never drunk spirits but she imagined that this must be what it was like to be drunk. She wanted to sing, to dance, to throw her head back and laugh for the sheer pleasure of being free, of being able to stay here for a little longer.

Helen moved to Ezekiel, her hand held out. 'Come. If we are not betrothed then there is no necessity for you to worry about what Lord Carnglase thinks. Take up your living, settle in. When I have finished here, when I am back in London – then, if you wish it, you may propose again and I will accept. Subject to Lord Carnglase's permission, of course.' Despite her best intentions she could not keep the dryness out of her voice. 'Ezekiel, is this not best for both of us?'

He turned away, his thin shoulders drooping. 'You wish the engagement at an end? You do not wish to marry me?' There was defeat in his voice, in the sag of his thin body.

'I do not wish to hold you to an engagement that will prevent you obtaining the living you so richly deserve,' she said robustly. 'Ezekiel, I do not wish to stand in your way in anything.'

He would not look at her, staring into the darkest corner at a sight only he could see. 'I had often thought – it had crossed my mind–' He swallowed, choked. 'I had considered that if, for any reason, our engagement was not to be – sometimes it seems to me that the Lord has called me for a different service, that if I were not to be a married man I would be...'

'What?' She found the fact that he had considered a future without her strangely hurtful. 'What are you trying to tell me?'

He turned to face her. 'If I am not to be married, I will join our mission overseas. I will go to convert the pagan.'

Helen stared at him. 'You can't!' Then, realising that she was impolite, she added hastily, 'Ezekiel, you are not strong. Those overseas posts – they ruin the health of the strongest of men.' She stared at him as he stood before her, noticing more strongly than ever before his thin frame, the stoop to his shoulders, the premature lines that etched his pale cheeks. 'Even life in the East End mission is too much for you,' she said, with rough anxiety. 'You cannot – you must not risk yourself abroad.'

'I must do as the Lord requires of me.' His chin was up although she could see that his lips were trembling slightly. 'If you will not be my wife as you have promised then I will go abroad and serve the Lord there.'

The excitement died out of her. 'You're asking me – you can't expect me to make such a decision!'

He nodded. 'I am promised to you and I will never break that vow. But if you desert me...'

Nineteen

'You'll catch your death of cold, out here.'

Agnes' voice was rough with anxiety but Helen did not turn. Arms clutched closely about her body she stood in the field, staring out across the valley. The sun was almost set; here on the hilltop the gorse blossoms seemed to burn in its golden rays but the valley bottom was already in shadow, the white smoke from the calciner falling heavily through the still air, filling it like mist.

'To leave here...' Helen's voice was scarcely audible. 'To go back to London...'

'That's what you must do.' Agnes' voice was rough. 'He's your man. You have to stay with him.'

Helen swung round. '*You* tell me that! You who–'

'That's different.' The older woman settled her hands on her thin hips, staring at Helen under dark, lowered brows. '*Your* man won't hit you nor desert you. *He* won't leave you to starve. He's a good man.'

'A good man.' Helen turned back to stare again across the valley. 'That's the trouble. He is a good man. Too good for me. And if I don't go with him he'll do as he says; go abroad, preach to the heathens, martyr himself.' She swung back, her face pale and contorted with the effort of holding back tears. 'I can't do that to him, Agnes. I can't let him do that.'

'No one's asking you to.' Agnes snorted. 'All you got to do is marry him and that'll be the end of all your worries. He'll look after you, earn you money, give you a home. What more do you want?'

'I don't know.' Helen stared out across the valley. 'Once, that was all I wanted. I thought I was lucky to be offered so much but now...' She sighed, waving an arm at the view before her. 'There's freedom here, space–'

'There isn't freedom,' Agnes interrupted. 'You just think that because you don't know no better.' She caught Helen by the shoulders, pulling her round, fingers biting into her soft flesh. 'You listen to me,' she snapped. 'You think you've done brem well keeping this here farm going but you haven't done *nothing!*'

She waved a thin arm across the field. 'You've kept the cows milked but you haven't made no cream nor butter. There's tatties growing in they there fields but the only ones pulled are the ones I get in for our supper. There's hay growing and no one to mow it, corn growing but no one to thrash 'un. Who's going to plough? Who's going to teal the fields come autumn?'

As Helen stared at her, white-faced with shock, Agnes said bitterly, 'This here farm's no job for a woman, not even one born to it which you're not. It's hard enough to make money on a farm if you're a man who knows what he's doing and works all hours God gives; you'll never manage.'

'But' – Helen needed to justify herself – 'I tried–'

'Trying's not enough,' Agnes broke in. 'Anyone who's had to work for a living knows that. You got to succeed. Or you starve.' She waved her hand at the field. 'Looks good now, doesn't it? But that's because your brother-in-law worked his guts out until his death. With him gone' – she shrugged – 'a year from now this field will be rank grass and thistles. Two years and it will be half moorland again. There's no freedom here, just hard work.'

She waved a finger in front of Helen's nose. 'Forget it, that's what I say. You've done your best. You've kept the farm going for a week or two. Maybe you'll get an offer for 'un now, maybe you won't. But your job now is to forget it, go to London, marry your man, live the life you was born to.'

She stared up at Helen, her eyes fierce. 'And you forget that doctor, too. What good has he ever done? Making up to a lady what he knows is already engaged to be married to another man. What sort of a gentleman is that?'

'But–' Helen began, moved by an obscure desire to defend Anthony Ledgerwood against the unexpected attack.

'You forget him,' Agnes said fiercely. 'And you forget this farm. Take Beth, go back to London, marry your man. And thank your lucky stars that you aren't stuck down here, killing yourself, trying to make a go of a farm that will break your heart and your body.' She snorted again. 'Freedom!' she snarled. 'There's no freedom for women in this world – and the sooner you realise it the happier you'll be.'

Helen wanted to shout, to scream that there was freedom, ought to be – *had* to be, somewhere – but she was dumb. All her life until now had only confirmed Agnes' words. She had been an unpaid servant to her grandmother, offering her services in exchange for board and lodging. Marriage to Ezekiel meant very much the same. If only she could have saved Beth from such an existence. But Agnes was right, she knew nothing of farming, had only intended to stay at the farm for a few weeks to break the jinx that people believed was on it. But now the cow had died, and another was still ill. In the eyes of the neighbours, the jinx remained.

But she couldn't stay any longer. With a sigh she accepted her fate, then turned and reached out, took Agnes' thin hand in hers. 'When I go to London,' she promised, 'you can come with me. Your husband will never find you there and you can get work. Grandmother will give you a reference, or Ezekiel can – a clergyman is always believed. You can have a new life.' She smiled tremulously. 'You, at least, can have freedom even if I can't.'

'There's no such thing,' Agnes said stoutly. 'Nor I don't believe in fairy tales.'

Helen's brows drew down. 'I mean it,' she said crossly.

'Maybe you do but I aren't cut out for a life like that. Whatever you say,' Agnes added sourly, 'I do know that I'll never get to London with you.'

'No,' said Ezekiel.

'But – but you *must!*' Helen stared at him, shocked by the uncompromising negative. 'I can't leave her here. I saved her life; I am responsible for her.'

'Saved her life?' He smiled thinly, crowlike against the background of the comfortable kitchen. 'My dear, this county is getting to you. You sound positively melodramatic.'

'But I did! At least,' Helen corrected herself, 'she saved mine too.' She took a deep breath. She had intended to keep Agnes' past a secret but if telling was necessary to get Ezekiel to agree to let her bring Agnes to London then that was what she would do.

The response was not what she had expected.

'Miss Schofield!' His lips thinned in distaste. 'Have your wits gone begging? Where are your standards, the principles with which you were reared?'

Helen stared at him in shock. 'P-principles?'

'This – person.' She noticed that he did not even dignify poor Agnes with the description of 'woman'. 'She breaks her holy vows to God that she made on her wedding day and deserts her husband, to whom she has promised to cleave, she–'

'He beat her,' Helen broke in fiercely. 'He beat her so hard that she lost the child she was carrying.'

He dismissed her objection with a wave of his hand. 'So she tells you. But is this true? Have you heard the story from him?'

'No, but–'

He broke in, smiling at her in a superior fashion that made her hackles rise. 'We men have the advantage of you charming ladies. We are taught logic, we are capable of analysis. We' – his smile grew more patronising – 'are not ruled by our hearts. We can judge by the facts.'

Fury made her hands shake. 'You think I did not?' She moved forward, eyes bright with anger. 'Ezekiel, I saw her! I saw her walk out into the sea–'

'Felo-de-se.' His voice was dismissive. 'You should have reported her to the constables. That is a sin against the laws of both God and man for which she would have been imprisoned.'

'She would have been dead! Oh, for heaven's sake!' Helen turned, walked up and down the kitchen, trying to calm her seething emotions in movement. 'What about the Good Samaritan?' she demanded, whirling round to stare at her fiancé. 'Did he stop to ask if the man he rescued had perhaps deserved his beating?'

'One does not question the word of the Lord.' Ezekiel Hardcourt's face was set. 'Miss Schofield, enough of this. You acted as you saw fit. I respect you for it even though

I do not agree with your actions. But now that you have had the benefit of my advice, I do not expect you to set yourself up in opposition to me. I have made my decision. This woman has broken the laws of man and of God and I do not consider that she is a suitable companion for you or your niece. I will not take her back to London with us and I will certainly not write her a reference. To do so would be to lend myself to a lie and as a man of the cloth I cannot do that.'

His face softened and he moved towards her. 'Come, Miss Schofield – Helen – do not let us disagree about such a person.' He took her hands in his and she almost shuddered at the touch of his cold fingers. 'For your sake I will not insist that she leaves immediately. Indeed, if she is as trustworthy as you say, I am willing to stretch a point and let her remain as a caretaker for the house until a tenant can be found.' He smiled down at her. 'There. You cannot say I am unreasonable, Helen. Indeed' – and he laughed – 'I can see myself turning into a most uxorious and compliant husband. I just hope that the Bishop never hears of it. He would be most disappointed in me.'

Her face set, Helen stood motionless, her hands unresponsive in his grasp. 'As you say, Mr Hardcourt,' she said expressionlessly.

Agnes moved away from the closed door that led into the kitchen. That Helen – clever as they come in some ways but so blind where men were concerned. This clergyman and the doctor – she didn't really seem to know what either of them were like.

Slowly, Agnes climbed the stairs to the room next to hers where Beth gurgled in her cradle, playing with her toes. The sight of her made Agnes' heart contract and she dropped to her knees beside the child, burying her head in the soft, sweet-smelling body.

Bitter tears burned unshed behind her lids. She should have had a child like this, she should have had a baby to care for, to love.

The loss still ached inside her. Even though she knew that if the child had lived her life would have been worse, in many ways she still longed for her, missed her, thought of her each day. With a child she would have been unable to leave George, unable to earn her own living, bound to her hated husband by unbreakable bonds – but it would have been worth it.

And now, beyond hope, almost beyond death, she had a new life, another child who pulled at her heart-strings. She stifled a sob and the baby gurgled, pulling at her hair, waving chubby legs in the air.

To have all this and then to lose it. But she had to, she knew that. Helen had strange, quixotic ideas. If she thought that by going to London she would be deserting Agnes she was quite capable of refusing to go. Agnes had ruined her own life; she would not be responsible for ruining Helen's.

'Agnes?' Helen's voice floated up the stairs, followed by the sound of her hurrying feet. 'Agnes!' The voice was sharper, as if the thought that Agnes might have run away had already occurred to her.

Agnes wiped her eyes roughly on her sleeve and cleared her throat. 'I'm here. I'm with the baby.'

She lifted the small, wriggling body out of the cot, holding her close, enjoying the feel and scent and sound of the child for the last time.

As Anthony rode into the stables where he kept his horse the ostler came forward. 'Evening, sir. Lovely animal this, if I may say so.'

'Beautiful, isn't she?' Anthony patted the glossy neck. The mare had cost more than he could afford but she had class in every inch of her. Who could doubt that he was a successful professional man while he was riding an animal like this? Even Helen's eyes had widened at the sight of her – and of him in his new coat. If only that damned parson hadn't arrived he could have been sure of her by now.

He dragged his thoughts away from Helen, aware that the ostler was still speaking. 'What did you say?'

'The account for the last month is still outstanding, sir.' The ostler coughed deprecatingly. 'Only an oversight, I'm sure. A busy man such as yourself has so much on his mind. But I am afraid that if the account is not settled,' – he patted the smooth neck as the mare nuzzled him – 'well, it would be a pity if an animal like this had to be stabled in some unsuitable yard.'

The vultures were closing in. Anthony felt a superstitious shiver. But, living as he did, the small traders were the last people to get their money.

If only he hadn't had such big gambling debts... But it was only in the clubs that he could still mix with the class of men to which he knew he belonged. Once he had married Helen and owned land – then he would be accepted as he should be. But not if he didn't pay his gambling debts. That went without saying. And he had had such bad luck recently. It had taken almost all the money from the calciner to settle what he owed this quarter and the rest he had spent on new clothes and the horse.

'You'll get your money tomorrow.' He turned on his heel, then swung back again as he caught sight of his tailor passing the open gateway to the livery yard. It would be fatal to let either man know that he was not Dr Ledgerwood's only debtor. 'Check the mare's shoes, will you? And give her more oats. I don't want her to lose condition.'

The coast was clear. He walked out of the yard with unhurried strides but his mind was racing. The cards had been against him for months. If only his luck would change.

He could still remember his run of luck while he had been designing the calciner. Enough to pay his share of the costs of building it. The fact that Robert had thought he would never meet his obligations made it all the sweeter. If only the profits hadn't been eaten up in his debts...

Mind you, the men knew. Last night, when the cards had fallen so badly, one had scoffed, 'Unlucky at cards – lucky in love,' and there had been a general laugh. They knew about him and Helen Schofield. And now that damned parson had turned up.

Anthony ran lightly up to his room, his feet too quiet to alert his landlady to his presence. But it would only be a matter of time.

Helen. She was the key to this. He had to marry Helen. For herself, for the land.

To stop her investigating the calciner.

Twenty

The feather tie was too hot. It clung to Helen's sweating body suffocatingly. Even with only a linen sheet on the bed she was too hot, too tied down, too confined.

Crossly, she sat up in bed. Her long linen nightdress had tied itself in knots around her body, the pile of feather pillows seemed to generate heat of their own accord. The whole room seemed to be airless, close.

Angrily, she pushed herself upright, sitting with her legs hanging over the side of the high bed. The servant girl had put her, that first night, into the main bedroom, once occupied by her sister and brother-in-law. Then it had seemed huge, the high, wooden bed enormous after the small cot in which she slept at home. Now, the whole room just seemed like a giant oven, baking in the air of the warm summer night.

After sunset, fresh air was bad for you – everyone knew that. But she could not endure the heat any more. Though she knew that the sense of oppression that so weighed her down and kept her lying hour after hour, wide-eyed and sleepless, had less to do with the heat and more with her imminent return to London.

Well, she could do nothing about that – but at least she could deal with the physical heat. She slid off the tall bed and marched to the window, throwing back the curtains and reaching up for the catch that secured the sash – and froze.

A small, dark figure was creeping down the lane.

No time even to dress. Her bare feet thudding on the old wooden boards of the bedroom, Helen raced for the door. There was no moon outside. It was sheer chance that she had looked out of the window while Agnes was close enough to be seen against the lighter gravel of the lane. Once she had got further away her dark clothes would merge into the blackness and Helen would never find her.

The stone flags in the kitchen struck cold against her feet but she did not stop, dragging open the heavy door and running through. The lane was only of beaten earth and the stones that littered it bit painfully into her bare feet but she had no time to care about that. At least her running steps were almost noiseless in the still night.

She was almost within touching distance of Agnes when the other woman became aware of her. One quick, frightened glance over her shoulder and she turned to sprint up the road. With a final, gasping effort

Helen threw herself forward, catching the woman's skirts in a frantic hand. 'Don't go, Agnes. For God's sake, stay.'

'Let me go!' Agnes tried to tug her skirts free from Helen's grasp. 'Leave me be.'

'I won't let you go!' Helen had to fight to get the words out. She clung to the woman's skirts with rigid fingers as she struggled to get her breath back. 'You mustn't go. I need you, Agnes. You've got to stay.'

'You don't need me.' Agnes voice was harsh with pain. 'You've got your man. You don't need me no more.'

'I do! I do!' Helen was almost crying. 'Please, Agnes, don't go. You've got to come with me. I need you to help with Beth, I need you for me!'

Agnes tugged again at her imprisoned skirt. Even in the dim light Helen could see tears sliding silently down her cheeks but there was no sign of them in her voice as she said bitterly, 'You can't have me even if you wanted. Not when your man tells you nay.'

There was a long silence. Finally Helen's fingers released their grip. 'You heard.' She could feel the despair washing over her.

There was no compromise in Agnes' face. 'I heard. He don't want me and he's your man. What he says goes.'

'But – what are you going to do?'

The other woman didn't answer, but one look at her cold, withdrawn face told Helen everything she needed to know. There was no future for Agnes. For her, there was nothing.

Helen's marriage meant Agnes' death.

'No!'

It came out a scream, ringing across the quiet countryside, echoing off the high Cornish hedges. 'You mustn't! I won't let you!'

'Your man–'

'I won't have him.' Helen stamped her bare foot on the ground. 'I won't let you do this. I can't let you do this. I'll stay here–'

'You got to marry him.' Agnes moved forward, shook Helen roughly, her fingers biting into the girl's arm. 'There's nothing for you here, nothing! He can give you security.'

'He'll give me nothing.' Helen stared at the thin face gazing so fixedly at her, then her expression softened and she smiled tremulously. 'Don't blame yourself, Agnes. I know you've done everything you can to get me to marry Ezekiel. Even this.' She waved her hand at the darkness that enclosed them like a private salon. 'Even running away like this you did for me.'

She sighed. 'But I can't do it, Agnes. I thought I could but I can't. I've changed. Cornwall, this farm – it's all changed me. I'm no longer the person I once was.'

'You've got to marry him.' Agnes shook

her fiercely. 'It's the only life for a woman, marriage. Whatever the man's like.'

Helen smiled, but sadly. 'Not for me, not any longer.' She took a deep breath of the clean air, heady with the tang of gorse and the faint smell of the distant sea. 'I can't go back, Agnes. I could never fit in again. For better or worse, this is my life now.'

She reached out and took the other woman's thin, rough hand in her own. 'Will you share it with me?'

The cows woke Helen, their frantic mooing funnelling into the bedroom like alarm calls.

Sleepily, she pushed herself upright in bed, pulling off her nightcap, rubbing her fingers through her plaited hair. She could tell by the light that she had slept late – and no wonder. First the excitement with Agnes and then the letter to Ezekiel. She had known that she had to write that before she went back to sleep.

But why were the cows making so much noise? She had grown used to the soft noises of the farmyard, could even sleep through the cockerel's crowing, but this was something completely different.

She slid from the bed and padded across to the window, wincing as her cut and bruised soles touched the floor, and moved aside the curtain.

She could see the cows in their usual

meadow by the lane. Usually, at this time, they would be moving easily through the field, their empty udders swinging, cropping grass, chewing cud. Now, they crowded against the gateposts and she could hear desperation in their bellows.

Were they all ill? Frantically, she poured cold water from the jug into the china basin and splashed her face in an attempt to rouse herself; then, not even bothering to dress, she pulled a shawl around her shoulders, thrust painful feet into her boots and ran downstairs.

Now that she knew a little more about the animals she could tell immediately from their swollen udders what was the matter. They hadn't been milked. They mooed at her and she could hear the need in their voices, see it in the tension that vibrated their bodies.

Where was Jenny? She had never been late before. Helen pulled open the gate, ushering the cows before her to the byre. Perhaps the girl had overslept. She walked slowly behind the cows, watching their painful waddle, legs astride their swollen udders. Only the sick cow seemed able to move freely, but she walked with her head down and her eyes dull and Helen noticed with concern that there were bare patches on the cow's hide where the hair had fallen out.

Concerned, she shut them into the barn, recklessly spreading some of last year's hay for them to eat. It would keep them occupied while she dressed and ran down to the cottage to get Jenny.

'She's sick as a shag.' Mrs Trahair's thin face was drawn with worry. 'I've had a brem awful time with her. Keeps wanting to get out to the farm, she do, and she's that wished and lairy! I'm afraid for my soul to let her up today and that's a fact.'

The child's bed was a rough cot: strings stretched over a wooden frame and covered with a straw-stuffed mattress. Jenny's face looked pale green against the bright red of her hair, her freckles standing out like a rash. A bowl by her bed and a faint smell of vomit reinforced her mother's words.

Quietly, Helen sat by the bed, pressing her hand against the child's forehead. It was hot and sweaty. 'Well, Jenny.' Helen made her voice as soft and light as she could. 'I'm sorry to see you ill like this. You must rest until you are completely better.'

The child turned restlessly, tears of weakness in her eyes. 'I tried to come, Miss. I did try.'

'Then you were a silly girl, weren't you?' Helen smiled at her. 'You'll get better much more quickly if you rest now.'

'But they cows?' Ignoring her restraining hand the girl struggled to sit up in bed.

'They got to be milked. They can't be left.'

'There's no need for you to worry,' Helen said calmly. 'I'll get someone else in to do it until you're better. And if the worst comes to the worst, I can always try myself. You know you've been teaching me.'

The child tossed painfully, her face almost the same colour as the greyish cover of her pillow. 'You can't do 'un. I've only let you try Daisy and she's easy. The others'll kick you to kingdom come. And you don't know nothing about stripping them or...' Her fingers plucked feebly at the covers. 'I'll come. I'll do 'un for you. I got to.'

'No, you haven't.' Helen pressed her back against the pillow before glancing at her mother. 'Have you called an apothecary?'

'Well, we thought it might just be a summer fever.' The woman wiped her hands down her apron. 'Children do get so ill and mend again while you blink.'

Helen stared at the pale face, the red hair dark with sweat. She knew so little about children. 'If you need a doctor–' she began.

'I reckon she'll be right as rain in a day or so.' Mrs Trahair bobbed a brief curtsy. 'She's a strong child. It's not like poor old Da.'

So much illness. No wonder the poor woman was looking worn out. 'If she gets worse...' Helen glanced at the child, looking smaller and younger than ever on her poor cot.

'I'll tell you, Miss.'

As she reached the door, Helen paused. 'Jenny, that sick cow–'

The child's body was suddenly convulsed with a spasm of pain. A low, agonising wail broke from her pale lips and she curled into a small ball, hugging her agony to herself like a sick animal. Her mother hurried to her side and Helen felt sympathetic tears start to her eyes – but there was nothing she could do. She was only in the way.

'There, sweetheart, there.' Mrs Trahair rocked the thin body comfortingly in her arms, her cheek against the child's sweating head. 'You were saying, Miss?'

'Nothing,' Helen said swiftly. 'She's too ill. There's nothing for her to worry about now. But if you want anything, you have only to ask.'

Was it an omen? she wondered, as she left the evil-smelling smoke of the calciner behind and started the steep climb up to the farmhouse. Was this a sign that her decision last night had been wrong?

She didn't have to stay here. She could explain to Agnes, tear up the letter, leave all these worries behind and settle for the easy life, a life where food was not a problem and where there would be servants and a suitable social position.

And destroy Beth's inheritance? She could not do it.

'My dear Miss Schofield!'

Anthony Ledgerwood hurried towards Helen as she hesitated at the kitchen door, his face a mask of horror. 'What have you done to yourself?'

If only she had known he was here she would never have come in. Her hand held across her face, Helen stared at him, appalled, while blood dripped steadily from under her shielding fingers to splash in a growing pool at her feet.

'Allow me.' A huge white handkerchief appeared like magic and was thrust into her hand, and he guided her gently across the room, settling her in the kitchen chair as if she were a princess. 'Lean forward while I find something...' His gaze wandered around the shining kitchen. 'Aha!' He reached for a copper jug and pressed its coldness against the back of her neck below her piled-up hair.

Helen relaxed under his gentle touch. She would not have had him see her like this for a hundred pounds but it was a relief to be able to leave her treatment in his capable hands, to know that he would make the decisions for a little while. She could feel her over-stretched nerves loosening at his command. But what must he think of her?

'A cow kicked be.' The words were hardly distinguishable, muffled by blood and linen and the swollen tissues of her nose. 'I was–'

'Quiet, please. You will do yourself no good at all by talking.' He looked around the kitchen. 'You have clean cloths?'

'Id the drawer.' She was shocked to see that his handkerchief was already soaked with gore and wanted to apologise but he quietened her with a gesture before moving with quiet competence around the kitchen.

In only a few seconds she had a towel in her hand to staunch the blood and he was wetting others in the sink. 'Here. Now lean back.'

The cool wetness of the towels was spread over her forehead, across the painful bridge of her nose. She closed her eyes, partly in relief, partly because of the embarrassment of seeing his handsome face so close above her that she could feel the fan of his breath upon her cheek.

'Just lie still, Miss Schofield. You have nothing to worry about.' The calm, reassuring voice made her want to burst into tears of relief. 'There is no real harm done. A blow to the nose will often cause such an effusion but it has done no real harm and may even do good by purging unhealthy humours.'

Helen lay still. He was so kind, so reassuring. And she needed reassurance. She could feel herself shaking all over, partly in shock from the pain and suddenness of the blow, partly from reaction.

Jenny had been right. The cows were not easy to milk. She had assumed that in their need to relieve their bursting udders they would be eager for her ministrations but they had seemed more edgy and restless than usual. Even Daisy was uncooperative, swishing her tail and raising her hind leg threateningly as Helen had tried to milk her.

By now she knew the characters of the cows, had deliberately started with the calmest and worked her way up. She probably hadn't got all the milk and she knew that that would lead to them producing less in future but at least she had relieved their discomfort.

It was Faith who had caused the trouble, kicking forward in the strange action that cows had and catching her on the bridge of her nose.

Tears and blood had started together, streaming down her face. Ignoring the upset bucket of milk she had staggered into the kitchen, only to find Anthony Ledgerwood there...

He leaned over her, swapping the towel for a new one, wrung out in cold water and she opened her eyes, smiling up at him in relief as the pain began to ebb. 'Thang you.'

He stroked her cheek with a gentle finger. 'No talking, Miss Schofield. Wait, if you please, until the haemorrhage has stopped.

There is no hurry. I only came to see how you did.'

No hurry. The relief was immense. And now that Doctor Ledgerwood was here she could tell him about Jenny, and he could take her letter to Ezekiel into Penzance.

Anthony Ledgerwood seemed to be the answer to all her prayers.

Helen leaned back with an easy mind.

Twenty-One

'You can't do it,' Agnes said fiercely.

'Oh, don't be foolish! If I don't who will?' Helen dragged on the elderly skirt she had found in a cupboard. 'I managed this morning. At least this time I am prepared for it.'

'Prepared for it! Prepared to get killed by some mad cow! You can't expect to have a doctor here next time you come in covered with blood.'

'I learned a lot from that,' Helen said shortly. 'Besides, we need the milk for Beth. The cow kicked the bucket over and I lost all this morning's milk.' She flexed her fingers ruefully. The muscles in her forearms twanged painfully. It wasn't that milking took strength but the repetitious, small movements of the fingers made her hands and arms ache. And she took so much longer than Jenny. But it had to be done.

'You could get your nose broken this time,' Agnes said fiercely. 'You could get your face ruined.'

'Or I could do it without having any trouble at all.' Helen's voice rose angrily in an attempt to hide the nervousness she was feeling. It had been bad enough to go out to milk the cows the first time, not knowing what to expect. Now that she had been kicked already, it took all her resolution to go back into the byre.

Perhaps she should give the animals something else to think about. They had not touched the hay, used as they were to the fresh green grass but at one end of the shed there were breast-high stone containers covered with heavy wooden lids and she remembered seeing some sort of cereal in there. If she gave the cows some of that...

She tied a rough apron around herself and laughed as she saw her reflection in the looking-glass. 'My grandmother would never recognise me. I look a fright.'

'You look like a working woman,' Agnes said shortly, 'and that's what you'll be if you don't make it up with that there vicar. It's always easier to go down than it is to get yourself back up again.'

'It's too late,' Helen said calmly. 'I gave a letter to Doctor Ledgerwood to take to Penzance. I am no longer betrothed.'

Gone! The news echoed throughout the district. That strange Miss Schofield what took on her brother-in-law's farm has jilted her parson and he's gone.

Workmen who had never even seen Helen discussed it over drinks in the local inns. The gentry discussed it over six-course dinners. Servants carried the news with the post and the fish. Before Ezekiel had even left the county the whole district knew that he had been thrown over. And throughout the district there was only one opinion.

'She's a brem fool,' the ostler muttered to the farrier. 'A singularly foolish young woman,' the local vicar confided to his lady. 'Daft as a brush,' the fisherman announced loudly to the crowded bar. And they thought of Anthony Ledgerwood's handsome face and smiled knowingly.

Locally, they added, 'It's that farm. 'Tes brem unlucky.' With a dead cow and the broken engagement added to the list of misfortunes at Tregurtha Farm, Mr Brownfield, the attorney, would find no takers for land.

Only in the Polglase household did the news meet with a different reception.

'I told you that I'd do it,' Anthony Ledgerwood announced, exalted. 'No problems now. She's given the clergyman the push and now the way is clear for me. I'll be a landowner yet, sister mine. And I'll make my fortune from the calciner.'

'If she goes to Robert...' Theo gnawed her lower lip, less pleased by the news than her brother. Not that she didn't want Anthony to marry a woman with land; as he had said, that was the only way to re-establish himself as a gentleman. But why did it have to be *her?*

'About the sickness in the valley?' He waved a dismissive hand. 'I'm the medical expert. Robert will believe what I say. The trouble is, the child who was doing her milking has become ill. When I was there she was trying to milk the cows herself. A lady like that! And one of them, needless to say, played up and gave her a kick in the face.'

'Did it break her nose?' Theo asked hopefully.

He turned on her. 'Don't be such a bitch! Don't you realise, you fool, that I am still not home and dry. Even though she has broken her engagement to that dried stick of a vicar she could still take the child back to London and then where will I be?'

The words echoed round her head. 'She could still go back to London.' Thoughtfully, Theo asked, 'How can she stay if she has no one to milk the cows?'

'She could sell them or hire a cowman by

the day until the child is better.' Anthony shrugged. 'I don't think running the farm is her main concern. At least she has a reliable servant to look after her. With the rumours I have heard of the farm's bad luck, I doubt if she could get another servant to stay.'

'No.' said Theo thoughtfully, 'that would certainly be more of a problem for her.'

Muscles and ligaments twanged in her forearms as Helen sat by the cow and put the wooden bucket in place. Twice a day. How could she do it? Gingerly she felt her nose, still sore and swollen from this morning. Pray heaven that the cows would be quieter now they were used to her.

Carefully, concentrating, she began to milk. Daisy shifted uneasily but did not kick and Helen felt her confidence grow. Perhaps she was getting better. As long as her forearms didn't cramp up...

'Hello?' A man's voice from the yard. 'Is there anyone here?'

George, Helen thought with a start that made the cow lift her leg threateningly, then relief washed over her as she recognised the voice. 'In here, Mr Polglase.'

Immediately she had spoken she regretted, it. To be seen like this, milking a cow – and in her oldest clothes – it went against every instruction regarding ladylike behaviour that her grandmother had ever given her. But it was too late now. Repressing her dismay, she turned her head and smiled pleasantly at Robert Polglase as he stood hesitating in the doorway. 'Excuse me for not getting up. As you can see I am somewhat occupied at present.'

He moved forward instantly. 'I heard at the mine that Nat Trahair's sister was ill and remembered that she worked for you. I had hoped that you had found another helper.'

'Unfortunately not.' There was a pause while she racked her brains for a new topic of conversation but before she could fix on one he had excused himself and left. Helen felt a brief flutter of disappointment but before she had time to rationalise it he was back, a three legged stool in one hand, a wooden bucket in the other.

He paused at the doorway and removed his fine black coat and waistcoat, rolling up the sleeves of his shirt to display strong arms. 'You had better tell me which cow is the easiest to start with. It is a long time since I last milked a cow.'

'You can't do that!' She was scandalised.

He grinned at her, looking younger and more carefree without his formal coat. 'And why not? If you can then I certainly can.'

'But they're not your cows,' she protested

'Nor yours, strictly speaking.' Faith swung her head to snuffle at him and he took it as an invitation, settling himself beside her, thrusting his dark head into her tawny side. 'You may lose more milk than you gain, Miss Schofield. I am likely to be kicked out of the door at any moment.' But he did not sound as if the prospect frightened him.

'You are probably less likely than I am.' And indeed, already she could hear the milk singing into his bucket. She breathed a sigh of relief, stopping for a second to flex her aching fingers. 'But–' It was ridiculous, sitting together in a cowshed, talking to each other as if they were in at a formal salon. 'Won't you call me Helen? Somehow, I feel as if I have known you for a long time.'

'It's the way we were introduced,' he said lightly. 'There's nothing like shooting a man to get on easy terms with him.'

She laughed, glad that he could not see the blush on her face then, hearing the steady spurt of milk, she added, 'You put me to shame with your skill. You are a far better at milking than I.'

'It comes of not being born a gentleman.' She could hear the anger in his voice and he must have communicated it to the cow, too, because Faith swung her head round angrily. He soothed her easily. 'We shared a cow with another family when I was a boy, before my father became rich. That's why I have such an ungentlemanly accomplishment.'

She hated his sensitivity about his background. 'My uncle the Earl–' Helen stopped herself in time, started again. 'An uncle of mine who owns a large estate was made by his father to learn all the jobs of all the men who worked on the estate, from milking to shoeing a horse, so that when he inherited the land he would know if they were doing their jobs properly.' She paused in her milking to try to shake some life back into her hands. 'Unfortunately,' she added drily, 'the same principle doesn't apply to the women of the family.'

A long silence and she could feel he was digesting this information; then Robert said, 'It would have been different if he owned a factory.'

'Well, I don't expect that he would have wanted his son to work on the production line,' she agreed, 'but he would certainly have expected him to know the principles of how it all worked.'

Again, the pause. The singing of the milk was softer now and she could tell that he had already almost finished milking Faith even though he had started after her. Finally he pulled the wooden bucket from under the cow's feet and got to his feet, giving the animal a friendly slap on the rump. He moved to stand over Helen. 'I – I know a fair amount about mining.' He sounded half defensive, half ashamed.

Daisy was finished now. Helen stripped the last few drops of milk then sighed with relief, stretching her tight hands and shoulders. She smiled up at Robert. 'That is good. I think that it is wrong for men to employ people and know nothing of their working conditions.'

As she stood he took the heavy milk bucket from her. 'I'll carry that to the dairy for you while you choose my next cow.'

'No,' she protested. 'Really, you have already done too much.'

He moved easily to the doorway, scarcely bothered by the heavy buckets that so weighed her down. 'Nonsense. Anyway, that's what friends are for – to help out in times of trouble.'

Friends. Yes, that was how she thought of him. A friend. As much a friend as Agnes or Jenny really, which was strange because she hadn't seen very much of him. But when they did meet they were as much at ease together as though they had known each other for years. He wasn't as good-looking as Anthony Ledgerwood, he didn't make her pulse race as Anthony could, but she knew that she could trust him. It was a comforting thought.

It was only after she had waved him goodbye and watched him walk down the darkening lane that she remembered something she should have asked his advice about.

Blossom. Heavily, Helen walked across the yard to the byre where she had penned the cow separately. The cow stood listlessly in the dim light, the corn that Helen had given her still uneaten. Helen reached out, rubbed the animal's ears, stroked her hand across the bare patches that disfigured the cow's skin.

Blossom was dying. Even she could see that. Helen sighed. She had agreed that Jenny should have the other cow put down but she had hoped against hope that Blossom would recover. Now that hope was gone. To keep this animal alive any longer was a cruelty. She laid her arm comfortingly along the animal's stringy neck. So many failures. So many worries. So many deaths.

She buried her head in the cow's mangy hide, feeling tears pricking at her lids. It was so dreadful to order another creature's death. And with Jenny ill, she didn't even know how to set about it, who to contact.

Resolutely, she straightened her shoulders. The town of Madron was only a couple of miles down the road. Someone there would be able to help her. Or if she passed another farm she could make herself known. They might even have a cowman who would be willing to take on the milking for a few days. It would only be a few days, she told herself. Jenny was young, healthy. Children suddenly got these violent fevers and then, a few days later, they were their usual selves again.

Not like this poor dairy cow at all.

'I'll kill 'un for you, Miss, no problem.'

Helen winced at the farrier's bluntness. Still, at least Fred Zelah was the right man for the job. Both the farmers she had spoken to on her way here had recommended him, even though neither had been able to offer her the services of a cowman, even for a few days.

''Tes the bad luck of the place, see,' the more forthright had told her, stopping for a second in his industrious probing of his ear with a straw. 'No one don't want to go there in case it do alight on them.'

'It isn't unlucky.' she said crossly. 'I've been living there and I'm all right.'

But the farmer had shaken his head. 'There's yer cows,' he pointed out. 'Can't say that that isn't bad luck.'

But at least the farrier seemed to have no qualms about bad luck, or perhaps, she thought, watching him apply a red-hot shoe to a horse, he believed that, with all the horseshoes he had around him, he could laugh at ill luck.

Smoke, white and choking, reminding her of the smoke from the calciner, poured up around him from the horse's hoof. Through it he said, 'On her feet, is she?'

Helen thought of the wasted, sorry animal. 'She's not capable of walking far.'

'As long as she's on her feet she'll walk all right, don't 'ee worry about that. I knows how to get them along.' He took the shoe away from the hoof and dropped it into a trough of cold water where it steamed and hissed briefly. 'I'll be along later this evening then.'

So short a time for the poor animal. Helen felt guilt rise inside her and turned away, fighting with the temptation to countermand her order. Logically, she knew that it was kindest to put the animal out of its misery but emotionally...

As she moved away the farrier shouted after her, 'Same as the other one is it? Only I got to know for the dogs, see?'

'Dogs?' She turned back, eyebrows raised.

'Sir Ivan's hounds. Runs the Western Hunt he do and takes all my dead animals. But he were brem cross about yer last cow. Didn't like the rotten liver, see, or the holes in the lining of the stomach.' He spat accurately into the water trough. 'Treats they hounds like children he do. And feeds 'em better than some folks round here feed their children.'

Helen paused. No lady would ever dream of discussing these subjects. She knew she should turn and walk away, erase the thought of an animal's insides from her mind. Only when they were cleaned and cooked and on a table could a lady ever admit to the fact that there were pieces inside an animal's skin. But here, at last, was a fact, something that might point to the reason for the animal's death.

'I don't know what the cow is dying of, Mr Zelah,' she admitted, 'but perhaps, after you have – done what you have to, you could have a look...'

Her voice tailed off but he followed her chain of thought readily enough. 'Want me to see if it's the same thing, do 'ee? That's all right, my 'andsome. I'll do that for 'ee. And I'll pop in on my way back from the kennels tomorrow and let 'ee know, shall I?'

His enthusiasm for his grisly task made her feel ill. She had to swallow hard before she could agree. But facts were facts. It was all very well for ignorant farmers to blame everything from her brother-in-law's accident to the death of the cow on bad luck but Helen was educated, intelligent. The two things were fundamentally different.

The best way to lift the jinx on the farm was to find out why things were happening.

And stop them.

Even as she knocked on the door Theo knew that she was acting irrationally, but she could not help herself. Helen had taken over her mind, entangling herself through all Theo's other preoccupations like some kind of malignant bindweed.

First Robert and then Anthony. What was there about this woman that so captivated them? They both said that she wasn't beautiful but Theo didn't believe them. How could she have so much influence if she wasn't beautiful? Beauty was all. She, who had been blessed from birth with good looks, knew that.

No answer. She knocked again, louder. Where was everyone? If her servants didn't respond more quickly than this she would have sacked them long ago. She hammered again, her daintily gloved hand banging the knocker against the wood as if it were Helen's face.

Finally, footsteps.

Slow, faltering, they stopped the other side of the door. 'Yes? Who is it?' A woman's voice, sounding frightened.

Theo was in no mood to play games with a servant. 'Open the door at once, my good woman.' Even through the wood she had recognised the commonness of the voice.

The door creaked open and she stared at the thin woman with a child in her arms. 'About time. I wish to see your mistress.'

'She isn't in, madam.' A brief curtsy that showed that the woman had had some exposure to polite society. 'I don't know how long she'll be gone. It may be a brem long time.'

'I won't wait.' Not in this poky farmhouse

with a smelly yard at the back. Theo turned away.

Behind her the servant called out, 'Can I give Miss Schofield a message, Mrs Polglase?'

'No. No message.' Theo began to walk down the lane, eyeing the overgrown hedges, the rough track disparagingly. What lady would live in a place like this? Anthony must have been teasing her.

It was only when she got to the end of the lane that the servant's words came back to her. She had called her 'Mrs Polglase'. How had a servant known who she was? Yet she had seemed faintly familiar, now Theo came to think of it.

It was only as she was entering her own house that she tracked down the elusive memory. Clothes, that was it. She had ordered a new gown and it hadn't fitted. Madame Elise had called out one of the seamstresses from the hole they worked in at the back to help put matters right.

She pulled off her bonnet and handed it brusquely to the maid, sitting before the looking-glass to make sure that her hair had not been disarrayed under the minute lacy cap she wore to denote her status as a married woman.

'Tell the coachman I want him tomorrow, Briggs. I want to go to Penzance, to see Madame Elise.'

Twenty-Two

'She's so ill.' With Beth clasped tightly in her arms, Helen rocked to and fro in her chair, her eyes unfocused.

She could still see the small room in front of her, the child. In only twenty-four hours Jenny seemed to have become smaller, shrunken, her eyes deep in her head. Even her red hair seemed to have lost its lustre. Her father, hovering awkwardly around, merely emphasised her illness by his clear skin and shining thatch.

'So she won't be doing no milking for a while, then?' Agnes raised an enquiring eyebrow from the nettle soup that she was making for Beth 'to clear her blood'.

'She doesn't look as if she'll ever milk another cow.' Helen's arms tightened automatically around Beth and the baby gave a discontented squirm. 'I asked – I offered to get Doctor Ledgerwood but they refused. They said it was a childhood fever, that it would pass. But supposing it doesn't, Agnes? Supposing she dies?'

'Children get these things,' Agnes said comfortably. 'Dying one minute and running round like a teetotum the next.' She nodded at Beth. 'You'll find out soon enough.'

'But there was her grandfather. And now Jenny...' Helen bit her lip. 'Sometimes I think that the locals are right when they say this farm is cursed. The grandfather, Jenny, my cows, my brother-in-law and sister, my–' she swallowed, '–my engagement.'

'Regretting it, are 'ee?' Agnes thumped the heavy iron pot onto a trivet on the table. 'Well, I'm local but it seems to me that there's no such thing as good luck and bad luck. There's only people. People and the choices they make.'

'You're saying I shouldn't have broken off my engagement? But–'

'I've said that all along,' Agnes broke in. 'And there's my situation – but that isn't luck. That was marrying the wrong man. And your sister and her husband. It weren't bad luck, it were a fact of life. Drive too fast and you'll break your neck. Wherever he'd lived that would have happened. And if he'd lived here till he were a hundred and drove like a sensible man he *might* have lived here 'til he were a hundred.' She picked up a knife and began to scrape new potatoes for their dinner.

The steady scrape of the knife and the smell of hot food was somehow comforting. Helen felt her nerves untwist. 'We never did find out why he was driving like that,' she said, playing with Beth's fingers, admiring their tiny nails, the perfect winkles. 'But there are others. What about old Mr Trahair?'

'An old man. He'd lived a good age, especially for a miner. Just 'cos he lives on the edge of your land there's no reason for him not to die. Old age, that doctor said it were, and he should know. And Jenny don't have the same thing, does she?'

'Old age?' Helen almost laughed. 'Oh, you mean the symptoms. No, she's not yellow or anything like that. Just very sick and weak.'

Fool, she told herself. Imagining things. It was just tiredness, that was all. She who had never had to take charge of anything was responsible for Agnes, a baby, a farm, cattle. The work seemed never-ending. But, through it all, she was happier that she had ever been. Happiest of all, she admitted to herself, because she had broken off her engagement. The sense of freedom astonished her.

She knew that she had probably thrown away the only chance she would ever have to make a respectable marriage but she didn't care. Only for Ezekiel did she feel a slight sadness. But if he chose to risk his life by going abroad to work in a mission that was his responsibility, the little voice in her head pointed out. She could only make decisions that concerned her. Ezekiel was responsible for his own decisions.

Agnes stirred the pot of stew. 'You going to milk they cows?'

'I'll have to, won't I? It's too much to expect that I'll get help tonight.' Robert had been more than kind to help her with the milking but she couldn't expect it again. The thought made her feel suddenly low. With a sigh Helen got to her feet and put Beth into her cradle then paused as there was a knock at the door.

Robert! She thought, then, heart sinking, George? She and Agnes exchanged glances. 'I'll go.' Surely there was no danger of Agnes' husband finding her now, but even so...

'Mr Zelah.' Helen glanced at the empty cart behind him. 'You've – er–' She could find no polite way of asking what she wanted to know.

'Cow's been killed and gutted and taken to the kennels.' He had no such worries. 'You said you was interested in her innards.' He hefted a sack from the back of the cart. 'I got they here to show 'ee.'

She swallowed. 'Perhaps if you just tell me. Were they the same?'

'Worse, if anything.' There was a ghoulish delight in his voice. 'Good job I knew to take they bits out or I could have lost a customer for the rest of my life. If you could see what a mess that there stomach was...'

He lifted the sack invitingly.

'No, I thank you.' Helen gazed fixedly over his shoulder. 'Then there were – ah – holes?'

'All over. Black they were. And a smoke in her stomach like you wouldn't believe.'

She didn't. 'Smoke? In the *stomach?*' Perhaps, she thought, he didn't know the difference between the stomach and lungs. He was only a farrier, although, she realised, farriers often acted as animal doctors in the country.

'Well, that what it did look like. None in the lungs, mind you,' he added, answering her thought unconsciously. 'And that foam round her mouth? Did you smell 'un?'

'Er, no.' Had there been foam around the cow's mouth? A little, perhaps. But she wasn't familiar enough with the animals yet to know what was normal and what wasn't.

'Stank, it did.' Again the stomach churning relish. 'Onions,' he added with lip-smacking satisfaction.

'But I don't feed the cows on onions.' Even she knew enough for that. She pondered, trying to make sense of what he had told her. 'Do you know – have you ever seen this before?'

He sucked at a lone brown tooth in the front of his top jaw. 'Not in a cow, I haven't, but a horse now – I seen that once.' He stared ruminatively across the farmyard.

'Well?'

'It were old, mind.' He was in no hurry to tell her, seeming to drag the information from somewhere deep in his memory. 'Worked the whim up Wheal Misery.' Seeing her blank expression, he explained, 'He pulled the ore up to grass at a mine.'

'And?'

'Just the same, he were. They reckoned t'were when they was burning the tin, see. Reckoned he ate what he shouldn't. Very quiet summer like this. No wind even up St Just and you can usually count days like that on the fingers of one hand.'

His words rang a bell. 'When you say "burning tin"–'

'Getting rid of the arsenic, like.' He nodded towards the valley. 'Just like what they say they're doing down there.'

'Her husband was here again, looking for her. He seemed annoyed.' Madame Elise, with a practised twist of her arm, sent a couple of yards of flowered silk flying from the bolt to lie across the counter in a multi-coloured stream.

Leaning forward in her bent wooden chair, Theo fingered it thoughtfully, her mind racing. The woman might affect the French name of 'Madame Elise' for business purposes but the best she could achieve in real life was a local accent overlaid by an artificial twang that she imagined was upper-class. Normally Theo shut her ears to it, interested only in the fact that she could make clothes that looked at least as though they came from Bath and, occasionally, even from London. Paris chic, Theo knew, was beyond her, but who in this godforsaken part of the world would recognise real Parisian chic even if they saw it?

Theo pulled the end of the material over her arm, examining the way it draped. 'So, she has left her husband.'

'And me! Without a word of warning, mind, or an apology. Walked out! And me with a month's work piled up in the back room.' Indignation flattened the pretentious accent and brought out the Cornish. 'If I could get my hands on her...'

For a moment Theo was tempted, but what, after all, could the woman do?

Whereas a husband – there was almost no limit to the powers God and the law had given to a husband. Especially over an errant wife. 'Is he still around? Would I know him?'

'He was here when you called in last time, as I recall.' Madame Elise's mouth twisted disparagingly. 'Not the type of person I am accustomed to in my emporium.'

Theo had a vague memory of a man being hustled out as she had waited. 'I–' she struggled for an excuse, '–I promised her a present for the work she did on my gown. If her husband would like to collect it sometime–'

She could see the disbelief in the woman's face. That she should want to reward a seamstress! Theo hurried on, 'I would be grateful if you would tell him if you see him again. Now...' Only one way to stop the woman speculating. 'I'll have this. Made into an afternoon dress, I think.'

It was ugly material, almost common, and Theo knew she would never wear it, but there was nothing like ordering clothes to get Madame Elise's attention. As long as she didn't forget about the message.

'I can show you if you like.' Fred Zelah turned back to the cart with enthusiasm. 'Even a lady like you what doesn't know her tripe from her sweetbreads could see what was wrong with this here stomach.'

'No.' Helen wished her voice hadn't squeaked quite so much. The ladylike part of her wanted to throw up her hands in horror. And the other part of her brain whispered coolly: Perhaps he's wrong. A second opinion?

But she wouldn't be the one who was going to give it. Not even for the doubtful privilege of seeing smoke in a stomach. 'There wouldn't be any point in showing me, Mr Zelah.' Her voice was suddenly steadier. 'It occurs to me, however, that there may perhaps be someone else in the district who could confirm what you have discovered.'

The farrier pushed his greasy black hat further back on his head and scratched at his thinning hair with an enthusiasm that suggested a dog with fleas. 'Well, Miss, they say that there's a veterinary surgeon up Truro way somewhere. Perhaps he might know. But I have heard tell that he's a young man and a stranger from up-country so he might never have seen no arsenic poisoning afore. And 'tis a brem long way to Truro. In this hot weather that there stomach–'

'Quite,' broke in Helen quickly, her heart sinking. She was certain that Mr Zelah was an honest man but, when all was said, he was only an uneducated farrier. She dare not rely on his word alone if she were to challenge Robert Polglase about the calciner. 'And there's no one else?'

He rubbed his hands down his leather apron, split at the bottom so that he could straddle the legs of horses while he was shoeing them. 'Well, not as knows about animals, no. I reckon I'm about the best round here. Getting the animals for the kennels and all.'

'Yes, of course. I didn't mean...' Helen's voice tailed off. 'Well, if you will tell me what I owe you, Mr Zelah,' she added, her heart sinking as she thought of the dwindling store of coins in the drawer in her bedroom.

To her surprise, he said, 'My wife did say to ask for some eggs.' He licked his lips. 'I don't know what it were but Mr Trethowan's eggs always was more tasty than anyone else's in the district. Reckon it were that gert rooster they got.'

Brought up in London Helen had not realised the extent that barter played in the rural economy. 'You can have some eggs and welcome,' she said. 'We have more than we know what to do with. And if you come with me now you can see me pick them up, still warm from the hen.'

He helped her collect the eggs, chasing the sitting hens away with a boldness that made Helen feel ashamed of her more gentle methods. It was only when he was seated in his cart and she had handed up the basket of eggs to him that he suddenly said, 'I don't know of no people round here who knows more of 'osses than I do, but it's come to mind that there might be someone who could help you.'

'Yes?' Her voice was suddenly breathless.

'One of they mining captains was telling me. They got to have their tin graded and all. He talked about some people what could find out what almost anything was made out of.'

Her heart thudding, Helen asked eagerly, 'And is there someone like that around here?'

'In Penzance. Sparrow and Tregenza their name is if I remember right.' He lifted his voice. 'Here, Miss, you'll need the stomach if you want to go to them.' He waved the bloodstained sack at Helen.

But she was already running through the door, careless of the fact that her lifted skirts gave him a wholly satisfying glimpse of her ankles.

The back room of the Regent Hotel was filled with the quietness of men occupied in their favourite pursuits.

The slap of cards on baize, the muffled bets and tinkle as coins were pushed across the table, the soft-footed waiters with their trays of shining glasses – Anthony sometimes thought that no music ever written could be as satisfying as these sounds.

Now, he wondered. 'I'll have to write you an IOU, Mat.' He managed to sound as if it was a minor matter. 'You've run me off my feet, you rascal. And I bet now you'll stay away for weeks just to stop me getting my revenge.'

Not that he could. Not until he had some money. Anthony could feel the sweat prickling under his arms. Dear God, why hadn't he stayed away tonight? Why had he pushed his luck?

Mat Pender slapped him on the back. 'Never mind, Ledgerwood. I've never known you to be down for long at cards. Besides, you know what they say? "Unlucky at cards, lucky at love." We've all heard about the young lady out at the farm.'

Anthony ground his teeth. He wanted to take the man by the throat and shake him. Helen was too good to have her name bandied around the clubs like this. But he dare not. He knew that their eyes were all on him, that his financial situation was probably well known. Marriage to a woman with a farm – that possibility was probably all that had given Mat Pender the confidence to accept his IOU. Now that Ezekiel Hardcourt had been sent packing they would be expecting him to make a move – had probably laid odds on it already if he knew them.

God help him if Helen didn't accept.

'Sparrow and Tregenza.' She pulled the drawer out of the dresser with a jerk and emptied it by the simple expedient of turning it upside-down over the kitchen table.

Agnes watched, open-mouthed, as the papers slithered over the whole surface, cascading off the edges like a snowstorm. 'My soul and body! What's got into you?

You're all of a motion like a Mulfra toad on a red-hot shovel!'

'Sparrow and Tregenza.' Helen picked up a handful of papers and sorted through them, then threw them back into the drawer and grabbed another lot. 'Sparrow and Tregenza. I know I've seen that name.' She glanced up as the door was filled by the figure of Fred Zelah, the sack in his hand. 'Oh, that *is* kind of you. I almost forgot. Um, if you could just leave it in the porch...'

'Best I put 'un in the dairy where 'tis a bit cooler, miss. And make sure you keep the doors and winders shut or you'll have every cat in the district after 'un. Not to mention foxes.'

Agnes stared after him as he left, the bloodstained sack swinging casually from one horny hand. 'What did he have in there, for heaven's sake?'

'The cow's stomach and liver, I think.' Helen hurled another handful of letters into the drawer. 'I'm sure I saw something.'

'Well,' Agnes snorted. 'I reckon you're both of you daft as a brush. Why he should think you'd want to keep the stomach from that poor old cow I don't know.'

'But I do,' Helen insisted, still intent on sorting through the letters. 'It's vital that I–'

She stopped, her mouth open, eyes fixed on the piece of paper in her hand.

'Well,' Agnes asked. 'Vital that you what?'

When Helen looked up, her face was white and the hand holding the paper shook. 'I've found it!' Her voice was little more than a whisper. 'I've found the paper.'

'Well?'

She read out. "Dear Sir, et cetera, et cetera. Analysis of the stomach lining of the horse confirms the presence of large amounts of arsenic. In addition, a discussion with my cousin, Mr Phillips, a Bachelor of Medicine of Oxford University who happens to be staying in the town, confirms that the symptoms you describe – hair loss, pining away, the purple spots on the outside of the stomach and the rottenness of the inner coat – are all accepted symptoms of arsenic poisoning."

She laid the paper down on the table with a shaking hand. 'It is dated two days before my sister died, Agnes. Two days. You realise what this means?'

She tapped the paper with a quivering finger. 'My brother-in-law had just received this letter before he went for that last drive. That was why he was going so fast, Agnes. That was why he was driving dangerously.'

She reached out and her fingernails bit into Agnes' thin arms. 'He was out of his mind with fury, Agnes. He was driving to see the man who had poisoned his beloved animals.'

Twenty-Three

'But supposing it is arsenic poisoning?' Helen asked.

Anthony Ledgerwood laughed. 'My dear Miss Schofield, it is obvious that you are not a local. Everyone around here knows that there is arsenic everywhere in this part of Cornwall and it doesn't do us any harm at all.' He laughed again. 'Good heavens, I even use arsenic in medicines. The arsenic that is used for poisoning is highly concentrated, refined.'

'But it could be,' Helen insisted. 'You can hardly say that Jenny is suffering from old age like her grandfather.'

Anthony Ledgerwood said calmly, 'As I have never examined the young person, I would never dream of giving an opinion one way or the other.' He moved forward, his hands outstretched. 'Come, Miss Schofield, the strain is affecting you. You are letting your imagination run wild. The child is probably suffering from no more than a childish colic. Probably she has been scrumping green apples but she dare not admit it or she knows she would be whipped.'

His hands were warm on hers, his face smiled down at her kindly. His words were so reasonable, so likely. Helen felt herself weakening. Agnes had said almost the same. After all, the rest of the family were well. 'But the cows–?' she began.

'My dear,' – he was close to her now, leaning over her 'Sparrow and Tregenza is very reputable but it is a mining firm. They know nothing of animals. As I said, the ground here is full of arsenic. What could be more likely than that you would find arsenic if you tested the stomach of any animal grazed in the area?'

She wavered, wanting to believe him. 'But the doctor – the farrier–'

His fingers tightened on hers. 'The farrier is a good man but uneducated. I doubt if he can write his own name. And these uneducated men have strange beliefs, beliefs which you and I, Miss Schofield,' – he was closer than ever – 'would never consider for a second. And as for the doctor' – he released one of her hands and snapped his fingers – 'I am also a Bachelor of Medicine, Miss Schofield, but I would never have the temerity to say what a cow's stomach should look like. God made men and he made animals and we are not the same.'

He dropped his hand and it stole round her waist. Helen was aware that her breathing had almost stopped while her heart hammered deafeningly in her ears. She knew she should say something, move away, but she seemed rooted to the ground.

'My dear Miss Schofield, may I, dare I say, Helen?' His voice was low, thrilling. She could feel it vibrating through every fibre of her being. 'Forgive me, but I know – I am not unaware of your situation.' He was so close to her now she could feel the fan of his breath on her cheek, though she could not lift her eyes to him. 'If,' – his voice was soft, hesitant – 'if your heart is not forever broken, if you feel that in time you could love another, Helen, my dearest, could you, would you, consider that there is another who loves you, whose heart has been yours since the first moment he saw you?'

Deep inside, so deep that she could hardly hear it, a faint voice jeered, 'On the beach? He certainly didn't fall in love with you then!' but she would not listen. His voice was all she wanted to hear. His voice, saying things she had only dreamed of, his touch, so gentle, so compelling. She swallowed, the sound seeming to echo around the empty kitchen.

His arm tightened around her waist, pulling her into his side. The faint, masculine smell of him was all around her, filling her body with every breath that she took.

Gentle, insistent, his words throbbed through her body. 'I know that this is not the time, I am aware that I should not have spoken so soon, but Helen, dearest, it has hurt me to the quick to see you struggling so bravely, to see you taking on a burden which is beyond your strength and yet making every effort to carry it.'

He raised one of her hands to his lips, kissing the once-white fingers that showed the marks of her struggles over the past weeks: the torn cuticles, the small scratches from the hay and straw. 'If you knew, if I could only tell you how I long to lift this burden from your shoulders, how I want to let you rest in the circle of my arms, free forever from the worries and duties that are wearing you down, are quelling the light in your beautiful eyes.'

He lifted his mouth from her hands. He was staring straight into her face, his blue eyes gleaming in the evening sunlight. 'Helen, dearest, give me an answer, at the least tell me that I have a chance, that I can still hope that some day you will be mine?'

She had to answer, she had to say something. The whole kitchen seemed to be suffused with a golden light; his blue eyes filled the universe. The birds outside sang a prothalamion.

'Oh, Mr Ledgerwood!'

The garlic stench of the calciner filled Robert's nostrils as he pushed open the rickety gate that led to the Trahairs' front door. He had never realised how bad it was. Perhaps he should offer the Trahairs another cottage, further away. Even being convenient for work didn't mitigate living with a smell like this all the time.

Mrs Trahair opened the door, bobbing a curtsy, apologising even before he had said 'Good evening' for the state of the house, the lack of suitable food, almost for existing.

'I was told that your daughter was ill and came to enquire.' He could hear the stiffness in his voice. His father would have chucked the woman under the chin, shouldered his way in and sat down without waiting to be invited. Robert would stand, cringing at the woman's deference, wanting to be accepted and knowing that everything he did and said merely emphasised the distance between them.

Helen didn't have his problem but then, she was a real lady while he... He tightened his lips, forcing himself to forget Theo's cutting remarks. They were man and wife, weren't they? They were together for the rest of their lives. 'The child? Jenny?' he asked, remembering that Helen had talked about her.

'Brem poorly. She's that wished. But if 'ee'd like to come in and see her she'd be that honoured.'

Honoured! Poor little brat. 'I won't disturb her,' he said quickly. They'd probably haul the poor child out of bed to make a curtsy. 'But have you had a doctor for her? Is there anything you need, anything I can do?'

She denied any need as he had known she would. In desperation he asked for Nat. At least they could talk man-to-man. But Nat came out full of apologies for not being at work.

'For God's sake, man!' Robert finally lost his temper. 'Can't you see I don't give a damn about whether you were there or not?' Then, more quietly, 'If your sister is ill your place is here beside her, with your parents. But I wanted to ask – your mother said that she didn't need anything but there must be something I can do. Shall I send my brother-in-law along to examine the child?'

'He didn't do no good for Granda,' Nat said sourly.

'Oh, but surely–' Robert stared at him in horror. 'This isn't the same thing at all. Your grandfather was an old man.' Then, seeing the look on Nat's face, he lowered his voice. 'You think that? You think she has the same problem?'

Dear God! Not an epidemic. There were too many scourges against which medicine had no defence: cholera, diphtheria, typhoid – and he had been here. And to the funeral, too. What would Theo say if she knew? For her sake he had better stay away from her for a few days. Just in case.

He said, with sudden resolution, 'I'll get Doctor Ledgerwood to call. He saw your grandfather, he is the best man to tell us if they are both suffering from the same thing. I'll send him a message as soon as I get home.'

But Nat was staring over his shoulder. 'There's no need,' he said. 'He's here already.' He spat. 'Jest like crows, doctors are, always gathering round the sick and dying.' He turned on his heel and walked back inside.

Robert went to meet him. 'You've heard?'

'Helen Schofield told me.' Robert felt his hairs rise at the easy familiarity. 'I said I'd have a look in on the child.'

'I'll wait for you.' Anthony would know if there was likely to be any danger to Theo.

'I'd be grateful.' Anthony pulled off his top hat and ducked his head to go under the lintel, glancing back over his shoulder. 'I've news you should hear as soon as possible.'

Robert stared after his disappearing figure, feeling cold. Anthony had just come from the farm. Pray God there was no illness there as well.

'Is it the same as old Mr Trahair had?' Robert demanded as soon as Anthony came ducking out of the cottage.

The doctor paused to adjust his shiny top

hat. New, Robert couldn't help noticing. Bought, probably, with the profits from the calciner. 'Of course not.' His voice was easy, unconcerned. 'She's got a bellyache, that's all. Probably stolen green apples out of your orchard.'

'She's welcome to them if that is all it is.' But Robert couldn't help remembering the worried look on Nat's face. He wasn't a man to fuss over nothing. 'You're sure the child isn't dying?'

Anthony snorted. 'That child is as tough as old boots. All these miners' brats are.' He raised an eyebrow at Robert. 'I can't imagine your father getting himself into a lather about such a thing.'

Robert's lips tightened. Now that Theo had given the game away he could see through the games she and her brother played. On the one hand they upbraided him for not being a gentleman born and bred, on the other they told him that he wasn't the man his father was. The fact that both charges were true made him aware of the contempt in which they held him.

He sighed and turned his mind back to Jenny. 'Should I move her from that cottage, do you think?'

For once he had got the better of Anthony. The doctor goggled at him. 'What the – why on earth should you?'

'Oh, that smell. It can't be very nice for

the poor child.' Robert coughed. 'I have to say–' He took a deep breath. 'I hadn't realised how bad the smell from the calciner would be,' he admitted, shame-faced. 'You don't think – it isn't that that is causing the illness?'

Anthony threw back his head and laughed. 'For heaven's sake, man! What about her father? He works at the place, up to his ears in arsenic dust most of the time, and there's nothing the matter with him!'

'No, you're right.' Robert gave an embarrassed laugh. 'The funny thing is, I said exactly the same to Miss Schofield at the funeral. And you would know if there was any problem, wouldn't you?'

'Exactly,' Anthony said with confidence. 'I am a trained physician, knowledgeable in physiology, pharmacology, chemistry and many more branches of science that I can remember offhand.' He paused, then said, 'Have you thought any more about expanding the calciner?'

Robert rubbed a worried hand through his brown curls. 'I have,' he admitted. 'But I haven't reached a decision yet.'

'But it makes sense, you know.' Anthony turned to him eagerly. 'Think of the profits we made with just that one furnace. If we had two we could get twice as much. And we do not just have to roast the black arsenic soot from the chimneys on the mines, you know. There are lumps of arsenic oxide in those mines and the men know enough to pick them out. We can offer a special price for them, apart from the worth of the tin they raise. If we roast the arsenic like that we can earn even more money.'

'But a new furnace would cost money. And I don't have it.' Robert could feel himself being pushed again down a path he did not want to follow.

'Pshaw!' Anthony waved an airy hand. 'Borrow it from the bank. With the figures you can give them about the expenses and profits of the existing calciner they'll fall over themselves to lend it to you.'

'And if the bottom suddenly falls out of the market?'

'Ridiculous!' Anthony snorted. 'Think what the arsenic is used for: sheep dips, pest control, colouring wallpaper and cloth and glass – all needs which will expand in the future, not contract. Why,' he laughed heartily at the thought, 'I wouldn't be surprised if soon every Tom, Dick and Harry will be papering their walls. Even if they do live in a hovel like the Trahairs.'

'I could do with the money,' Robert admitted. Though, if he were honest, he could have lived on a fraction of his present income. It was Theo who kept them poor. If she wanted something she made his life miserable until she got it.

'*I* could do with the money,' Anthony said. 'Probably more than you, old man. Which leads me to what I was going to say to you.'

He stopped in the middle of the road, smiling broadly at Robert. 'Congratulate me. I have just proposed to the woman of my dreams and have been accepted.'

Robert was startled. He had never heard Anthony even talk of the possibility of marriage. 'Really. Who is it?' This would be something to talk over with Theo.

'Miss Schofield,' said Anthony, his face glowing with satisfaction; then, more sharply, 'What's the matter? Why are you looking at me like that?'

'He asked me! He asked me!' Helen caught Agnes in her arms as the older woman came through the door into the kitchen, whirling her around at top speed. 'Agnes, I am to marry Doctor Ledgerwood.'

'And you think that's a reason to rejoice, do you?' Agnes' face was colder than ever, her eyes hard and angry. 'You haven't got the sense you was born with! Marrying a man like that!'

'But–' Helen stopped, staring. 'What's wrong with him? Why shouldn't I marry him?' She stood in the centre of the kitchen, her arms by her sides, her happiness dissolving in the face of the other woman's coldness.

'Why should you?' Agnes demanded. 'And, come to that, why should he marry you?'

Helen felt the glow inside her increase again. 'Exactly,' she said. 'He's so good-looking, a professional man, respected. I – I have nothing. I'm not good-looking, I'm not rich. Yet he wants to marry me. Me!' She began to dance around the kitchen again. 'It's like – like Anne Elliot and Captain Wentworth and everybody all rolled into one. He loves me. He said so. And he must because there's no other reason to marry me, is there?'

Agnes snorted. 'No other reason! And you with this gert farm.'

'Which isn't making money,' Helen reminded her. 'And it isn't mine. It's Beth's. I have nothing. Nothing.'

'And if she dies?' Agnes demanded. 'Who gets it then? You, if I'm not mistaken. And then there's the works. He's involved in those, don't forget. And I bet you said about that there cow before he proposed, didn't you?'

'Well, I...' Helen stood still. 'Well, what if I did?' she asked, recovering. 'He was very helpful.'

'Helpful?' Agnes pulled the bread out of the giant crockery pot in which it was kept and began to slice it, the knife cutting through the bread with vicious strokes.

‘’Course he were helpful, you gert lummock,’ she said furiously. ‘If you kick up a fuss he’ll lose the money what he gets from it and that wouldn’t suit him, not head over heels in debt like what he is.’

‘Don’t be foolish.’

‘Foolish, am I? And him a gambler and all. If he’s so good-looking why idn’t he married already?’ She pointed the knife straight at Helen’s pale face. ‘I can tell ’ee that. Because they do know him round here and there idn’t a gentleman will let his daughter marry a man like that, no matter how pretty his face is.’

‘You’re just saying that!’ Helen’s face was red now with fury. ‘You’re just jealous. Because you married a man who was no good you think all men are. But you’re wrong about him. Wrong! He’s a good man. Kind. He’s gone to see Jenny – just because I asked him to. Without payment. And you’re wrong about the debt, too. He’s got new clothes, a new horse. He earns a good living. And he loves me for myself. Just for me.’

Anger shook her hands, curled her fingers. If she stayed any longer, she thought, she would burst into tears out of sheer fury. She turned, storming to the doorway.

‘Where are you going?’ Agnes demanded.

‘To milk the cows. They need me, at least.’ With a swirl of her skirt Helen was out of the kitchen. The door slammed behind her, making the plates on the dresser rattle.

Alone, Agnes dropped the bread knife and stared down at the table, her shoulders sagging. Fool that she was! It never did any good to abuse the man a woman loved. If only she had not been panicked into telling the truth. Because Helen needed to be told, needed to be warned. But now her only chance was gone. Helen would never listen to her again on the subject of Anthony Ledgerwood.

Wearily, she picked up the knife again. Everything she did in her life always went wrong. She would have given her life to save Helen and now she had just ruined her chance to do the one thing that would really help her.

Her whole life. A failure.

The knife glittered in the rays of the afternoon sun.

Twenty-Four

The cow kicked forward, her cloven hind hoof missing Helen's swiftly withdrawn head by a fraction.

Calm yourself, she told herself, firmly. Relax. She knew that it was because she was so angry with Agnes that they were reacting like this. Already, in the few days that she had been milking them, they had come to accept her although the milk they were giving was falling off. Helen sighed and rose from the three-legged stool she had been using, pulling it aside while she went to look out across the valley.

The smoke from the calciner filled the valley bottom. Thank God she couldn't smell it up here. But the sight brought back her concerns.

Anthony had told her that the information in the letter was all wrong, that the calciner was quite safe – and who should know better than he did? He had helped design it, after all, and he was a doctor. He had treated old Mr Trahair and had volunteered to see Jenny. If they were suffering from arsenic poisoning he would be the first to know about it.

The thought of him calmed her again. He was so handsome, so kind. The way he had volunteered to go to Jenny when he had learned she was ill. Helen had not expected it, had, in fact, mentioned that she was going to get another doctor to see the child. Not because she didn't think Anthony would do it but because she didn't want to impose upon him. But he had immediately offered his services – free! Had gone straight there.

She sighed with happiness. Already the burdens that had weighed her down were lifting. Now she had someone to rely on. Anthony Ledgerwood would help her. He would make Jenny better and then she would again look after the animals, milk the cows...

Helen sighed and turned back. That was all in the future. For now the milking was her responsibility. But at least the cows had calmed down in her absence. And so had she.

Helen pulled the stool back into place and settled down with her head buried in the musty-smelling flank of the cow. Carefully, remembering what Jenny had taught her, she began to milk, closing her finger and thumb firmly around the top of each teat then closing the other fingers to strip out the milk that was in it, then the next, then the next.

She started to get back into the rhythm and the milk began to sing as it squirted into the wooden bucket, just as if she were a real milkmaid.

It was silly to get herself worked up about Agnes. After her experiences with her husband, it was only to be expected that Agnes would dislike and distrust all men. And she was probably jealous, as well. Anthony Ledgerwood was so good-looking, so tall and handsome and well-dressed. He was a man from a dream. Her mind wandered off her milking and the cow raised a threatening hoof, bringing her back to the present. Concentrate, she told herself firmly. She didn't want another kick.

It was only when she went into the cool of the dairy, the heavy wooden bucket banging against her legs at every step, that she saw the bloodstained sack with its contents.

'I won't come back with you.' Anthony could not face Theo tonight.

He knew what she would be like: bitter, jealous. She had always been close to him, far closer than she was to Robert, and his feeling for Helen had shocked her to the core. Far better to let Robert tell her the news and face her wrath.

Besides, whatever his feelings for Helen, he had to marry her. And soon. Only by marrying her could he stop her investigating the calciner.

If it could be proved that people had died because of it – but that was nonsense, he told himself as he strode easily down the road. He was a doctor – who would doubt his word? He had treated old Mr Trahair, and now Jenny. Their symptoms were completely different. And arsenic poisoning was notoriously difficult to diagnose. Even tests for arsenic were dubious and if the body of the old man was exhumed – that would do no one any good. With all the arsenic around naturally any cadaver from the graveyard would be contaminated with the stuff. No. Whatever his private concerns, no one could pin a charge of poisoning onto him.

It was those damned cows – if that could be proved... He slashed viciously at the white heads of the cow parsley with his stick. Merely a civil suit, of course, but that could be worse. If Robert closed the calciner...

He could feel the tension in his chest, constricting his breathing. How soon could he marry Helen? He had to keep her quiet. Without the money from the calciner he would be ruined. Even now, he knew, it was only the possibility of marriage, the promise of the next profits from the calciner, that was allowing him to keep his head above the water. If Robert could be persuaded to expand the works all might yet be well. But if Helen went to him, told him what she suspected – Robert was a soft fool. He was likely to close the works on her word alone.

He had to stop that.

'You look very lovely. As always.'

Despite the ache in his heart Robert was determined that he would keep his resolution to be nice to Theo, treating her as he always had. After all, marriage was for life.

To let unkind remarks fester, to mope about them, keeping them always in mind until they grew and coloured every aspect of a relationship – that was the way to make a hell for oneself. Better to pretend it had never happened, to try to continue as if everything was as it always had been. It was a poor substitute for the love and respect that he had once thought they shared but it was better than the alternative.

He leaned over and touched Theo's cheek lightly with his lip. She smelled of violets and roses and her skin was as soft as swans-down.

Her smile seemed more constrained than of old but perhaps she, too, was finding it difficult to pretend to their old relationship. 'We're alone tonight for once, Robert. Anthony seems to have decided that he has something better to do with his time than eat with us.'

He glanced at her but there was no knowing smile on her face, no arch lift to her eyebrows. Robert groaned, tempted to say nothing, to let Anthony break the news of his engagement himself. Theo knew him too well. He would never be able to hide from her the fact that he disliked this engagement from the depths of his heart.

Helen Schofield was too good, too honest, to be married to a scoundrel like Anthony Ledgerwood. Robert had been at school with him, had known him since they were boys together. Anthony was attractive, amusing, intelligent. He was also a gambler and, Robert suspected, a liar. He had certainly had liaisons with other women. That would not normally have damned him forever – many young men, too poor to marry, had an arrangement with a complaisant woman, usually older – but there had been rumours in Penzance that Anthony's liaisons had all ended acrimoniously, and that he had not been generous to the women concerned as befitted a gentleman.

No, Theo would see immediately that he was unhappy with this engagement and it was more than likely that she would immediately jump to the wrong conclusions. Robert knew from past experience that to justify himself by putting any blame on Anthony would be asking for trouble. Brother and sister could fight like cat and dog but they defended each other to the hilt against any third party.

The butler appeared to announce dinner and Robert breathed a sigh of relief. Such personal information could not be divulged in front of the servants, in any case. He took Theo's arm, leading her into the dining room, holding her chair for her. 'The Trahairs seem to be having more than their fair share of bad luck. The grandfather has just died and now the little girl is ill.'

She lifted her head quickly. 'You didn't go there?'

'Not into the house. I just enquired at the door.'

She stared at him. 'You might consider me. Heaven only knows what people like that might be suffering from. And you could bring it into the house.'

Her lack of sympathy angered him but he said peaceably, 'Your brother was there. He seemed to think it was just a childish fever.'

'Anthony? Then why didn't he come back with you?' She stared at him under lowered brows. 'I hope you didn't quarrel?'

All conversational avenues seemed to lead to danger. Somehow he got through the dinner by discussing the news of Sir Robert Peel's fall from his horse and his illness. It was only after the servants had placed the puddings and fruit on the table and retired that he had to say, 'I have news for you which I hope you will find pleasing.' He took a deep breath. 'Your brother has just told me that he has become engaged to Helen Schofield.'

Her surprisingly dark brows drew down, almost hiding her great blue eyes. 'What?' Her voice was an outraged whisper.

Hiding his true feelings, he said cheerfully, 'She will make him a wonderful wife. She is a real lady. You will like her. And she will be a companion for you, I imagine.' He tried to ignore the set look to her face, the thin line of her mouth. 'I imagine that he will be introducing you to her as soon as possible.'

She rose slowly to her feet, her face white. 'A companion?' she hissed. 'For me?' She crumpled the linen napkin in her hands like a dishrag and flung it down wildly so that it flopped into the custard. 'I wouldn't speak to that – to that – bitch, if she were the last person on this earth.'

'My dear Miss Schofield!'

Helen could not tell if the little attorney were more shocked or admiring of her actions. She lifted her chin, staring him straight in the eye. 'It seemed best to get confirmation. There are two opinions after all.'

Inwardly, she felt a frisson of shame, but it was not because she had just walked three miles into Penzance with a cow's stomach swinging awkwardly in a sack at her side and delivered it to a firm of chemists. It was the fact that she had not taken Anthony Ledgerwood's word as final that made her want to hang her head.

What sort of woman was she to doubt a man like him? What sort of wife would she make if she dared to set up her opinion in opposition to his? But she could not help it. That sack, sitting in the cool dairy, had played on her mind.

At milking, last night, she had pretended to herself that she hadn't seen it but, in bed, it kept appearing before her closed lids in all its horrible sogginess. What if Anthony Ledgerwood were wrong? He was handsome, attractive, he made her pulses race as poor Ezekiel had never done, but what if...

Agnes had said no more but her tight lips and withdrawn face had told Helen what she was thinking. Caught by a pretty face! It was an expression she had heard used of young men before now but just suppose...

In the small hours she had reached her conclusion. She would check his word just this once. After all, the farrier had gone out of his way to be helpful. She owed it to him to establish the facts.

And once she had proved to herself that Anthony Ledgerwood was right she would never doubt his word again, she promised herself. And he would be proved right. He was clever, educated, honest. There was no real doubt that he could be mistaken.

But she still didn't understand why she had left Sparrow and Tregenza's and come here. Because, of course, when it was proved that there was no arsenic in the stomach...

'What if arsenic is found in the stomach?' Her question almost took her by surprise. It was as if the other part of her brain had taken over now, as if the cynical, disbelieving side was in control.

Mr Brownfield set his fingers together, staring at her across the scarred wood of his desk. Despite the bright sunshine outside it was dim in here, the light subdued by its passage through the years of grime that encrusted the small, thick panes. In the dark corners, deed boxes lurked, their names unreadable in the gloom. Only the attorney's white collar glowed in the subdued light.

'Sparrow and Tregenza are very reputable, very reputable indeed.' He gazed at her intently. 'If they say that there is arsenic present, then I think you may take it as accurate. They are used by many of the mining companies around here for their technical expertise.'

It wasn't what she wanted to hear. Part of her mind, the part that was still giddy with delight at her engagement, tried to shut out the unwelcome news. The other, the half her grandmother had tried to drive away, asked, 'And what are my options if the arsenic is confirmed?'

He thought. 'You have three that I can see. First, obviously, you should speak to Mr Polglase. As the owner he is the only one who can either close down the calciner or adapt it so that it does not cause a nuisance.'

'Oh, well...' She could feel herself smiling with relief. Robert Polglase was a friend. He was kind, honourable, he cared about others. All she had to do was tell him and–

As if he had read her mind Mr Brownfield said, 'You may not find him easy to convince.'

Her head jerked up. 'Oh, but surely...'

He rose to his feet, short and round, his hands tucked under the back of his coat, his stomach straining forward, so that he looked like a small bird hopping about the room. 'You must understand, Miss Schofield, that the price of tin is in the doldrums at present.'

It meant nothing to her. 'But this is an arsenic works.'

'Quite. And, if the rumours I hear in the club are correct, it is only the profit from the calciner that is enabling him to keep the mines working. It may be that however much he has sympathy with you, he cannot, for economic reasons, close the calciner down. To do so will throw his entire work force out of work.'

'But–' She stopped, appalled. 'But surely...'

He shrugged. 'If I may proffer my advice, Miss Schofield, I would recommend that you go to Mr Polglase and tell him of your concerns. It is possible' – he quirked a bushy eyebrow at her – 'and this is *not* what I would recommend to him as a man of law, but it is possible that, being a kind-hearted man, he will ignore the legal position and offer you recompense.' He cleared his throat. 'If that were to happen I would recommend that you take it.'

She was on her feet. 'But you can't suggest that! It isn't the money – it's all the other things. The suffering of those poor animals, the death of my brother-in-law and sister, old Mr Trahair, Jenny's illness – how can you say I should just take the money and forget what has happened?'

He cleared his throat. 'You may believe that some or all of these events are linked to the calciner but as your attorney I am bound to point out that you have evidence only for the death of one cow – two if the arsenic is found in this other animal.'

'But if they died because of the arsenic then all the other deaths must follow on,' she said hotly. 'Besides, you have forgotten; I am trying to sell or lease the farm. Who will buy it if any animal on it is likely to be poisoned? What you are suggesting means that my niece's inheritance will be worthless.'

He looked down, fiddling with some papers on his desk, stacking them one above the other until the edges were perfectly aligned. 'That is my advice to you.'

'And if I don't take it, what then? Is there anything else I can do?'

There was a long pause before he said reluctantly, 'I can only suggest two other courses of action. The first is to charge Mr Polglase under the criminal law with creating and continuing a public nuisance. The second–'

She didn't bother to wait for the second. 'That is easy,' she said, feeling relief flood through her. 'What he is doing is obviously a nuisance.'

'Not so fast!' He held up a warning hand. 'The wording of the charge is that he is creating a *public* nuisance. That means that it must affect a group of people, not just yourself.'

'But he *is*,' she said eagerly. 'I told you. The Trahairs are suffering too. The smells, the illness – of course it is a public nuisance!'

'The Trahairs,' he reminded her drily, 'all work for Mr Polglase, either in the mine or the calciner itself.' He sat down and stared at her through gold-rimmed spectacles. 'Do you really think that they would choose to take their own employer to court, knowing that, whatever the outcome, they would certainly lose their jobs?'

Her excitement died. For a few seconds she struggled with her feelings; then she asked, 'And the third course of action?'

'The third course of action is that you take out a private prosecution against Mr Polglase to halt the production of the nuisance.'

Slowly she raised her head and looked at him but he raised a warning hand.

'Before you answer, Miss Schofield, may I just say one thing?'

He sighed. 'You do not have the funds to finance such an action.'

'You've been some brem long time.'

Helen dropped wearily into the kitchen chair and rested her head on the palms of her hands. 'I waited for the results of the analysis.' The sky was darkening towards evening, the mooing of the cows warned her that they should have been milked by now but she felt exhaustion dragging through her body. Every step on the way home had been an effort; now she felt that she just wanted to put her head on the table and forget her troubles in sleep.

Agnes poured water into the teapot. 'You've missed yer young man.'

'Have I?' Even that had no power to rouse her now. He was just another problem. They crowded round her, growing bigger and more frightening every time she looked at them until she felt herself hemmed in, surrounded, suffocated by their looming presence.

A cup of tea appeared before her and she reached out gratefully. 'Actually, Agnes,' she confessed, 'under the circumstances I'm glad he came early, while I wasn't here.'

'Are you?' the other woman snorted. 'Well, I aren't! And I'll tell you why.'

She stood over Helen, her arms akimbo, looking down at her. 'If he'd come a bit later maybe he could have had a look at poor little Beth.'

'What?' Helen looked up, her face white. 'What do you mean? What's the matter with her?'

Agnes sighed. 'She's sick as a shag, that's what's the matter. And bloody Doctor Ledgerwood had been and gone before she started.'

'My dear Helen, you really are worrying unnecessarily.'

Helen looked up into Anthony Ledgerwood's handsome face and wished she could feel reassured. 'But there is so much illness. Old Mr Trahair, Jenny and now Beth.'

She glanced down at the mewling child in her arms. It had been frightening to see how swiftly the child had gone downhill. Already, the tiny face seemed older, fallen in, the eyes dull. She had hated having to ask Nat if he would go for the doctor, not with Jenny so ill as well, but she had been left with no choice.

He lifted her chin with his long fingers until she was forced to look him in the face. 'I have told you before, Helen, those illnesses are not the same. Nor is Beth's.' He smiled at her, his blue eyes kind. 'I *am* a doctor, you know. Why won't you believe me?'

She hadn't meant to say anything, had meant to mull things over before she broached the subject with him, but she had no time now for niceties, not with Beth so ill. 'I took the cow's stomach in to Sparrow and Tregenza today.'

The bald words seemed to have a weight of their own. They almost resounded round the silent room. Strange, she thought, staring up at the doctor; he hadn't seemed to move a muscle of his face but suddenly the blue eyes were cold rather than kind, his smile a wolfish baring of teeth. She shivered, pulling the child's body closer to her own.

His laugh seemed to come from a long way away. 'There's no reason for you not to. I was only trying to save you money. Now you'll just have to wait for weeks to learn what I told you yesterday was true.'

She wished she didn't have to say it. 'They gave me the results today.' Her voice seemed to creak through her dry throat. 'They said it was arsenic.'

'And I told you,' he said, calmly, 'that arsenic is found all over the area. Probably every animal you tested would prove positive for it.'

Yesterday she had been so happy. She said, 'I told them that. They went to the abattoir behind the Terrace and got another cow's stomach. It came from Madron.'

There was no doubt about him now. The kind smile was gone, the handsome face drawn, with deeply carved lines from nose to chin. 'You don't trust me.'

She could tell that he made an effort at sounding hurt, at sounding disappointed, but all she could hear was condemnation. Sadly, she raised her head.

'I don't trust you,' she confirmed. Her eyes were burning with unshed tears, her throat ached with tightness. She would have given anything not to have had this conversation, not to have to say the things she must. She forced her labouring lungs to take a deep breath.

'I haven't trusted you since I got the results of the test on the second cow. They found no trace of arsenic.'

He stared at her for a long second, his teeth bared, then he turned, took his hat, and left.

Helen stared down at the sick child, rocking her gently in her arms.

Yesterday she had been so happy.

Twenty-Five

It felt like betrayal even to approach Robert Polglase, and the welcome he gave Helen as she entered his study only made her feel more like a Judas than ever. 'What a pleasant change to be able to welcome you to *my* home for once, Helen.' He held out his hand, smiling at her. 'I seem to have spent half my life at the farm recently drinking your tea. You must let me offer you some refreshments in return.'

His welcome was reassuring but she could not respond, not with the letters from Sparrow and Tregenza weighing down her reticule. He must have read something in her manner because his hand dropped and he scanned her face anxiously. 'Are you well? You look–' He made a helpless gesture, at a loss to know how to tell her politely that she was not looking well.

As if she needed reminding of the dark circles under her eyes and her pale cheeks. 'Mr Polglase–' He gestured abruptly and she corrected herself. 'Robert. I have – I think I have bad news for you.' She fumbled in her reticule and pulled out the letter from Sparrow and Tregenza that she had found in the kitchen drawer. 'I would be obliged if you would read that.'

She sat as he read it, lowering herself into the red leather chair facing his desk. Weariness and depression hammered in her head. She felt beyond sleeping, beyond sensible thought. She was only keeping to her course of action now by sheer will-power.

He finished the letter and she saw him double-check the date and the addressee. 'This letter–'

She interrupted him. 'I believe that this letter is the cause of my sister and brother-in-law's death. I think that it was on receipt of this letter that they decided to put a stop to what was causing the deaths of their cattle.'

She raised her head. 'I think they were driving to see you.'

He tapped the paper. 'You think my calciner was responsible for the death of this horse? But there is arsenic all around here, Helen. The horse might have picked it up anywhere.'

She reached into the reticule again, laid the report she had received only yesterday from Sparrow and Tregenza on the desk. 'And then there's this.'

Again he read it carefully, checking back on details as he went along. 'This second cow?'

Tiredness dragged at her. 'It was used as a control. Doc–' She interrupted herself, started again. 'I had been told previously that arsenic was all around so I asked them to perform a similar test on another cow from this area. The second cow came from Madron, only a mile from the farm.'

'And it showed no sign of arsenic.' He stood, began to walk uneasily around the room.

To her tired eyes he seemed more of a stranger to this luxurious room than she was herself. His clothes were of good quality but no tailor could hide the ungentlemanly width of his shoulders, the strength in his thighs. Against the rich velvet curtains he looked more like a gamekeeper, summoned to his master's office for some offence. Don't let his appearance put you off, she reminded herself. He is the owner; this is his problem.

He turned. 'I hope you are wrong. In fact, Helen, I have to tell you that you are almost certainly mistaken. The calciner cannot be causing this. It was designed by Anthony Ledgerwood and as a doctor, he would obviously ensure that there was no danger to health.' He smiled at her. 'We discussed this at the funeral, I remember. I really thought that I had convinced you then.'

'These letters have unconvinced me.' Helen took a deep breath, holding herself straighter. 'And there is more.'

He tapped the papers on his desk. 'More animals ill?'

'People,' she said briefly. 'Old Mr Trahair, Jenny and now' – her voice cracked – 'Beth.' She turned her head, hiding the sudden tears that burned at her lids.

'I am sorry.' He reached out and touched her shoulder lightly and she had to resist the impulse to turn and bury her face in his shoulder. 'She is such a lovely child, so happy.' Then he stopped. Looking up at him she could see the change come over his face. 'But, Helen, there is no possibility that the calciner can be responsible for these illnesses. Anthony – Doctor Ledgerwood treated old Mr Trahair and he has visited Jenny. He is certain that they are suffering from different problems and in neither case has he even suggested that they might have been caused by arsenic.'

'Well, he wouldn't, would he?' The other half of her brain, taking over again. Helen cringed inside at the rudeness but it had to be said.

Robert was staring at her as if he couldn't believe his ears. 'You don't believe him?'

She shook her head.

'But, forgive me, I understood...' He tailed off, started again. 'I thought that you and he–'

This time she did rescue him. Head high,

her pale face carefully schooled to show no emotion, she stated calmly, 'Doctor Ledgerwood and I are no longer engaged.'

For a second she thought she saw something, almost like relief, show on his face. Then he bowed his head. 'I am sorry.' But no more, she noticed. No pleading for his brother-in-law, no persuasions or regrets. Just the simple statement, the bare minimum that politeness demanded. Even amid her other preoccupations she wondered about it, but forced the thought away as he went on, 'But that does not affect anything. Anthony is a reputable doctor. He would never design a calciner that was not safe.'

A slight noise behind her warned Helen that the door had opened but she ignored it. 'But this illness? The cows? The horse?' She leaned towards him. 'Robert, you cannot ignore the facts. It *must* be the calciner that is causing all these problems.'

He had his back to her, staring out of the window. 'But, my God!' His voice sounded appalled. 'If this is true–'

'Of course it isn't true.'

They both swung round. Behind her, Helen saw a young, fashionable woman, beautifully dressed, her face contorted with rage. 'What rubbish are you letting this woman come out with? Really, Robert, I have no patience with you.'

Helen rose, bobbed a swift curtsy. 'Mrs

Polglase, I have evidence that your calciner–'

Theo broke in swiftly, 'Evidence? Madam, that calciner was designed by my brother and it is operated by my husband. How dare you insinuate that they are operating something which is not safe?'

Helen glanced at Robert for support but he was silent, staring at his hands. Theo stepped forward. 'Leave this house at once. We don't need troublemakers like you around. And if I ever hear you saying that our calciner is unsafe you will be sued for every penny. Do you understand?'

Helen glanced again at Robert but he remained silent, withdrawn.

Betrayal gnawed at her heart but Helen would not let it show on her face. Head high, she dropped a stately curtsy.

'I came to you first because I believed in your probity.' She spoke directly to Robert, ignoring the outraged gasp of his wife. 'I thought you were my friend. I thought that you would listen to reason.'

He raised his head but before he could speak Theo had intervened again. 'Out.' Theo caught at her arm. 'Get out at once before I have the servants throw you out.'

'Robert.' Helen's voice was pleading, her heart breaking. 'Mr Polglase, please, you've seen the reports–'

'Are you going?' Theo gripped her arm.

'Robert, tell this woman to go. She has no right to come here, insulting us in our own home.'

Helen shook her arm free, made one last effort. 'Please. Beth's life may be at stake. Please listen.'

He did not raise his head. Staring at the desktop, his voice thick and heavy, Robert Polglase said slowly, 'I think you had better go.'

Helen stared at him, unwilling to believe what she had heard. She had trusted him, liked him, had believed that he was her friend. And now... It was all vain, all a lie. She was wrong about him, wrong as she had been wrong about Ezekiel, about Anthony. But even Anthony's betrayal had not hurt her as this did.

Vaguely, she could hear Theo's voice, shrill, complaining, but it did not penetrate through the depths of her despair.

Like an automaton she turned away from the man she had thought of as a true friend. Her head high, her heart breaking, Helen left the room with stately tread.

The apothecary was old and shabby, his cheeks embroidered with broken veins. 'I'll need payment first.'

Sighing, Helen counted out the money. It would be impossible to find a greater contrast to Anthony Ledgerwood. But Doctor

Tregarron was trained; he would, at least, give a second opinion. He took the money in a grimy hand. 'Which patient do you want me to visit first?'

'My niece.' Beth was failing so swiftly, shrinking, dying, it seemed, before her very eyes. 'I will have to tell the parents of the other girl to expect you.'

She told him the name of the farm and his head jerked up. 'More bad luck, eh?' He eyed her inquisitively. 'And so you're the young lady who jilted the curate?'

Helen felt her face redden with embarrassment. She could only hope that Anthony Ledgerwood had told no one except Robert Polglase about their short-lived engagement. You wouldn't have to be superstitious to believe that losing two suitors in less than a week was very unlucky.

Sighing again, she set off to walk to the Trahairs to tell them of what she had discovered.

'And don't you come back! We don't need no vagabonds like you around.'

'I'm going, I'm going.' George Penhaligon took up the small bundle that was all he had left and hurried down the steps, his one-time landlady's farewell screeches ringing in his ears.

All down the street doors popped open, women stood on their top steps, thick arms akimbo above rough cotton aprons, watching him leave with that air of righteous superiority which women seemed able to adopt in the face of all the evidence.

Damn them all. Damn all women – and especially Aggie. Humiliation dampened the back of his shirt as he walked stiff-legged under their jeering gaze. This was all Aggie's fault, all of it. He stored it up in the hot, inner recesses of his mind, ready for when he saw her again.

When, not if. That damned vision had reassured him of that, at least. Not that it wasn't the immediate cause of his present troubles.

He ground his teeth, feeling the vibration through the very bones of his skull. If the seeing had gone as he had planned, if he had given the reassuring, comforting message he had prepared, none of this would have happened. But the vision of Agnes with the knife in her side – how could he recover quickly from that? It wasn't humanly possible.

So he had left, shocked, stumbling. And the word had gone round. 'That Penhaligon – he's no good. Just a fraud. Can't see anything.'

George turned the corner, out of sight of the women who had seen his humiliation, then dropped his bundle to wipe his sweating hands down the sides of his trousers. Aggie. The name echoed in his brain. She had brought him to this. Thrown out of his lodgings, wanted by the constables. Even the men in the public houses refused to play with him any more. Word about that had got around too.

He knew he should leave the area, go upcountry. Truro, perhaps, or Bodmin – he hadn't been there for a while. But the jail was at Bodmin. Under the circumstances the further he was from that jail, the better. Besides, Aggie was around here somewhere, he knew it. He could almost taste her presence. Not close. Not in the town itself but near, near...

The vision he had seen of her came again to mind and he smiled, cracked his knuckles, then shouldered his bundle. After all the trouble she had caused he would be glad to see her when he had a knife in his hand. After all, a man who has killed once...

But finding her was the first thing. If she was still around she must be living somewhere, earning her living. She might even have some money.

The dress shop, he decided. So many stories flew round in a place like this it was quite likely that if she had been seen, news would have got back to Madame Elise. And if not – he would visit the butter market again. With luck that girl still hadn't learned to keep an eye on her takings.

‘’Ere, I aren’t going to do that!’ Mrs Trahair stared at Helen as if she had suggested the other woman should walk through Penzance naked.

‘You only have to back up what I say to the constables,’ Helen repeated patiently. ‘It won’t be difficult. You just have to tell the truth about Jenny and your father-in-law.’

‘And what good would that do?’ she demanded, her red hands clutching the edge of the deal table. ‘That wouldn’t bring Da back, nor it won’t save Jenny.’

‘We might save Jenny,’ Helen said. ‘If Doctor Tregarron–’

‘I’m not having he! Drinks like a fish, he do. Besides, what’s wrong with young Doctor Ledgerwood? You was all for having him round last thing I heard.’

‘I thought a second opinion might be advisable,’ Helen said diplomatically. ‘And Doctor Tregarron was the first doctor I tried. Besides, if it *is* the arsenic–’

‘Course it idn’t!’ Mrs Trahair’s red face grew redder yet. ‘Da’s been working there fer months, and all with no more than a tiddy piece of cotton wool stuck up his nose and he’s all right.’

‘But if it *is* the calciner that is causing Jenny’s sickness, you’ll want it stopped.’ Why did Mrs Trahair make it so difficult? Helen wondered. Or was it just that she herself was over-tired? She longed to get back to Beth, to see for herself if the child was better but she had to sort this out first.

'Have it stopped?' Mrs Trahair's voice rose in a screech. 'What do you mean, "have it stopped?"'

'Well, closed down until...'

'And throw our Da out of a job?' Mrs Trahair moved out from behind the table, her face furious. 'That there calciner belongs to Mr Polglase, it do. All this family have worked for he and his family ever since his da paid out his first wages. We're not going to shut down his calciner. Whatever do you think we are?'

'But if it's killing people–' Helen protested.

'And who says it's killing people? Not Doctor Ledgerwood and he should know better than you.' She stepped forward, her face belligerent. 'You come down here with yer fancy ways and think you can tell us all what to do.' She raised her voice. 'Nat, you come here at once.'

He moved forward from where he had been hanging over the small cot by the fire in which Jenny's small figure was huddled. 'What is it, Ma?'

His mother turned to him, wringing her hands in agitation. 'You heard what she said! You heard her! Trying to put our Da out of a job. And ruin Mr Polglase, more than likely.'

She pointed a shaking finger at Helen. 'You get her out of here. You throw her out. And tell her that if she ever shows her face here again I'll – I'll–'

'It's all right. I'll go.' Helen knew when she was beaten. 'But I'll send Doctor Tregarron–'

'You'll do no such thing! We don't hold no truck with the likes of he! Nor with you neither!' As Helen and Nat left the tiny cottage she slammed the door viciously behind them.

Everything was going wrong. In a final attempt to put things right Helen turned to the broad young man by her side. 'Nat, you heard what I said and you love Jenny. Can't you persuade your mother to at least let Doctor Tregarron have a look at her? It can't do any harm and it might save her life.'

He looked down at her, his face twisted in anguish. 'God knows, I don't want Jenny to die, Miss, but I don't reckon Doctor Tregarron can save her if Doctor Ledgerwood can't. He's brother to Mr Polglase's wife. He'd do his best for us.'

How could she tell him? How could she explain that that very fact might be the reason for this problem? But she dared not. Mr Brownfield had explained it all very carefully to her. Whatever she did, she must not slander Robert Polglase or his brother-in-law or she would be the one in prison.

Frantically, she felt in her reticule. 'Can you read, Nat?' When he shook his head she explained about the letter, what she had done about the cow's stomach, read both letters out loud to him. 'Now do you see?'

He said slowly, 'But cows are different from people. We don't eat grass. And we've been eating new tatties out of our garden, all of us, for weeks now but it's only Jenny what's ill. How do you account for that?'

Helen pushed her bonnet back and ran a distracted hand through her hair, lifting the damp strands away from her sweating forehead. 'I don't know, Nat. But if the arsenic from the calciner can affect the cows, surely it can affect people.'

He was still pursuing his slow thoughts. 'And our Da. Up to his knees in it he is and he's well enough. Never been better.'

'I don't know,' she said again. She longed to persuade him. He was younger, more open to new ideas. 'Please, Nat, try at least to let Doctor Tregarron see Jenny.' If she, at least, could be saved...

He pursed his lips. 'Ma says 'tes just a summer fever, and Doctor Ledgerwood says the same.'

'But if it isn't?' she pressed. 'If this is a chance to save her life?'

He was silent for several moments then said, 'I'll see what I can do. But 'tes a pity it was Doctor Tregarron you set on. Ma never could abide he.'

'Then get someone else,' she insisted. 'I'll pay.' Her heart dropped at the thought of yet more money going out. Always out, never in. But the memory of the small body, curled up in the tiny cottage by the fire, reproached her. Poor Jenny, her light almost extinguished, her red hair almost black with sweat, her face a greenish blur. 'And get them quickly.' How long could the child hold on?

And at home there was Beth. Little Beth, for whose sake she had been doing all this. Helen took her leave of Nat and turned up the steep track to the farmhouse, almost running despite her tiredness, her black skirts lifted clear of her aching feet.

Pray God Doctor Tregarron would be able to save the child.

Twenty-Six

'No! No!'

Helen stopped abruptly at the entrance to the farmyard. In front of her the farmhouse cowered under its thatched roof, its eyes blind.

'No!' The lowered blinds, the pulled curtains could mean only one thing. 'No, it can't be true. It mustn't be.'

Her feet were too heavy to lift. She could not move, could not cross the yard, enter the sightless house. She did not want to know, did not want to have the news confirmed. Shaking, she stood alone in the gateway. Cold shudders ran through her body and she could hear her teeth chattering. Please God, don't let it be true. I'll do anything, just don't let this be true. Let it be a mistake, a cruel joke, anything. But not this, not Beth.

The sky above her was black, the house threatening. The whole world seemed strangely silent, as if it was holding its breath, as if it, too, was in mourning...

'No!' Suddenly she was running, stumbling on feet which did not belong to her, her eyes blinded by tears. Stones caught at her feet as if trying to hold her back, her skirts wound round her legs as if they were trying to stop her. Every step took a world of effort, every breath was a hard-fought battle.

The house loomed before her bleary eyes, rising suddenly from the gloom, and she cannoned into a doorpost, knocking herself backwards, reeling. It didn't want her to enter, either; it didn't want her to have to face the truth.

Her trembling hands fumbled with the latch, fighting it as if it were an enemy. She had to be there. She had to be with Beth. As if it read her mind it gave way with a rush, scraping her knuckles raw. But the physical pain was unnoticeable, masked by her mental anguish.

Disregarding the dripping blood Helen staggered on legs that didn't belong to her, rebounding off walls, lurching wildly, hands reaching, fumbling, for anything that would help her to struggle – slowly, painfully – to the stairs, to the room, to the cot...

'No!' She flung herself forward, reaching for the small body, so tiny, shrunken now in death. She picked it up, hugged it to her, rocking, rocking, clutching it tight, tight, as if the heat of her body could make it warm again, as if her breath on its cheek could make it breathe again.

'Oh, Beth. Beth.' Her tears flowed unstoppably now, wetting the baby's white cheeks. Pain gripped her heart, squeezing until she could have screamed with the anguish of it. A life, a child, dead; dead while in her care; dead while under her protection. Dead.

She had envisaged such a future for the baby; love, happiness, laughter. She had worked her fingers to the bone so that this tiny creature could have a future. And that future had been stolen from her.

There would be no love for Beth; there would be no laughter. Just an empty hole in damp earth, just loneliness, just dissolution. She rocked harder, faster, dry sobs hiccuping through her body, her mouth open, gasping for air, desperate to give this small morsel of humanity comfort in whatever eternity it was in.

There was an arm around her shoulders, a hand touching hers. She had a feeling that they had been there for some time.

Slowly, with difficulty, she lifted her head. Agnes was there, her eyes red with weeping. Her face was as stiff and cold as ever but Helen could see beyond the façade now.

The other woman's hands were cold on hers, almost as cold as Beth's hands that Helen fondled as she rocked the child. 'Leave her be, love. She's better where she is. No one can hurt her now.'

Helen stroked the white cheek. 'She had so little. There was all this life out here for her, all this happiness. And she's dead. It's been taken from her before she even knew what happiness was. She's been robbed.'

'Life isn't all happiness.' Agnes voice was suddenly rough. 'There's pain and sickness here as well as good times.'

'She'd have had happiness,' Helen insisted. 'I would have made sure of that.'

She looked sadly down into the tiny face then, sighing, laid the body back in its cot, pulling the blankets up as if, even now, to keep the chill of the grave from the baby as long as possible. 'I had hoped the doctor could have saved her.'

'She were gone before he come.' Agnes, too, leaned over and twitched a corner of the blanket into place. 'He just shrugged and said these things happen and don't forget to register the death.' She swallowed. 'He were so – calm about it all.'

'Oh, Agnes.' Helen reached out and held the other woman. 'It must have been dreadful for you. And you all alone here. If only I had been here – if only I had got the doctor first–'

Agnes sniffed hard, rubbing her hand roughly across her eyes as Helen steered her tenderly out of the room. 'I reckon it wouldn't have done no good what you did. She were on her way out yesterday, I reckon. A small child – they aren't strong enough to stand much. Like flowers in the field, they are. Wither and die at the first touch of frost.'

'But she shouldn't have died!' Helen closed the door and, as if that frail barrier were enough to stop her from disturbing the dead baby's eternal sleep, she allowed her voice to rise, let the anger she had been keeping at bay flood through her. 'She was healthy. Strong. There was nothing wrong with her.'

'There never is anything wrong with them – until they die.' Agnes' voice was weighed down by bitter experience. 'God calls them and they go.'

'But not this time!' Helen swung round and hammered her fist into the wall of the passage, denting the plaster. 'Beth was killed. Murdered! By that damned calciner.'

'Here, my handsome, don't 'ee take on so.' Agnes reached out and took Helen's hands in hers, then gasped. 'You let me tend to these. What have you been doing to yourself?'

'What?' Helen came to with a start and stared at her hands. The knuckles of both were raw and bleeding. 'I don't know.' She shrugged the other woman aside. 'I don't matter. It's Beth that matters. Beth and–' She stopped dead. 'Oh, dear God!'

'Now what's the matter?'

'Jenny.' Helen reached out with her bleeding hands and clutched Agnes, shaking her to and fro with the violence of her passion. 'Jenny mustn't die, Agnes. She mustn't have her future taken from her too. I can't be responsible for her death as well.'

She picked up her skirts and began to run down the stairs.

'Here, where are you going? You're not responsible for Beth's death, you gert lummock. You couldn't have looked after her better if she were your own,' Agnes called after her.

'If she's dead then I didn't look after her

well enough.' There was a bottomless lake of desolation in Helen's heart. She would never forgive herself for Beth's death, never. However long she lived. But if she could save Jenny...

Clutching her skirts with bleeding, swollen hands, she ran from the house.

'Madam, you must be mad.'

The doctor's eyes blazed with anger. 'To suggest such a thing. Even to think it!' He shook his head, his hands waving aimlessly as he tried to find words to express his horror at her request. 'It's – it's – perverted.'

'It has to be done.' Helen gripped her hands tightly together, forcing herself to speak calmly. 'God only knows I don't like the idea any more than you do–'

'But you do!' His shaking finger pointed straight at her face and it took all her resolution not to back away from his fury. 'What you ask is a crime against all good feeling. An abomination.' He wiped his hand across his forehead. 'My only excuse for you, madam, is that you must be deranged by grief.'

She gritted her teeth. 'I am not deranged. But the death of this baby is important because–'

He interrupted her, leaning forward furiously across the scarred surface of his desk. 'The death of every baby is important, madam. To their families, as to God. Even to me. And do you know how many children that I have attended have died? Have you any conception of the total?' he shouted at her face.

Helpless in the face of his violence she could only shake her head dumbly.

'Nor have I,' he snapped. 'It runs into hundreds. Thousands, possibly. And–' he dropped his voice, leaned closer, his lips drawn back from his teeth, '–do you know how many of those parents have made the request that you have just made?'

She was about to answer when he brought his fist down on the desk, making papers and inkwell jump into the air. 'None,' he yelled. 'Not one.'

Helen took a deep breath, made her stand. 'I have a reason for this. I wish to find out what my niece died of.'

'You wish to find...' Words failed him. He dropped his head into his hands. She could see the bald spot on his head, the small flakes of dandruff that clung to the thinning strands. Then, slowly, he raised his face.

'In case you haven't realised it yet, my answer to your request is no.'

She took a deep breath. 'Then I shall have to go to another doctor.'

He laughed hollowly. 'You will be wasting your time. There is not a medical man in Penzance, in *Cornwall*, damn it, who would accede to your request. Dear God,' – he actually shuddered – 'to cut open a dead child! You must be mad.'

'But if it establishes what caused her death–'

He shouted her down. 'No!'

'If by doing it we can save another's life–'

'No!'

'Another child's–'

'No! No! No!' He stood, pointed at the door. 'You sicken me.' His voice vibrated with distaste. 'You make me want to vomit. Now go. And I swear, if I hear, if I even suspect, that you have visited any other medical man in the area with your perverted and disgusting request I shall have you committed to the nearest lunatic asylum. Now go.'

Helen went, her head drooping. The disgust that Doctor Tregarron had expressed had been nothing to the disgust she had felt when the idea (oh, God! that free-thinking, independent part of her mind!) had first come to her. The thought of anyone taking Beth's dead body and–

Even now she recoiled from the vision but she had forced herself on. If by this terrible desecration of the baby's dead body she saved another child's life, then surely it would be worth it? God, she was sure, would not reject an innocent for something that happened to her body after her death.

But the doctor's rejection of her had taken its toll. It had taken every ounce of her willpower to make the request of him. His threat did not dissuade her but she knew that she was physically unable to go through another scene like that. Besides, what would be the good? His violent rejection of her idea would almost certainly be mirrored by every other doctor in the town. They would not do it.

Her feet dragged. At home, the cows were waiting to be milked. At home, Agnes waited, needing comforting, Helen knew, as much as she did herself. At home, the dead body of Beth waited her, a silent reproach for her failure.

She felt exhausted. She must have walked thirteen or fourteen miles today, she realised as she forced her weary legs to climb the hill into Madron. At least, this time, she could go the direct route to the farm. There was no reason, now, to go round by the Trahairs.

It was as she was walking down the lane to the farm that she saw Nat walking up the hill towards her, his head bowed. More bad news. She sighed. So he had not been able to persuade his mother to have a doctor to see Jenny. She waited for him, almost grateful, despite her tiredness, for the chance to put off for a few moments longer her entry into the farmhouse.

He glanced up as he turned into the lane and saw her, pulling off his shapeless hat automatically. Then his eyes went to the farmhouse and he stopped. 'You've heard already, then? I was coming to tell you.'

'Tell me what?' Then she followed his gaze, saw the blank-eyed windows, realised what he meant. 'Oh, no.' It was a prayer. 'Please, no. Not Jenny too?'

He nodded. 'She died a couple of hours ago. I thought I'd better tell you.'

Twenty-Seven

'This is hardly an economic proposal, Mr Polglase.' Mr Blacklock put his fingertips together and gazed at Robert across the vast expanse of his desk.

Bankers! Robert cursed the whole set of them under his breath. He had been pleased at first that his meeting was with old Mr Blacklock: Robert had been at school with the son and wouldn't have trusted him as far as he could throw him. Old Mr Blacklock was failing fast, his body scarcely more than skin and bones; but his mind, damn it, was as sharp as ever.

'I only wish to close the calciner for a short time,' Robert protested. 'There are–'

he struggled for an explanation that would satisfy the old man, 'there are technical difficulties.' He leaned forward, forcing confidence into his voice. 'If we close the calciner and rebuild the chimney so that it is higher, we will retain more of the arsenic. That means that we will increase our profits in the long term.'

Blacklock showed no signs of softening. 'And in the short term?' He pulled a ledger towards him. 'As I understand it, Mr Polglase, it is only the income from the calciner that is allowing you to continue to run the mine – and service the loan which you have from us.' He glanced at the page, raised sharp but sunken eyes to Robert's face. 'And I presume you wish to borrow money to increase the height of the tower?'

'Well–' Robert shifted uneasily in his chair. 'Now that you mention it...'

Damn it, why couldn't he act with ease in these situations? Why couldn't he stroll in, throw down his hat, 'Look here, old boy, bit of a problem. Just a small loan.'

Not that that would work with this vulture. The banker wrote some figures on a piece of paper, his handwriting too small and crabbed for Robert to be able to read it upside down. 'Why do you need to make the tower higher, Mr Polglase?'

Damn the man. Straight to the point. And if he answered, the next question would be,

'And why didn't you build it taller in the first place?' And the only answer to that that Robert could honestly give would be, 'Because I was a blind fool.'

He had spent the time since Helen had left visiting friends of his father – smelters, miners – probing, asking. Not telling – he did not want the true scale of the problem to become known – but even his questions must have left some of the canny old men wondering.

And they had all agreed. 'Some gert chimney, you'd need to catch all that there arsenic,' they told him. 'How high did you say yours was?' And they'd shaken their heads. 'You'd get a better retrieval rate with a higher chimney.' 'You be losing a fair old whack of yer arsenic with it that short.' 'Why ever didn't you build 'un bigger, boy?'

And he knew why. With every reply the knowledge sank deeper and deeper into his soul, eating like poison into his self-respect. He had done it because Anthony had advised him to. *And Anthony had known at the time that the chimney was too short.*

The conclusion was inescapable. Some had worked it out on torn bits of paper bags; some had smoked, pursing their lips and gazing vaguely at the sky before they had given their answer; some had argued from theory – but the results were the same. The chimney should have been half as high again. And possibly, as an old friend of his father's had pointed out, careful not to meet Robert's eye, if it were in, say, a deep valley with shelter from the prevailing wind, perhaps double the height.

If these men had known it then Anthony must have also been aware of the fact. He was trained, educated. He had investigated the possibility of the calciner, the costs, the likely profits, and put the figures to Robert. And he had deliberately skimped on the building, knowing that this would also reduce the profits. Why?

There was only one reason.

Robert had agreed that Anthony could have fifty per cent of the profits if he put up a fifth of the building price.

Robert writhed in his seat. He had only agreed to such a division for two reasons. Because Theo had wanted it. And because he was certain that Anthony could not raise the money.

It was all he could do not to groan out loud as the full extent of his betrayal sank home.

His wife, his best friend and brother-in-law. The two people he had believed he could trust to the ends of the earth. They had conspired against him. They had cheated him. She had made him agree to the ruinous bargain and Anthony had deliberately skimped on the building so that he could pay his agreed portion of the costs.

They had made a criminal of him.

If Helen was right then he had been responsible for the ruin of her farm, the death of cattle and horses, *the death of old Mr Trahair.*

He remembered Theo, standing beside him in his study yesterday, arguing. 'There is no evidence. This allegation is slanderous. The calciner is safe.'

But she must have known. They must both have known.

The look of disdain on Helen's face as she left had been like a spear through the heart.

She had been so dignified, so straight. Her head had been high, her pallor enhanced by the mourning she still wore for her sister. His heart had gone out to her. He longed to help her, to comfort her, to throw caution and legal arguments to the wind and offer her compensation, apologies, promises.

But Theo was there. Theo was the woman he had once loved. Theo was the woman he had promised before God to put before all others. He could not betray her. He had to–

'Mr Polglase? Are you listening?'

Robert jerked himself back to the present. 'I am sorry. My mind was wandering.'

Blacklock frowned. 'It is not surprising that you find your finances in a tangle if you pay so little attention to them.'

Robert opened his mouth but what could

he say? 'It is not lack of attention, but too much trust'? He lowered his gaze. 'I'm sorry. If you could repeat what you said, please.'

Blacklock gave him a despairing look but announced, 'I am willing to give you the increased loan you asked for which will allow you to rebuild the chimney on the calciner and keep your mine going in the meantime.'

It was more than he had believed possible. Robert opened his mouth to express his thanks but Blacklock went on, 'All I require is the deeds to your house as collateral.'

The bloodsucker! The house was worth double the total of all his loans to Blacklock's. But that was Blacklock all over. He'd made a fortune out of other people's misfortunes. But his house! The house his father had built. The house that Theo had married him for.

He struggled, knowing that it was no use, that he had to have the money. 'But that means – if I default–'

'You lose your home.' Blacklock smiled thinly. 'That is my offer. Do you require time to think about it?'

Seated at one end of the kitchen table Nat struggled to convey the depth of his feelings in a voice thick with tears.

'She were so lovely, see, so–' His thick

hands described helpless circles in the air as he struggled for a word to describe his sister. 'So – valiant.'

As if embarrassed by his sudden flight into poetry he buried his red face in his thick arms, shielding himself even from Helen's sympathetic gaze.

She blinked. 'You're right, Nat. That is the perfect word for Jenny. Valiant.' She reached out and touched his thick, hairy forearm gently, swallowing the lump in her throat. Already the farm seemed empty, lifeless, without her.

To know that never again would the tiny figure, hair flaming in the sunshine, stomp round the corner on bare feet, her arm companionably around the neck of a cow, asking, 'Haven't you cleaned that there bucket yet, Helen?' Never again to see her lopsided grin as she hitched her skirts higher above the farmyard muck, hear her trenchant comments on Helen's first attempts at milking – 'Awkward as a cow with a musket, you are' – never to be on the receiving end of a grin that lit up her plain, face – Helen bowed her head to hide her brimming eyes.

Nat reached for her hand. 'You too?'

She nodded, sniffing. 'I loved her, I really did. She – she made life here bearable. Whatever was wrong she always rose to the challenge.' Her voice broke. 'I put so much onto her,' she mourned. 'I let her take too much responsibility.'

'You couldn't have stopped her if there was animals around,' he comforted her. 'No one could. Mad on them, she were. Always was, from a child.' His face crumpled suddenly. 'I loved 'er, too,' he whispered, his voice rough with emotion. 'She were the youngest after me and we grew up together. Always so full of life and now...' He lowered his face on his arms, his shoulders shaking.

'That damned calciner.' Helen had never sworn before in her whole life but no other word could express her hatred of the building. 'Spewing out its filth, corrupting, poisoning everything it touches.' Even Beth, even her friendship with Robert.

Agnes stood at the table. A folded sheet softened the surface and on it, carefully, gently, she was ironing the clothes that Beth would be buried in.

'There's no point in fighting it; there's nothing to be done.' She raised red-rimmed eyes from the delicate lace frill around the edge of a bonnet that she was straightening with shaking fingers. 'The gentry are all the same. They live in their grand houses while we–' her voice broke and she steadied it with an effort, '–we live and die like animals in our hovels. And what do they care, as long as they have their money and their gee-gaws?'

Nat slammed his fist on to the table,

making the crockery rattle and slopping beer from the tankard Agnes had poured him onto the white deal table. 'I care!' His voice was hoarse with emotion. 'I care a brem lot. She were my sister. She were the light of my life and she's dead! Dead before her time! And your babby too. Both of them. Dead and gone. And there's nothing we can do about it.'

'Anthony.' Theo flung herself into her brother's arms. 'I haven't seen you for an age. Why haven't you called?'

He held her from him, gazing down at her with the half-humorous quirk of his mouth that was so typical of him. 'What's the matter, sister mine? Bored? You don't usually greet me like this.'

She pulled him into the drawing room out of hearing of the butler. 'Bored out of my life,' she said petulantly. 'I haven't seen anyone for days. Even Robert is out all the time. And you?' She pushed him into the chair, stood over him. 'What do you mean by getting engaged to that girl at the farm and leaving Robert to break the news? What way is that to treat your sister?'

He was silent, staring at the carpet. In the afternoon sunlight she could see that his face was thinner, that there were lines running from nose to mouth, dark shadows under his eyes. Her heart constricted with fear. If Anthony was looking older – if her handsome, laughing brother was also showing signs of age – what hope had she? She shot a quick glance at her reflection in the looking-glass over the fire but she was looking as lovely as ever. Relieved, she turned her attention back to her brother. 'What is it? What's the matter? You're looking' – she could not bring herself to say the word 'old' – 'unwell.'

He raised haggard eyes to her. 'I am not engaged to Helen Schofield.'

She snorted. 'Typical of Robert! Though how even a fool like him could get such a thing wrong–'

'You don't understand.' His voice was harsh and she stopped, staring at him. 'I was engaged but she – broke it off.'

For a second Theo could not get her breath. 'She broke it off!' It was unbelievable. 'Engaged to you and she broke it off?' Fury on her brother's behalf surged through her. She clenched her fists. 'How dare she? How dare she? Who does she think she is? Jilting my brother!'

Then, seeing his face, she flung her arms around him, hugging him. 'Never mind. A handsome man like you can do far better for yourself than her. There are much better brides for you around, much richer, much prettier–'

He threw her off, rising to his feet as if he

couldn't bear her touch any longer. 'Can't you understand? Don't you ever listen to what I tell you?' His face was contorted suddenly, as it had been when he was a young boy. 'I–' His voice rasped awkwardly. 'I loved her. It wasn't just the land, not this time. It was her. I wanted to marry Helen Schofield for herself.'

She stared at him, feeling that the carpet was undulating under her feet. 'But – I've seen her. She was here. She's not even pretty...'

'For God's sake, Theo!' Anthony slammed his hand down on the mantelpiece, making the ornaments rattle. 'What's that got to do with it?'

She could hardly believe her ears. 'But – but–' If beauty wasn't important, then what was?

He moved across to her in one quick stride and grabbed her by the shoulders, shaking her. 'That woman has character, breeding, standards. Even though you may have the morals of an alley cat surely you can appreciate what she is? How superior she is to either of us?'

'But she isn't even rich,' Theo protested, struggling to understand.

He laughed, shortly. 'No. And do you know, I would have married her if she didn't have a penny to her name.' He ran his fingers through his fair hair, disturbing the careful arrangement of his locks. 'Me!' He snorted with derision at himself 'Me, with the debtor's prison hanging over me and creditors hammering at the door. And I'd have married her anyway.'

She hadn't realised his financial problems were as bad as he said. Certainly, he didn't look poor. His black frock coat was new, his linen impeccable even on a hot day like this. Suddenly protective, she reached out to him, laying a slender white hand on his dark sleeve. 'There's no problem, Anthony. I'll get the money from Robert. He won't let you get sent to prison for debt.'

'Robert!' The laugh caught in his throat. 'Sister mine, you just don't understand. Robert doesn't have the money to save me. He may not even have the money to save himself.'

'It isn't right!' Helen sat straighter, her face set with fury. 'Money should make no difference. People should have rights, whoever they are.'

Agnes snorted. 'You just say that because you aren't really poor. Not like us. You've got no money but you've got rich relations, relations with power and influence. You've got an education. It's the likes of us what can't do nothing. The law is all on the side of the rich and them with learning.'

Helen wanted to protest but she knew it

was true. If she had the money to pay for a private prosecution she could stop the calciner herself. It was too late for Beth and Jenny but there were other children out there, other old people who deserved to live out their allotted span. She lowered her head in her hands, feeling despair wash over her. That calciner was evil. And she knew it. 'Oh God!' Her anguish was choking her. 'If there was something I could do. I would tear that calciner down brick from brick with my bare hands if I thought it would do any good, but it won't.'

She raised her head and met Nat's gaze, tears sliding unheeded down her pale cheeks. 'There's nothing I can do. Nothing!'

But there was a new look in Nat's eyes, a sudden excitement in his face as he said, 'There is something...'

George Penhaligon watched Theo carefully. 'Why?' he demanded.

The message from the shop had been almost too good to be true and he had hesitated a long time before following it up, suspecting a trap. But his reception had been friendly. Too friendly. The woman was too eager and excited. George could feel his nervousness growing. Something was going on that he did not understand – yet.

His simple question seemed to throw Theo off balance. 'Why?' She struggled visibly for a reason. 'Well, I just – I–' she pulled herself together with an effort. 'The law says that your wife has no right to desert you like this and as I know where she is I thought it right to tell you.'

George stared at the woman in front of him. As a confidence trickster himself he had developed an ear for knowing when people were lying and this woman radiated untruthfulness. But even without that, he wouldn't have believed her. He hadn't been born yesterday. All these bitches stuck together, whatever the law said. Even his own sister had once supported Aggie against himself.

'That idn't enough,' he said firmly. He kept his eyes on her, trying not to be intimidated by the soft carpet; the furniture, so clean, so pretty; the knick-knacks that covered every surface, any one of which would have kept him in drink for a month. 'There's got to be another reason.'

Theo raised her chin, so smooth, so delightful. Her neck was a white column that he longed to kiss, to sink his teeth into in a passionate love bite. Why could he never have a woman like this? Her voice when she spoke was haughty. 'Are you daring to say that I am lying?'

He'd dare anything for a couple of hours with a body like hers. 'Yes,' he said uncompromisingly, determined not to be browbeaten by her. There was something behind this strange desire to rat on another woman and he wouldn't act until he knew what it was. He was nobody's dupe. Besides, where someone wanted something there was always room for a little manipulation.

Especially where someone wanted something as badly as she did. Her need was palpable. Under normal circumstances she would have thrown him out for his insolence. Under normal circumstances she wouldn't have let him in the house. Yet he had seen the relief in her face when he had been announced and now she was scarcely reacting to his rudeness, her great blue eyes troubled and doubting as she stared at him, her emotions running across her beautiful face like a cat's-paw over a still sea.

He decided to test how far he could push her. He sat himself down on the velvet chair, watched her mouth open to protest then close again, smiled to himself. 'Look, Missis.' He crossed one leg over the other, wriggled himself more comfortably into the seat. 'Why don't you tell me what it is you're after?' He tried a reassuring smile. 'Mebbe you and me might find we got a common cause in all this somewhere, eh?'

He had almost pushed her too far. Theo's voice was frosty as she said, 'I can imagine no possible common interest between the two of us.'

'But there is one, idn't there? My Aggie, for a start.' God, but she was lovely! All that yellow hair and a waist he could put his hands around. Lucky old Mr Polglase having that in bed with him every night. He leaned forward. 'I aren't saying I'm not interested in what you got to tell me, I just want to know why. And,' he said quickly, as she opened her mouth, 'I do know it's more than your desire to see the law kept so you needn't spin me that one again.'

'You have no right to know my reasons for anything I do.' But he heard the uncertainty in her voice and rejoiced. He was on to something here, something he might be able to turn to his advantage. After all, he already knew that Aggie was somewhere close at hand. It wouldn't take him long to track his wife down now he knew where to look even if Mrs Smoothbody here wouldn't tell him. But, with the proper leverage, he might get more out of her than just the information – money, perhaps.

He leaned forward. 'Come on, Missus, tell me why.' His voice was friendly, wheedling. 'We're both in this together, aren't we?'

She looked as if she would have preferred not to be but after a moment's hesitation she said, 'Your wife is working for – a person. I would rather that that person did not have your wife working there.'

The words were careful, hiding as much as

they gave away, but he was experienced at getting information out of people. The trick was to get them started. Once they had told you the first thing it was easier for them to tell you the next.

He stared at his dusty boots, thinking. 'My taking Aggie away won't stop her getting in another woman.' The easiest way to elicit information was not to ask questions but to make statements.

She fell for it as they all did. 'But it will!' Her voice was eager, animated. 'The farm is thought unlucky. Once your wife has gone the – person – will be all alone with a small child. She will have to leave then.'

She? A child? There was enough information in that sentence alone to enable him to find the right place by the end of the day. But he wanted to know more. He eyed Theo carefully, taking in her perfectly coiffured hair, her clothes that exactly matched her blue eyes. God had been good to her when he gave out beauty but no one looked like that without a hell of a lot of effort. And no one who was that vain would tolerate a husband's straying.

Dropping his eyes to his boots again, he stated, 'But husbands have been known to provide other accommodation for a – person – if they find themselves without a servant. Especially if there is a child involved.'

'Fool!' She was on her feet, her voice quivering with fury. 'Of course it is not my husband's child. How dare you think such a thing!' He half expected her to tug the embroidered bell-pull, have him thrown out, but to his interest she didn't. She must want something *awfully* badly.

She sat, holding onto her temper with a visible effort. 'That woman has jilted my brother. Is that reason enough for you? And I want her out of here, out of the farm, out of the district.' Her voice grew shriller as emotion broke through, tightening her lips. Perhaps Mr Polglase didn't have such a fun time with this little lady after all.

He suppressed a satisfied smile. 'I can help you there, Missis. No problem.' He hesitated artistically. 'I can take my wife away, no problem, but it might be possible to – give the woman extra reasons for leaving, if you get my meaning. I could make it too uncomfortable for her to stay on here as long as you don't have any objection if the female were to be – hurt?'

From the look on her face she wouldn't have objected if he had said he would kill the cow. 'Well,' he went on, his voice gaining in confidence, 'I think I'm your man. I just need two things from you. One is the address of this here farm.'

'And the other?'

Now he couldn't keep the grin from his

face. 'The other is money, Missis. I'm not doing anything illegal without getting paid for it – and getting paid well.'

Robert had waited until after dinner to tell her. He had waited until the tea had been brought into the drawing room, until Theo had settled herself in her favourite chair, until there was no danger of the servants overhearing. And then he told her.

'I am closing the calciner.'

Coming out of the blue it took a second before she appreciated what he had said. He could see the realisation dawn, the widening of the great blue eyes, the sudden tension that tightened her cheeks. 'What?'

He took a deep breath. 'I am closing the calciner. For a time. To make the chimney taller.'

'But the income?' Trust Theo to latch on to money first thing. 'We need the income.'

It was he who needed the income to keep the mine going. Holding on to his temper he said, 'I am borrowing from the bank to pay for the bigger chimney. And to pay the men's wages at the mine.' Another deep breath. Legally, it was none of her business but she was his wife. He owed it to her to tell her what he was planning. 'I am going to put up this house as surety.'

She was on her feet, face white except for two red spots over the cheekbones so that he realised for the first time that she used rouge. 'You can't do that!' Her voice was a screech. 'You can't risk my house like that.'

'Our house, Theo.' A sudden vision of his mother came to mind. She would never have minded if his father had done this. They had discussed everything together and often they had disagreed, but once he had made his decision she had supported him all the way.

Theo turned on him, her face contorted. 'It's my house. I live here. You're never here. Never around. You'd be quite happy living in a *cottage!*' She made it sound like the ultimate in insults, which it probably was to her.

He said calmly, 'I hope that the calciner will only be closed for a short time. Once it is reopened we should make bigger profits because the arsenic which is presently coming out of the chimney will stay in the works and can be sold.'

'Sold!' she hissed. 'And how much difference will that make? Not enough to pay for the cost of the chimney. And you're risking my house for that?'

Keeping his temper with an effort, Robert said quietly, 'There should be no danger of our losing the house. But even if there were, I would still have to do it.' He moved towards her, holding out his hands beseechingly. 'Theo, people are dying out there. An old man, children. I cannot let that happen.'

'But you don't know it's the fault of the calciner,' she snapped. 'People of that class die all the time. Why should I lose my house because of it?'

His anger was growing uncontrollably. 'If you lose your house, Theo,' Robert said, 'it will be because your brother cheated me when it was built. He deliberately built the chimney too low to save money. Just so that he could meet our agreement about sharing the profits equally. The agreement *you* persuaded me into, Theo. Think about that. If you lose your house it is because you and your brother put profits before the safety of other people.'

'Other people!' Her voice was a harridan-like shriek. 'You don't care about other people. The only person you are thinking of is that bitch at the farm.'

'Leave Helen out of this,' he began.

'How can I leave her out? She's the one who's caused all these problems. She's the one who's got you and Anthony both running round her like dogs after a bitch in heat, she's the one–'

He moved forward, caught her wrist. 'I said, leave her out of this.'

She dragged her hand from his grasp. 'She's not even pretty! She's nothing! Nothing! And you are throwing me out of my house because of her!'

'I'm not throwing you out of anywhere, for

God's sake.' He took a deep breath, fighting for self-control. 'She has simply alerted me to a problem.' He looked at her sadly. 'Theo, for heaven's sake! You're my wife. You have no reason to feel like this about Helen.'

'Helen! Helen! I hate that name! And I hate her!' Theo swung round the room, the deep blue satin of her dress shining softly in the lamplight. 'She turns on her charms and you and Anthony rush around her like flies round a jam pot. And then she uses you.

'Oh, yes, she does,' she went on as Robert tried to interrupt. 'Uses you and then throws you away. Like Anthony who she dropped like a hot potato as soon as that niece of hers became ill. As the owner of the farm–'

'Owner?' He took a step forward, his face paling. 'But her niece Beth–'

'Is dead or dying, according to Anthony,' Theo snapped. 'And the desirable Helen is now the owner of a farm and too proud to want to marry a poor country doctor. Oh no. She's lifting her sights now.'

'Beth, dead.' Robert sank into the chair. 'Oh, dear God, I didn't know.' He glanced up. 'It wasn't – she didn't die because of–'

Theo said cruelly, 'She probably killed the child herself in order to inherit the farm.'

'That's ridiculous!' He was on his feet. 'How dare you even think that! She loved the child, doted on her! And what good would the farm do her anyway? Thanks to the calciner it's worthless. Worthless! And now she's lost that little baby. Poor woman.'

'Poor woman!' Theo snapped. 'What about me? At least she's got a roof over her head. I'm your wife and you are not sparing a thought for me and what I might be suffering.'

'Suffering? You'll never suffer,' he said bitterly. 'You have to care about other people to really suffer. And you don't do that, Theo. I know that now. You don't even care about me.'

'Why should I care about you?' she snapped. 'A good-for-nothing oaf. A fool. A jumped-up peasant with only your money to make you acceptable. And now you don't even have that.'

He looked at her sadly. 'It seems to me,' he said, his voice suddenly quiet, 'that I don't have anything. And that includes the love of my wife.'

And he turned and left her.

Twenty-Eight

'Explosives? Here?'

The small lamp Nat was holding swung slowly around a shed Helen had previously only glanced inside. Of all the machinery stored there the only thing she had recognised was a plough. Now, the strange machines sent weird shadows leaping wildly around the shed, and the cobwebs overhead extended dusty fingers, swaying in the night air.

Nat gave a grunt of satisfaction. 'There they are. See?' He swung the lantern and Helen saw three small casks piled in the corner of the shed, half hidden by the plough.

'John Trethowan bought 'un off me. We was going to blow up they rocks in the upper meadow back there so that his gert horse could plough up the whole lot without stopping.' Nat handed the lantern to her then pulled one of the casks out and, taking it to the doorway where there was more room, he levered the top off. Black powder trickled through his fingers and Helen's nose twitched at the smell of it. 'Yes, 'tes all here, right enough.'

Helen felt nervous just being so close to explosives. 'But where did you get the stuff from?'

Nat looked at her as if she were mad. 'I'm a miner, aren't I?'

'I thought,' she said vaguely, her eyes on the cask at her feet, 'that you used picks.'

'Picks!' His voice vibrated with scorn. 'We aren't digging out coal.' He almost spat out the word. 'Deep in the granite, tin is, and we have to blast 'un out.' He snorted again. "'Tes hard enough, God knows, just drilling holes to put the explosives in, but picks!'

'I'm sorry.' Helen dragged her eyes away from the cask. To think that she had been sleeping here all this time, not knowing that just yards away there was all this explosive... 'Is it safe?' she asked nervously.

'Unless you get a spark in it,' he said and she jumped nervously backwards swinging the lantern as far away as possible. He laughed shortly. 'It idn't that bad. I do work with a candle on my helmet down the mine and I'm still alive to talk about it – though there's plenty as aren't.'

'So how–'

He showed her some cord. 'It's a fuse, see. You put one end in the powder, set light to the other and run like hell.' He saw her face and amended his words. 'I were joking, miss. 'Tes quite safe if you know what you're doing.'

Helen fingered the cord, fighting with her conscience. To stop the poison spreading – yes, that was good, but to bankrupt Robert Polglase? 'You really think that we could blow up the calciner?'

The calciner had to be stopped, she reminded herself. There was no other alternative. How many animals and people had already died because of it? How many more would die in the future? Helen took a deep breath. She could not stand by and let other people suffer and die because she lacked the strength of mind to act. But to bankrupt Robert Polglase – to commit a crime of this magnitude–

Nat's hands clenched convulsively. 'I could do it, no trouble. That damned works deserves to be destroyed. And Robert Polglase with it. He's nothing but a bloody murderer.'

'I'm sure he didn't do it deliberately.' Helen felt moved by an obscure wish to defend Robert Polglase.

She felt the fuse cord again, her mind racing. The calciner had killed Beth and Jenny. If nothing were done, how many other children would die? But to blow it up...

The penalties for crimes against property were vicious – until recently, transportation and hanging had been common punishments for theft although in these enlightened times imprisonment was the rule. But to blow up a place which employed men – to deliberately destroy a profitable business...

Helen swallowed. It had to be done, she reminded herself She had no other legal way of stopping the calciner, and if Robert Polglase was bankrupted as a result... She brought her mind swiftly back on track. It had to be stopped whatever the cost to herself. Besides, what had she to look forward to in life? Living with her grandmother in genteel poverty then, after the old woman's death, life as a slave being a companion to rich old women. At least this way she would keep her self-respect, this way she would know that she had done what she believed was her duty.

'Could I blow the works up by myself?'

She was scarcely aware that she had spoken the words aloud until she heard Nat's contemptuous snort. 'You? You got to know about explosives, see. You got to put them where the blast will do the most harm. And you don't even know nothing about the works, do 'ee?' He raised an eyebrow at her. 'You can't just put these here kegs any old place and expect them to do much harm. And you can't just blow the works up any old time either. When the lambreth is full there's tons of arsenic in there. Blow it up at the wrong time and you'll poison half of Cornwall, I reckon.'

Her heart sank. But there had to be a way. 'If you would teach me, tell me what to do...'

Nat stared at her across the cask of death. 'Tell you? It were my sister that were killed, as well as your Beth. I'm bloody well going to blow it up myself.'

But she would take the responsibility, Helen decided. After it was done, she would go to Robert, she would tell him what she had done and why. And she would make sure that Nat wouldn't suffer. He was a young man with a life ahead of him, prospects, a family who needed him.

She opened her mouth to say this when he took her breath away by adding, thoughtfully, 'And it's got to be done tonight.'

'Oh, not tonight.' Helen felt panic rise within her. It was too soon. She needed time. 'I – I – we can't just blow it up like that.'

Nat shook his head stubbornly. 'They turned the furnace off a couple of days ago so that they could collect all the powder and barrel 'un up. And there have been carts coming and going all day up the far lane, which means that the place is as free of powder as it will ever be.'

Tonight. She would have liked to have buried Beth first, said her proper goodbyes to Agnes, written a letter to her grandmother – but all these things were trifles, she told herself furiously. What was most important was that never again would a family mourn the loss of a child, dead before its time because of the calciner.

She took a deep breath. 'Tonight,' she agreed.

Robert was out of the door before she realised he was going.

Suddenly, Theo felt afraid. She had come to take him for granted, certain that through smiles or guile she could make him do as she wanted. But this was a new Robert; stronger, resolute, no longer asking her permission but making up his own mind, going his own way.

'Robert. Robert.' She gathered up her dark blue satin skirts and ran after him, struggling momentarily with the doorknob. 'Robert, where are you going?'

But the only answer was the slam of the front door.

He had gone out. He had left her. But she could guess his intention. He was going to see *that woman.* He was going to tell her that he was agreeing to her ridiculous demands.

Anger and jealously burned in her stomach like acid. How dare he. How dare he! She'd show them. She was the most beautiful woman in west Cornwall. She wasn't going to be made to look a fool by losing her husband to some plain-faced bitch with no money or style. She'd find them and stop them. Tell them both what she thought of them. She wouldn't sit quietly at home while her husband made love to another woman.

Her slippers almost silent on the polished stairs, Theo ran for her shawl.

Alone in his rooms, Anthony lifted the glass

of brandy to his lips.

Despair. Now he knew the real meaning of the word; now at last he could understand his father, the reason he had shot his brains out. Despair.

No Helen. And without her – what? His debts were already too great to pay and once the story of the calciner got around his reputation would be in shreds. No profession; no money, no wife.

No future.

He swallowed the glass of liquor, not even tasting it as it burned its way down his throat. The small, mean room, which he occupied as seldom as possible, seemed to close around him like a prison cell.

A gentleman. That was all he had ever wanted to be. It was his birthright, wasn't it? He deserved it. He had the looks, the manners, the education of a gentleman. He had all the attributes – except money.

He poured more brandy, the glass ringing as his shaking hands banged it against the edge of the decanter. Robert was a gentleman – just. In his case money and a big house were enough to offset a money-grabbing oaf of a father while Anthony–

He had been up against it before but there had always been a way out. At the least he had always had the stakes to go gambling, to trust his future to the turn of a card, the roll of a ball.

And now, nothing. His future was in Helen's hands. It was what he had wanted – but not like this. Not like this at all.

They had said in the clubs that the child was dead and Anthony knew what that meant. Beth's death would drive Helen to close the calciner down whatever the cost to herself.

And whatever the cost to him. He swallowed more brandy, staring blankly at the embroidered fire-screen that covered the empty fireplace. There would only be one way to stop Helen now.

To kill her.

And he could not do it. He poured more brandy, drank it, trying to hide from himself the depth of his self-loathing.

A gentleman! He didn't have the money to be a gentleman, he didn't have the land.

But he did have one gentlemanly instinct. He could not knowingly harm a woman.

It would not be long before everyone knew. If Robert told Theo, their servants would know, then it would spread out through the whole district. No marriage for Doctor Ledgerwood.

And the calciner – that would get abroad too. The chemists who had done the analysis, the farrier, the slaughterhouse man – all would know about her enquiry, about the results, and they would pass the word on.

How long before it came to the ears of his debtors?

Not long. Not long at all.

A knock on the front door, the heavy steps of his landlady on the stairs. 'A – person – to see you, Doctor.'

He drained his glass for the last time, put it carefully down on the table beside the chair.

'I will come immediately, Mrs Stringer.'

Back straight, head up, step firm, he walked down the stairs.

A gentleman.

'Ready, are you?' In the dimness of the shed Helen could just make out that Nat held two casks, one under each arm, as if they were small piglets.

She swallowed nervously, hating the idea of carrying explosive so close to her body. 'Of course,' she lied, wiping damp palms down the sides of her skirt, then bent and lifted the remaining cask.

''Twon't hurt 'ee. I do carry these here casks of powder up and down ladders every time I do go down the mine.'

Helen nodded, following him out into the yard, trying to act more confidently than she felt. She glanced up at the farmhouse, noting with relief that Agnes' window was dark. Agnes had enough troubles already; Helen did not want her to be implicated in this in any way. For a second she worried that the house was left empty and unlocked. But surely Agnes would not try to leave now? Not with Beth's tiny corpse still lying in the nursery.

Leaving the shelter of the shed she staggered slightly as the wind caught her. For the first time since she had come to Cornwall the weather had changed. Gale force winds drove black clouds tumbling across the sky, hiding the moon. She shivered, telling herself it was from the cold, it wasn't nerves, of course it wasn't nerves.

Out of the yard and she cast a last glance at the house. Still not too late to change her mind, still not too late – but she had to do it. For Beth. For Jenny. For other children who might eat food contaminated by the poison. She turned away and followed Nat's dimly seen figure down the lane.

Twenty-Nine

Stupid, stupid man! In her fury Theo wondered yet again what had ever possessed her to marry Robert Polglase. Surely, after their argument this evening, he wasn't just going to wander around the countryside in the dark? Any real man would have gone straight to his mistress, but then Robert...

She hesitated. The weather was changing, the calm days giving way to more blustery weather with clouds scudding fast across the sky. No weather for a lady to be out walking. Besides, perhaps she had been wrong; perhaps she had been misled by her jealousy... She stopped, shivering, and peered through the darkness, trying to make out Robert's figure. If he was simply walking off his anger...

Then he turned aside down the lane that led to the farm. Theo smiled in grim satisfaction and, wrapping her dark shawl more securely around her head as a protection against the buffeting of the wind, she followed him on soundless feet.

The wind and darkness were a relief to George Penhaligon. They acted as a shield to his own activities and made it less likely that other people would be wandering around at night.

Not that there were likely to be many people here, anyway, he decided with satisfaction. From his point of view the farmhouse was perfectly sited; away from the main road and with no other houses near. He cracked his knuckles cheerfully. He was doing what he had always planned and being paid for it as well. Life was good.

The wind gusted louder, sending dust and

hay flying around the farmyard. Even outside, he could hear the rattle of loose casement windows. Things couldn't be better. With the wind rattling the windows and moaning through the chimneys, Aggie and her friend would never hear him break in.

Moving quietly, keeping close to the walls just in case there were unfriendly eyes, George made his way to the front door. In the shadow of its porch no one would be able to see him work on the lock.

But when he lifted the latch the door opened quietly of its own accord.

Scarcely able to believe his luck, George stepped into the silent farmhouse.

In the bedroom overlooking the farmyard Agnes tossed and turned. She was never a good sleeper at the best of times. Too many years waiting for George to come home, too many nights wondering if the constables would come this time, or the debt collectors, or some angry husband.

She rolled over, pulling the blankets high around her ears to block out the noise of the wind, but her eyes were wide open as she stared into the darkness.

To close them meant to see Beth again, her tiny body smaller than ever in death. To see the petal face framed in the carefully goffered lace frill. Despite herself, Agnes felt her eyes fill with tears. Foolish. She hadn't cried when she had lost her own baby. But then she had been too ill, too weak, too afraid of George and his fists.

Now, in the peace of this house, the loss of the child that was not her own ripped her heart asunder. In these last weeks Beth and her welfare had been her first waking thought and, before going to bed, her last act had been to check on the child, breathe in her fragrance, bury her face in the sweet-smelling blankets that covered her, luxuriate in the tiny, lined hands, the immense eyelashes, the smile...

She rolled back again, pulling the pillow over her head. Never again to hold Beth in her arms, never to kiss her. Agnes stifled a groan. The child's death had left a hole in her life that could never be filled.

The wind howled around the farmhouse, and a sudden gust made the windows rattle. Agnes pulled the pillow closer, stifling the noise of the storm and her own sobs in the soft down.

'See, you has to put it where it's going to do some good. Leave it out in the open and nothing much won't happen. We got to make sure that this whole works is blown to high heaven.'

Helen nodded dumbly. Thank God for Nat. Even if she had known that the explosive existed she wouldn't have had any idea how to set about blowing up the calciner.

Nat had encountered no problems breaking the lock to get into the main part of the building. Here it all seemed quite normal. In the soft glow of a candle she could see an office, a battered desk with an untidy stack of paper held down by a large piece of rock, hooks on the wall for coats, a long trough.

Nat pointed. 'That's where they do wash all the muck off. 'Tes important, specially in this hot weather we've been having. Da do say that if you sweat with arsenic dust on you you do get brem awful sores.'

Helen nodded again, afraid to trust her voice. Now that they were actually here she could hardly breathe for fear. She looked down at the casks at her feet. So innocent-looking. As innocent-looking as this office.

Nat followed her glance. 'Three casks.' He eyed them speculatively. 'I reckon one under the furnace, one in the lambreth and one under the tower should do 'un.' He turned to Helen. 'You do the lambreth. It won't matter where you do put 'un in there. 'Tes all shut in, with low ceilings and all. Any explosion will be sure to blow a gert piece out.'

He pointed through a further doorway. Helen nodded and bent to pick up a cask but he stopped her. 'Don't go through there without yer cotton. You don't want to breathe the stuff.' He reached into a wrapping and withdrew a ball of fluffy white cotton wool. 'Put it into yer nostrils and yer ears. And make sure you do breathe through yer nose. You don't want this stuff in your chest if you can help it.'

She reached out and took the small ball. It seemed a small protection against something so deadly. 'Is this enough?' Her voice shook.

He shrugged casually. 'It's all Da do have and he seems to thrive on it.' He picked up a second cask. 'I'll put this under the furnace.' He grinned suddenly, his teeth white in the darkness. ''Tes a good thing the furnace has been out while they've been clearing out the arsenic. One small spark and this stuff is off.'

I wish he hadn't mentioned that, Helen thought as she pulled the ball of wool apart and pushed small pieces into her nostrils. It was difficult to get the balance right, she discovered. Too much and she wasn't able to breathe at all but she was afraid that too little would mean that she inhaled the deadly dust.

She picked up the candle he had left behind. One small spark... She eyed the cask nervously. Better to find out what was behind the door, find a place for the cask, then come back for it. She pushed open the further door.

She found herself in a long narrow room

that ran the whole length of the building. The far end was closed and barred by double doors, large enough to admit a horse and cart. Everywhere the floor was white with gritty arsenic dust which gathered in drifts against the bottom of the walls and powdered the thick window sills.

Along the windowless long wall, small open doorways gaped every few feet, and beside them, metal plates leaned against the bricks. Curious, she moved forward, holding the candle higher, and peered into the dark opening.

She had found the lambreth. Repeating the word to herself she could realise now that it was a Cornish corruption of the word 'labyrinth'. In the flickering light of the candle she could see that it was merely a long, low passage that wound to and fro up the length of the building. White powder on the floor and caught in cracks and irregularities of the walls showed that this was where the arsenic came from.

A sudden noise echoing out of the lambreth made her jump nervously before she realised that it was only Nat at the furnace. The whole tunnel was a giant chimney, she realised. The arsenic-bearing rock and crude arsenic was heated until it evaporated and was carried down this long chimney, cooling all the time, until it condensed back into the white powder that she saw everywhere around her. It was obvious that when the furnace was being used the metal plates were fixed in the openings to seal off the chimney from the room. Only when the furnace was out were they opened up so that the white arsenic could be shovelled out.

Helen swung round. Yes. There was a shovel and wheelbarrow, both bearing traces of the white powder. Lifting the candle higher she moved down the room. Further on there was a stone mill and paper-lined wooden barrels stencilled with the name 'Polglase Arsenic Works'.

Even now, when the filled barrels had just been sent off, there was still arsenic dust everywhere. Again she gave silent thanks for Nat and his knowledge. If the lambreth had been full, blowing up the calciner would have poisoned the whole countryside.

She moved back again to the lambreth. If Nat was going to blow up the furnace at one end and the chimney at the other, then for maximum damage she should place her cask in the centre of the lambreth.

But she wasn't going to carry the cask and a candle at the same time. She dripped a little melted wax onto the window sill and fixed the candle to it then went back for the cask and fuse.

It was no good. She had fought it as long as

she could. Soon, too soon, the child would be lost for her for ever and with her, Agnes feared, her only reason for living. Just once more to see the baby, just once more to gaze at her face, mourn again the life that had been lost, the potential for happiness, the potential for love.

She thrust back the blankets and, wrapping a shawl around her, moved silently to the nursery, anxious not to make any sound that would wake Helen. She had enough troubles to deal with; let her sleep while she could.

But even as she leaned over the cradle, trying in the darkness to make out the faint outlines of the child's face, she heard stealthy footsteps coming along the corridor.

Agnes froze. Helen was already worried about her, she knew. Although she had never said anything, Agnes knew that Helen found her obsession with the dead child strange and distasteful. She held her breath, standing motionless, praying that Helen wouldn't look in here.

There was the creak of a door opening. Agnes looked over her shoulder but the nursery door was still closed. The only other door in this part of the house led to an unused bedroom. Why would Helen be creeping in there in the middle of the night?

Her heart was suddenly pounding, her breathing harsh with fear. Eyes on the still closed door she listened, ears searching for every sound.

Click. Click.

Almost beyond the limit of hearing. If she hadn't been listening so intently she would never have heard the minute sound. But once heard it was instantly recognisable. It had punctuated her married life and haunted her nightmares. It had accompanied her worst moments of despair.

It was the sound of George, pulling his fingers to make the knuckles crack.

Again the creak of the door. He had finished in the room opposite. He would be coming here next. Fear sent her diving under the cot, into the only hiding space available, pressing her spine against the coldness of the wall, knuckles pressed against her mouth to try to still her frantic breathing.

A creak. From her hiding place she saw the door open slowly, saw a man's feet and legs standing in the doorway, moving forward across the floor. Towards her.

Robert shivered in the night air. It was foolish to wander around like this. Marriage was for ever. He couldn't get rid of Theo just by walking around. And here he was again at the end of the lane that led down to the farm. He hesitated. Helen and Agnes would be in bed by now. Best not to go anywhere near the farm in case one of them woke and saw him and became worried.

He turned aside, down the lane that led to the calciner. The calciner that Anthony had convinced him would solve all his problems. The calciner that would make him rich, let him give Theo what she wanted, keep the mine going until the price of tin rose again.

His lips tightened. All dreams, all fantasies. Instead of being the answer to his dreams the calciner had been the cause of his worst nightmares. Because of it he had learned exactly how much the wife he had once loved despised him, because of it he was burdened with guilt about the deaths of innocent people, because of it he was likely to lose both the mine and his home.

The night was dark but a small, yellow flicker caught his eye. A candle. But any candle would have blown out instantly in this wind. He squinted into the darkness, trying to place the tiny pinprick of light. Not at the Trahairs; their place was further down the valley, and the light was too still for a lantern. No, the only place could be the calciner.

But who could be there at this time of night? His curiosity aroused, he began to walk more quickly down the steep path. Behind him, her evening sandals silent on the beaten earth of the track, Theo followed.

The feet came nearer, nearer. Pressed against the cold wall, Agnes held her breath, expecting any minute to see them stop, to see the face of her hated husband peer down at her. She cringed, waiting for his gripping hand, his angry curse.

But the only sound was a brief expulsion of air before the feet began to move away, back towards the door, silently.

He was afraid of waking the child, Agnes realised. In the darkness he hadn't realised Beth was dead. She had pulled down the covering sheet to stare her fill at the tiny face before she had heard him.

Scarcely able to believe her luck she listened to the soft creak of his boots as he moved on up the corridor. He hadn't found her. But he would. He must know she was here. He would carry on looking until he found her – and the longer it took the angrier he would be. And there was Helen. What would he do to Helen? She knew George, knew the depths of his violence, the explosiveness of his anger. She had to warn Helen.

She crept to the door, eased it open. He was further down the corridor, his back to her as he pushed open the door to her room. The noise of the wind hid all sounds now that he was further away. She saw him take in the disorder of the room, register that someone slept there, saw him move slowly in – and took her chance.

Her bare feet silent on the old floorboards she flew down the corridor, past the head of the stairs, on into the other wing of the house. A glance over her shoulder showed her that he was still in her bedroom.

She pushed open the door. 'Helen. Helen.' Her quiet whisper seemed to echo round the house. But there was no answer from the bed, no mutter or rustle of a disturbed sleeper. She reached the window, pulled back the curtains, let what little light there was into the silent room. But the bed was undisturbed, the coverlet unmarked. Helen was not there.

It took a second for full understanding of her situation to dawn. She was alone in the house with George. A George who had hunted her down, who would certainly punish her for every second she had been away from him.

He must not catch her. Better death than that. Agnes did not know where Helen was but it did not matter. Her bed had not been slept in. She must have gone out of her own accord. Agnes turned to go too but the sight of Helen's spare boots, neatly laid out by the bottom of the bed, stopped her. She would need something on her feet if she went outside. She picked them up, peered out of the door. Still no sign of George.

The boots held in her hand Agnes fled silently down the stairs. Only in the kitchen did she pause for a second, rummaging in a drawer.

George would not take her again. If she had to she would kill him. And if that wasn't possible – she could always kill herself. She stopped in the shelter of the overhanging porch to thrust her feet into the boots then she was off, running down the lane, laces flying loose. Her window overlooked the farmyard. As long as George was still there he would not see her.

But a roar of rage from the house told her that her supposition was wrong. He had seen her. Even through the thick walls of the house she could hear the pounding of his feet as he raced after her.

She had intended to get to the main road but she had no time now. He would catch her long before she reached it.

The Trahairs' was the nearest house.

She swerved left and ran as fast as she could down the steep lane towards the bottom of the valley.

Thirty

Theo had expected Robert to walk straight into the farm. She had her plan all ready. She would hammer on the door, interrupt them, tell them both what she thought of them. Shame them. She had felt her toes curl in anticipation. She would be able to do what she liked with Robert after that. There would be no more of this independence she had seen growing recently, no more making up his own mind about things. He would be clay in her hands.

When he had paused at the end of the lane then set off down into the valley she feared that he had heard her. Had she scared him off? Uncertainly, she hesitated where the lanes diverged. Then there was a sound of running feet – a woman's running feet. Instantly, her fury grew again. They had arranged a tryst elsewhere – and the woman was late. Theo pulled back into the shadow of the hedge. The figure of a woman came closer, paused fractionally where the lanes diverged. For a second Theo was afraid that the woman was going to come up towards the main road and discover her but she turned, glanced back at the farmhouse, then plunged on down the track after Robert.

Walking silently, Theo went after her.

There was not much room in the chamber of the lambreth where she had chosen to put the explosive.

Crouching to keep her head away from the roof and aware that her skirts were sweeping up the remains of the white powder with every movement she made, Helen poured the black, gritty gunpowder from the cask onto the floor. Despite Nat's comments it still scared her to be so close and she could feel her hands sweating. A memory of his comment about the effect of arsenic on sweating skin did nothing to make her feel more comfortable. It was difficult to see what she was doing in the flickering light of the distant candle but nothing would have made her move it from its safe place on the window sill.

She tipped out the last of the powder, pouring it as far back in the small chamber as she could, then took the fuse cord Nat had given her. Even this contained a core of gunpowder wrapped in a cotton surround, the whole covered in pitch to keep out the wet. But should she just push one end into the gunpowder? How did you use a fuse? Better to get Nat to do this part, she decided, bunching the fuse in her hand.

She had just stepped out of the narrow space and was stretching her aching back when she stopped, abruptly.

A gust of wind blew along the floor, rattling the door into the office and sending the candle flame curtseying and flickering in the window. For a second her heart seemed to stop beating then she calmed herself. It was only Nat, come back to see how she was getting on.

She opened her mouth to call to him but before she could speak there was the sound of another voice. 'Hello? Is there anyone here?'

In a second she was across the room and had blown out the candle then back again, quick, quick, and she was squeezed into the tiny refuge provided by the lambreth before the door to the office was pushed open.

Even with the fear of George behind her, Agnes could not run for ever. The boots she had taken from Helen's bedroom flopped and rubbed at every step and the laces flapped wildly, flaying her ankles as she ran. She slowed, pressing her hand against her side to ease the pain from a stitch, her breath coming in harsh pants.

George would soon catch her if she stayed in this lane. She knew him of old. Despite his drinking and womanising he was fit and strong, able to keep going all day. She had never had much stamina. She cast a swift glance behind her but the twisting lane hid all sight of any pursuers. This was her chance. If she could get over the hedge she could stay hidden while she got her breath back.

The Cornish hedge was high, its top crowned by small bushes, but the grass and plants that covered it gave her something to pull herself up by and her feet found purchase on the rough stones that made the outer facing of the earth-filled bank. Ignoring the pain as unseen stinging nettles brushed the bare skin of her hands she hauled herself to the top. Still no one in sight. The only way through the dense scrub that covered the top of the hedge was by forcing herself bodily through it, ignoring the rip of tearing material as branches caught at her with delaying fingers.

A final heave and she was through, falling face first into the long grass of the field, flinging the knife from her as she fell lest she impale herself on it.

Agnes landed with a jolt that knocked the breath from her body and seemed to echo through the night. Frantically, she scrambled to her feet, huddling in the slight shelter provided by the bottom of the hedge. Had George heard her? Would he notice the gap in the bushes where she had thrust herself through? Trying to stifle her gasps she pressed into the bottom of the hedge, her whole body shaking in time with the beating of her heart.

It seemed an age before she heard the footsteps and she curled into a smaller ball, trying to make herself invisible. But there was something not right about them. They were too light, too quick to be George's heavy tread. Agnes lifted her head, straining her ears. The footsteps were nearer now, and recognisably those of a woman.

It had to be Helen, but she must be

warned. Under starless skies, George could easily make a mistake. Agnes rolled out from under the hedge. Already the quick, light footsteps were moving away, down the lane, almost noiseless on the earth. Agnes opened her mouth to shout a warning then shut it again.

These were George's footsteps. She would have recognised them anywhere. Not running any more but still striding onward, long legs eating up the ground. Fear held her motionless, silent, as they approached, passed, went on without a pause.

He hadn't seen where she had got over the hedge, thank God. But Helen was in danger. She had to make sure that he didn't hurt Helen. But she knew his strength, knew his anger. She had no chance against him without a weapon.

Frantically, Agnes began to search through the tall grass for the knife she had dropped.

Robert paused in the doorway. The candle he had seen must have been in here but it was not lit now. In the darkness the room was eerie and strange. Darker openings, like mouths to the lairs of wild animals, gaped along one side of the long room. He could almost imagine he could hear the stealthy rustle of an animal, crouched in its den.

Foolish, he chided himself. At most it

would be a rat. Though any animal would surely have been poisoned by the arsenic lying around. Even in the darkness he could see the traces of white powder on the floor. Then a silhouette on the window sill caught his eye and he moved forward. It *was* a candle. And – he touched the top cautiously – the wax was still soft and warm. Someone had been here.

But why? There was not even enough arsenic left to be worth stealing now that the filled barrels had been sent off for refining. He moved slowly up the room, stirring the traces of white powder with his foot. It looked so innocent, so pure. It was hard to believe that this powder was one of the deadliest substances used by man. He moved on, taking his last look at the calciner on which he had pinned so many hopes. It had seemed such a good idea, integrated so closely with the work of the mine.

He reached the end of the shed and despite his distress a small smile twisted the corners of his mouth. Here was more evidence of the mining influence. The wheelbarrow was typical of the ones the miners used, and even the shovel with its pointed end was the same. He picked it up then swung swiftly round. There had been a sudden gust of wind, a distant rustle and even as he looked the door into the office swung shut.

He had not been mistaken about the noise. There had been someone in here with him and now they had gone.

Dropping the shovel, he began to run back down the room with long strides.

Helen ran out of the calciner, bunching her skirts in her hand to free her feet. Her heart was thumping nervously. Who was that man who had almost caught her? Someone who had a right to be there? But Nat had told her that the works would be deserted until after the weekend when the furnace would be lit again and more ore delivered for refining.

Chimney or furnace? Furnace, she decided. Even if Nat was not there, there would be more places to hide. She moved to the end of the building where the raw materials were delivered. 'Nat?' Her voice was a hoarse whisper. 'Nat?'

He appeared almost at her feet, crawling out of one of the narrow mouths of the furnace, making her jump. 'Done it.' She could hear the satisfaction in his voice. 'Chimney and furnace both. They won't poison any more children after this.' He moved back and she could see the dull gleam of the fuse leading into the furnace itself.

He searched in his pockets for the tinderbox he kept. 'We'll get this up first, then the chimney. Have you done your bit all right?'

'Nat.' She shook him, trying to stop the flow of his talk. 'You can't do it. There's – there's someone in there.'

He looked at her and she could see the grimness in his face. 'I know,' he said. 'I saw him walk past me. Mr bloody Polglase. He's the one who killed my sister. He and his damn calciner can both go to hell together.' And he flicked the tinderbox with his thumb, making the flame leap high.

Agnes panted, her hands feeling frantically through the long grass. It had to be here somewhere; she hadn't thrown it far.

The steps were distant now, almost at the calciner. She searched swiftly, her heart in her mouth, expecting any moment to hear a woman's scream, George's shout of rage. It had to be here. It had to be.

The razor-sharp edge sliced viciously into the side of her hand but in her relief she hardly felt the pain. At last. She grabbed the handle then set off, running down the field. Quicker to get out at the bottom where the stream flowed than to try to force her way back over the hedge.

As she ran, she prayed, frantically, breathlessly. 'Let me be in time, dear God. Please let me be in time.'

'No!'

Helen lashed out, knocking the box from

Nat's hand and the flame extinguished as it dropped to the ground. 'No. You can't do it.'

'He killed my Jenny.' Nat's voice was harsh with pain. 'He killed her. I'm going to get him for that. I'm going to make he suffer like I do suffer.'

Helen felt her heart lurch with fear. 'You're mad.' It was the barest whisper. 'You can't go round killing people.'

'It's one of they things that is all right for gentry but not for the likes of us? Is that it?' He thrust his face into hers. 'All this–' he waved his hand around, encompassing the works, '–this here is to make sure that no more of that muck will be made. But it isn't revenge, it don't help my Jenny – dead and cold in her coffin back there.' His eyes blazed down at hers. 'What I want is a life for a life, like it says in the Good Book.'

'But–' Helen began then stopped. A door slammed inside the building, footsteps approached. She backed away from Nat and threw her head back. 'Robert! Go away. Get away from here. He's going to blow up the calciner.'

For a second the footsteps paused; then they came closer. 'Helen?' No doubt now that it was Robert. And he was walking straight to them.

She glanced at Nat. He was mad enough to light the fuse while they were all within range just as long as Robert would get killed as well. Part of her was paralysed with fear listening to the steps coming closer, closer; then her brain jolted her into action.

She bent, scooped up the tinderbox then ducked under Nat's outstretched arm and began to run. Behind her she heard Robert's shout but she could not stop. She had only a second's lead but with luck a second was all she would need. She paused, took her arm back and flung the tinderbox as far as she could towards the silvery music of the stream.

At the sound of the splash she felt the tension ooze out of her body. Robert was safe. There was no way Nat could light the fuse now. She turned to go back, then Nat was on her, shaking her angrily. 'You little bitch!'

'Let me go.' Her voice came out raggedly, through gritted teeth. 'Let me go at once.'

'Leave her alone.'

Robert's voice, from behind her, then there was a strong grip on her shoulder and she was pulled bodily away from Nat as Robert forced himself between them.

The man's figure was unrecognisable in the darkness but Robert did not care who he was. He had already identified Helen and the thought of anyone hurting her made his heart swell with unaccustomed fury. He did not understand what had been going on here but that did not matter. *No one* was going to lay a finger on Helen while he was around.

He could only make out the man's silhouette in the darkness but that was enough to enable him to see the blow that was swung at him and duck it. Half-forgotten boxing lessons at public school came flooding back and he automatically took up the defensive stance, fists raised.

Another haymaker of a blow. Again he ducked before jabbing his left fist into the man's midriff while his right drove up under his chin. He heard the man's teeth snap together with an audible click but it didn't stop him. His opponent was back again immediately, arms still flailing in the wide punches that were so easy to duck.

He wanted to punish the man for hurting Helen but his sense of fair play made him detest fighting a man so much less skilled than himself. Besides, Helen was safe now, he would make sure of that.

He ducked again. 'Stop it, man.' He could not bring himself to batter this stranger to unconsciousness. 'For heaven's sake, give up.'

His words were echoed from behind his back. Helen's voice, slightly breathless but with the old self-assurance in it, ordered sharply, 'Stop it, Nat. You're acting like a fool.'

Nat? But he had nothing to fear from Nat

Trahair. Robert dropped his guard. 'Good Lord, Nat. I didn't realise it was you I was fighting. It's Robert Polglase here.'

'I do know that.' And a punch he had never expected caught him on the side of the head and sent him tumbling, tumbling, head spinning.

'How could you?' Helen was on her knees in a second, cradling Robert's head in her arms. 'He was going to stop. How could you hit him?'

'Because he killed our Jenny.' Nat drew his foot back and a heavy boot slammed into Robert's side. 'He killed my Granda. He's a bleeding murderer.' He pulled his foot back for another blow.

'Stop it.' Helen leapt to her feet. 'Don't you dare do that to him.'

He kicked again. Helen gritted her teeth to stop screaming as the boot swung forward and was only slightly relieved when Robert rolled slightly with the blow. He was obviously not knocked out.

But she had seen Nat's boots before. Tough miner's boots with iron studs in them. A kick from a boot like that could easily break a rib. She ran at Nat, pulling at him, sobbing. 'Leave him alone.'

'Bloody murderer.' He elbowed her away, aiming another kick at the limp body on the ground.

Pulling was no good. Helen knew that she did not have the strength to prevent Nat from killing Robert if that was his wish. She left him, running back to the door of the office.

It was on the desk, a lump of crude rock weighing down a pile of papers. Probably, in good light, if you were knowledgeable, it would show interesting ores. Helen did not care; its weight was what she needed. She grabbed it and raced back, panting with fright.

Nat was astride Robert's still body now, hammering his head against the hard ground. 'Damned murdering gentry.'

Robert's skull could be fractured. Helen swung the rock hard at Nat's head, hitting him just behind the ear and he collapsed on to Robert's body with a sigh.

'Thank God.' She hoped that she had not killed him but Robert was her main concern. She leaned over and grabbed a handful of Nat's shirt, rolling him bodily off Robert's inert body. 'Robert, Robert. Are you all right?'

No answer. Frantically, she threw herself on top of him, resting her ear against his chest, struggling to hear his pulse. 'Robert.' She was almost in tears. If he was dead it was all her fault. 'Robert. Please, answer me.'

A movement. Slight, but there was no

mistaking it. She leaned over him. 'Robert.'

'Mm?' Muzzy but an answer of sorts. Tears of relief flowed freely now. 'Thank God.'

'Helen?' Still a mumble but it was clearer. He knew who she was. She sniffed, wiping away the tears that were dripping on to his face.

'You're crying.' He reached out and touched her face gently. 'Why are you crying?'

His voice was still slurred from the after-effects of the blow. Helen smiled. 'Because you're all right. Because–' she stopped for a sudden sob, '–because you're not dead.'

He reached up and touched his head. 'Nat.' He was struggling to focus on her. 'Nat hit me.'

'He wanted to kill you.'

He frowned, struggling to comprehend. 'You stopped him?'

'I – I knocked him out.' The relief was enormous. Robert was all right. Helen reached out a gentle finger and stroked his cheek. 'I couldn't let him hurt you. I couldn't.'

And he turned his face slightly and kissed her fingers.

The touch of his lips sent a shock through her system. For a second she could not move, she could not think. Then his arms reached up and pulled her to him, his lips were on hers and there was no future, no past, just him, his mouth, his arms, Robert Polglase. As she gave herself up to him her treacherous mind whispered softly, *you never felt like this with Ezekiel or Anthony.*

And a voice came out of the darkness.

'What are you doing with my husband, you slut?'

Thirty-One

The long grass tugged at her feet, tripping her. More than once Agnes sprawled in the darkness but she struggled on, her breath coming in agonised gasps.

She had to get to Helen. The thought drove her on when her breath and strength were exhausted. George was like a madman when he was angry, not caring who he hurt. She had to save Helen from him. The knife clutched in her sweating hand, Agnes forced herself onwards.

Guilt throbbed hotly through Helen's body as she jumped to her feet to confront the angry woman.

How could she forget herself like that? To act like a hussy, to kiss a married man, to say what she had done – it was sinful. Unforgivable.

She could feel the hot shame in her face like a brand of infamy. She wanted to die on the spot, to shrink inside herself, to melt away into the darkness.

It was a surprise to hear her voice – under the control of her disobedient brain – snapping, 'How dare you say such things? Can't you see that Mr Polglase has been hurt?'

'Hurt? And what were you doing to help? Kissing him better?'

The tartness in Theo's voice brought Helen out of her sense of shock. This was no grieving wife, her world falling in ruins about her ears; this was an angry and bitter woman whose pride had suffered more than her feelings.

Robert must have thought so too. He struggled up on to one elbow. 'What are you doing here, Theo? You haven't been *following* me?' His voice rose in disbelief.

'And why shouldn't I follow you?' Theo snapped. 'If you go sneaking out into the night to spend time with your fancy woman don't you think I should know about it?'

'I am not his fancy woman–' Helen began furiously.

'Oh, no? When all I hear is how wonderful Miss Schofield is, how clever, how polite and well-born.' Theo's voice rose in a parody of a genteel lisp. 'And I come here and find the polite and well-born lady cavorting in my husband's arms like a common shop-girl.'

'I do not–' Helen snapped, then stopped. Another voice broke in, deeper, angrier even than Theo's.

'Here are two bitches. Where's the third?'

George's anger burned in his gut like a white-hot flame. Not to have found Aggie yet, not to have got his hands on the cow and choked the life out of her...

But here were two other women; the way he was feeling they would do as well. Women were all the same, liars, thieves, each as bad as the other.

Theo's blonde hair shone in the darkness and he would bet a shilling that the other was the woman who had sheltered Aggie. 'Where's my wife?' he demanded. 'Where's Aggie?'

Theo was silent but the other woman stepped forward, chin raised. 'You'll never find her, Mr Penhaligon. Why don't you forget her? Haven't you tormented her enough?'

The easy superiority in her voice roused him to greater fury. She was only a woman after all, however educated and well-bred she was, while he was a man, a real man. He grabbed her by the arms, dragging her towards him until her face was inches from his own. 'Tell me where she is,' he hissed, 'or

I'll break every bone in your body.'

'I'll tell you nothing!' The contempt in her voice slashed at him.

'Leave her alone, you brute.' A dark figure he had not noticed on the ground moved, struggled to his feet. 'Let her go at once.'

George waited until he was upright, then, letting go of Helen with one hand, he punched the man in the face, putting into the blow all the suppressed anger that gnawed at his insides. It felt so good to have a means of letting it out; so good that, when Robert hit the ground, he lashed out with his foot, kicking him in the ribs, even though he would have bet that his punch had knocked the man out completely. The body lifted slightly with the force of his kick but did not otherwise move and George felt a surge of gratification. That would teach him! George could handle ten men like him any day – and their women.

Then the woman in his arms turned on him and he just had time to duck as her nails raked down his cheek. 'How dare you kick an injured man?' Her feet lashed out, striking his knees and ankles hard enough to hurt despite her hampering skirts, and when he shook her she lowered her head to bite at the arm that held her.

He slapped her hard across the face and her head fell back with a gasp. 'A little cat, eh?' He grinned. 'I've never had a sleek little posh cat like you before.' He pulled her towards him, feeling his body tighten at the thought of what he could do to her.

She turned her head away, straining to avoid him. 'For God's sake, Mrs Polglase, help me.'

He had to laugh. 'Help you? Silly bitch! Who do you think told me where my Aggie was?' He grinned wolfishly at the other woman. 'Want to watch while I earn my money by teaching this cow a lesson, Mrs Polglase?'

He pulled the girl towards him, slowly, watching her face, enjoying her growing despair as she realised that he was too strong for her, that all her struggles were useless. He held her against his body, lowering his mouth onto hers, excited by the revulsion he could read in her face. Then, suddenly, her eyes widened, she was staring over his shoulder.

Instinct made him fling her from him, swinging swiftly round, and the stab that Agnes had aimed at his back merely sliced through his coat.

'Aggie.' Fury burned brighter than ever, mixed with satisfaction. At last, his wife. At last, he could teach her a lesson, teach her something she would never forget and afterwards – there was still the pleasure to be had from her friend.

'Come here, Aggie, girl. Come here and

take your punishment like a good wife.' He moved forward.

'Don't you touch me!' Agnes' voice was shrill with fear but she still held the knife pointing at him. 'Don't you come any nearer.'

'Leave her alone!'

It was that damned girl again. Without looking round he flung out an arm and caught Helen on the side of the head, knocking her to the ground. He would deal with her later. It was Aggie he wanted now. 'Come here, woman.'

As he moved forward Aggie backed away. The knife blade shone in her trembling hand. 'Keep away. Keep away from us all.'

All? He laughed. As if a couple of women could stop a man like him, even if one of them did have a knife. He waited, judged his moment, leapt at Aggie – and fell forward as a heavy weight hit him on the back. That damned girl.

They fell in a tangle of arms and legs, Agnes' thin body under his own and the girl clawing and hammering at his back. 'Get off, you bloody bitch.' He twisted violently, his fist thudding heavily into Helen's head, and felt a surge of pleasure as he saw her fall back under the force of the blow. That would keep the cow quiet while he dealt with Aggie.

He was on his feet before she could recover, reaching down, grabbing Aggie's thin body, hauling her to her feet...

'Oh, Jesus Christ!'

The world had stopped. There was no sound, no motion. In front of him Aggie lay, her head bowed submissively like a good wife's, her hair coming loose from her night-time plait ... the knife protruding from her side.

The body fell from his nerveless fingers. 'I didn't do it.' His voice was a panic stricken whisper. 'It wasn't my fault. She fell, didn't she? She just fell!'

He turned to the two silent women, staring at him with white faces. 'It was an accident, wasn't it?' He could hear the pleading in his voice. 'You saw it was an accident.'

Silence, a long, long silence, then the girl cleared her throat, spoke. 'It was an accident.' Her voice was hoarse and breathless but he was grateful to her nevertheless. She wasn't that bad. She turned to the other woman who was still staring at him, her eyes wide with fright. 'It was an accident, wasn't it, Mrs Polglase? We both saw it.'

Theo moved, gathered her skirts with shaking hands, her mouth working. 'You killed her!' She stared from him to the body on the ground then back to him again, over and over. 'You killed your wife!'

'But it was an accident,' the girl insisted. 'Tell him that you realise it was just an accident.'

The once-beautiful mouth still worked, small muscles twitching at the corners. 'You killed her!' The voice rose hysterically. 'You killed your wife! You murdered her!'

He saw Helen make a move as if to stop her but it was too late. The word had been said. It dropped into the darkness with the sickening inevitability of an avalanche.

Murder.

He knew what that meant. Dear God, he had spent time enough thinking about it since those few frantic moments he had spent with the prostitute. Prison. Hanging. Death. He had lived with it every second, dreamed of it every night. Lying awake, wishing he could recall those few moments, praying that no one would ever pin it on him, seeing ahead of him the trial, the imprisonment, the hangman, the final walk.

He had decided then that he would not let himself be taken. He would not undergo the disgrace, the degradation; he would rather kill himself than that.

But that had been an easy decision. With every hour that passed, every day, the danger had grown less. No witnesses. No evidence. Not even a victim that anyone cared about.

This was different. He had killed in front of two women who could both recognise him. This time there would be no escape. Already he could smell the stench of the prison, see the silhouette of the gallows...

'No.' It was little more than a whisper. 'No!' Then determination woke in him. He would not be taken, locked up like a dog, hung, he would–

He would get rid of the witnesses.

The simplicity of it all made him gasp. So easy. After all, what had he got to lose? It was his life or theirs. He straightened, feeling hope flower within him, feeling clever again, all powerful, a real man.

Theo was still staring at him, her face working, but the other girl was cleverer. Suddenly she was running, skirts held high, feet pounding as she headed into the darkness.

He leapt after her, grabbed at her fleeing body, missed.

Then her feet were suddenly entangled in something and she was down, the breath knocked out of her by the violence of her fall.

'Silly bitch.' He reached out a hand to drag her to her feet then stopped. She had fallen because her feet had been caught up in a loop of cord. He picked it up and stood for a second, transported back, back to when he had first met Aggie, back to when he had been a struggling miner, in the days before he had learned that you could make far more money working with your brains than your body.

Fuse. He had handled it every day, down

in the mines at Camborne. But what was it doing here?

Fuse meant explosives. Someone had been setting explosives here.

His eyes gleamed. Despite everything, he hadn't fancied killing the women in cold blood but this – to set the fuse, light it and go – that would be easier, that would be no trouble at all. And the explosion would get rid of Aggie's body, too, and the men's. And no one would suspect him, no one at all.

He hauled Helen to her feet, hurried back to Theo. He had been half afraid that she would take her chance to make a run for it but the silly cow seemed frozen with fright. Where to put them?

He dragged them both to the building. Theo came easily, stumbling without a word, but the other she-cat needed a couple of good knocks before he could subdue her. Two metal doors, shut by a bar, caught his eye and he kicked the bar free and dragged one open.

This would do. Apart from the door the only exit was a window high in the wall. Not even the she-cat could climb to that. He flung them both inside and slammed the doors, dropping home the bar that held it shut. Almost immediately he heard a hammering from inside. The she-cat again. Well, let her hammer. She wouldn't get out of there.

But the men might recover consciousness. George made up his mind. Get Aggie and the men and put them with the women, then he would have plenty of time to find the explosives and set them off. But it was all of Cornwall to a Mounts Bay pilchard that the explosives were in the furnace already, right under where the women were. He cracked his knuckles contentedly. Things were going right at last.

Helen landed on the dark floor with a thud that made her teeth rattle. Her head was spinning from the violence of George's blows and it was several seconds before she could push herself to her knees. 'Stop him shutting the door,' she shouted to Theo but the woman seemed sunk in despair. Helen climbed to her feet and threw herself bodily at the doors but it was too late. Even as she reached them she heard the bar that closed them drop home and although she threw her weight against them, the doors remained firmly shut.

The room stank of smoke and garlic and she realised that George must have put them in part of the furnace building under which Nat had already set the gunpowder. The whole place could explode at any moment. She felt her flesh shrink at the thought, then she calmed herself. George would not want any witnesses to what happened. He would want Robert, at least, in here with them when the gunpowder went off, and that meant that he would have to open the doors at least once more. It was up to her to make the most of that opportunity.

The only window was high up on the wall and the overcast sky meant that little light percolated through but she could see some shapes leaning against the wall. She moved towards them, then tripped as her foot caught in a raised part of the floor and fell headlong again, knocking herself breathless. But she was near enough now to see what the shape had been. A rake.

Stiffly, she climbed to her feet and picked it up. It was too light and too long to be a good weapon but it was the only one she had. She hefted it experimentally. If only Theo would co-operate...

'Mrs Polglase.' Theo did not answer. She was standing where George had pushed her, her breath coming fast and unevenly, her hands constantly running down and down her full skirts as if she wanted to wipe her palms clean of everything she had ever touched.

'Mrs Polglase.' Helen shook her lightly. 'Mrs Polglase, you have to help me.' No response. Theo might not have heard her for all the notice she took. Helen tried again. 'Mrs Polglase, if you don't help me that man will blow up the calciner with us in it.

You must help me.'

That, at least, got through. Theo's mouth opened to become an 'O' of terror and a low, hair-raising wail began deep in her throat. Helen shook her again, more roughly. 'Help me. It's our only chance.'

'Chance?' The voice was weak and breathless with fear but at least she was listening.

'We have to stop that man. When he opens the doors–'

Theo's wide, staring eyes became riveted on the entrance. 'He's coming in here?' Her voice rose hysterically.

She had no time to deal with this. 'Listen,' Helen said fiercely. 'When the doors open, you must be lying down across the room, pretending to be hurt, do you understand? Groan or scream. Try to get him to come to you and I'll' – she swallowed – 'I'll try to knock him out. Then we can escape.'

It had only the slightest chance of working, she knew. George was quite likely to ignore them even if they were dying, but it was the only thing she could think of. She pulled Theo forward, pushed her down into position on the floor. 'Remember. When he begins to open the doors, scream as if you are badly hurt.'

Helen positioned herself against the wall by the doors, the rake held over her head. If she could get in just one good blow it might be enough.

The bar outside rattled free. She flattened herself against the wall. 'Scream,' she hissed.

Theo's scream was ninety per cent hysteria but that did not matter. It rose to a mind-numbing pitch, echoing off the stone walls, shaking down dust from the rafters above them. Helen stood motionless, waiting for George to come through the door.

Instead an arm swept round the doorpost, feeling for her.

He had expected a trap! She brought the rake down but she was too slow, too late. He grabbed her clothes, pulling her easily out of her hiding place, and jerked the rake from her in one easy movement. 'You have to be cleverer than that to beat George Penhaligon.' He threw the rake behind him, easily, pulling her closer.

'Run, Mrs Polglase, run,' she screamed, then he brought his fist up in a blow and she knew no more.

Thirty-Two

Hearing came back first. Long before Robert could open his eyes, long before he dared to move, he was aware of sounds. At first they were meaningless, echoing through his aching head with no rhyme or reason; then, slowly, the meanings coalesced, the words linked into sentences.

The pain in his ribs made it difficult to breathe, impossible to move. He lay still, hoping that the man would not realise that he was conscious, waiting to gain strength.

Strength! He felt as if he would never again have the strength to even lift his head, let alone stand. But he needed strength if he was to save the women, strength and determination. Dear God, if he was their hope, why wasn't he fitter? How could he achieve anything in this state? Eyes closed, his teeth buried in his lip, he tried to suppress the nausea that threatened to give him away.

He could see the hunched shape that was Nat, lying still a few yards away. Desperately he tried to get up but at every movement his stomach and head swam. But he had to move. He was their only hope. He managed a couple of feet crawling on hands and knees, every movement sending spasms of agony through his side.

The slam of the bar being slotted back into place gave him warning of the man's return and he sank thankfully to the ground, eyes closed. He was aware of the man's approach, aware of him standing over Nat, listening, and now moving towards himself...

Robert lay still, trying to imitate Nat's

ragged breathing. Please God, don't let the man see he had recovered. One kick, one punch to the head and Robert knew that he would lapse into unconsciousness again.

An age, and then the man moved away, bustled around. Robert dared not move, dared not even lift his head to see what he was doing. Then he came back and Robert heard the sounds of a body being dragged to the building, but when he looked again Nat was still there, and still, to Robert's despair, showing no signs of regaining consciousness. As soon as it seemed safe Robert tried to move and this time it was easier. His legs were rubbery but they held him up, just. Doubled over like an old man he lurched to the nearest cover, a pile of anthracite, and sank down behind it trying not to breathe too deeply.

Theo's scream ripped through the night like a crimson slash. Despite his hurt, Robert found himself on his feet, fists clenched. Then the screams stopped and there was a silence. Every instinct told him to go to his wife's aid but he knew that to do so would seal all their death warrants. He was too hurt to fight George face to face. Fists clenched, he waited, head bowed, praying.

Again the footsteps, again the sound of a body being dragged. Nat, this time. He could hear the panting and grunts of effort as the man struggled with his thick-set weight. Robert knew that he was to be the last one and then...

Think. If he was too hurt to be able to fight the man he would have to outsmart him. Helen had said that the calciner had been mined. Nat would have done that and Nat was a miner. He knew his explosives and although Robert had never worked as a miner he had grown up with them, he had heard them talking. He knew how they thought.

In the furnace. The anthracite was shovelled in under a large plate on which the arsenic was heated until it evaporated. If the explosives were put under that they would blow the whole place up – and the women were right above it. They would have no chance if he didn't act.

He cast a swift glance at the man, still dragging Nat's body across the ground then ran, stooping low, in a wide circle that would bring him back to the entrance to the furnace.

He had to get rid of the explosives and the only way to do that was to crawl inside the firebox itself.

It was low and pitch black but he dared not light a match. Even the spark off an iron-shod boot would set off gunpowder. He crawled forwards, ignoring the stabbing pain in his side, feeling with his hands.

There. A winding, tarry cord caught under his searching fingers. The fuse. He pulled it from the gunpowder – and stopped.

Faintly, from outside, he heard an angry shout. His absence had been discovered. Robert thought swiftly. The man might lose his nerve and run away but that seemed unlikely. Far likelier that he would either try to hunt Robert down or, if he knew about them, set off the explosives. And that meant he would have to come into the firebox.

Heart pounding, Robert crawled deeper into the depths of the furnace until he was pressed up against the back wall. He could only hope that the man knew enough about explosives not to come looking with a lighted match. But in this restricted space they could only be feet away from each other at most.

Eyes staring into the darkness, Robert waited.

Helen groaned as she opened her eyes into darkness. Her head was splitting and she could feel the pain of a bruise along her jaw but when she tried to rub it her hand would not move. It took her several seconds before the awful truth dawned; her hands were tied behind her back.

'Mrs Polglase?' It was difficult to talk through her battered face.

'Don't you talk to me!' Theo's voice rose

hysterically. 'Look at the mess we're in now, tied up in here with a dead *body.*'

Oh, Aggie. Helen blinked away tears as the loss of her friend hit her again. 'Anyone else?'

As if in answer the doors opened again and George appeared, dragging Nat's heavy body. He dumped it unceremoniously just by the doors. 'Don't be impatient, ladies, it won't be for much longer.'

'You're going to let us out?' Hope throbbed through Theo's voice.

George laughed. 'Out? You're even more stupid than I thought, Missis. The only place you're going is up.' He slammed the doors shut again, banging the retaining bar home.

Helen climbed awkwardly to her feet. Without her hands to move her skirts out of the way she stumbled and tripped, almost falling before she could make her way to the two figures lying motionless on the floor. 'Nat? Nat?'

But he made no move and his breathing did not alter when she pushed him gently with her foot in an effort to rouse him.

'Up?' Theo demanded. 'What did he mean by "up"?'

'He's going to blow up the calciner.' Helen had no time to spare for Theo; her whole being was concentrated on the problem of getting out of here.

'He's going to blow us...' Theo's voice

reached a full-bodied shriek. 'He can't! He can't! He mustn't. That's–' she struggled for words, '–that's illegal.'

'You tell him that,' Helen snapped. She moved to the doors and stood listening. Robert was their only hope. Once George put him in here the end would come soon.

There was a roar of anger from outside and her heart leapt. But Robert had been badly injured, she had seen that herself. He couldn't fight George. He might have gone for help but in that case George was likely to fire the explosives immediately and trust to luck to get away. They had to get out.

'Are your hands tied?' she asked. Theo was too far gone in hysterics to respond but squinting through the darkness Helen could see the answer in the other woman's stiff stance.

Get free. That was the first thing. She needed to cut the cords that tied her hands. She glanced around the room. Nat might have a knife but, bound as she was, she would never be able to turn his stocky body so that she could reach it.

There is a knife. The side of her brain that seemed to work independently from her, the side that thought the unthinkable, prodded her, forcing the thought into her mind. There is a knife.

Oh, no! Helen felt herself go cold with horror. She couldn't do it. She couldn't.

Not even to save her life.

But she had contemplated the idea. To die just because she was squeamish – to be responsible for other people's death because she was finicky...

But Agnes was my friend. You can't expect me...

The voice in her head was silent. It had offered its advice. It was down to Helen.

Perhaps Theo – Helen dismissed the thought immediately. She would never do such a thing.

Taking a deep breath Helen moved to Agnes' body. She was lying half on her back, only the handle of the knife protruding from her side. What if she were still alive? Helen wondered. She had read of wounded soldiers who had lived until the sword was removed from the wound. Could she be responsible for taking Agnes' last chance if she was still alive? Even to save the rest of them?

The thought of touching the body made her feel sick. But Agnes was my friend, she reminded herself. I touched her in life. How can I fear her dead? Turning her back to bring her tied hands closer to the other woman Helen lay down beside her, stretched out shaking fingers.

The skin was already cooler than in life, the texture less yielding. Her fingers fumbled over the woman's hands, found the thin wrists, searched for a pulse.

Nothing.

This was it then. Do the unthinkable. Closing her mind to the impiety of her act Helen moved her fingers higher, backing her body until it was pressing against Agnes' cold corpse, trying to reach the hilt of the knife.

Her fingers touched the wooden handle but could not get a grip on it. She had to wriggle herself half on to the dead body before she could get a grip on the knife, feeling the harsh stickiness of drying blood against her hands.

Pull. But the knife did not move. She pulled again and again. Come, please come. She could feel tears trickling down her face. Please, Agnes, let me have the knife. I don't want to do this. I don't want to hurt you. The stench of blood was all around her, the cold rubbery body moved and jerked in rhythm with her pulls. Come.

And it came. Just an inch but that was enough for now. Helen could feel its blade rasping against bone as it moved and the horror of it nearly made her let go but she had to have the knife. It was their only chance.

She raised her hands so that her bound wrists were over the tiny section of blood-stained, reeking blade that protruded from Agnes' side and cut the cords.

Closer, closer. Unable to move, unable to breathe, Robert waited. Darkness and silence were his only hope. Closer still. He must be over the damn gunpowder by now. What was he looking for?

Silence from the man. Had he heard him? Had he realised Robert was there. Silent, waiting? He moved again but backwards now, towards the opening. Was he going? Or, Robert felt himself break out in a cold sweat at the thought, had he come into the furnace *to set another fuse in the explosive powder?*

He dared not move. He waited, envisaging the scene outside if his thought had been correct. The man would light the fuse, then run. The spark would race down the cord, spitting and spluttering. Robert knew he had a race against time. Move too soon and the man would hear him. Even if Robert put out the spark the man would simply come in, deal with him and relight it. Move too late...

The spark would be easy to see but where, in this darkness, did the gunpowder lie? Even a small spill at the entrance to the furnace might be enough to make the whole place explode. Robert held his breath.

There. The small spark, running with horrifying speed through the darkness. Ignoring the pain in his ribs, Robert hurled himself towards it...

'No! You can't!' Theo cringed back against the wall of the room, her eyes on the blood-stained knife.

'For God's sake! We could all be blown up at any minute.' Helen had no patience with her. Pulling the knife right out of Agnes' body was the worst thing she had ever had to do in her life. The memory of the way she had had to put her foot against the woman's side to get it out would stay with her all her life but she had known that even in their present peril Theo would never have lain on that cold corpse to cut her own bonds.

She caught the other woman roughly, turning her around so that she could slash through the cords that bound her. All the time Helen could feel her flesh cringing; every second she expected the floor to erupt in an explosion of pain and death.

The second Theo was free she was on her feet, running for the door, sobbing with fright and relief. Helen moved to follow her then stopped. It wasn't them alone. She could not leave Nat to die here, not while they escaped. He was moaning now but he was still a dead weight. She eyed him speculatively. She and Theo might manage to drag him outside between them, if Theo could be persuaded to help.

'Mrs Polglase.' She was afraid to shout too loud in case George heard. 'Mrs Polglase.'

But Theo was at the doors, hammering her fists uselessly on the hard wood.

'We can't get out,' she screamed, throwing herself onto Helen in an agony of fright. 'We're locked in. We're going to die.'

The ashes slid and compacted under his knees, his toes could not get a purchase and skidded. And all the time the spark, a bright meteor, burned its way across his retinas as it raced towards the explosives.

No time to try anything fancy. Expecting every second to be his last Robert threw himself bodily on to the racing spark, clutching at it with frantic hands, trying to quench its life by the weight of his body, smother it in his clothes. For a second he felt the burn in his hands then – blessed darkness. Scarcely daring to breathe, he opened his fingers, ready at the first sign of life to roll again on the lighted fuse. But the cord was dark, the fire extinguished.

Relief made him weak. For a second he dropped his head on his arms, breathing a brief prayer of thanks then he was on the move again. The women must be terrified. He had to help them.

At the opening to the firebox he paused. No sign of the man. But he couldn't be far away. Suppose he came back when he realised that the gunpowder hadn't gone off? Robert moved back into the darkness, pulled what was left of the fuse from the powder, stuffed it into his pocket then hurried to the door through which the women had been taken.

But the bar was down and someone had driven a wedge between it and the supports. He would need a hammer or something similar to release it. He rattled it impotently, but as he opened his mouth to shout reassurance to Helen and Theo a hard body hit him from the side, sending him sprawling onto the ground, and a voice in his ear said, 'You won't get away this time, you bastard.'

'We have to get out.' Helen ran to the window but it was too high to reach. She moved back to the door – and her foot caught, almost tripping her.

In the dark the large metal cover was almost impossible to see. She knelt beside it, trying to pry her fingers under the edge, moving around slowly, feeling for a place where she could get some purchase.

There. She could only lift it a couple of inches. She moved back to the door. George hadn't bothered to take away the rake, obviously thinking they would be unable to use it again. She knelt again by the plate and raised it far enough to slip the rake handle underneath, then, using it as a lever, she forced the cover a little way back across the dirty floor.

The hole was pitch black. She probed, using the rake handle. The hole was less than two feet deep but, further prodding with the rake, it seemed to extend under the room they were in.

This must be the place where the arsenic was actually heated, she realised. The arsenic soot was loaded into the furnace from this room and the rake must have been used to spread it around. And under it the explosives had been laid. It was almost certain that they would be killed here in this room if the gunpowder exploded – but she was horribly certain that if she were down that hole she would definitely die.

But there had been no sign from Robert. Either he had escaped or else George had dealt with him separately – and at any moment the whole building would blow up.

'I'm going down there.' She sat on the edge of the hole, lowering her legs into space.

'There's a way out?' Theo's voice was high with hope.

'I don't know. But there's no other way.' How long did it take to blow something up? Perhaps George did not have matches. But the calciner had a furnace; there was sure to be means of producing a flame somewhere here. She dared not wait.

With a brief prayer she closed her eyes and let herself slip into the darkness.

Robert fell with a gasp as pain from his ribs speared through him. Automatically he spread his hands, trying to cushion the fall – and his clutching hands fell on something hard. The rock that Helen had used to hit Nat with. He could see her now, flinging it from her in horror as she threw herself on to him. It was a good omen.

He grabbed it, twisting painfully as the man leaned over him, then he reached up and the rock thudded into the side of the man's head.

Because of his position he hadn't been able to get any force behind the blow but it was enough to send George reeling back, his hands over his face. But he hadn't been badly hurt and Robert knew that he had to make the most of this small chance. Gritting his teeth against the pain from his cracked ribs he climbed to his feet and set off at a stumbling run.

Within a few paces he could hear the thud of footsteps behind him. Once George got him Robert knew that he was too weak to fight back. And with the fuse in his pockets and his silver box of matches – he had to get away.

The steps were getting nearer. Unable to outrun him, Robert dived through the first door he saw, the door into the office. No help there. Through the next door – and the blank mouths of the lambreth called to him. It wasn't called a labyrinth for nothing. The long passage wandered forward and back, dark and inviting. George would know that he was in there, of course, but it would take him some time to actually find him.

Robert ran as far down the long room as he dared, then, judging his moment by the rapidly nearing footsteps, he dived into one of the dark mouths and moved to the back to stand behind the small part of the tunnel that ran round the back of the dividing wall. Standing sideways, knees bent to keep his head from brushing the low roof, he could not be seen from the mouth of the lambreth, even if George was immediately opposite it.

He heard the footsteps slow, halt. An angry voice said, 'I do know you're in there. You might as well come out, 'cos it'll just be the worse for you if I do have to come and get you.'

Robert grinned in the darkness, trying to stifle his breathing. The footsteps came on again, moving up the long room, and Robert could imagine George peering into every opening. Then it must have occurred to him that if he came too far into the room Robert could get behind him and make for the door because he moved back again.

''Tes a blamed silly thing you're doing.' Robert could hear the frustration in his voice. 'Don't you think you're going to get away with it.'

Not for ever, Robert decided, but when death was the alternative, every extra minute was precious.

George had obviously worked out his strategy. Robert heard him duck into the first of the lambreth's mouths, hurry back, round the bend at the back, forward to the next mouth then out into the room again to check that Robert hadn't made a dash for it. A few second's pause then back into the second mouth.

Robert cursed under his breath. The man was intelligent. This way he would herd Robert up the lambreth until he was caught in the last chamber and then...

There was no point in just waiting to be caught, even if taking preventative action only delayed the evil for a few minutes more. Timing his movements so that his cautious footsteps were covered by George's heavier ones, Robert began to move up the lambreth, chamber by chamber.

His foot knocked against a small keg and he winced at the noise he had made. But what was a keg doing here? He dipped his hand down, felt the familiar small kegs used by the miners to carry gunpowder.

Nat must have been intending to blow up the lambreth as well. It was too dark to see clearly but surely the powder on the floor was darker here? Someone had poured the powder from the keg intending to blow up the lambreth, but this site was less well prepared; there was no fuse cord inserted into the explosive. He grinned, and pulled the remains of the furnace's fuse from his pocket. There was only a short length left but that should be enough, that and the rock that he was still holding like a lucky charm.

This chamber was half-way up the lambreth. It was not an ideal place for an explosion. With one side open to the long room, much of the force would come outwards, dissipate itself without much damage. The back and side walls of that chamber might blow out but that should be all. And, most importantly, the chamber was well away from the furnace. The women should be all right as should he himself, as long as he could put several walls of the lambreth between him and the explosion.

He cocked his head, listening. George's feet were getting closer. He did not have much time. Bending, he thrust one end of the fuse well into the gunpowder leading the fuse away around a twist of the tunnel. Now!

He lit the fuse with a match from his silver box, waiting until the sound of George's feet showed that he had just dived back into another chamber of the lambreth, then

Robert ran out into the long room.

How long had he got? He had to get this just right. He ran silently down the room away from the door past one, two, three open chambers. Time was passing, the fuse was short. He dared not wait any longer.

Halting at the mouth of the next chamber he turned and flung the stone, making it bounce off the wall of the long room opposite the chamber holding the explosive then, not waiting to see if his ruse worked, he hurried into the lambreth and crouched down, head buried in his arms, counting.

He had got to six when the world erupted around him.

There was a door to the space she had lowered herself into. It was little more than an access hatch but Helen did not care and she kicked it open, not caring about the noise. Speed was what was important now. If George was still around they would all be dead soon anyway.

She ran to the door of the room where they had been imprisoned, struggled uselessly with the jammed bar, cursing him. But the wedge could be moved, with the right equipment.

She raced for the office, grabbed a metal ruler and ran back, levered the rock out and dragged out the retaining bar.

'Thank God.' Theo forced her way past

Helen. 'I thought I was going to die in there.' She started across the yard but Helen grabbed her arm.

'Wait. Nat's still in there. Between us we can get him out.'

'Who cares?' Theo pulled herself free. 'I'm not staying here to be blown up.' And she gathered up her full skirts and ran through the gateway.

Helen followed her as far as the path that ran beside the works. 'Mrs Polglase. Please–'

And the world exploded in a volcano of noise and heat. As Helen was blown to the ground she had a last glimpse of Theo's body flying through the air, limbs flung wide as the whole side of the lambreth blew out.

Thirty-Three

'Ashes to ashes.'

The earth landed heavily on the tiny white coffin, marring its virginal purity. Alone by the graveside, Helen caught her bottom lip between her teeth, struggling for composure.

'Dust to dust.' She could feel the sob coming up from the depths of her body, forcing its way out with all the inevitability of a volcano. Poor Beth. She had failed her so completely. Failed them all. Beth. Agnes. Jenny. Theo. It would have been better for all of them if she had never been born.

'Are you all right, Miss Schofield?'

She blinked, dragging her mind back to the present with all its awfulness. 'Yes, thank you, Vicar.' What else was there to say? The desolation in her heart made her shiver despite the warmth of the day. Cold, cold, cold. But not as cold as Beth, as Agnes. She forced herself to listen to the Vicar.

'God will support you in your sorrow, my dear. God will help you.'

She forced a smile, nodded meaninglessly. No one could help, no one. She was all alone. Just her, following the tiny white coffin the undertakers had brought to the church. And in two days time, it would be just her again, following Agnes' body on this last, sad journey. And then – London. Her grandmother. The tiny house, the cluttered rooms, the claustrophobic hopeless future – for ever and ever.

She turned away. Behind her, she saw with surprise, there were others, distantly apart. Just a handful. Now she remembered the soft chorus of 'Amens' to the prayers from the back of the church. She recognised Mr Browfield, the attorney, the farrier who had found the signs of arsenic in the cow and another familiar figure, standing at the back.

'My sincere condolences, Miss Schofield.'

Oh, God! She had more guilt towards this man than to anyone. The memory of those brief seconds in the yard of the calciner haunted her. 'Thank you, Mr Polglase.' The black veil hid her embarrassment as well as her grief. Her fingers, in the black gloves, twisted, clenched, fell slack. She inclined her head, moved away.

And he moved with her. Decently apart. Indeed, too far apart. She realised that he was accompanying her out of kindness; his sympathy had always taken a practical turn.

It was necessary that she should say something. She cleared her throat. 'I am sorry about the calciner, Mr Polglase. Believe me, I had not intended–'

He gestured angrily. 'It was my fault. I should have made sure the calciner was safe. By the time I realised...' His voice trailed away.

Silence. What was there to say? Side by side they walked down the road. There was room between them for another person, Helen thought, then realised. There was another person. Theo, unseen, walked between them, a greater obstacle in death that she had ever been in life.

She made another effort, searching for the correct social formula, for the words her grandmother would expect her to say, the artificial, dishonest words that had never been necessary between them before. 'It is good of you, Mr Polglase, to come to this funeral with your wife so recently deceased.'

Again the gesture, angry, cutting her off. They walked on in silence, Theo unseen but ever-present between them.

It was he who finally broke the impasse. 'I – I loved my wife.' His voice was harsh with pain.

Dismay and anguish flooded through her. She didn't want to hear this! But she understood his need. To talk of the dead – to relive the happy hours – she had felt the same. But other people did not want the embarrassment of hearing it. Only a close friend would understand, would listen.

And he had been a good friend to her. Despite their misunderstanding about the calciner he had been her best friend – until she had ruined it, until that moment of madness at the calciner when she had forgotten her training, her upbringing, her common sense, and thrown herself at him, kissed him, held him...

She knew that it could never be forgotten. It would always be there, that time when she had taken advantage of his half-conscious state and let her true feelings show. She hadn't even realised herself until then what he had meant to her, what she had felt about him. And now, because of her actions, they must be parted for ever. She could almost hear Theo's ghostly laughter from beyond the grave.

But if she loved him, she should help him, whatever her own feelings. She, took a deep, steadying breath. "You knew her a long time?'

'Since I was a boy. Anthony Ledgerwood was my best friend at school and I went home with him one holidays and there she was.' His voice grated with agony. 'She was so beautiful, so alive, always laughing, always smiling. I thought she was an angel come to earth. And I fell in love with her the moment I saw her.'

The pain was like a knife in her heart. Oh, God, how much of this could she bear? She forced her clenched fingers to relax, swallowed the choking lump in her throat. 'I only saw her that once – but she was very beautiful.'

Out of the corner of her eye she saw him nod briefly. 'Always the most beautiful. Wherever she was, no matter what company she kept, she was almost the most beautiful, the best-dressed woman there.'

Helen glanced down at her clothes. Agnes had been skilled but she knew that her blacks could not compare with Theo's fine raiment. And she was not beautiful. Not even as beautiful as Mary, her sister, whose untimely death had brought about this whole disaster. She blinked hard under her thick veil.

'What are you – have you any plans for the future?' Had he seen her pain and tactfully changed the subject?

She shrugged. 'Agnes' funeral is the day after tomorrow. Then I shall go back to London.' Despite the camouflage of her veil she turned her head away. 'There is nothing for me here.'

Silence. Still the invisible Theo marched between them. 'And – you?' She had to make herself ask.

His shoulders sagged. 'I don't know. With the calciner gone the best part of my income has disappeared and the mine is losing money. I don't know what I shall do. I can't see any future at all.'

She recognised his desolation, the counterpart of her own. But he had a life ahead of him. He must not sink into lethargy, despair.

'You cannot give up.' She stopped, looking him straight in the face for the first time. 'You do not simply have responsibilities to yourself. You have your employees to think of: men, whole families who rely on you. You have to go on.'

He gave a strange laugh, half cry, half groan. 'And what do I do for money? Where can a man in my position get money from?

Already the bank is threatening to foreclose on the mine and I have had to sell my wife's jewellery to get my brother-in-law out of debtor's prison. I was–' his voice cracked, '–I was arranging to borrow more money against the deeds of the house but even that may not be enough now. And they won't give me anything like the value of the place.'

She was silent. Finance, business; she knew nothing of them.

She had *intended* to be silent. But she heard a voice that was recognisably her own saying staunchly, 'Then sell it.'

That maverick mind of hers. She cursed silently. What right had she to advise him? Why did she have to think the unthinkable?

He was staring at her. 'Sell my house? But without it...' He spread his hands hopelessly and she knew what he was trying to avoid saying. For a man like him, born of common parents, property and wealth were the only claims he had to being a part of genteel society. Without them, he would sink hastily back to the level of shopkeepers, engineers, schoolmasters, all the rag-tag of people who lived out their lives between the gentry above and the poverty-stricken working classes below.

But right was right. 'What does that matter?' she demanded fiercely. 'What does such a small thing matter when set against the lives of these people? You said it is worth more than you can borrow against it. Well, then, sell it. Get every penny you can for it. And build a calciner you can be proud of, one that will set the standard for others to come.'

She stared straight at him. 'These people depend on you,' she said harshly. 'They need you. Think about the Trahairs, about Nat. He's injured, but he'll get better. And he'll need a job. And his father. If you go down you'll drag them all with you. Think about that!'

He was silent, not looking at her now, staring over his shoulder into the distance, as if she no longer existed for him. 'And – what if I want to marry again?'

Helen closed her eyes. Oh, God, this was too much to bear. She could feel the tears seeping out, running down her cheeks. But her veil was thick; he would never notice. She waited until she was sure that her tears would not sound in her voice before saying, 'A woman who loved you would not care. A woman who loved you would live with you in a hovel.'

Another long silence. Surreptitiously, she licked the tears that ran past her mouth.

He said abruptly, 'Theo would not have married me if I had lived in a hovel.'

She was sure he was right but there was nothing she could say in reply and she had already had more pain than she could stand.

She turned, began to walk away.

He caught at her arm, swinging her round to face him once more.

'Theo would not have married me if I had lived in a hovel,' he repeated, his voice harsh. 'She married me for that house, the house my father and mother had bought when they became rich. They were never accepted in society but they sent me away to school, had me raised like a gentleman, did everything they could so that I could be accepted as they never were.'

'I – I'm sorry.' She should have realised how much the house meant to him.

He was still holding her arm, the fingers digging into her flesh. 'Theo only married me for the house.' His voice was rasping with unshed tears. 'She wanted the money, the position, the house that my parents sacrificed themselves for. She wanted all that – but she didn't want me!'

Helen shook her head in helpless sympathy, unable to speak.

'And you tell me that a woman would marry me without any of those things!'

She felt lost, unsure. But he was – *had* been, she corrected herself – her friend. She owed it to him to help him, to give him the best advice she could. She swallowed. 'A woman who loved you,' she said clearly, determinedly, 'would marry you. Even if you didn't have the house and money.'

He stared at her, seemingly trying to see beneath the thick veil. 'Would you?'

What had she done to deserve such pain? Her lips trembled. 'Yes.' She dared not say more. She could feel a sob gathering, trying to force her to give herself away.

He moved towards her. Too late, she realised what he was going to do. His hands reached out, lifted the veil. She stood before him, tear stained, lips trembling, no place to hide.

'Will you?'

For a second she did not understand him; then her glance flew up to meet his, hope, stupid, impossible hope, shaking her.

'Will you?' he asked again, and his voice was soft and compassionate.

She had no breath to answer him with. Only her lips could move, silently forming the word.

'Yes.'

He was still, staring at her, frowning slightly. 'I shall be in black gloves for a year.' The commonplace phrase brought her back to earth. 'I shall need somewhere to live if I sell the house. Could I rent the farm from you?'

She could only nod, still struggling to come to terms with the changing circumstances.

He went on, 'It will be convenient for the calciner. With the money from the house, I can enlarge it, get more output–' He glanced at her. 'It will be safe, this time,' he assured her. 'I shall make sure of it.'

He wasn't asking her, she realised, he was telling her. At last he had come into his real inheritance; not the house or money, but the ability to run a business, to take responsibility, to make his own decisions.

She said weakly, 'I am sure you will do very well.'

His hand took hers. 'When I come out of black gloves, we could be married then.'

She nodded.

'And, if in the meantime, I come to London,' – his lips curved into the start of a smile – 'if I were to present myself at your grandmother's house, would you see me?'

She was still too stunned to be able to think of the proper answer, but the wild, uncontrollable part of her brain knew what to do.

To her astonishment she heard her voice saying, 'Yes! Yes!' Then her arms came up round his neck as his lips came down tenderly, gently, on to hers.